The Collected Short Stories of

Kazi Nazrul Islam

The Collected Short Stories of

Kazi Nazrul Islam

Edited by

Syed Manzoorul Islam
Kaustav Chakraborty

Orient BlackSwan

THE COLLECTED SHORT STORIES OF KAZI NAZRUL ISLAM

ORIENT BLACKSWAN PRIVATE LIMITED

Registered Office
3-6-752 Himayatnagar, Hyderabad 500 029, Telangana, India
E-mail: centraloffice@orientblackswan.com

Other Offices
Bengaluru, Chennai, Guwahati, Hyderabad, Kolkata,
Mumbai, New Delhi, Noida, Patna

First published 2024

ISBN 978-93-5442-712-1

042454

Typeset in Calisto MT 10/12 *by*
Shine Graphics, Delhi 110 094

Printed at
Kensington Printing & Packaging, Noida 201 301

Published by
Orient Blackswan Private Limited
3-6-752, Himayatnagar, Hyderabad 500 029, Telangana, India
E-mail: info@orientblackswan.com

CONTENTS

UNANTHOLOGISED STORIES

ACKNOWLEDGEMENTS

This book is the outcome of a project sponsored by the Nazrul Centre for Social and Cultural Studies, Kazi Nazrul University, Asansol, West Bengal. We are grateful to Professor Sadhan Chakrabarti, Dr Swati Guha, Dr Somenath Mukherjee and Dr Gourav Chowdhury for their inspiration, guidance and help. Without their relentless support, it would not have been possible to undertake this transnational project of translating the short stories of Kazi Nazrul Islam into English. We are thankful to Dr Srikanta Roy Chowdhury, Assistant Professor of History, Southfield College, Darjeeling, for introducing us to Kazi Nazrul University. Professor Sumita Chakrabarti, former Nazrul Chair Professor, Burdwan University, has been very kind in clarifying some of our doubts. She has also provided us with relevant study materials. We must also thank Professor Fakrul Alam, Professor Niaz Zaman, Professor Ipshita Chanda, Dr Gulshan Ara and Ekram Ahmed for helping us in times of crisis. Dr Ketaki Datta and Dr Saurav Dasthakur have also helped us with the contacts of some of the translators. We are indebted to Arka Deb, our journalist friend who is also a Nazrul researcher, for his constant support. Professor Anindita Mukhopadhyay deserves special thanks for her comments and inputs in the 'Introduction'. We are thankful to late Kalyani Kazi, Anirban Kazi, Arindam Kazi and Khilkhil Kazi for granting us copyright permissions. We also thank Mitali Chakravarty for giving us permission to use the English translation of 'Hena' that was first published in *Borderless Journal.*

Words fall short in expressing our gratitude to all the translators. They have accepted the challenge of translating Nazrul, which is indeed a difficult task. Without their cooperation, engagement and patience it would not have been possible to complete this task. We thank Sreenath Sreedharan, Namrata Kartik and all the other members of Orient BlackSwan for all their efforts that have gone into this book. It has to be admitted that Namrata has accomplished the task of co-translator. Without her critical insight in making creative alterations, this book would not have acquired its current uniformity.

PUBLISHER'S ACKNOWLEDGEMENTS

'Harvest of Sorrow' by Kazi Nazrul Islam, translated from the original Bengali by Sarker Hasan Al Zayed. Used with permission of the translator.

'Hena' by Kazi Nazrul Islam, first published as 'Hena: A Short Story by Nazrul' translated by Sohana Manzoor, *Borderless Journal*, May 25, 2023, https://borderlessjournal.com/2023/05/25/hena-a-short-story-by-nazrul/. Used with permission of the publisher.

'In the Relentless Rain', by Kazi Nazrul Islam, translated from the original Bengali by Masrufa Ayesha Nusrat. Used with permission of the translator.

'Half Asleep' by Kazi Nazrul Islam, translated from the original Bengali by Nishat Atiya. Used with permission of the translator.

'Insatiate Desire' by Kazi Nazrul Islam, translated from the original Bengali by Sreetanwi Chakraborty. Used with permission of the translator.

'Letter from a Political Prisoner' by Kazi Nazrul Islam, translated from the original Bengali by Anindita Mukhopadhyay. Used with permission of the translator.

'The Agony of the Destitute' by Kazi Nazrul Islam, translated from the original Bengali by Jackie Kabir. Used with permission of the translator.

'Autobiography of a Vagabond', translated from the original Bengali by Amita Ray. Used with permission of the translator.

'Meher Negar' by Kazi Nazrul Islam, translated from the original Bengali by Marzia Rahman. Used with permission of the translator.

'Evening Star' by Kazi Nazrul Islam, translated from the original Bengali by Priyanka Chatterjee. Used with permission of the translator.

'Rakshasi' by Kazi Nazrul Islam, translated from the original Bengali by Sutanuka Ghosh Roy. Used with permission of the translator.

'Salek' by Kazi Nazrul Islam, translated from the original Bengali by Fakrul Alam. Used with permission of the translator.

'The Widow' by Kazi Nazrul Islam, translated from the original Bengali by Sudeshna Majumdar. Used with permission of the translator.

'The Restless Traveller' by Kazi Nazrul Islam, translated from the original Bengali by Dhrubajyoti Sarkar. Used with permission of the translator.

'The Lotus-Cobras' by Kazi Nazrul Islam, translated from the original Bengali by Sucharita Sarkar. Used with permission of the translator.

'The King of the Djinns' by Kazi Nazrul Islam, translated from the original Bengali by Saurav Dasthakur. Used with permission of the translator.

'The Volcano' by Kazi Nazrul Islam, translated from the original Bengali by Gulshan Ara. Used with permission of the translator.

'The Shiuli Mala' by Kazi Nazrul Islam, translated from the original Bengali by Pritam Bandyopadhyay. Used with permission of the translator.

'Letter from a Lost Boy' by Kazi Nazrul Islam, translated from the original Bengali by Ketaki Datta. Used with permission of the translator.

'The Hawk-Cuckoo from the Woods' by Kazi Nazrul Islam, translated from the original Bengali by Parjanya Sen. Used with permission of the translator.

NAZRUL: A TIMELINE

1899 Zahida Khatun gives birth to Nazrul on 24 May in Churulia village, Bardhaman district, West Bengal in British India; nicknamed Dukhu Mia.

1908 His father, Kazi Fakir Ahmed, dies.

1909 Gets a religious education in the village lower primary school.

Works as the caretaker of the local mosque.

Starts composing as a member of the local theatre troupe which performs folk musicals called 'leto'.

1912 Leaves his school, Nabin Chandra Institution at Mathrun.

Works as a cook, and then in a bakery and a tea stall.

1914 Admitted to Darirampur School in Mymensingh district in Class Seven.

1915 Admitted to Searsole Raj High School, Raniganj and studies till Class Ten.

1917 Leaves school in September before matriculation and joins the 49th Bengal Regiment of the British Indian Army.

Gets military training in Karachi Cantonment.

The socialist revolution in Russia impacts him and is manifested in major poetical works like *Sammobadi* (*Egalitarian*, 1925) and *Sarbohara* (*Proletariat*, 1926).

1919 First short story 'Baundeler Attokahini' ('Autobiography of a Vagabond') is published in *Saogat*.

'Hena' is published in *Bongiyo Mussalman Sahitya Potrika*. 'Shami Hara' ('The Widow') is also published in *Saogat* later that year.

1920 Returns to Kolkata in March.

His career as a journalist begins with the publication of the evening edition of the daily 'Nabojug' along with Muzaffar Ahmad as his co-editor in July.

The short stories 'Byathar Daan' ('Harvest of Sorrow'), 'Awtripto Kamona' ('Insatiate Desire') and 'Rajbondhir Chitthi' ('Letter from a Political Prisoner') are published in *Bongiyo Mussalman Sahitya Potrika*.

'Badal Borishone' ('In the Relentless Rain') is published in *Moslem Bharat*.

'Ghumer Ghore' ('Half Asleep'), 'Rikter Bedon' ('The Agony of the Destitute') and 'Mehar Negar' are published in *Noor*.

'Salek' is published in *Bokul*.

'Duronto Pothik' ('The Restless Traveller') is published in *Moslem Bharat*.

1921 In June, his first marriage with Sayida Khatun alias Nargis at Daulatpur, Comilla is abandoned.

Meets Rabindranath Tagore at Shantiniketan in October.

Joins the Non Cooperation Movement at Comilla in November.

The publication of two poems, 'Bidrohi' and 'Kamal Pasha' brings immediate fame. 'Shaajher Tara' ('Evening Star') is published in *Bongiyo Mussalman Sahita Potrika*. 'Rakkhushi' ('Rakhshasi') is published in *Saogat*.

1922 First anthology of short stories, *Byathar Daan* (*Harvest of Sorrow*) is published in March.

Launches a bi-weekly magazine, *Dhumketu*.

In September, the political poem 'Anondomoyir Agomonay' ('On the Arrival of Durga') is published, for which he is charged with sedition and arrested.

In an October issue of *Dhumketu* he makes a demand for the complete independence of India.

Ognibina (*Veena of Fire*), a collection of poems and *Jugobani* (*Voice of the Age*), a collection of essays, are published. *Jugobani* is immediately banned by the Bengal government, with the ban being withdrawn in 1977.

The short story 'Hara Chheler Chitthi' ('Letter from a Lost Boy') is published in *Aloka*.

1923 Sentenced to a year in prison.

Tagore dedicates his musical play *Bashonto* (*Spring*) to him.

Goes on a hunger strike to protest against the harassment of political prisoners. Tagore sends the telegram: 'Give up hunger strike, our literature claims you'. Released in December.

The anthology of poems *Dolon Chaapa* (*White Ginger Lily*) is published.

1924 Weds Ashalata alias Promila Debi, a Hindu woman.

Publishes two anthologies of poems, *Bisher Baashi* (*The Poisonous Flute*) and *Bhangar Gaan* (*Song of Demolition*): both of them are proscribed by the government.

His first son Azad Kamal is born only to die prematurely.

1925 Labour Swaraj Party is formed within the Indian National Congress and Nazrul becomes an active member.

He launches *Langol* (*Plough*), the first magazine dealing with the issues of class struggle in Bangla.

Publishes *Chittonama* and *Chhayanot*, two collections of poems—the first one is in memory of Congress leader Chittaranjan Das.

Rikter Bedon (*The Agony of the Destitute*), his second volume of short stories, is published in January.

1926 Communal riots in Calcutta in April. Meets Tagore and discusses issues related to Hindu–Muslim relations; sings before Tagore.

Moves to Krishnanagar; gets more involved in active politics.

Second son Bulbul is born in September. Goes through acute financial crisis. Starts composing ghazals in Bangla.

Durdiner Jatri (*Traveller of Adverse Times*), a collection of essays, along with two volumes of poetry, *Poober Hawa* (*Eastern Wind*) and *Jhinge Phool* (*Ridge Gourd Flower*), are published. *Jhinge Phool* is written for children.

1927 Visits Dhaka and attends the first conference of the Muslim Sahityo Shamaj in Dhaka University.

Disagreement with Tagore on the issues related to aesthetics and poetic diction.

The literary magazine *Shonibarer Chitthi* (*The Saturday Letters*) starts publishing parodies of his writings.

Baadhon Hara (*Unfettered*), the first epistolary novel in Bangla; *Rudro Mongol* (*The Benevolent Rudra*), a collection of essays; and *Phoni Manosha* (*Manosha, the Snake*), a collection of poems, are published.

1928 Mother dies in May.

Bulbul, an anthology of songs, is published.

Association with HMV Gramophone Company begins; they start recording songs composed by him along with his recitations.

Shifts from Krishnanagar back to Calcutta.

Criticised by a section of conservative Muslim literary persons for his interfaith practice (as manifested in his composition of Islamic songs along with songs dedicated to Kali known as Shyama Sangeet, and bhajans and kirtans dedicated to Krishna) while supported by many others.

The poetry books *Shindhu-Hindol* (*An Ocean Swing*) and *Jinjir* (*Chain*) are published. *Shonchita*, a collection of his select poems, is published.

1929 A national reception in his honour is held at Albert Hall, Calcutta, on 15 December in the presence of Subhash Chandra Bose.

His third son, Kazi Sabyasachi, is born.

Publishes the book of songs, *Chokher Chaatok* (*The Swallow that Longs for the Eyes*), and two collections of poems, *Chakrobaak* (*Chakor*) and *Shondhya* (*Evening*).

1930 Publishes *Proloy Shikha* (*Apocalyptic Flame*), a collection of poems, on account of which he is sentenced to six months imprisonment.

Under the Gandhi–Irwin pact the case is dismissed and he is released.

Begins association with All India Radio, Calcutta.

His son Bulbul passes away.

Mrityu-Khudha (*Death-Hunger*), a novel; *Nazrul Geetika* (*Songs of Nazrul*), a collection of songs; *Rubaiyat-e-Hafiz*, a book of translations of Hafiz's poems; and *Jhilimili* (*Sparkles*), an anthology of plays, are published.

The short story 'Pawddo Gokhro' ('The Lotus-Cobras') is published in *Dunduvi*.

'Jiner Badsha' ('The King of the Djinns'), 'Ogni-giri' ('The Volcano') and 'Shiulimala' ('The Shiuli Mala') all published in *Saogat*.

1931 He starts getting involved with theatre and cinema.

His youngest son Kazi Aniruddha is born.

Publishes *Kuhelika* (*Mystery*), a novel, and *Chondrobindu* (*Crescent Moon*), a collection of songs.

Shiulimala (*The Shiuli Mala*), an anthology of short stories is published in October. 'Aleya' ('Will-o'-the-wisp'), an opera composed by him, is performed.

1932 *Sur-Saki* (*Musician*), *Zulfiqar* (*Sword*) and *Bono-Geeti* (*Forest-Song*), anthologies of songs, are published.

1933 Acts in the film *Dhrubo*. Emerges as a music director.

Kavya-Ampara, his translation of thirty sections of the Quran in verse, is published. *Gul-Bagicha* (*Flower Garden*), a collection of songs and *Putuler Biye* (*Marriage of Dolls*), collection of children's plays, are published.

1934 *Geeti-Shatodol* (*Lotus of Music*) and *Ganer Mala* (*Garland of Songs*), two volumes of collected songs; *Shurolipi* (*Tune-Script*) and *Shuromukur* (*Tune-Mirror*), volumes of the notations to Nazrul's songs are published.

1935 *Maktab Sahitya* (*Elementary Literature*), his textbook written for elementary school students, is published.

1938–39 Writes scripts for films like *Vidyapati* and *Shapuray*.

Nirjhar (*Fountain*), his collected poems, is published.

1940 The shock of his youngest son's demise and the broken health of his wife, makes him inclined towards yoga sadhana.

1941 Tagore dies. Nazrul composes poems in his memory.

1942 Falls sick during a radio program in July, resulting in a gradual loss of voice and memory.

1944 A special issue on Nazrul is published in Buddhadeb Bose's journal, *Kobita*.

1945 Awarded the Jagottarini Medal by Calcutta University.

1946 The first book critically assessing Nazrul's works is published by Kazi Abdul Wajud, titled *Nazrul Protima*.

1953 Sent to London on behalf of the Government of India for treatment. Returns due to no improvement.

1960 Awarded the Padma Bhushan by the Government of India.

1962 Pramila Devi, his wife, dies.

1969 Awarded a D.Litt by Rabindra Bharati University, Kolkata.

1972 In a mutual decision taken by the Indian government and the government of the newly-formed, independent state of Bangladesh, he is asked to relocate to Dhaka.

1974 Awarded a D.Litt by Dhaka University.

1975 Admitted to hospital.

1976 Given Bangladeshi citizenship.

Awarded the title of Ekushey Padak by the Bangladesh government.

Passes way on 29 August; buried on the premises of Dhaka University.

1981 The short story 'Baner Papiya' ('The Hawk-Cuckoo from the Woods') is published posthumously in *Kafela*.

1987 Declared the National Poet of Bangladesh.

A CRITICAL INTRODUCTION TO NAZRUL'S SHORT STORIES

Syed Manzoorul Islam & Kaustav Chakraborty

A writer critically deals with society, but society deals equally critically with the writer as well; perhaps, in a more powerful manner. For it is the societal politics of critical responses towards the writer and their compositions that renders judgement on whether the writer is 'good' or 'bad'.

Kazi Nazrul Islam has been a very popular writer in his own time and beyond. Yet, as William Radice observes, it is unfortunate that the literati compare Nazrul 'adversely with Rabindranath Tagore even now' (qtd. in Chakrabarti 141). Thus, Tagore's comment that Nazrul 'tried to shave with a sword' still circulates in literary circles. However, it is undisputed that Nazrul's creative world 'has great energy, and originality, and ... values that ... are courageous, positive and life-enhancing' (141). Nazrul's legacy stands testimony to the unfortunate reality that classifies an author as a weak writer based on critical mis-evaluation despite their immense popularity. Hence, the societal politics of critical response towards an artist has to be understood in terms of the aesthetic 'norms' based on which a piece of human creativity is ultimately categorised as 'good' or 'bad'.

The standardisation of aesthetic 'norms', as revealed by studies in the sociology of art, is intimately related to the politics of sustaining the hierarchical structures of society. The acceptance of the Dalit literary canon after decades of resistance and repression, resulting in bringing heretofore unnoticed authors gradually out of the 'waiting rooms of history', typically demonstrates how the evaluation of a writer changes along with sociopolitical movements and debates that challenge societal hierarchies and ultimately redefine aesthetic parameters as well. Characterising Nazrul as merely 'crudely rhetorical, tub-thumping, sprawling, sentimental, vulgar' (141) needs to be understood in terms of the politics of marginalisation that resulted from Nazrul's major differences with literary connoisseurs in Kolkata—the cultural hub of the Bangla elite.

Nazrul represents a range of social 'others': born into a humble, rural family and identifying mostly with the poor and suffering classes, he is the 'other' of the elite Kolkata bhadralok. Nazrul's hybridised language makes him an 'other' for the spokespeople of linguistic nationalism And most importantly, because of his self-location on the cusp of Hindu and Muslim religious identities, he has often been treated as an 'other' by puritans from both communities. It is, therefore, not surprising that literary critics who were his contemporaries also perceived him as an 'other' with regards to mainstream literary ethos—an outlook that has been internalised by succeeding generations of critics as well. Those literary critics who reinforced the norms propagated by Tagore—a man from the upper class with friends and fans from the West—and his followers as the 'normative' aesthetics of Bangla literature and culture, placed Nazrul outside the orbit of 'good', sophisticated writers. It has been rightly pointed out by Radice that, unlike Nazrul—whose writing reflects a cross-cultural heritage and inter-civilisational correlation—'Tagore ... despite his bid for universality, conspicuously failed to incorporate Muslim tradition into his writing' (141). Yet the Nobel Laureate and founder of Visva-Bharati has become accepted worldwide as the epitome of 'a cultural universal' of Bangla literature, while Nazrul's literary works have been dismissed more and more as an aberration. The politics of publication and visibility that is revealed through the manifold translations of Tagore's Bangla texts into other languages, as opposed to the paucity of translated texts of Nazrul's works, further adds to the myth of infantilising Nazrul as a writer. This translation of Nazrul's collected short stories is an attempt at de-emphasising these myths about his writing and is aimed at underscoring Nazrul's merit as a literary, non-conformist rebel and a transgressor of 'normative' aesthetics that have been formulated with the intention of keeping social hierarchies intact.

While maintaining that novel writing is a human invention, unlike 'the divine art' of the story, Isak Dinesen argues that it is the story alone as an art form which 'has authority to answer that cry of heart of its characters, that one cry of heart of each of them: "Who am I?"' (26). In Nazrul's stories one comes across characters from different civilisational and cultural backgrounds—Hindu, Muslim, Afghan, Bedouin, French, people from Bangla- and Hindi-speaking regions, and many others—and in their search to understand who they actually are, they provide readers with a plurality of perspectives. For the Soi-ma in 'The Widow', the significance of the self lies in sacrificing the person who is one's most beloved. For Allah-Rakha in 'The King of the Djinns', the self seems to derive meaningfulness only by attaining the object of his love. For the Kazi in 'Salek', the meaning of life lies in overcoming one's ego under the guidance of a dervish. Sabur in 'The Volcano' feels that his meaning of life lies in the assertion of the self, while to Romola in 'The Hawk-Cuckoo from the Woods', loving the elements of nature and seeking solace by singing bhakti kirtans seems to be the sole purpose of life. For the narrator of 'The Agony of the Destitute', identity is centered round the notion of a martial way of life. According to the protagonist of 'The Restless Traveller', existence is meaningful through a struggle for liberation. For Moti of 'Insatiate Desire', it is blind attachment to an abusive love that adds meaning to life, while Bindi in 'Rakshasi' undertakes a protest against her humiliation and the ultimate killing of the object of abuse and shame to assert her true self. Apart from this plurality of perspectives regarding the meaning and purpose of identity and existence, readers from different parts of the world will be delighted by Nazrul's non-communal liberality as manifested through these short stories. Narzul, as Abu Rushd observes, is a writer 'not of any sect, nor of any narrow ideological or economic system' (qtd. in Chakrabarti 140).

Translating Nazrul's stories has transformed the translators as well. More than the differences of expression between Bangla and English while translating Nazrul, we, as editors and translators, have had to pay attention to the heterogeneity of cultural aspects related to several religious and linguistic traditions. While dealing with 'The Hawk-Cuckoo from the Woods' there is a need to understand Vaishnavism. To understand 'The Volcano' and 'Salek', a close acquaintance with Islam and Sufism is a must. Engaging with 'Rakshasi' and 'The Volcano' is only possible after a thorough grounding in an understanding of the locational and regional variations of Bangla extant across West Bengal and Bangladesh. Above all, Nazrul's use of Hindi, Urdu and Persian compels the translators to arrive at a 'point between languages, between people (and between peoples), where the differences between them can be more fully seen and more nearly comprehended' (White, J.B. 230). Thus, a translator—along with overcoming a bias towards homogeneity by becoming acquainted with the heterogeneous differences of civilisations and cultures as depicted by Nazrul—eventually comes to a realisation about the foreignness of the self and human sociality. As a translator of Nazrul, one is bound to start engaging with differences in order to respond to the reality of differences that Nazrul has dealt with so deftly, and with such passion. This ultimately helps one understand that, antithetical to the notion of merely providing of equivalents from Bangla to English, translating Nazrul is an endeavour to communicate as a foreigner to foreigners—as Naoki Sakai has rightly pointed out—by recognising the 'plurality' of 'one humanity'. Translation is not about reinforcing or erasing differences but 'is a political labor to overcome points of incommensurability in the social' in order to provide us 'with insights into how cartography and the schematism of configuration contribute to our critical analysis of social relations' (Sakai 29, 33).

CONTEXT, TRAITS AND TRANSLATION

'My Sundar has first come to me in the form of short stories', writes Nazrul about his muse, 'then as poems. Thereafter as songs, tunes, rhythms and emotions. The occasional advent has also been in the form of novels, plays and prose writings' (Islam 3: 37). The prominent characteristics of Kazi Nazrul Islam's short stories are simplicity, vivacity, and emotionality. He writes,

> In order to exert an everlasting influence on Bangla literature, at the very beginning we have to get rid of our passivity and introduce in our writing a wavelike *vivacity* of the fountain and a liberty of *simplicity*.... Literature is the expression of the life of *emotions*, the one who doesn't have emotions and has become inert, how can that person create writing that is alive with emotions?... The unrestrained flow of literature should be accompanied by a delight in the flow, a stream like swiftness and wavelike echoing-music and liveliness (1: 188, emphasis ours).

Nazrul's resistance against a separate 'literary' diction and style finds reflection in the remarks that he has made in 'Muslims in Bangla Literature': 'However subtle a discussion an author initiates, it should allow any person of the world to say that the discussion is the reflection of the innermost words of the person's own mind.... This is how world-literature is created; this is known as universality in literature' (1: 389).

Nazrul's aesthetics of simplicity finds manifestation through non-urban settings; detailed descriptions of rural landscapes and village folk; a portrayal of the quotidian; use of local languages; and rejection of complex plots. Above all, it is the poetics of the familiar that enhances Nazrul's aesthetics of simplicity. Vivacity in Nazrul's stories has been achieved by his depiction of things that demand energy and enthusiasm: battling, dancing, singing, jesting, making people frightened, doing social work, snake charming, travelling to distant lands, and so on. The recurrent use of onomatopoeia also adds to the vivacity of the narratives. Emotionality, often somewhat excessively, pervades all of his compositions in general and the short stories in particular. Emotionality is the consequence of Nazrul's unformatted spontaneity. He can elaborate on the same expression in different ways, to the extent of making it seem repetitive. This spontaneity of emotion is also reflected in his juxtaposition of a word with its synonym. For example, in 'The Agony of the Destitute' Nazrul uses 'green', 'unripe' and 'immature' one after the other to describe the protagonist. In this regard, one should keep in mind his fascination for dialogic communication rather than a depiction of incidents—some of the stories are framed entirely as soliloquies or monologues. Some others fall into the epistolary genre which lends itself to such emotional overflows reasonably well.

Nazrul's genius lies in the fact that beneath all the simplicity, emotionality and spontaneity, grave concerns surface with regards to issues that are relevant even in our times. His wholehearted embrace of the interfaith and inter-civilisational aspects of culture and society that are practiced on a daily basis—unlike other literary maestros of his times, including Tagore—in language that possesses multiple registers, makes of his oeuvre a model which modern readers can draw upon to gain perspective on the trap of the singularity of identity, which forms the basis of othering. The international settings and cross-civilisational lingo of Nazrul's stories should make us more conscious of ourselves as 'singular-plural' and inspire us towards cultivating in our ideas as well as expressions, 'an indefinite plurality of singularities': 'Being cannot *be* anything but being-with-one-another, circulating in the *with* and as the *with* of this singularly plural coexistence.' (Nancy 3; emphasis in original).

In his essay 'Deposition of the State Prisoner' Nazrul has complained, 'The royal-translator appointed by the ruler translated [my] message into the words of the state-language but did not translate its essence.... the translator's intention is to please the king, but my writings have revealed truth, strength and vivacity' (Islam 1: 432). Keeping this in mind, the translators of this book have tried to retain the essence of the original text in their translations.

There are a few points where the translations are different from the original. At times, Nazrul tends to make his sentences quite long while in the grips of strong emotion. These longer sentences have been broken up into shorter ones by the translators. In this translation, we have tried to replace archaic words with simple words as much as possible, in order to make the stories readable by and enjoyable for contemporary readers. Translation from Bangla into English is not a new phenomenon in Bangla literature. Hence, there is an advantage to be had in such translations because readers have become acquainted with many Bangla-specific words, like 're', 'oi', and so on. Even so, some of the vernacular terms and expressions that have been retained in the translated text are explained in footnotes. Nazrul is essentially multilingual—he uses Hindi, Urdu, Arabic and Persian words along with Bangla. In his essay, 'Muslims in Bangla Literature', Nazrul has remarked, 'Now we too must try to generate universality in our literary creations. However, not by ignoring or losing the particularities of our own nation and community' (1: 390).

Accordingly, an effort has been made to uphold this multilingualism and regional flavour in the English translation as well. Therefore, instead of choosing the English equivalents of Bangla words, we have preferred to opt for words from vernacular languages which are now part of the English lexicon. For example, instead of translating 'putrobodhu', as 'daughter-in-law', we have used the Hindi word 'bahu', which is now incorporated into English as per the *Oxford English Dictionary*. Similarly, we have not provided any explanations of the terms like 'baba', 'baap', 'hai', 'veena' and many others, that are now included in English dictionaries.

Nazrul has also referred to ragas and raginis like Anandabhairavi, Asavari, Bageshri, Bhairav, Bhairavi, Bibhas, and many others. The Bangla names of flowers like bakam, bakul, nargis, polash, shiuli, and many others have been retained along with those of trees like ashoka, ashwatha, neem, piyal, and so on. In the endeavour to make Nazrul accessible to a greater number of connoisseurs of literature, enough care has been taken so that the 'truth', 'strength' and 'vivacity' of Nazrul's writing remain unspoiled.

HARVEST OF SORROW: THEMES AND CONCERNS

'Harvest of Sorrow', the eponymous opening story of the collection is a story which is a collage of tales narrated by the three characters: Dara, Bedoura and Saiful Mulk. Dara, who is located in Iran's Golestan, narrates his tale of love, separation and devotion to his motherland through a series of reminiscences. Then we hear the same set of events narrated from Bedoura's perspective. Then follows the account narrated by Saiful Mulk who is portrayed as a sinner who tempted Bedoura into losing her virginity, and then overcome with guilt joins the freedom struggle where he encounters Dara. What follows is a tale of redemption, loss and transcendence of physical love to a more spiritual kind of love.

Dara's hesitance in accepting Bedoura because of her physical contact with Saiful Mulk and his sense of guilt because of Bedoura's wrath—which has its origin in her loss of virginity—show how patriarchy operates through both men and women. Moreover, the fact that both Dara and Saiful Mulk's 'manliness' is wounded by their incapacity to be ideal men in the sphere of love and so they ultimately decide to go to war, reveals how warfare serves to prove one's 'manliness': 'War does not challenge women to prove that they are women, whereas wars have been historically symbolized as the touchstone of "manliness". The concept of war as a proving ground of manliness has centered on the notion of combat, which is understood to be the ultimate test of masculinity, and thus crucial to the ideological structure of patriarchy' (Cock 235–36).

Nazrul's war-fixation can be approached in two different ways. On the one hand—reminding us of Ashis Nandy's views that in colonial culture the 'identification with the aggressor bounds the rulers and the ruled in an unbreakable dyadic relationship'—the warmongering protagonists of Nazrul's anti-imperialist stories provide testimony to the observation that in their enmity against the British, colonised people 'saw their salvation in becoming more like the British ... They may not have fully shared the British idea of the martial races' but 'they did resurrect the ideology of the martial races latent in the traditional ... Ksatriyahood' (Nandy 7). On the other hand, as Abhishek Sarkar has observed, it is 'Nazrul's attempt to inscribe the Bengali-speaking Muslims into an urbane, middle-class, literary space under the broader rubric of Bengali identity and also in adherence to transnational Islam', that has resulted in his recurrent depiction of the 'Great War' which has allowed him to explore 'the discourse of patriotism' through 'a military re-modelling of Bengali masculinity' (Sarkar 1).

War zones, to us, also seem to be a real and fatal reverberation of Nazrul's own emotional tempests. War zones as a physical escape from clashes in the mind becomes a trope in Nazrul's writings. As a projection of masculine mental turmoil in real time, the fact that these wars were often launched by Western imperialism across the globe, is irrelevant. Even though Nazrul is a confirmed anti-British seditionist and rebel, the war zones in his stories are romantically sundered from their imperialist context and are turned into fields of battle that are echoes of far more violent battlefields raging in his mind. Nazrul was also a communist and the Bolshevik Revolution had a great impact on his early writings. Muzaffar Ahmad, one of the founders of the Indian Communist Party, has written about how 'In the original draft written by Nazrul, Dara and Saiful Mulk were shown to have joined the 'Red Army', but since the utterance of the word 'Red Army' was a crime in the colonial India, he replaced it by depicting them as the 'soldiers of freedom' (Ahmad 101).

'Hena' is the second story of the collection *Harvest of Sorrow*. The entire story is narrated by Sohrab. The theme of this story is also love and war—both internal and external battle. The plot is almost similar in many ways to that of the preceding story. But some of the unique speculations made by Sohrab are significant. Sohrab's seeming obsession with war makes him feel that 'If the entire world could come under one (and only) such military regime, then it would become so beautiful that even calling it a heaven on earth would not be enough!' (23, in this volume). Through this brief utterance, Nazrul seems to expose how military training actually tries to glamourise and normativise hegemony, in the name of discipline and order. Sohrab expresses his admiration for the Western world but is still critical of them. On the one hand he admires the strict discipline exercised by the British, while on the other hand he criticises the preconceived notion of the French that non-Europeans are incapable of accomplishing things as brilliantly as only Europeans can. Sohrab also feels sad at the conservative treatment that the women of Indian subcontinent receive, in contrast with the freedom that a woman enjoys in the West.

Hena's initial indifference to Sohrab despite the official recognition of his heroic deeds in foreign battlefields, and Sohrab's success in attaining Hena's love only after his surrendering to the service of his own nation, makes Sohrab an epitome of 'cosmopolitan patriotism'. Like Nazrul, who fought as a soldier in foreign lands but primarily dedicated himself to India's struggle for freedom, Sohrab too represents those cosmopolitans who 'can be patriots', 'loving our homelands', and 'as cosmopolitans, defend the right of the others' (Appiah 622, 629). Muzaffar Ahmad has rightly observed that in these stories, 'Apart from nationalism there is a manifestation of internationalism. This has to be regarded as a new aspect in our literature' (100).

'In the Relentless Rain' is basically a story of love between strangers. The author doesn't provide us the names of the lovers—rather both the lovers are addressed as dark-skinned: Kajaria/Kajri and Shyamal. The wandering Shyamal, the narrator of the story, meets Kajaria during a festival celebrating the monsoon. His love remains unrequited as she feels it is impossible for anyone to fall in love with her because of her complexion. The story ends on a tragic but positive note, where Shyamal expresses how he can always feel Kajaria's presence in the dark clouds of the monsoon, even after her death. The story makes extensive use of music to convey the pangs of love and separation. It not only offers a critique of the prejudice against dark skin but highlights the gendered aspect of the prejudice as well. The male, Shyamal, is not made to internalise the fallacy of equating fairness with light or fair skin, while it is the woman who is made to suffer self-contempt by internalising this pernicious 'stigma'.

The next story, 'Half Asleep', is divided into two parts: Azhar's story and Pari's story. Azhar's story is mainly about his sacrifices. The reasons he puts forward justifying his detachment from love are meant to make him seem magnanimous and evolved. Like a true cosmopolitan, he says that by joining the war he has been able to make the world his home. Echoing the transcendental outlook of various endogenous traditions of philosophy that—apart from a few exceptions—considers the body as a hindrance to the elevation of the soul, Azhar also favours detachment from sensuousness and a renunciation of carnal pleasures towards attaining a greater pleasure: 'a freedom from body-bondage ... does not merely provide a negative happiness of freedom from miseries, it is a state of positive joy' (Lal 29–30). The problem, however, lies in the fact that Azhar takes his decision to end their relationship alone and thereafter seems to infantilise Pari, in a typical patriarchal manner, by accusing her of not being able to understand his high thoughts. Moreover, by fixing a marriage between Pari and one of his friends, Azhar ensures Pari's confinement within the household structure, as if it is the only domain where a female must be. The fact that he renounces the same household structure by perceiving it as detrimental for his elevated existence reveals that, for Azhar it is the male alone who can live a life that he considers to be superior. To us, Pari's story is more interesting in terms of the unique portrayal of the mindscapes of its characters. Pari's husband is characterised by a simple and inherent magnanimity which offers a sharp contrast to Azhar's theatrical performance of high-mindedness. Pari's assertion that she will not betray her role as a loving wife without pretending to erase the love that she has for her former lover, shows how Nazrul is offering a critique of the conventional notion of 'loyalty' according to which women—embodying the traits of Sati—are expected to acknowledge that their 'highest religion' is not to serve, or even emotionally adore, anyone except 'their own husbands as their gods' (Coomaraswamy 126).

The first person narrator of 'Insatiate Desire' soliloquises on a saga of disunited love: where the narrator falls in love with his childhood friend after she is sequestered upon coming of age, feigns disinterest in her when her marriage is arranged to another man to her shock, and characterises his own actions as stemming from the most noble impulses. Underneath this uncomplicated story, Nazrul focuses on the complications of the much hyped 'macho' role that often becomes a compulsion for men to play, even if in a performative manner. The unreasonable violence that the narrator afflicts on Moti as a child, and Moti's asking him to beat her in case he hasn't done so in a long while, reveals how society engineers a boy becoming a 'rough and tough' man. It is this internalised hypermasculinity that prevents a male from showing weakness, particularly in front of a female. The narrator's confession about how he has to bring back his 'arrogance', 'a cruel, ruthless smile' to stop 'an outburst of sobs' before Moti shows the extent of damage that societal admiration for hypermasculinity wreaks on a male. He is unable to speak out about his sense of loss and as a supra-man, needs to satisfy his wounded ego with the deception of sacrifice as magnanimity—not only of his own happiness, but in the process, the happiness of the woman associated with him as well.

The final piece of the volume, 'Letter from a Political Prisoner', is an epistolary story of a political prisoner, who has also been diagnosed with fatal tuberculosis. The story is addressed to the lady of his dreams, Manashi, who does not seem to have reciprocated his love. The story is an elaborate description of the mindscape of the prisoner—how all his hopes of getting love and care from Manashi have remained unfulfilled despite his whole-hearted devotion to her. In doing so it brings out the contrast between the inner longing of a man who, from the outside, may be regarded as a brave political prisoner. The letter ends with the writer's signature 'Shri Dhumketu', reminding us of a famous poem by Nazrul as well as the title of the magazine he edited, in which he had published his demand for India's complete freedom from British rule—as a result of which, like the protagonist of this story, he was sentenced to a year in prison. The recipient of this letter being named Manashi also reminds us that the collection *Harvest of Sorrow* was dedicated by Nazrul to his 'Manashi':

> Manashi—the woman of my dreams!
> I had taken your hair pins
> For which you didn't forgive me.
> So I atoned, and my heart
> Is now marked with incisions.

Apart from these autobiographical resemblances, the story is important as it deals with the patriarchal and gendered biases of even nationalist revolutionaries who, otherwise, fight against oppression and otherisation. The political prisoner writes, 'I hold the female race in very high respect . . . but my consistent complaint against them is that they do not give much value to men's love, and ignore and insult their feelings. . . . This is what lies behind much of what society is afflicted with. The proud woman, glorying in her youth and beauty, tramples underfoot one who would have given her the status of queen and devi in his heart and home' (82, this volume) The misogynistic generalisation underscores the gendered aspects of anticolonial nationalism that often 'induces nostalgia for a romanticized past when men "controlled the land and women" without interference from European men' (White, A. 863). Shri Dhumketu's furious blaming of his dream woman for not responding to the demands of his love, without understanding that as a woman Manashi too has a right of choice, reveals the fact that the nationalist anticolonial movement and the women's liberation movement are not identical, though they are interrelated (Maitse).

THE AGONY OF THE DESTITUTE: KEY ISSUES

In the preface to *The Agony of the Destitute*, which is also the title of the first story of this collection, Mohammad Mozammel Haq declares,

> Amid the turmoil of the war, a young poet reflected on his visionary land which he illuminated with these figurative expressions. It fell on someone like me, not competent for the job, to remove the Mesopotamian dust from them and take care of them. It's my incapability that had stopped these creative outbursts from reaching the readers. I am responsible for the injustice done to both the poet and the readers. I have made my atonement today. (Islam 2: 231).

The story, 'The Agony of the Destitute', is a glorification of war but in the process it also raises questions related to war and gender. The first-person account begins with a description of the 'brave boys of Bengal' marching towards war. The narrator's reluctance to meet his beloved and his forceful arguments with his mother while joining this military contingent can be understood via the gendered stand of warfare: 'Combat readiness, male bonding, and social cohesion are achieved through military training by emphasizing the otherness of both women and the enemy: women represent the weaker sex, home and hearth, ... while the enemy represents the weaker force to be dominated and conquered' (White, A. 866). Hence, a soldiering man should keep away from females so that he may cut off his domestic bonds, without which he cannot dominate the enemy. The soldier-narrator asserts: 'Those who would sacrifice their lives for the country would first have to be become celibate, forgo all sensory passions' (94, this volume). A series of events and a love interest in foreign lands adds to the theme of gender and war. The story ends on a tragic note with the narrator killing the Bedouin woman, Gul who loves him, as she becomes the enemy. Yet Gul expresses her peace at dying in the arms of her beloved. The narrator's sacrificing of his love life for his hypermasculine preference for war is overshadowed by Gul's 'female masculinity' when she accepts the sacrifice of her life out of her preference for love.

In sharp contrast to the narrator-protagonist of 'The Agony of the Destitute' who detaches himself from domesticity in order to join war, the protagonist of the very next story, 'Autobiography of a Vagabond', suffers a tragic end to his domestic life and thereafter, joins the army and eventually dies while fighting in Baghdad. Though the story is called an 'autobiography', it is actually the meta-narrator—the person to whom the 'vagabond' protagonist confessed his life story—who reproduces the account verbatim after the protagonist's death. The protagonist's progress from a drunkard to a soldier reveals how warfare seems to have produced a greater intoxication among Nazrul's contemporaries, including himself (he served in the British Army, joining the Bengali Regiment), as a way to demonstrate the martial prowess of the Bengali race. The reason behind the obsession towards military masculinity seems to be to counter the stereotypical rendering of Bengali men as not manly enough by Europeans: '. . . the physical organization of the Bengali is feeble even to effeminacy' (Macaulay 566).

'Meher Negar', the third story of the volume, is another tale of war and conflicts in love. Yusuf Khan, the protagonist, is a Pathan from the mountains of Waziristan who meets Meher Negar (whose actual name is Gulshan), the woman whom he has seen and loved in his dream, after reaching a distant land to learn music. She feels unworthy of his love because she is the daughter of a courtesan. She bids him goodbye and he bids goodbye to his life as a musician and joins the War of Independence for Afghanistan. Yusuf's militant patriotism, however, fails to make him forget his love. Hence, he visits Meher Negar one last time, only to discover that she is no more. What has remained are the words written in blood on Gulshan's tombstone, asking the traveller not to hate her but to wait until he is able to unite with her in the next world. The striking feature of this story is that it offers a critical study about the deployment of art in two completely opposing directions. In Yusuf's case, love for art has motivated him to come to a distant land in search of a music teacher, and in the process also leads him to discover the woman of his dreams in the real world. Music becomes the vehicle through which he achieves self-actualisation. In the case of Yusuf's music teacher, his artistry has brought him fame and honour: he is regarded as ustad—the maestro. However, in case of Khurshedjan Baiji, Gulshan's mother, the artistic skill of the dancer–musician becomes the instrument of enforcing female prostitution. In this context, where in real life women with a talent for dance and music are often exploited through forced prostitution, Yusuf's dreaming of Gulshan, as Meher Negar, in the form of a supernatural being with a veena in her hands appears to be an incisive, almost satirical, comment on gendering in art.

As an allegorical piece of writing, 'Evening Star' is about a man's love for a distant beloved that is ultimately futile because of the probable demise of his beloved. The Morning Star is symbolically used to represent the faraway lady love of the narrator, who is represented as a traveller. He is all alone in his journey of life. In between he comes across other females who are symbolically represented as Sleep and Languor, but none of them have become his life partner. The interesting feature of this story is the shift from the surreal to the real world towards the end, when the traveller returns to his home and meets his sister-in-law. She asks him about his bride as she has heard that the traveller has got married. The narrator–traveller points at the Evening Star. She then seems to understand the meaning of his symbolic marriage and seems to share in his pain. The pain that is shared by the sister-in-law convinces the reader about the reality of the protagonist's pain, even though it is not certain if the object of the pain is a creation of the wanderer's romantic imagination.

'Rakshasi' is written in the language spoken by the Bagdi community of the Birbhum district in West Bengal. It has not been entirely possible to retain the distinctiveness of the language in English translation, but the narrative style and vigour do make it distinct from the other stories. Similar to a dramatic monologue, this story is an address by the speaker to her friend, Makhon, from whom the readers do not hear anything but can feel her presence. The speaker, Bindi, is a woman who complains to her friend about how society has stigmatised her as a demoness because she has killed her husband in order to save him from abandoning her and getting remarried to a notorious girl—an action for which he would have been made to suffer in hell. Bindi contemplates the fact that as a wife it is her moral duty to prevent her husband from committing a sin for which he will have to suffer eternally in hell. Their society ostracises the entire family and no one is willing to marry her daughter. She ends by asking whether it is her fault that she is so angry at the treatment meted out to her and her loved ones by society or it is the heartless society that is to be blamed for not recognising the circumstances that have wrought her into an enraged woman. The story reveals the societal stigma associated not only with being a widow, but also with a woman who dares to invert the conventional image of a weak and voiceless wife abiding by the actions of an authoritarian husband. As Bindi has failed to perform the conventional role of a Sita, she is labelled as a rakshasi. The fact that society ostracises Bindi's entire family, even after her imprisonment as a penalty for her crime, highlights the stigma attached to a former convict by treating the person as a lifetime criminal.

'Salek' is a short moral story where, through a series of events, a dervish (later revealed to be Hafiz) shows an arrogant Kazi the path to salvation; the former becomes the latter's salek or the one who shows the way. Nazrul has luminously shown the mystical intersection of things that apparently seem to be contradictory: what is considered to be sacrilege following the ways of the world is often a step towards salvation. The story delineates the Sufi proclamation of 'withdrawal from this-worldly demands, *tark-i-duniya*, with the same kind of intensity as the madness of Majnun and yet superior to him, for the latter sacrificed his life for a perishable Layla, whereas Sufis devoted themselves to an eternal God' (Aquil 27). The Kazi exemplifies that the shunning of 'attachment to this world, whether private or public' lies at the core of Sufism, along with a call for 'soul-searching, remembrance of God beyond ritual prayers in mosques, ... and wandering around as dervishes' (64). Following the dervish, the Kazi himself ends up becoming a Sufi salek, reminding us of a composition by Rumi:

> I wander aimlessly
> the ruins of my life
> my old self a stranger to me
>
> (Chopra 51)

In 'The Widow', Begum, the narrator, speaks of her sorrowful youth, her happy married life and the miseries of her widowhood to her friend, Salima. The story challenges multiple stereotypes that are often associated with the women of South Asia. It portrays Begum's mother-in-law as a progressive woman who can easily overcome and resist societal taboos related to class discrimination. She also exhibits tremendous fortitude, unlike the typical characterisation of an anxious mother, in dedicating her only son to God at his imminent end. Begum too becomes a rebel by not conforming to the conventional socio-religious customs prescribed for a widow. Stating explicitly that despite her hardships on account of the death of her husband she is not going to commit suicide, which she condemns as weakness, she represents a suffering widow who, nevertheless, refuses to be submissive.

Nazrul classifies 'The Restless Traveller' (the concluding tale of the volume) as a short sketch. This impressionistic story is centered round the urge towards finding freedom by restless youth. The traveller is portrayed as a champion of liberty who inspires thousands of other young people to follow him in a risky and noble move for freedom. The elders are apprehensive, but the young ones are ready to surrender themselves for the sake of the independence of the nation. The protagonist finally becomes a martyr in the struggle for freedom, but he is not the only one—there are many others who have given their lives prior to him, and there are millions of his followers who continue with his ideology and spirit. By not specifying the identity of the traveller or the territory for which he is struggling, Nazrul puts forward the restless traveller as a global icon of the universal aspiration for liberation and decolonisation: 'For once raise your voice and say O valiant, "We are all free, all sovereign" .... Violently twisting off the chains of your hands, legs and necks, O valiant say, "We are all free, all sovereigns". You will find then and there that all your chains, all fetters are broken into pieces' (Islam 2: 405–06).

THE SHIULI MALA: TALES OF ANXIETY AND INTIMACY

The opening story of the volume, 'The Lotus-Cobras', is about Zohra and her human and nonhuman intimacies. Zohra is married to Arif, the descendant of a zamindar family that has lost its riches a few generations back. With her arrival, the family's fortunes start to miraculously become better. She even finds a treasure trove of ancient gold coins that sets the family in the lap of luxury. It is with the 'lotus-cobras' that guard the treasure that Zohra forges an intensely maternal relationship, a relationship that causes great consternation amongst her in-laws, her husband and her own parents. Through many twists and turns including the loss of a twin pregnancy, the story ends with Zohra's death on seeing her beloved snakes killed. This story is important from ecocritical perspectives. According to many environmentalists and conservationists, the perception of personhood in nonhuman elements of nature seems to be one of the means of enhancing one's ecological sensitivity (Milton 51). Zohra's maternal dealings with the venomous cobras highlights Nazrul's ecological concerns, similar to the tenets of Deep Ecology which stress on a human being's sense of belonging with nonhuman nature as 'a necessary condition for a viable approach to building an eco-philosophy. In Deep Ecology, the wholeness and integrity of person/planet together with the principle of what Arne Naess calls "biological equalitarianism" are the most important ideas' (Devall 133). In the portrayal of Zohra's attachment with her serpent sons, Nazrul seems to be very close to the essence of posthumanism where radical posthuman subjectivity is understood on the basis of an intersectional ethics of plurality.

Zohra differs from her husband and in-laws who seem to have internalised anthropocentrism's compartmentalised methods of association among species. In her 'open-ended', 'interrelational' and 'trans-species' mode of 'becoming' (Braidotti 89), Zohra embodies the posthuman plea of rejecting stark individualism for the sake of establishing multiple belongings with multiple others, including nonhuman entities. Further, Zohra's apparently absurd motherly concern for the snakes as opposed to the apparently reasonable hostility of her husband and in-laws towards the cobras—forgetting that these snakes have caused them no harm and are the actual custodians of the pot of gold that has brought them prosperity—converge with the ecofeminist endeavour of exposing how our 'tradition has resulted in devaluing whatever is associated with women, emotion, animals, nature, and the body, while simultaneously elevating in value those things associated with men, reason, humans, culture, and the mind' (Gaard 5).

'The King of the Djinns' is a tragicomic story about how Allah-Rakha, the protagonist, resorts to a series of tricks in order to get married to Chan Bhanu, the woman he desires. Ranging from threatening to set fire to his father's crops to resorting to impersonating a djinn, Allah-Rakha tries many things to fulfil his goal, but ultimately fails. The significance of the story lies in the paradox that is highlighted through Allah-Rakha's failure to terrify Chan Bhanu's future father-in-law, Chheraz Halder. On the one hand, Chheraz Halder upholds a certain rational thinking that helps him see through Allah-Rakha's tricks, as opposed to the majority of people from Allah-Rakha's village who are fooled by the latter's tricks because of their romantic faith in the supernatural. On the other hand, one wonders about the merit of such unenchanted rationality that causes a person to become so utilitarian that he arranges his son's marriage to a girl, not by valuing the human skills and qualities of his would-be daughter-in-law, but on the basis of her utility in enhancing his capital.

'The Volcano' deals with the disaster that is caused by the sudden eruption of repressed anger and egotistic pride, similar to the calamity that results from an abrupt discharge of lava from a dormant volcano. Sabur, the humble, helpful and uncomplaining protagonist of the story, is severely bullied by a neighbourhood gang of boys. In order to impress his benefactor's daughter, Nurjahan, after being castigated by her for not standing up for himself, he resolves to act like a man. His resolve leads to one of the bullies being killed when Sabur tries to defend himself for the first time, ending in his imprisonment, Nurjahan's contrition at being the one to goad Sabur into action and his benefactor's guilt and subsequent atonement at Mecca. The story is a study of the anxiety of manliness. Sabur lacks all the socially acceptable markers of masculinity. He is not assertive by nature; rather he is obedient and enjoys the company of his room and does not fight back even when provoked—all of which are labelled feminine qualities by society. Nurjahan, as the character who draws attention to this gendered role, mistakes his politeness as weakness and his modesty as a lack of manliness. Sabur remains indifferent about his inability to fit into the societal framework of manliness and does not respond to the taunts and bullying until he falls in love with Nurjahan. His ego is hurt at the thought that the woman of his dreams will hate him unless he proves himself to be manly enough. This anxiety of manliness which society compels individuals to internalise—both male and female—becomes a hurdle that one has to cross in order to overcome the anxiety of intimacy. Sabur and Nurjahan do overcome their anxiety of intimacy despite their difference in class—Nurjahan's father too starts thinking of a possible marriage between her and Sabur—but not before Sabur's performative machismo has severe consequences. Through the story, Nazrul has portrayed the perils of the fixation on machismo which becomes stereotyped as the only form of ideal manhood.

'The Shiuli Mala' is the concluding story of the volume and is a testimony to Nazrul's love for the trope of separated lovers or unrequited love. It primarily deals with a platonic and disunited love between Azhar, a well-known chess player, and Shiuli, the daughter of another brilliant chess player, Professor Chowdhury. Structured as a flashback, Azhar narrates the story to his friends who are part of a regular chess adda. The entire story, with its setting in Shillong and ending in a voluntary separation, reminds us of Tagore's 'The Last Poem' (*Shesher Kobita*). Like Azhar, Amit the poet-lover of Tagore's novel, decides not to transform his love for Labonyo, his beloved, into marriage, so that the memory of their love remains forever as a truth of imperishable beauty, unlike the manner in which he and his beloved can never escape in real life from the wreck of time and change.

UNANTHOLOGISED STORIES

'Letter from a Lost Boy' is an epistolary account of a boy who writes to his mother about some incidents in his life that have occurred since he had left her until the time of his return. He narrates his personal losses, being made aware of the plight of child brides through the situation his sister seems to find herself in, and the perils of widowhood he has witnessed in the life of his aunt. He ends the letter by expressing his gratitude to his mother and all the women in life, along with the assurance that he will serve them through his life.

The story is a critique of child marriage and the consequent early widowhood that brings never-ending misery in the life of a woman. The most important characteristic of this story is that, it is autobiographical in nature. Arun Kumar Basu has written that,

> In the middle of March-April 1921, Chaitra 1327, Ali Akbar Khan along with Nazrul have travelled to Comilla via Chattogram Mail. It seems that the first conflict in the drama of Nazrul's youthful days has approached him.... Taking Nazrul with him, Ali Akbar

> Khan has become a guest in the house of Indrakumar Sengupta at Comilla. Indrakumar is a key figure of the aristocratic family of Comilla; his son Birendrakumar has been Ali Akbar's classmate in the district school. Ali used to address Birojashundori, the mother of Birendrakumar, as "ma". Birendrakumar has two unmarried nieces, Kamala and Anjali. Adjacent to the house, like a joint family, stays Giribala, the widow of Indrakumar's late elder brother. She also has a daughter of Kamal–Anjali's age, named Duli or Ashalata. Henceforth, Birojashundori has also become Nazrul's mother (Basu 65).

The mother in this epistolary story is none other than Birojashundori. The 'mashi-ma' is based on Giribala, as 'Nazrul used to address Indrakumar's widowed sister-in-law, Giribala Debi, as mashi-ma' (Sengupta 78). In the story there is a reference to Kamala. Pramila is another name for Giribala's daughter, who later on becomes Nazrul's wife. In the story the protagonist says that the date on which his journey began was an inauspicious one. This actually hints at a crisis through which Nazrul had to pass because of his association with Ali Akbar Khan's niece, Sayida Khatun alias Nargis at Daulatpur. Nazrul and Nargis were supposed to get married, but 'Disappointed due to various reasons Nazrul, carrying the guilt of an incomplete wedding, left the marriage ceremony. That very night taking Birendrakumar along with him ... Nazrul left Daulatpur and started heading towards Comilla on foot' (Basu 69). From Bandhon Sengupta we come to know that, 'economically and emotionally exhausted, he [Nazrul] was in terrible anguish which compelled him to stay for nineteen days at a stretch in the household of the Sengupta family' (Sengupta 85). The disagreement between the protagonist and his mother that is hinted at in the story is also reminiscent of a disagreement between Nazrul and his mother; a disagreement that led to Nazrul staying away from his mother until she died.

The last story in this collection, 'The Hawk-Cuckoo from the Woods', reminds us of 'The Lotus-Cobras'. Like 'The Lotus-Cobras', the story is about the marital discord between Dushasan Mitra and his wife Romola that widens after Romola becomes too attached to an injured hawk-cuckoo. Her husband feels agitated by her gradual disconnect from their conjugal life. On top of that, Romola, who has been trained in singing devotional kirtan songs, ends up teaching the bird, through her songs, to utter the names of her gods. For her, the bird's uttering of 'Radha Krishna' is not a mere imitation, but a form of 'naam-kirtan'—the repeated recitation of the name (or the various names) of divinity as a means of spiritual elevation. The selfless love she has for the bird becomes a manifestation of Romola's bhakti. Romola's linking of the bird with divinity reminds us of a song by the Baul saint, Lalon Fakir:

> The unknown bird in the cage...
> how does it fly in and out?
> Catch it, I would, if I could...
> and put my mind's chains on its feet
>
> (Chatterjee)

The story ends with Romola flaying her husband for throwing the bird away, finding and hugging the dying bird to her heart and plunging into the waters of the Padma. Romola's perception of the bird as her deity and her total abandonment of societal norms on account of her complete surrender to reunite with Krishna through the 'Hari-Bola' bird, brings to mind a composition by the Vaishnava poet, Chandidas:

> . . . I see
> his sorrow and deep love
> and I am tormented.
> I would set fire to my house
> for him, I would bear
> the scorn of the world.
>
> (Dimock and Levertov 22)

Apart from an exploration of spirituality, Nazrul reveals his unique understanding of human psychology through the character of Mr Mitra. It is not possible to confine Mr Mitra within the prototype of a dominant patriarch. Rather, his jealousy regarding Romola's obsessive love for the bird can be best understood by his remarks, 'I know your father is very rich! My wealth, my job—everything is granted by him! True, you can leave me whenever you want! You can even remarry' (254, this volume). It is the burden of this great indebtedness that makes Mr Mitra suffer from a lack of confidence. Consequently, any indication of aloofness from Romola hurts his ego and makes him vengeful, because 'Great indebtedness does not make people thankful, but vengeful instead' (Nietzsche 68).

RECLAIMING NAZRUL AND HIS STORIES

James Procter has alerted us to a trend of minoritising difference by perceiving it as a deviation from the majoritarian ethos: 'the processes by which we become indifferent to difference have to be recognized as a crucial part of the postcolonial project' (78). In postcolonial South Asian countries, under the pretext of the nation-building, the culture of the majority seems to be projected as the homogenous 'national' culture and differences are treated as trivial, minor or even 'anti-national'. Nazrul's short stories are marked with 'differences'—the characters are more cosmopolitan than national, more fluid in their faith than expected by spokespersons of ethno-religious nationalism, and exhibit little discrimination based on differences of class, caste and species. The difference in our attitude towards Nazrul versus his other contemporaries says something about our indifference towards the perception of differences in the majoritarian social order prevalent in postcolonial societies. A proper evaluation of Nazrul as a writer is possible only by understanding that, as opposed to the imitation of the majoritarian notion of aesthetics or simply abiding by the traditional formulas of aesthetic enquiry, Nazrul's aesthetics of experience are based on celebrating the differences in everyday life that are concrete, common, familiar but lived, and is an important decolonising endeavour. Narrating the micropolitics of everyday life, Nazrul offers 'a critique of superior activities' (Lefebvre 109) out of the conviction that such 'superior' activities are a part of the neocolonial scheme of inattention to the needs of the marginalised and the ordinary. Besides providing glimpses of underrepresented lives, it is hoped that this translation of Nazrul's short stories of extraordinary celebrations of the ordinary will also allow readers from all over the world to ponder how, in our pursuit of knowing the unfamiliar and the extraordinary, we have become those people who 'in general, do not know their own lives very well, or know them inadequately' (116).

Kazi Nazrul Islam was interested and invested in the literatures of different cultures. In the essay 'Contemporary World-Literature', Nazrul begins by dividing the major literary figures of the world into two categories. In the first group of 'dreamers', he places writers like Shelley, Milton, Yeats and Tagore who 'try to soar high above the dusty earth and search for heaven, their feet never touch the dust of the earth; soaring higher—further higher, they sing the songs of the land of dreams' (Islam 7: 22). In the other group Nazrul places 'the offspring of the soil' like Benavente, Gorky and Bernard Shaw, who 'cling to this earthy world with immense affection—the way a child overwhelmingly embraces their mother during the dark hours and frightening nights' (22). In the same essay, Nazrul also formulates a third category of writers, like Leonid Andreyev and Knut Hamsun, who lie between these two extremes of dreamers and realists:

> Lying on the lap of the mother of soil, this person listens to the tales of heaven ... This person is such a child who thinks that heaven and earth are not co-wives, but are sisters. Like the mother, the aunt-heaven is not sorrowful; she is a majestic queen full of wealth ... This child knows that his own heavenly relatives, the gods, do not have any sorrow ... but that does not invoke malice. The child sings a painful song sitting in one's own room—makes the unhappy mother listen to it.... the soil turns clayey with his tears, but the child does not make a ball of clay to throw at heaven out of rage. (23)

In which category can we place Nazrul? Is there a need to formulate a different category altogether in order to position him? We leave it to the readers of these translated stories of Nazrul to decide.

NOTE

Apart from the lines quoted from the stories of Nazrul, all translations, unless otherwise specified, are ours.

WORKS CITED

Ahmad, Muzaffar. *Kazi Nazrul Islam: Smritikatha*. National Book Agency Private Limited, 1975.

Appiah, K.A. "Cosmopolitan Patriots". *Critical Inquiry*, vol. 23, 1997, pp. 617–39.

Aquil, Raziuddin. *Lovers of God: Sufism and the Politics of Islam in Medieval India*. Routledge, 2020.

Basu, Arun Kumar. *Nazrul Jiboni*. Ananda Publishers, 2016.

Braidotti, Rosi. *The Posthuman*. Polity, 2013.

Chakrabarti, Sumita, editor. *Kazi Nazrul Islam/Kabitar Janma: Patthaker Anvesa*. Nazrul Centre for Social and Cultural Studies, Kazi Nazrul University, 2020.

Chatterjee, Sudipto. "Songs of Lalon Phokir : 3". *Parabaas*, 27 Dec 2007, https://www.parabaas.com/translation/database/translations/poems/lalon_sudipt 3.html. Accessed 20 January 2024.

Chopra, Deepak, editor. *The Love Poems of Rumi*. Harmony Books, 1998.

Cock, Jacklyn. *Colonels and Cadres: War and Gender in South Africa*. OUP, 1991.

Coomaraswamy, Ananda K. "Sati: A Vindication of the Hindu Woman". *The Sociological Review*, vol. 6, no. 2, 1913, pp. 117–35.

Devall, Bill. "The Deep Ecology Movement". *Key Concepts in Critical Theory: Ecology*, edited by Carolyn Merchant, Humanities P, 1994.

Dimock, Edward C., and Denise Levertov. *In Praise of Krishna: Songs from the Bengali*. Double Day & Company, Inc., 1967.

Dinesen, Isak. "The Cardinal's First Tale". *Last Tales*, Random House, 1957, pp. 3–27.

Gaard, Greta, editor. *Ecofeminism: Women, Animals, Nature*. Temple UP, 1993.

Islam, Kazi Nazrul. *Nazrul Rachnaboli*, edited by Rafiqul Islam, Abul Kalam Monzur Morshed, Abul Kashem Fazlul Haq, Mohammad Mahfuz Ullah, Abdul Mannan Syed and Nurul Islam, Bangla Academy, 2006. 12 vols.

Lal, B.K. *Contemporary Indian Philosophy*. Motilal Banarsidass, 1978.

Lefebvre, Henri. *Critique of Everyday Life: The One-Volume Edition*. Verso, 2014.

Macaulay, T.B. *Critical, Historical and Miscellaneous Essays and Poems*, vol. 2, Estes and Lauriat, 1880.

Maitse, Teboho, and Jen Marchbank. "Revealing Silence: Voices from South Africa". *States of Conflict: Gender, Violence and Resistance*, edited by Susie Jacobs, Ruth Jacobson, and Jennifer Marchbank, Zed, 2000, pp. 119–24.

Milton, Kay. *Loving Nature: Towards an Ecology of Emotion*. Routledge, 2002.

Nancy, Jean-Luc. *Being Singular Plural*. Translated by Robert Richardson and Anne O'Byrne, Stanford UP, 2000.

Nandy, Ashis. *The Intimate Enemy: Loss and Recovery of Self under Colonialism*. Oxford UP, 1983.

Nietzsche, Friedrich. *Thus Spake Zarathustra*. Cambridge UP, 2006.

Procter, James. "The Postcolonial Everyday". *New Formations*, no. 58, 2006, pp. 62–80.

Sakai, Naoki. "Translation and the Figure of Border: Toward the Apprehension of Translation as a Social Action". *Profession*, vol. 11, no. 1, 2010, pp. 25–34.

Sarkar, Abhishek. "The Great War, Communal Identity and Personal Emotions in the Fiction of Kazi Nazrul Islam". *South Asian History and Culture*, vol. 10, no. 3, 2019, pp. 1–16.

Sengupta, Bandhon. *Samagro Nazrul Jibon*. Paschim Banga Kazi Nazrul Islam Akademi, 2018.

White, Aaronette M. "All the Men Are Fighting for Freedom, All the Women Are Mourning Their Men, but Some of Us Carried Guns: A Raced-Gendered Analysis of Fanon's Psychological Perspectives on War". *War and Terror I: Raced-Gendered Logics and Effects in Conflict Zones*, special issue of *Signs*, vol. 32, no. 4, edited by Mary Hawkesworth and Karen Alexender, 2007, pp. 857–84.

White, James Boyd. *Justice as Translation: An Essay in Cultural and Legal Criticism*. U of Chicago P, 1994.

HARVEST OF SORROW

ONE

HARVEST OF SORROW

Translated by Sarker Hasan Al Zayed

DARA'S STORY

Golestan

Golestan! I have come back into your arms after a long time. Ah, my earthen mother! How tranquil is your lap! Standing in the empty yard, the first thing I recall is my doting mother, her adoring kisses, her unending, baseless anxieties, her agonised affection for me ... that plain and simple lullaby:

> Fairy mashi[1] and pishi[2] of slumber, make us fall asleep,
> We'll give you a box full of paan, stuff your cheeks and eat up![3]

I remember those innumerable implorations and affectionate exchanges between the two of us—mother and son ... Where is my mother now?

Sometimes, I ponder whether this blind, maternal love made it difficult for me to know my other, more significant, mother—the nation. I do not know if my mother can hear me from heaven, but I can say, without doubt, that I have come to recognise my superior mother—my homeland—because I lost my biological mother; because the shackles of motherly love broke apart when she died. But I have to also confess that I learned to love my greater mother only later; earlier I had given my whole-hearted respect, devotion and love only to my human mother. I am not belittling my biological mother, by the way.

---

[1] Mother's sister.

[2] Father's sister.

[3] A popular Bengali lullaby.

In a sense, she remains superior. She was the one who had taught me how to love. She was the one who struck the sweet tune of affection in my soul. She was the one who had taught me to respond in this manner to crucial or casual calls! She was the one who showed me the way; all I did was follow. People think I am crazy! They think I have chosen a thorny path to self-destruction! But my mother knew my destination. And now only I know what it is.

Do people hate me? Aha! that's what I want. But there will be a time when people will know the truth about me. That day, they will shed tears of sympathy. I probably won't get the opportunity to see it after all, and, unlike a child deprived of affection, will not weep in private. Perhaps, I will be on the other side of life by then, beyond anguish and tears.

Chaman[4]

Achcha ma! Why did you light the fire of unhappiness in my heart, while you found peace in your afterlife? I implored, I protested: no—no—no, I would not bear this burden, this sin; but why didn't you listen? Smiling, you waved it aside, as if you knew what was brewing inside me. Who is responsible for burdening me with Bedoura? My work is delayed! I can't even hide anywhere peacefully!

I know now that you forced me to wear this flower-fetter on the day of your departure so that my restless soul would settle down. That garland has turned into the source of my suffering! I have the strength to tear apart an iron shackle, but I don't have the heart to crush this flower-cuff that you left me with. It is easy to meet strength with strength; but who's going to hurt what is tender and delicate? I can't take the pounding of that delicate thing anymore!

Unfortunate Bedoura! Do you remember that day—Ma's last day? That grim hour? A glum messenger of Death waiting near Ma's head and her sorrowful face reflecting shades of an apathetic contentment! Do you remember how the last drops of her life turned into tears and fell on our foreheads like blessings? Those sacred teardrops were as

---

[4] Chaman is used here in two senses: the headquarters of Killa Abdullah district in Pakistan, and as the Urdu word for garden. It is interesting to note that 'Golestan' and 'Bostan' also mean 'garden' in Persian, while being used as place names in this narrative.

iridescent with agony as they were clad in tenderness! Your curly, black, unkempt hair, partly drenched in our tears, covered my face, entwined around my hand and neck. Ma put your tender, leaf-like hands on mine, and, crying, told me, 'Dara, promise me—you will never abandon Bedoura.'

Almost indistinctly, she whispered her last words, 'Son! She doesn't have anyone. I have raised this motherless child with so much love that she has become very sensitive, even pampered . . .'

How desperate and despairing her bidding! How deep her conviction in the power of love!

Do you remember Bedoura, how love blossomed in our teenage hearts and how the faint rays of attraction turned into sunrise? Our desperate hearts howled in pain, although we were sitting side by side. Do you remember? I used to think that having you by my side was the most painful thing in the world. No? Then why did our smiles dry up within seconds when we sat together in the vineyards of Golestan? Why were our hearts filled with a deep, sacred silence? Why did our souls quiver in inexplicable pain, time and again? Why did our eyes fill with tears . . .

Now, I have resolved this mystery Bedoura. After spending so many days lamenting your absence, I have moved closer to you rather than pulling back. I lost you because I found you so easily. Only a lovelorn soul knows how intense the happiness of detachment is. No one else can express in words what pleasurable agony it is when the heart pines for the beloved crying, 'piya piya'. Of all the pleasures in life, that of detachment is the most intense.

And what about the memory of that day? It truly hurt my soul, resonating like a deep wound. I still remember that day—Phagun[5] lit the sky, breeze, fruits, flowers, leaves with fire . . . and, most importantly, the hearts of young men and women!

The grapes hanging from the vines were so juicy and delicate that they looked like sixteen-year-old badshahi fairy princesses with perfect bodies! The pears appeared rosy, like the blushing cheeks of beautiful women. Pomegranate seeds spurted from their skins like the red pouting lips of teenage girls, so juicy were they. In flowering pistachio orchards,

[5] Phagun or Phalgun is the eleventh month in the Bengali calendar and the month of spring.

bulbuls were holding their Nowruz carnival. Newlywed koel and doel brides were rehearsing their songs from the hidden, topmost branches of trees, so that they could enthral their young husbands.... Intoxicated by the fragrance wafting in on the brisk southern breeze, you leaned against my chest. Putting aside the Bulbul of Shiraz's diwan,[6] I contemplated ordering your naughty locks, as tears kept rolling down our eyes.

The sweet discontent of our union was beautifully turning the pages of the first chapter of our lives. Then everything came undone, just as the pages of an open book are ravaged by a storm.... How I had to struggle to put those pages in order, Bedoura!

But I don't mind because I have found you again in Chaman. You are mine.

It reminds me of a line by a Bengali poet,[7]

You're mine, only mine
In my lonesome world you reign!

Then came the hour of separation, Bedoura! Do you remember? I was reciting that verse composed by the Bulbul of Shiraz,

One Spring morning I saw in the garden,
A bee, lying prostrate amidst the scattered pollen
Of a newly bloomed lotus and profusely crying,
Disrupting, all of a sudden, my flower picking!
I asked—'For what sorrow do you cry, bee, my brother,
From the very bosom of your beloved flower?'
Lighting up the lotus with his tears and kisses,
Said the bee, 'O poet, this juncture is apt for shedding tears.
After so many days, having found the desired one,
My tears gush in the agonising pleasure of pain!'

And at that moment, your uncle came and forcefully took you away; he did not believe a single word I said. Smiling disdainfully, he declared that as long as he was alive, he would not allow you to be with a homeless and penniless fellow like me.

---

[6] This refers to the Persian poet Hafiz, as he was born in Shiraz and his compositions were said to be as captivating as the melody of the bulbul; the diwan is a collection of shorter poems.

[7] This is a reference to Rabindranath Tagore and his song, 'Tumi shondhar megh mala' ('You are the beauteous garland of evening-clouds'; *Swarabitan* 10).

Seeing tears in my eyes, he said that I had lost my mind reading crazy Persian poets. Hearing you haplessly implore him, he claimed I had cast a spell on you.

For many days, I wandered around that powerfully flowing mountain spring. When I came to my senses, I saw that the carnival of the Basant festival[8] continued. Except, you weren't there. I saw the imprint of your alta-dyed[9] feet gradually vanishing in the waters of the spring, and the broken pieces of your colourful glass bangles being veiled by grains of sand.

Sometimes, forgetfully, I would call out 'Bedoura!' . . . An echo, sounding howl-like, 'ra—ah—ah!', died out midway.

I discovered all the mountains and forests of Baluchistan and Afghanistan, but I could not locate your spring-side hut.

One morning, I saw a mad man in a vast open field, looking at the sky, jumping upwards, and trying to catch something in his clutching fingers. I felt like laughing out loud. Eventually, I asked him, 'Brother jumping-jack! Are you trying to catch the sky-grasshopper by jumping up and down?'

He became more hyper, jumping up and down and singing,

I threw a knife from this side, but it struck a banana plant
My knee bleeds and baba re! my eyes are gone!

This would have made a dead man laugh. Although heartbroken, I laughed loudly, 'Bhai, are you a poet?'

This made him very happy. Swinging his hair in the air, he said, 'Yes, yes, exactly!'

'But your couplets don't rhyme!'

'It doesn't matter. What's important is that your knee too is bleeding.' Saying that, he embarrassed me by starting to kiss my cheeks where my new beard had begun to show. He said, 'When you try to grab the colour blue, believing that the azure of the air is in fact the indigo sky, then it moves away from you, saying, "I'm not the sky, I'm air. I'm empty. You can't catch me. You already have me. Still, if you come to catch me thinking I'm not there, that would be a dreadful mistake."'

---

[8] Spring-festival suggests the overall carnival of spring as well as the particular festival of Holi.

[9] A red dye that women use to decorate their feet with.

My loud laughter became silent. I thought—yes that's right. The person who resides in my soul, why am I labouring so hard to possess them?

I sobbed for the last time in my dilapidated house: 'Bedoura, you are in my soul—in every blood-cell of my heart.'

Believing strongly in those words, I went to Hindustan disguised as a Kamliwale[10]; an eccentric walking through its streets and narrow lanes. I thought my life would be spent this way, but how could that happen? Once again, I found myself back in Golestan. My hut had turned to dust, but the imprints of your feet near the spring were still visible. Those imprints told me you had come looking for me, and had gone crying from one place to another, unable to find me!

That mad man came again to tell me that after blooming like a flower, you were slowly withering away in Chaman.

In Chaman, I recognised you from afar. But why did you run away when you saw me? Oh! How you hid yourself behind those date trees running pell-mell as if drunk! How uncontrollable tears fell from your eyes! So much grief in those sad, sad eyes!

But where did you go?

Bedoura, where are you?

BEDOURA'S STORY

Bostan

O ma! What a pale, sad sky! That deluge earlier, was it the infinite sky weeping? No, no, why would the vast sky cry? Even if it did—unlike our selfish and sinful weeping—its teardrops are not warm and unsavoury. Have you noticed how cold it is!

But have I been dreaming? I literally ran from Chaman to Bostan! Let it be. It is as if my soul has returned to my body.... Ah silly-billy! Why do I feel like crying? Why is this grief welling up? There is no greater troublemaker than the human mind—my aching mind is the cause of all my pains! What? Am I crying because I saw him? Why is it such a big deal?

---

[10] It literally means a madman, or a man wrapped in blanket. However, as a title this is also used for the Prophet Muhammad, as well as Krishna in South Asia.

I knew he would come back. But why so late? Why at this hour? The flower stalk of my youth is now blossomless! Oh, how will I set up a bridal bed on the shore of death in this evil hour? If you had to come, why didn't you come a few days early? I wouldn't have had to avoid you then! That day, when I saw you in the dried-up garden in Chaman, I would have jumped on you and said, 'Come dear! come back to me!'

We womenfolk cry very easily but men can't. Their chests are tight, as if they have buried their emotions under a stone. When such men fail to control their emotions and tears roll down their eyes, what woman can hold hers back? I don't know anyone who can!

When our eyes met after all these days, they moistened, lighting up with emotions, entreaties, complaints, hurts! Yes, all that! And how, shaking and reeling, whispering 'Bedoura,' he fell into a thorny date palm! Seeing him in that state, I simply covered my eyes with both my hands and ran as fast and far as I could. How heartless of me!

So many old memories are surfacing today! We used to meet in Golestan like a pair of bulbuls: pouting in togetherness, suffering from the detachment of being in union (despite our togetherness), and shedding tears of joy! It hurts to even think of those days! Then that scoundrel dragged me from my betrothed's chest. With a great deal of effort, I escaped his grip and came back to look for my beloved! Oh! What haven't I done to get him back! Where was he then?

Then a struggle ensued, both external and internal! Inside me, the embers of burning husks flickered. And outside? The stray breezes of Phalgun lit a fire of intense desire! That's when, God knows from where, Saiful Mulk appeared in my life like a comet, singing the seductive raga of love in my ears—just like that sharp fourth note of Bhairavi, love is also marked by immaculate melancholic gravity!

And how intense, sharp and unkind that foul desire was! The pleasure one derives by fulfilling this carnal desire is as malignant as a pishacha! Its blaze only burns us down like the raga Deepak! Yet, in the new spring of our lives, it consumes each and every one of us at least once. If there is no serene symphony of Megh Malhar to soothe us, Deepak will set us ablaze—there will be no respite!

That's why, when someone desired me in my youth, I could not suppress my physical instinct. I went blind! My lord, where were you on that day? No one admonished me! Hai! I think I died that day. It was on that day I turned into a beggar and turned to the street. In those days of free-fall, such dense darkness concealed my eyes and not an iota of light tried to penetrate it—as it does now. Perhaps, if a single ray of light could chase out all the darkness, I could see the king of kings who reigns in my soul.

I didn't understand then why I fell—I still don't. Everything seems muddled up! Who will understand if I say my love—the love that is hidden in my heart, the love that is sacred—will forever remain so, unscathed, and no amount of torture can dent it? Who will forgive me? Yet, I continue to say that love is sacred, invincible, and eternal; vice always corrupts, and is weak and short-lived.

Oh ma! What unbearable pain in my chest, in every single rib! What silly things have I been talking about until now? Exactly like a dream, no? ... Vice is short-lived. Just as the river leaves behind a slick of mud after the flood, so vice leaves behind a thick covering of misgiving—doesn't misgiving last for a very short time or does it, for many people, last throughout their lives? Even when a wrongdoer like me manages to change, my disrepute sticks to me like mud forever! Even the full moon cannot conceal its blemishes! How painful even this repentance for sin is! As if thousands of needles are piercing the soft corners of my chest simultaneously...

Again, I remember that devil, Saiful Mulk—the man who led me down the garden path. He is a khaja[11] made of spoiled and bitter jaggery! If he were here right now, I would tear him to pieces with my nails!

We are women—even when a trivial thing happens, we tend to think our souls have been corrupted and always regret our deeds. We also tend to assume that men are not bothered by small misdeeds. That they do not regret wrongdoings as intensely as we do. When my thirst for lust dried up, and it dawned on me that I had swallowed poison mistaking it for ambrosia, that moment the sacred love inside me welled up like an unstoppable force. That powerful awareness expressed itself through the anger in my eyes. Since that day—on that day, to be precise—Saiful Mulk became so lowly all of a sudden! An inexorable sense of shame mixed with loathing came over him, twisting his mouth! He looked at me from a distance with fearful eyes, raising his hands and

[11] A crunchy, layered sweet that is prepared with flour and sugar.

screaming, 'Khoda![12] I will atone for this sin with my life. Just give me your blessing so I can sacrifice my life for the sake of goodness!'

Then he fell at my feet like a madman and pleaded, 'Devi, forgive this devil! A goddess retains her godliness forever. It isn't contaminated by external transgressions. It becomes greater and shines brighter when tested by conflict! What am I? Me?! Oh, oh, oh!' He started running away after saying so. I don't know whether he has stopped running.

What is it? Why is my mind urging me to see, for once, if my love is alright after falling senseless into the thorny date palms? . . . No, no more! I can't suffer this heartache anymore—I simply cannot! Yes, I will go there and see him. One last time. I will tell him, 'O dear! That Bedoura of yours is not there anymore. She has died—dead! Her life has flown out of her body, searching for you! You're looking for her in vain! Bedoura is no more!—no—no more!'

After that—after that? If he still wants me to be with him even after that, what will I say? What will I do? No, even then I will remain stiff like a piece of wood and tell him, 'Please don't, don't touch me my deva! Just don't touch me! Don't insult your sanctity by touching this sinful body!'

O ma! How painful! It is as if someone is piercing my chest with a knife, cutting my heart into pieces . . .

DARA'S STORY

Golestan

Are you that same Golestan? Why do you look so ugly today? Your flowers are not as beautiful. A hellish stench rises from their guts! Your sky is not as generous as it used to be. Someone has distorted it, making it opaque. It seems as though your southern breeze has hundreds and thousands of pieces of glass hidden in it and your whole body is in pain!

What did you do Bedoura? Bedoura! No, the pain that you caused me—this hurtful betrayal from my beloved, dearer than life, must have happened because of the benevolence of Khoda. I will never forget, my Khoda, that you are unquestionably magnanimous, and the pain

---

[12] Khoda/Khuda/Khodatalla: Persian words for the Almighty.

and happiness that you give to your subjects are all the same, full of blessings! Your deeds cannot be uncaring, and no one but you know what lies in the future! How much consolation does this bring to the soul of a heartsick one!

Yes, but why does my heart not accept this? Why do I think this is a serious blow? When a thirsty chatak[13] flies close to the sky, pleading 'crystal water, crystal water', and the heartless cloud strikes the bird with thunder, laughing lightning, why do we think the cloud is very cruel? Why?

I am yet to understand who I am. I used to think that I was a great man—towering! Today I realise that I am no better than the lowliest man! Like him, my mind is mean and narrow! Else, why couldn't I simply forgive Bedoura's mistake? It does not matter how great the mistake was! Her body may have been contaminated, but her soul is as full of goodness and purity as it was! Even with this knowledge I couldn't forgive her. This is my fault, for I am still narrow minded. I thought to forgive her because I wanted to look generous, but that is not how it should happen. Because it did not come from my heart! No—I have to change and become pure. I will go back to her only when I have changed, else I won't. Oh, how lowly I am! When I heard from Bedoura about her fall, I too reached the brink of hell. I thought I would take revenge on her by fulfilling my hidden desires. But then, someone held my hand, brought me back from the road to hell and wiped my tears! In a soothing voice they said, 'Bhai, this is not revenge on Bedoura. This is your revenge on your own self.' It struck me: this is so true! Overcome by bitterness, I was about to destroy myself! This brought me back.

I went to meet Bedoura and told her, 'If I can ever learn to forgive you from my heart, then we will meet again. Or else, this is our last meeting! I am lying if I compel myself to tell you that I have forgiven you. I cannot embrace a falsehood like that. I want the colours of my love to be able to replace my soul's darkness.'

With tears in her eyes, Bedoura smiled and said, 'You have to come back my love, you must come back! Your doubt will be removed in a few days. Then you will see how our love has become deeper and

---

[13] A bird that is believed to be a harbinger of the monsoon as it drinks only drops of rain that fall.

holier, cleansed of its dark stains! I will wait for you by this scanty fountain in the garden, singing and making flower garlands. And you will wear them. The puja that has ensued from so much pain cannot be for nothing, my love!'

Where do I go now? What path will she take? You, my constant fellow-traveller, where are you now?

SAIFUL MULK'S STORY

I am that Shaitan, that sinner, who led a devi down the wrong path. I thought I would join this World War—any side engaged in the conflict—and bring my wretched life to an end as fast as possible. Then? What else then? What happens to all sinners will happen to me as well.

When a sinner is punished, they find solace in believing they have not been unjustly punished; that they deserved it. But if they are not punished, their conscience keeps biting them, which is even worse than infernal torment.

What I wished for did not happen! I roamed about and finally joined this band of freedom fighters.[14] The soldiers were extremely happy having a foreigner join them. They thought their selfless ideology had gained ground in different parts of the world. Fondly taking me in seemed to prove how motivated they were by fighting for the oppressed and the wretched of the world against their oppressors—and I, too, now belonged to this magnanimous community! My dark heart can now enjoy a little bit of the light of satisfaction!

Khoda, I have come to understand today that you do not detest the sinner; rather, you take pity on them. You have kept all doors open for them. Even a sinner's life is necessary. Even such a life can be used to set alight the wick of the lamp of goodness. Sinners are not contemptible or untouchable!

But what do I see? How did Dara come to be here? When I asked him later, he said, 'I didn't find a better job in the world. That's why I have joined this group.'

---

[14] This refers to the Afghan force that fought against the British in the War of Independence for Afghanistan, also known as the Third Anglo-Afghan War (6 May–8 August 1919).

How subdued he has become after getting hurt again and again. I must ask for his forgiveness; or else, I will not find forgiveness anywhere. I am the one who started the fire of grief in his life. I am the one who has made him homeless.

. . . Dara is fighting the battle with unimaginable courage. Everyone thinks that someone who works so tirelessly for the well-being of the world, spilling his own blood for others, must be a true hero, and his a heroic race! Not a single day goes by when he does not face one kind of injury or another. He pays no attention. It is as if he is attacking injustice with a deep, endless thirst for war and the single-mindedness of death. As long as he is of sound mind, who can persuade him to return from the battlefield! What stubborn determination! I understand this is not simply a fight against an external enemy, but an internal one too; a failed effort to get rid of the pain inside. I know it will either bear extremely toxic fruit or yield that which is calm and beautiful.

For the last few days, bombs and airplanes have become his consistent companions. How does this crazy young man withstand all these assaults from both inside and outside so stoically? As though he has left behind his fear in the Arabian Sea!

He is a commander now. God knows what dissatisfaction has started to grow in his heart and show in his facial expressions! He is injured daily, but who can reason with him to go to the hospital! Asking the gunner to go and rest, he assumes his role and shells the enemy with his broken hand. Although he is the commander, he carries bags full of grenades and bombs in his hands like an ordinary soldier, along with buckets of liquid fire on his back—and, of course, a revolver in his hand. How can I describe how happy he seems to be spilling blood and killing people! He says the smaller the number of enslaved people on earth the better.

I am really surprised. Has he gone mad for real!

* * *

What did you do Khoda! What did you do? Even after so much suffering and pain, you turned poor Dara blind and deaf? I was afraid that his pishacha-like war-thirst would end in something like this! We do not understand the meaning of your leela, All Merciful! You made the bomb blind his eyes and destroy his hearing, while keeping a sinner like me safe and sound. Am I supposed to see even this as a sign of your mercy? Please let me understand, O Lord, what kind of mercy this is! I have broken this blind man's only cane of comfort! Are you going to keep my body intact, so that you can dice my soul into pieces? O Supreme Righteousness! Is this your punishment for me—a world full of distress?

* * *

Even on this joyful day of triumph, the victory flag hoisted atop our imperial palace is shaking and quivering! Instead of the celebratory sounds of the trumpet, what we hear is a heart wrenching waltz of wails, stopping and slowly trudging out! The trumpet's brazen sound is breaking down again and again! Today is Dara's farewell! When he stood in front of his soldiers—injured, blind and deaf, leaning on my shoulder—all the freedom fighters began to break down! Words cannot express how sad it is to see tough soldiers weep this way. The leader of the freedom fighters—with tears in his voice—said, 'Bhai Darabi, we have no tradition of rewarding soldiers with honours like "Victoria Cross" or "Military Cross" because we cannot reward ourselves for our work. The reward for our sacrifices and good deeds is the wellbeing of the people of the world. But those who sacrifice like you, show courage like you, are the only ones who are esteemed as heroes by us.'

The leader choked. Wiping his tears with his sleeves, continued, 'You have been blinded, deafened, and your whole body is covered by deep scars. We say, this is your greatest reward! As someone no one had even heard of, you came to sacrifice your life for the people of the world! In return, what Khoda has given you on His own—these scars, that look frightful from the outside—are the greatest rewards anyone can ever have! What can we human beings give you? "Allah is great and He rewards humans for their good deeds"—is what is written in our holy Quran. So, fearless soldier, our hero, perhaps all the happiness of the world is secretly contained in the depth of your blindness and deafness! I hope Khoda gives you peace!'

Dara made a vain attempt to see the soldiers with his blind eyes. Suppressing his tears, all he could say was, 'Goodbye my fearless, righteous brothers!'

I came back to this same Golestan with blind Dara! This is the only consolation of my failed life—serving this stoic hero! Dara has forgiven me, embraced me as a friend! The barren life of this unfortunate youth has at last begun to blossom with meaning! At last, true love has made him generous, making him indulgent like the eternal sky! On our way back home, I asked him, 'Achcha bhai, have you been able to forgive Bedoura?'

In a tearful voice he sang a ghazal by Rumi,

My love! I have built a great
Mosque of love with
The stones you hurled at me!

I believe children are the most innocent things in this world. The magnanimity of love has turned Dara into an innocent little child. How his face lights up with an easy smile, and how he cries without any hesitation! Doesn't it bring tears to the eyes of the most heartless person? The other day I told him smiling, 'O bhai, do you see any sign of mercy in your blindness and deafness?"

He said, 'Foolish! That I could forgive you all—that the lowliness of my mind has been erased—has been possible because I lost my sight. It has happened because my external eyes and ears are not functional! Even a blind person can see and that seeing comes from the inside, extra-sensory. The whole world now seems full of the beauty of my beloved and the eternal sunshine of her smiles! Do you know what I hear with these deaf ears? Only the sweet sound of our amorous, secret conversations and the runu-jhunu of the anklets on her feet!—I am intoxicated by these things.' Overwhelmed, he started singing,[15]

If someone else you love, if you do not come back,
Then I hope you get what you want, no matter how terribly I ache!

What my heart longs for, is you, it's only you,
In this world I have nothing, no one else but you!

It was as if, by its flat third and seventh note, the overwhelming sorrow of Kanada raga took shape and whimpered endlessly! How substantial is the composed assurance and sacrifice in this song!

[15] These lines are borrowed from the song 'Amar poranjaha chaye' ('What my heart longs for') from Tagore's musical drama, *Mayar Khela* (*The Game of Illusion*).

The most surprising thing that happened was Bedoura also forgave me. When she told me about it, it did not sound affected or unusual. It seemed as though she had truly forgiven me from her heart!

You are great Khoda! You are with those who do not have anyone. Touched by the magic wands of these lovers, I too have lost my stigma, my inhibitions!

How sweet and beautiful it is today, on this day of idle work!

BEDOURA'S STORY

Golestan

The other side of the stream

He has forgiven me with an open heart, from deep inside his soul! His forgiveness has been unconditional, with no hesitancy. I knew it would happen. That's why I spent my mornings and evenings happily waiting for him! I have surrendered my days of waiting, flower wreaths put together in seclusion, and tear-soaked songs of separation at his feet. What he has gifted me in return, after picking up those wreaths and wearing them, is my harvest of sorrow!

He said, 'Bedoura! Desire and love are two completely separate things. Desire is an intense, temporary excitement and love is patient, peaceful and eternal. That neither the instinct for desire nor the satisfaction of it can cover the love etched in the heart, is an eternal truth. Those sad souls who do not slowly sink into love, believe in it, make a big mistake, and no one is as unfortunate—has as restless a life—as them. No matter how hard the clouds try to swallow up the sun on rainy days, they cannot. They can only hide it for a while. The sun lies too far from the reach of the clouds! These clouds cannot even understand how and when the sun's rays penetrate their thick covering and reach the surface of the earth. Neither can we. Once the cloud covering moves away, the sun smiles and shines even brighter. Because there is no harm caused to the sun—it knows it will still be what it always has been. The only beings affected by this are us—those on the planet. But does it mean that the rain cloud should stop coming? It won't touch the sky? It will come. It is in its nature; no one can stop it from doing so. But even in those days of heavy rain, one has to rise above the clouds to find the sunshine. It is not an easy task, and is not even necessary.

Desire is just like a rain cloud; and love is like the sun—burning bright in our hearts, unwaveringly!

Desire may have polluted your body, but it could not corrupt your soul. Besides, you would not have been able to know me better, understand me more intimately, if these things had not happened. The wind outside cannot extinguish the light of love; rather, it only accentuates it. And my blindness and deafness? Do not cry for them, Bedoura. I would not have got you back if this had not happened!'

The bulbuls flew off from the flowering apple tree, wailing, 'piya piya'.

Once again, he said, 'Listen Bedoura, tonight is our last night together—our honeymoon night. When the sun rises, you will go to the other side of the stream, and I will stay on this side. We will sing songs of separation from both sides to fill our hearts with sadness. And, the happiness of that pain will bring us back together, bonded stronger than ever.'

Since then, I have been living on the other side of the mountain spring.

I sigh in anguish when, on quiet and melancholy evenings, in a deep, soft voice he begins to hum a weary ragini that comes crying to this side of the stream,

> As the day departs, all the lamps of my woe I'll light up to offer
> The puja for my heartache is not yet over![16]

---

[16] The opening lines of a Rabindranath Tagore song (*Swarabitan* 16).

TWO

HENA

Translated by Sohana Manzoor

France

A trench in Verdun

Oh! This must be what they call a rain of fire! And the roaring sound of artillery—guroom, droom, doom! Not a speck of blue can be seen—as if the whole sky has been set on fire! The thick rain of fire that pours down from exploding cannonballs and bombs is so intense that if these were real raindrops trickling from the blue eyes of the sky, the entire world would be flooded just in a day! And if these 'droom—droom' sounds that are louder and more intense than any thunderbolt, would continue like this, peoples' eardrums would split, turning them deaf. Today, we soldiers could only recall the song that is sung during Holi celebrations:

> Today we will play Holi with our swords,
> From all over the world are gathered here the soldiers.
> Shields playing trumpets, cannonballs the water guns.
> The ammunitions sprinkle colours; the battle is intense!

It is true: the ammunition has turned sky and ground completely red. Reddest of all is the congealed blood on the bayonetted chests of the unfortunate ones! All red! No other colour but red! As the soldiers fall one by one, each one a martyr, they lie on the ground dressed in red like bridegrooms.

Oh! The worst of all is the smoky smell. Baap re baap—how revolting! It is enough to turn your stomach. Aren't human beings the best of all creations? Then why kill them in these ugly and terrifying ways? When inanimate lead bullets hit someone's bones, they explode with horrid force and tear through flesh.

If only human beings used their intelligence in more productive ways; they could have become akin to angels!

Ah! This heart-rending thirst! The friend lying next to me, rifle slipping from his hand, cannot be awakened even if a thousand cannons roar by his ear. No general can ever make him obey orders. After seven days of tiresome fighting at a stretch in this muddy trench, he has finally attained such profound peace! A soothing touch of contentment lingers on his cold and dry lips!

Whatever it is—now I feel extremely thirsty. Let me take the water bottle from his waist and take a sip to cooldown! I haven't had a drop of water since yesterday. No one cared to offer me a drink. Ah! Ah! This one sip feels so sweet after such deep thirst! My Lewis gun doesn't work anymore. It grew tired after days of continuous shooting. I will take the gun off my deceased friend then! If his mother, sister or wife were here, they would surely have cradled his broken skull on their laps and cried their hearts out! Well, I guess in a few minutes, a heavy shell of twenty to twenty-five maunds[1] will land in front of trench and bury the two of us. It won't be too bad!

Yes, I find it really funny as I think of the women, crying! Shit man, all of us will die one day; both you and me! Why cry over this universal, utterly normal, utterly inevitable thing?

I am going through so much pain, so much hardship, receiving so many wounds, but my heart is filled with the joy of a pishacha! I cannot draw this feeling with this wooden pencil! There is often a joy that lies asleep at the heart of extreme pain which we can't really feel.

And is this habit of writing, something bad? I have been swimming in fire, with scores of dead bodies under my feet and bombs dropped from aircraft bursting over my head—doom, doom, doom—while twenty yards from me artillery shells are exploding—guroom, guroom—and rifle and machine-gun bullets zoom past—sho, sho, sho. Still, deep inside, I felt restless because I couldn't write down my innermost thoughts for the last seven days! But today, I feel relieved that I can start writing again!

Ah! Let me rest for a while, leaning against my dead friend! Oh, it feels so good! . . .

[1] A unit of weight used in British India and Central Asia, with one maund being roughly equivalent to 37 kilos.

An unknown young girl from this distant land across the sea gave me some pickles and two slices of bread with butter which I haven't had time to eat. The women of this country look at us with affection and pity! Ha-ha-ha-hah! Look at the bread here—dry and roasted! Let's see if the bread is tougher than my teeth! I have no other option but to eat these—my stomach is burning! At least the pickle is still quite fresh!

The girl was thirteen or fourteen (in our country she would be wedded by now, if not already a mother!), put her hands around my neck and kissed me. As she said, 'Dada, you must drive the enemy out with full force', I broke out into a pure, sad smile!

Ah! I can finally see the sky: a strip of blue behind a mass of heavy clouds. It is so beautiful—like a pair of tear-filled, blue eyes.

Anyway, I will write down my other thoughts later. The spirit of my dead friend must be mad at me by now. What, friend? You want a drop of water? See how he is staring at me! No yaar—no, your beloved is waiting for you with a glass of sharbat in the other world. Aha, I must not deprive her of the pleasure of serving her lover!

I seem to remember so many things today. But no—no! There's nothing to remember! These are all lies! Let me pick up the Lewis gun and start shooting! I see some of those who are helping me have stolen a nap!

Oi—oi, I can hear the sound of footsteps there! They are all marching—jhawp–jhawp–jhawp! Left–right–left! The rhythm is so melodious! Perhaps, this is the other regiment coming to relieve us from duty!

Ooh! A moment of distraction has allowed a bullet to bruise my arm! Let me dress it. I hate those nurses. If a woman takes care of me without loving me, why should I accept it?

Ah! A war shows how killing others can be so addictive.

The man who has fallen beside me is far stronger and healthier than me. But I have also seen how the mind can be stronger than the body.

This Lewis gun is shooting about six to seven hundred rounds-per-minute. If only I could know how many I have killed! Let it be—but the two Lewis guns at each corner are keeping the enemies confined to their position. You can hear the loud groans of the enemy as they die in droves! How terribly beautiful is this youth's delight at death!

France

A tent on the banks of the Seine

I have slept for all of forty-eight hours in the last two days. And now I have to get dressed for battle and go out to destroy Khoda's creation. This killing game is the right kind of training for a stone-hearted, hard-headed person like me.

Today that foreign girl took me to visit her house. How clean and pretty looking are the houses here! The girl has clearly fallen in love with me. And I, too, have begun to love her. In our country, people would have said that the girl has gone bad! They would not have liked to see a young, unmarried girl going out with a young man of twenty or twenty-one.

People look at love in such ugly ways these days. Are they human beings or vultures? There is so much sin in the world. How have people become so petty? The sky above is so vast and blue, but beneath the same sky human beings are so mean and narrow-minded!

Fire, you keep raining down—jham, jham, jham! Let the curse of Khoda float down the river like frozen chunks of ice—jhoop, jhoop, jhoop! Oh! the horn of Israfil![2] Blow and freeze the world with your sound—om, om, om! Strike, oh! thunder of apocalypse, inside human brains, through bombs and the artillery shells—droom, droom, droom! And let the whole earth and sky fall on the heads of those who slander love and blight the flowers.

If I dressed one of my countrymen the way I am dressed now and pushed him down, I am sure he wouldn't be able to get up, no matter how hard he tried. I am highly amused at my current bulky and sluggish look!

A dippy friend commented, 'What a salty figure!'

Aha! What a kooky adjective! Someone seemed to reply, 'The bullock looks exactly like a catla fish!'

France

A thick forest near Paris

All of a sudden, we were sent to this dense forest yesterday. I have no clue why we were ordered to fall back! This is the beauty of military

[2] An angel of music who blows his trumpet to signal the Day of Judgement.

life—an order is given and you're told 'Get it done!' You can never ask 'Why do I have to do this?' It's an order—bas!

If you say, 'I will die' a stern reply comes in thunder-grim voice, 'As long as you breathe, keep doing your duty. If you fall dead on your right foot while marching, let your left foot keep pace!'

Ah! There is an enchantment in obeying orders, in this blind obedience, even at the cost of one's life! What tenderness lies at the heart of thunder! If the entire world were to come under one (and only one) such military regime, then it would become so beautiful that even calling it heaven on earth would not be enough!

The British nation is so great now because of the discipline they exercise in everything they do. They walk so tall that we never see the crown of their heads, no matter how hard we crane our necks—letting our turbans fall off in doing so! To speak frankly, their global empire is like a huge clock that is always correct and faultless. Its two hands run in strict and rule-bound precision. The clock is oiled every day, so there is no speck of rust anywhere.

We were the ones who chased the Germans to the Hindenburg Line and then we had to retreat so far! Only the maker of the clock knows which hand has to move at what pace; the hands don't know anything. But the hands have to keep ticking because they are continuously driven by a spring from the rear!

We badly need a disciplined, clockwork system like this. This reckless nation of ours really needs to be tied up and disciplined; otherwise, there is no hope of it rising anytime in the future! How can it function if everybody wants to be the leader of the nation!

Oh, the artillery shells rain on us even at this distance! This is really uncanny! The war is being fought so far away, but cannonballs are dropping on us in the forest!

Well, an elephant might think it is the biggest animal in the world, but even a mosquito can cause it enough harm with a single bite to its head.

It's cool in this shady darkness here, guarded by the trees and bushes. How my heart had been yearning for this solace in darkness!

Hai! The darkness seems to trigger so many fond memories!—But no! Let me just climb the tree and see if the enemy is hiding nearby.

How charming that distant ice-covered river looks from the tree! But there are also some big houses around which shells have torn through, leaving ugly gaping holes! This game of creation and destruction reminds me of my childhood when we used to build clay dollhouses with such enthusiasm. After we were done playing, we used to crush them with our feet and sing,

> Gleefully with our hands we made them
> Gleefully with our feet we broke them!

The cannonballs are flying through the air and dropping on distant planes. From my vantage point, they look like falling stars.

Oh, the 'bow-bow' sound the fighter planes make! The way they climb and dive at breakneck speed—it looks as if an expert kite-flyer is manoeuvring his fighter-kite to hurtle through the sky in search of a rival. That plane is ours! The German zeppelins look more like big, flying caterpillars from a distance.

Anyway, let me get a bit of pickle out of my haversack. The foreign girl is so far away from me today, but the fruit pickle seems to retain her touch! Oh crap! Why do I keep thinking of all this gibberish? For no reason, it feels as if seven ghosts are biting and squeezing my soul!

Ha-ha-ha-hah! What do I see there? A friend is trying to take a nap in that tree. See, he has tied himself to a branch quite tightly with his belt. If he somehow falls into the water below, it will be quite a hassle for him! But then why not? Oh Allah, let him fall, do—om!

Should I shoot a bullet past his ear? Aha-ha, no! Poor thing! Let him sleep awhile. Nobody except me has such cursed eyes that remain untouched by sleep, or a blasted mind which sickens thinking about the goings-on in the world!

It's night—quite deep in the night, I guess! I will have to stay here, crouching, till dawn.... Perhaps when I am old (if I live that long!), these trials will turn out to be sweet memories.

The light of this almost full moon creates patterns of light and shadow in the forest below, making the forest look like a giant cheetah.

The heavy dark clouds, just two hands above my head, are slowly drifting away to some unknown destination. A few drops of cool water fall on my head, 'top-top-top'! Ah, how cheerlessly chill these drops feel!

The moon is hidden by one cloud, then shoots out and hides behind another—like a game of peekaboo played by beauties in the glass palace of some king. Who is running in the sky now? The clouds or the moon? I would say the clouds, but a child might say the moon. Who is right?

How lovely the play of light and shadow!

What is that bird cooing in the distance? The dulcet bird songs in this country seem to evoke a sweet laziness. I find them intoxicating.

In this light and shadow, I remember so many things! Oh, remembering her is full of pain!

'I love you so much, Hena.'

She shook her silky, raven-black hair and replied, 'But Sohrab, I haven't been able to love you.'

That day, bright saffron flowers seemed to be playing a bloody Holi in the gardens of Baluchistan. Unmindfully, I broke a walnut branch, collected some chandelier flowers from the deodar tree and threw them at her feet!

A few tears trickled down from her dark eyes lined with Istanbul kohl. Her face turned redder than her henna-dyed hands!

I picked up a bunch of raw plums and threw them at the bulbul sitting in the bush of screwpine flowers. The bird stopped singing and flew away.

What human beings think is the closest to them, turns out to be the farthest! This is indeed a profound mystery!

Hena! Hena!! What a pity!!!

Hindenburg Line

Oh! What is this place? I can almost believe that this is an underground land of djinns and fairies! Can a trench built during wartime really be as huge as a city full of houses? Who could have imagined this? What a gigantic venture deep down underground! This is indeed another wonder of the world! One can live as luxuriously as the nawabs of Bengal in this place!

But I did not come here for the peace it offers! I did not ask for comfort. I wanted only misery, only pain, only suffering! I am not made for enjoyment and comfort. I would have to seek another path then. It's like living under the tamarind tree while trying to escape tasting sour things.

Uh-oh! I need to be active. I want to drown myself in work. What an embarrassing comfort!

I've heard that iron turns into steel when forged in fire. Does this apply to human beings as well? Or are we just 'baptised'?

Freed from its restraints, my mind has once again fled to that room surrounded by grape vines and pomegranate shrubs! I recall those days . . .

'Hena, I'm about to jump into a fire that burns to set a country free. I am burning inside and wish that I burn on the outside as well! Maybe I will never return. But what do I have? What support will I get while I travel? What will I hold onto while I live in that foreign land?!'

Hena's henna-dyed fingers trembled like young shoots in my hands. She replied in a clear voice, 'But that's not how your life becomes meaningful, Sohrab! This is just your hot blood! You're clinging to a lie! Please try to accept it! . . .I've not been able to love you yet.'

All is empty! Nothing remains! A gusty wind blew through the thick tamarisk trees and cried, 'ah–ah–ah!'.

When the first battalion of our Baluchi Regiment No.127 started from Quetta, one of my friends, a young Bengali doctor, sang while sitting under an apple tree,

With what deceit now will you win that person back,
The one you bade farewell to with a tearful look.
In the middle of this languid air,
In the flower garden at this dark hour,
Under the bakul tree, don't you recall the one you like?
With what deceit, alas, will you win that person back!
The honeymoon of the full moon
Repeats itself now and then,
But the one who has gone, does not come back!
With what more deceit will you win this person back![3]

How weak I am! No wonder I did not want to come to this place! Listen—I cannot continue with this nawabi life!

The fellows in my regiment think no one is as carefree and happy as I am. It's because I laugh a lot. Hai! does anybody know how much 'crimson' is hidden in the heart of the henna leaf!

---

[3] The following song is a slightly altered version of one of Tagore's songs from the musical drama, *Mayar Khela* (*The Game of Illusion*).

I played 'Home home, sweet, sweet home' on the piano and sang along so beautifully that the French were amazed! It is as if we are not human beings and therefore, it's absolutely astonishing if we could do anything as brilliantly as them! We have to break such preconceived notions.

Hindenburg Line

What else can I do if there's no work? I have to find something to do. So last night I crawled for about a couple of miles and cut through much of the German barbed wire. No one seemed to notice.

My commanding officer said, 'You'll be rewarded for this.'

I have become a havildar today.

After all, it's not such a bad game!

I met that foreign girl once again! She has grown much prettier in these last two years! She told me directly that (if I had no objection) she would like to have me as her partner! I told her, 'No, that's not possible!'

I said to myself, 'A blind man loses his cane only once. Again? No way. I have had enough.'

The way her blue eyes filled with tears and her bosom heaved made even a stone-hearted person like me cry!

She controlled herself and said, 'But you'll allow me to love you? Like a brother at least . . .'

I am just a godforsaken, footloose and fancy-free boy. So, I showed a lot of interest and replied, 'Yes, of course!' Then she left, bidding me adieu. She never came back. I recollect, 'But the one who has gone, does not come back' . . . Oh!

Anyway, the day was well-spent with the Gurkhas. These Gurkhas are really like big babies. I would not have believed that grown men could be so naive and innocent. These Gurkhas and their brothers-in-law, the Garhwalis—both races turn into killing machines on the battlefield! Each of them turns into a Barbary lion—a sher-e-babbar. Even the Germans throw away their rifles and run off at the sight of their khukris.[4] If these two groups did not exist, we would never have been able to achieve this much. Only a handful of them are still alive.

---

[4] The Gurkha knife with a distinctive curved edge.

Regiment after regiment have completely perished! And yet, the few that are still alive are so full of life, as if nothing happened!

Nobody can make them understand what a great feat they have achieved. And those tall and sturdy Sikhs—what betrayers they have turned out to be! Some shot themselves in the arm and ended up in the hospital.

Oh my! There is a battalion 'march' going on in the trench. We are marching to the beat of a French band! Left–right–left! Jhawp–jhawp–jhawp! A thousand people are marching at the same pace—all at once. How amazing!

Baluchistan
My cottage in Quetta
In the grapevine garden

What is wrong with me? I am trying to answer this today, sitting in the walnut and pear garden.

All our Indian soldiers have returned home, and so have I. How happily those two years passed by!

I am looking at the blue, rain-washed sky, and am reminded of the wide blue eyes of that young French woman. I remember her silky curly hair when I look at the yaks. And those ripe grapes—aren't they exactly like her sparkling tears?

After becoming an officer, I also received the title 'Sardar Bahadur'. My commander would not let go of me. How could I make him understand that I was not there to purchase a permanent bond? I did not cross the seas with any high ideals. I only went to purify myself in fire—to hide myself too.

And I never thought I would return here of all places. But I had to—it seems I am tied to this land by an umbilical cord!

I have no one and nothing. And yet, I often feel everything is here. What purblind comfort am I trying to find?

I have not hurt anybody; nobody hurt me. Then why was I reluctant to come back? But that's the conceit of unspeakable agony—I can't articulate it well enough.

Hena! Hena! shabaash! There's no one around, still, the wind carries a broken echo 'na–na–na'.

The brook still flows down the hill; only, the girl, whose henna-dyed footprints are still etched on the stone-steps, is no longer there.

There are so many small-small things lying around that remind me of the scent of her soft touch.

Hena! Hena! Hena! . . . Again that echo, 'na–na–na'!

Peshawar

Discovered—discovered! I found her today. Hena! Hena! I saw you today, here in Peshawar! Why do hide such enormous truth behind those lies, even now?

She watched me from a distance and cried. She did not utter a word; she only looked at me and wept . . .

At such meetings, tears are the most articulate language of the heart. Today she has told me again that she could not bring herself to love me.

The moment she uttered 'no', her voice sounded so dejected that even the morning air became mournful!

The biggest puzzle in this world is the mind of a woman!

Kabul

Dakka camp

When I heard that the great man Emir Habibullah Khan[5] had been martyred, I felt that the Hindu Kush had collapsed, and Mount Suleiman been torn out from its base!

What am I supposed to do now? For ten days I kept thinking. Such a difficult task!

Nah! I decided that I would fight for the Emir.[6] Why? Well, there isn't an answer to that question. But let me say candidly that I do not consider the British my enemy. They are my best friends. Even if I say that I joined this war to protect the weak, even if it meant sacrificing my life, it wouldn't quite be the right answer.

Even I do not understand my own whims!

That morning, someone seemed to have set fire to the pomegranates. Oh! Perhaps, that was blood from the hearts of many young men like me!

---

[5] Emir Habibullah Khan was a relatively progressive ruler who ruled Afghanistan until 20 February 1919 when he was assassinated.

[6] Emir Amanullah Khan, the son of Emir Habibullah Khan, who ascended the throne after his father's death and declared Afghanistan's independence from Great Britain, resulting in the outbreak of the Third Anglo-Afghan War.

The vast sky had paused after crying incessantly. Its eyes are still hazy; it would start crying again. A broken-hearted cuckoo had also been weeping somewhere; its eyes red and its 'oohu—oohu' call ringing out through the damp winds of the autumnal morning. Someone on the other side of the dried-up river was playing Asavari on the shehnai. In its meend[7] echoed the doleful cries of so many suppressed souls! I felt its sadness more than anyone else. The strong smell of henna flowers intoxicated me!

'Hena, I am going to war again, to fight for the Emir. I won't come back. Even if I live, I won't come back.'

Hena buried her head in my chest and cried, 'Sohrab, my love! Yes, go there! Now is the time to tell you how much I love you! I won't hide the truth of my heart anymore with this sham. I won't cause my love further pain . . .'

I understood. She was a warrior-woman, an Afghan daughter. Despite being an Afghan, I have spent my entire life as a foreigner; she wanted me to sacrifice my life at the feet of our motherland.

O, the heart of a woman! How could you hide yourself like this, Hena?

What perseverance! How could such a soft-hearted woman be so tough?

Hena! Hena!!

Kabul

My body has taken five bullets. But until the moment I lost consciousness, I defended my soldiers with all my strength!

Khoda! If protecting my country with my blood makes me a martyr, then I am a martyr. I have done my duty until the very end of my life!

I came back. Hena followed me like a shadow. How could she hold so much love that flowed like a rapid rushing down the mountain, within her fragile ribcage!

* * *

---

[7] A gliding, usually slow, movement from one note to another, practiced in Indian classical music.

The Emir has given me a place in his court. I am a commander in his army.

And Hena? Here is Hena, sleeping by my side, clinging to my chest ... Her heart still fluttering with some unknown fear! Her sighs pervading the wind with acute dissatisfaction.

Ah! the poor girl has also been badly wounded like me! Slept? Let her sleep! No, no, we'll sleep together! O Khoda! don't give us any more pain by waking us up from this pleasurable sleep!

Hena! Hena!! Na—na—ah!

THREE

IN THE RELENTLESS RAIN

Translated by Masrufa Ayesha Nusrat

In the blink of an eye, an acquaintance

Listening to the rain pitter-patter, it occurred to me that my sorrows are somehow deeply connected with the rhythmic sound of monsoon downpours!

There is a deep forest before me. A few peacocks are fanning their tails, and a flock of herons are flying overhead. What excitement gives the kadam flowers goosebumps when they are in full bloom? What intense fragrance makes the whole body of the forest sway in such intoxication!

Isn't it the month of Shravan?[1] Ah, no wonder my heart has turned heavy with the pain of the rain!

It happened three years ago. My vagabond life has torn apart my memories of her like a lotus cluster caught in a storm. Sometimes I recall a word or a slight touch that lies hidden in my bereaved heart! The jui buds in my mind-forest never burst into full bloom, and the shiuli stalks become limp! Tears well in my eyes along with the thunder and gloom of the day, as I recall another Shravan day when the clouds roared the same way!

It was the fifth day before the Shravan full moon, just like today. I had lost my way and wandered here—Kalinjar. That day the town was bustling with the kajri[2] festival, singing to celebrate the monsoon. The sky was overcast with light clouds wandering aimlessly, like me, in its

---

[1] The fourth month in the Bengali calendar and the second month of the monsoon season.

[2] A genre of North Indian folk song, prevalent mostly in Uttar Pradesh and Bihar, which is sung to celebrate the monsoon.

limitless expanse. Between the banks of clouds, a slice of blue sky subtly emerged like the sorrowful kajal-smeared eyes of my beloved, weeping away! It was then that I met her. I was exhausted, and about to rest near the outskirts of Kalinjar in a woodland. The moment I set my eyes on her, she seemed so familiar, as if I had known her for ages—and lost her somewhere! She stared back. I wondered what she saw in my eyes. With a young paddy sheaf in her hand, half covering her face, she asked in her local language, 'O re pardesiya,[3] where is your home?'

Her melodious voice filled me with bewildered ecstasy and made my blood dance with excitement.

Why did her voice sound so familiar? Who was tricking my mind? It was as if the east wind blew past me moaning, 'Hai! the lost traveller! Hai! the homeless one!' Like a mass of weightless clouds in strong wind, a bevy of beautiful young kajri singers filled the air with the melody of Malhar, '*Ghoonghat pat khol aare sawaliya*! Take off your veil, there comes your dark, handsome Shyamal!'

The group of young women stopped in the blink of an eye as they saw her standing close by me. They let their hair down, swung their arms, flung their aachol[4] in the air and sang, 'Hey Kajaria (kajal-eyed)! Your dark, handsome Shyamal has already arrived, right?'

She moved towards them and answered in a trembling voice, 'Nahi re, sajaniya, no! He is just a gallant outlander!'

A woman from the group almost snatched her words from her mouth and retorted, 'But he's seized your heart, right?'

She blushed. Unable to hide her discomfiture she stole away, but not before casting an oblique, reproachful look at me!

From the bend of the road, I could see the waves of their paddy-coloured saris and the fluttering edges of their sky-blue dupattas. I could smell the sweet, damp, earthy fragrance from the loosened strands of their hair. Amidst all those beautiful faces, only Kajaria's small dark face gleamed in my mind—like the perfectly engraved face of a devi carved in black stone by an artist! The sweetness of her lightening-swift movements repeatedly stroked the clouds of my mind.

---

[3] Foreigner/outlander

[4] It means the end of the sari; but it has multiple connotations of affection and concern, dependence, protectiveness, and so on.

Standing on the road under a deodar tree with a swing tied to it, I could think of only one thing—just one, or even half a look, could turn someone utterly unknown into an acquaintance for a lifetime!

Tryst of hurt feelings

The next day I stood in an amla orchard and was brooding over that chance meeting. Where did I lose the bride of my fancy? When did I leave her on the ferryboat of the sorrowful Poorvi raga? I tried to recollect all my memories of her but could not. How was it that the moment I set eyes on her I recognised her as the woman of my heart? She flashed in the glimmering of my eyes and said, 'You are the one I have cherished all my life! Oh my dear! you are the treasure for whom I have done endless sadhana!'

I wandered deep down memory lane, hoping to find an answer. Just then, I heard a group of pretty, playful women walking past me, gustily singing a tuneful kajri,

> The sky grew dark, roared in fury did the thunderstorm clouds, re Hari![5]
>
> Rim-jhim rim-jhim rang the endless rain, my heart trembled again and again, O Rama!
>
> Tears ran down my cheeks and smudged the kajal of my eyes, re Hari!

The monsoon clouds cleared. Their deep-voiced gamaks[6] resounded in my mind—'... smudged the kajal of my eyes, re Hari!' Oh dear, the kajal in my eyes is getting smudged! You foolishly shed tears for which unknown person, O! you, this foreign woman? It is beyond her realisation, and her heart's comprehension!

Again the clouds—eternally cherished and healers of all my sorrows—thundered. The peacock's sharp cry combined with the chatak's longing for rainwater kept reverberating: 'pour some water, pour some more!' Hai, the perpetual suffering of this eternal thirst! Couldn't all the seawater quench your endless thirst?

---

[5] Hari is one of the thousand names of Vishnu.

[6] A term in Indian classical music for a sound created by repeatedly traversing the distance between two particular notes.

In my mind's ear I could hear the whisper of a faint memory—you have always been a chatak and your thirst can never be quenched!

On the one hand, the aroma of damp earth and the sultry scent of khus-khus felt stifling. On the other, the sweet fragrance of lotus and kadam flowers mixed with the maddening perfume of half-bloomed keya, juthi, jasmine buds, and some withered shefali and bakul flowers spread a pleasant drowsiness. The pangs of the monsoon cast a deep unspoken look at me and proclaimed,

> You can tell your mate on a day like this,
> On such a dark day of heavy showers![7]

Hai! what to say? Whom to say it to? This restless nut knows nothing yet longs to say something—wants to have someone close to his heart! As the messenger-cloud came to convey the whereabouts of this restless one's runaway beloved and left him a note on her exchanges with the cloud, he conveyed this tribute to the meghdoot,

> O come, in the wet, thick clouds and the relentless rain![8]

Today, once more I remembered what she had said at our parting, 'We'll meet again, but you might not even recognise me then!'

My heart swelled with remembered pain. When my rain cloud-complexioned Kajaria went past, glancing at me, I remembered again and again—'You might not even recognise me then!'

So, I called out to her 'See! I have recognised you by the way you looked at me!'

Kajaria covered her face with her hair and left. She too had recognised me; I could see it in the way she refused to look at me ...

So, I set out in search of her once more. I could hear the young women's song floating from the nearby forest like a fountain, rolling and rippling with the melody of Malhar and Hindola—'The rain falls down and again, the clouds come rolling into the month of Shravan!'

I stood in the middle of the road and saw thousands of fountains crazily cascading down, jham–jham–jham! It was as if a thousand frolicking girls wearing bells on their ankles were running about the

---

[7] Opening lines of a Rabindranath Tagore song (*Swarabitan* 11).

[8] A slightly altered version of the opening line of a Tagore song (*Swarabitan* 11).

courtyard of the sky! I went to the forest and watched the young women getting drenched in the rain, in a festive mood, riding on swings tied to the branches of deodar and bakul trees and singing kajri. How they revelled in rain and storm! Unbound and free, each appeared like an embodiment of wild nature. How lovely was this liberating fusion of the unstoppable raga of the primordial mind's eternal youth with wild and restless nature! The booming Shravan clouds plucked chords from my heart's veena. I could feel the tide of my youth rising. My mad soul flew swift as the wind, like the beautiful women's hair swinging towards the clouds—Hai! Where? At what distant frontier does it stop!

The swinging girls sang of kajal clouds and blue sky. Others with dangling braided hair stood on dark-green durba grass, singing about tender grass and green paddy, matching beats with the mridangam. Their hearts were touched by the lyrics about the clouds.... The grand festivity of the clouds brought tears to my eyes. I saw Kajaria's dark beauty once again—she had got down from her swing and was looking at me with her familiar, tearful eyes. The moment she caught me watching her, she swung and chanted, 'O sajaniya, the handsome outlander has turned up!' Her confidant Motia swayed closer to her, giggling like drizzling rain and retorted, 'O you dark Kajaria, yes, this darkly handsome Shyamal is only yours!'

Kajaria caught Motia's hair and pulled her down; then quickly hid behind a bakul tree nearby.

I was wondering if this was how a human and a cloud spoke to each other. This must have been the way a yearning yaksha asked a cloud to be his messenger and sent heart-wrenching notes to his beloved who was suffering the pangs of separation! Thus my tear-drenched mind embraced the black cloud as a dear friend!

I was startled to see her at my side. What infinite horizon her unblinking sight had come to rest upon, only she knew. Standing beside her, I felt it was just the two of us nestling in the lap of the clouds. There was no one else; only clouds above, beneath, and all around us. In that endless cloud-expanse, she held me in her cloud-hued arm and looked intently at my face with her cloud-like eyes. In that familiar place, right over there, we may have met for the first time—it was also where we had our fits of pique and separated. The very moment this memory popped up in the unknown recesses of our hearts, we became a part of each other's existence. What we could not have expressed in all the tears of our lives, was achieved in a split second, amid the rain and storm, simply staring at each other; two unblinking pairs of eyes . . .

'Kajri, I've finally found you after searching for so many lifetimes!'

She was listening intently to the heartfelt music of the rains and my voice seemed to startle her back to reality. Like a frightened doe, she suddenly looked around in bewilderment and let out a plaintive cry! Without waiting, she left, crying. On her way she said, 'Na re, my handsome outlander, don't you see I am so dark!' She tried to say something else, but her voice choked with intense hurt and resentment!

I did not see her for an entire year.

Tonight, in the frenzy of Shravan, my heart ached with the painful memory of our parting. The feeble lamp burning at my bedside had flickered low; the wavering light reminding me of many things in the lonely room—hai! now I had no one to hurt me that way! Only one who has experienced those bittersweet lover's exchanges will understand my pain! One who has not been bereft, will never understand the mental state of a lovelorn soul; never!

She had told me, 'Look at me, traveller from another land! I am intensely dark like kajal, so people tease me and call me Kajaria! I can endure and ignore them—I have that strength. But why are you so cruel? Why are you taunting me by saying you are in love with me? O my Shyamal! Why are you hurting this unfortunate girl? How can I hide my shame and humiliation? I know I am dark and ugly, but what right do you have, O pardesi, to tempt me with your lies? Chhi chhi! You should not love me. I cannot be loved; you just cannot love me! Don't attack my vulnerabilities and cause me more pain, Shyamal! You are not insulting me; but insulting my love. No one can bear it. Farewell, Shyamal, farewell!'

I thought to myself, 'My dear sensitive, delicate girl! Your hurt feelings, your pride and rage have blinded you, and so you do not want to accept the plain truth. I too am as dark as you. You called me Shyamal, which means dark; but why did you then call me handsome? The way you see beauty in me, I too find you beautiful. I have found my most desired one in your dark beauty, as if after an endless search. If you have no right over me, then why is my love unbearable while others' taunts couldn't hurt you? What right do you have over me, which lets you boldly ignore anyone else's affronts except mine? How can you trample my heart and leave me? You cannot be sentimental about me if you do not have any faith in my love! I can only be angry with, and be genuinely hurt by, someone whom I know would value my sentiments and over whom I have rights. Only then can I have great confidence that the person would tolerate my unnecessary fits of rancour because that person loves me . . .'

She left without apprehending any of this! She didn't even know against whom she nursed such strong resentment—probably some of her anger was directed towards the creator who had given her a dark complexion. Her heart swollen with sorrow, like a deeply wounded chick, she fell at the feet of the unfathomable creator and accused him, 'O Lord, why did you have to make me so ugly and dark and send me into this world? Would your bountiful pitcher have become exhausted if you had used a minuscule portion from it to create me? If you made me so dark, then why did you make my love glow so bright? And you make me more ashamed by allowing someone fall in love with me!'

Hai! She never realised that true beauty cannot be perceived in the external world, but rather deep inside—not in one's physicality but in one's heart.

I noticed something new that day. As long as she hadn't felt she was the recipient of anyone's love, there had been no outburst of pent-up resentments. But the moment she realised that someone had fallen for her, she couldn't hold them back anymore and let them gush out with anguished cries of pain. Alas! her overwhelming resentment and hurt made her stay away from the person whom she loved and was loved by.

When love becomes so strong, there is pleasure in avoiding your lover's company! No one has experienced this pleasurable pain the way I have!

Oh! Everything that I had to say seemed to just die within me! I don't think I can tell her any of this in this lifetime.

A timeless separation!

Here is what happened the following year.

I met Kajaria again in a valley named Birohi, between the hills of Mirzapur. It was the third day before the dark moon of

Bhadra.[9] Another dark cloudy night. It was also the penultimate day of kajri, the monsoon celebration. The last monsoon rains fell and played their parting music; the leaves and sheaves of young paddy in the fields were swaying in harmony with the rhythm of the rain and paying their tribute to the season for the last time. None of them had any idea when and where they would ever meet again; in which field, beyond which line of palmyra forest. The kajal in the beautiful women's eyes had lost its lustre; their voices sounded downcast and exhausted; their small, pretty faces looked like sunburnt new leaves of the sal tree. They were sad because the next day would be the last day of monsoon celebration—the festival they had yearned for throughout the year. Who knew if they would be meeting their sakhis again next year? Perhaps some of these familiar faces would disappear, never to be seen again in any corner of the earth.

Livid lightning flashed like sharp knives and made the golden strands of the swings glitter. Kajri came running to me, held my right hand between her soft hands and placed it on her bosom.

'Shyamal! My beloved outlander, I recognise you now! You are real! You do love me! You surely love me! You really do!'

Her moist and shrunken eyes fixed their bright gaze on me, and I could see a deep love sparkling in them like the humid, sunny sky of an autumnal morning! Ah! She had finally come to terms with her truth after enduring our long separation! I could not help the tears rolling down my cheeks as I took in her slender vine-like figure! After an unstoppable and unruly tear fell on her pale cheek, she looked at me pitifully and sat down at my feet! The bakul twigs and shiuli leaves sprinkled flowers and leaves on her head in solace!

Motia then told me that Kajaria had gone to bathe in the Jamuna on the fifth morning of Shravan, just like she had done the previous year, and to bring back some soil to help the young saplings blossom. Until then, she had carefully covered the saplings with her wet and tattered dupatta. She would say every day, 'Motia re, this time my beloved pardesi will come again! I can even hear his travelling song!'

That day, on the third of Bhadra, she had brought some of the new paddy sheaves as a gift for me and immersed the rest in the river.

I clasped her hand and said, 'Kajri, don't ever leave me again!'

---

[9] The fifth month of the Bengali calendar, and the first month of early autumn.

A pale, half smile played about the corners of her dry lips for an instant, then faded. She untied her aachol with a lot of difficulty and unpacked the green paddy sheaves she had saved so carefully, gave me a full look with her tear-filled eyes; then, placing her tired arms on my shoulders, tucked the paddy sheaves behind my ears. Her face lit up with a pure smile as she took a deep breath of satisfaction. It seemed to me that she had never smiled a more rewarding and livelier smile.

After a while, something occurred to her and her face turned white in pain. She cried out, 'No, Shyamal, no, I really must go! Let me leave with the full pride of your overflowing love for me!'

Her tired head sank into my embrace. I drew her close to my heart—the most desirable wealth I had craved for in my whole life. She whimpered, 'Oh! Oh! Oh!', as she summoned a burst of blowing rain and storm and her disconsolate cries rang around me!

I think her pride at getting more than she had ever desired did not permit her to live. She embraced death and went to the creator of her dark beauty! Now she'll be waiting for me on another road with her basket of eternal beauty!

Dark-skinned people seem to be highly sensitive. They seem to feel they can never be loved for their dark complexion and cannot believe it if they are loved. This is the biggest tragedy of their life.

A rain-drenched memory of my beloved

Shravan has arrived once more, just like that year. I still remember the kajri, 'Oh dark one, let down your veil!'

Hai, my pardesi sawaliya! Your veil was never lifted, and never will be!

Now when the waves of rain crash down before my tired eyes, Poorvi flows in the air, filled with the sorrow of separation of all the lovers of the world; proud Malhar moans with acute pain like the howling wind tearing through solid darkness—oh my dear, I see no road open before me!—not a single road! It rains in painful torrents, relentlessly. Where are you, my beloved, at this moment? You chose to appear before me in rain and storm during this year's monsoon; you spoke deep in my heart! My lost beloved! I can hear all the secret words you once whispered in my ears in the monsoon rains!

Your beauty is deep indigo—like the color of bright and freshly powdered antimony in your eyes. My dear, the dark beauty in your tearful eyes seemed to lightly brush kajal in my eyes just now! O my restless darling from the kingdom of clouds whom I have lost again and again! This time I have tied you with the strings of my tears! Where will you go now? You have unfettered this iron chain many times, naughty bird of the forest! Now I have secured you with my tears, you can never flee! I have found you again in the bosom of the dark blue clouds, in this young, green durba grass, and in the color of the wet paddy's song! Oh, Shyamali, my dusky young lady! Where can you hide the beauty of your darkness that glitters like Shyam?[10] That azure sky, this emerald field and the path lost in the horizon—that is where your Shyam-like beauty is eternally spread. So, on this Shravan morning, I sit in the paddy field and sing,

> O the enchantress of my eyes—you have arrived.
> On opening my heart, what did I behold!
> Along the shiuli-strewn grounds,
> Over heaps of fallen flowers,
> In the dew-wet fields of grass,
> With your feet dyed in red!
> The enchantress of my eyes has arrived![11]

When I woke up, it was still raining relentlessly in thousands of cascading streams—jham-jham-jham! The clouds had stored so much water! The ocean-sky seemed to have turned upside down, and there was no respite from the incessant showers!

I shivered in the rain and saw a multitude of blue lotuses blooming in the cobalt lake of my mind . . .

---

[10] Another name for Krishna referencing his dark skin.

[11] A Rabindranath Tagore song (*Swarabitan* 50).

FOUR

HALF ASLEEP

Translated by Nishat Atiya

AZHAR'S STORY

Africa
Camp near a Saharan oasis

I am awake. But I feel I could sleep some more.... My long night has ended, my dreams too; and with that my heart has also broken!

But the eternal memory she has left behind has no end. No—no, just like the intermittent flow of a desert stream, her memory has filled my empty, barren heart with soothing solace. O! my desert stream, flow on amid the overwhelming and searing emptiness, leaving behind cool, green shadows along the thin, long line you traverse. You don't even know how this thin, sacred course of yours has kept alive a huge tract of the desert. But keep the sacred flow anyway, O! pure, slender spring; please, flow on!

They say the darkest hour before sunrise is pleasant for everyone; and so the pure ecstasy of a newly born morning waking up to the tune of raga Todi enlivens the earth, spreading about the universe its wings of symphony like mated swans preparing for a romantic waltz. And yet for all that, I would rather the night not end with the dawn. I cannot endure the light—it is burning my eyes! How inauspicious this dawn of mine is!

The day breaks. The restless chirping of forest birds echo from distant woodlands, growing faint as the birds fly away. Flowers blossom among the foliage, dotting the branches of green trees! The wind rises too, whistling alongside a bulbul bird, while the honeybees float abuzz, all covered with fine pollen and dancing with the ghazals and dadra taal[1] of the accompanist breeze. The koel, doel and papiya birds start to sing in chorus,

> I'm slain, I'm slain by your charm, O beautiful!
> How do I receive you, with what welcome ritual![2]

Which stranger's voice, filled with the meend of Bhairavi, sings out a startling note: 'O townspeople, wake up!' The somnolent world then shakes off its laziness with a waking response!

You are pretty, and so the infinite universe is full of charm and glory.[3]

Abandoned and desperate, I was the only miserable being left on the far side of it all. This fragile, weary frame of mine, while seeking refuge in the bowels of an endless abyss, tried to pose like a fresh, moist teardrop sprayed over the plump cheeks of a smiling sunny day! I think the morning-lass hardly noticed whether she shed a solitary droplet last night while grieving her loss of an imaginary affair in the whims of her dream—although, she still bore the holy remnants of its memory, like a slight scar against her pale forehead!

Shaken out of a quiet slumber, I hear many voices outside rejoicing in unison, 'Oi, it's already dawn!' A mighty gust of wind makes sure the news is heard even in the quietest corners of the world. All then rise, shine and start casually. I, on the other hand, refuse to get out of bed, although awake! A fitful deluge of late regrets keeps me anxious, day and night.

All doors have opened wide; but how about this one in a boneyard, turned upside down with no way out?—No, it is a sin to even attempt and unlatch the door, as the mind of this grave is filled with a boneyard-of-skeletons and a heart-full-of-anguish, that has remained, and shall always be so, within the mind of the grave! Let it be bhai, allow it to lie down with its teeth sunk deep into the dirt. If you are hurt as you cross the same path, just leave behind a silent sigh and nothing more!

* * *

---

[1] Dadra taal is a rhythmic cycle of six beats having a 3/3 rhythmic structure or meter.

[2] These lines are taken from a Rabindranath Tagore song (*Swarabitan* 16).

[3] The line is borrowed, with slight alteration, from a song written by Bengali poet and music composer Rajanikanta Sen (1865–1910).

Achcha, does my putting down of thoughts on paper by hiding from others, bode well for me? Nah, I cannot decide yet, whether it is good or bad! Also, yes, the thin layer of mistiness I am spreading on my words, is it voluntary or born out of compulsion?

This leads me to say that indeed, I have been a living conundrum to many, and this is how I always want to be—to bury the source of my sorrow under a rock and fence it by weaving a cryptic illusion; immerse the suffering of my heart under the notes of my clamorous songs! Because people may laugh thinking chhi!—can a soldier afford to be so feeble!

Na, na—the very prospect of it fills my breast with an overwhelming shame! But it is also true that if I leave these words behind the veil of a melancholy miasma, this pain will not make sense to anybody. And if some idle mind tries to do that, I cannot be blamed for that.

Oh, the nonsense of it all! Who, I wonder, would ever want to read this story? Why am I writing then? Am I still writing? It is only human to seek sympathy in pain, or else life as we know it becomes unbearable with its burdens of pain! If a consoling friend is told the story of affliction, and it draws his tearful sympathy, the intense pain does lessen. Besides, no matter how much a volcano tries to contain the fire within, the waves of fire eventually become overwhelming. When that happens, can a rocky mountain stop its eruption? Never. The more desperate attempts to resist its course, the more the rigid rocks at the heart of the mountain are turned into debris by the hot, flying lava. Now, who dares to stop that irresistible flow?

Yes, one needs to remember that just as the last storm of vapour flies from the heart of the volcano, it becomes quiet and unmoving! It then looks as if the silent mass of rocks has no complaint against anyone in the whole world! A magnanimous mass of solitude lies uninterrupted and in peace! ... Ah! That is much better.

Achcha, despite my tough, pitiless exterior, are there no pair of eyes that become moist in response to the pain that flows underneath the arid expanse of the desert of my heart, like the Phalgu river? How harassed and cursed a life I live! Somewhere a pair of tear-filled eyes could have been available for me! But I don't want it, right?

Na bhai, na! What is more painful than anything else is the fear of rejection and ridicule. So, I don't want to put my grieving heart to shame—I don't! It might even sully the sacred memory. I won't be able to endure that. And yet a bit of solace has become the most desired thing in my prosaic life. What consoles me nowadays is my effort to write—it's like drawing a melancholy figure in shadowy outlines on the white pages of my private journal. These black letters on the white pages and the graceful waves of music are the two things that offer, and will offer, solace-kheer in my burning life!

Now I hold no grudge against anyone in the world! But I have a fair share of words reserved only for Khoda! It is you who have made me destitute; you are the one who has dispersed my safe haven of affection in the winds so that I could call the entire world my home—and now, you cannot act like a stranger—you cannot ignore me anymore. Now if you cannot respond to my entreaties and unjust demands, then say, who else can? O! inscrutable ever-benevolent Lord, now you're my everything!

* * *

Yes, now I should keep these in writing. Who knows when a mortar shell from the enemy troop lands on my chest and after a sudden sharp pain, will turn me silent; motionless forever! Like the way I have raised my head like a tiny bubble floating on the battle-ocean, in an eye blink, all my hopes, enthusiasm, distresses and agonies might disappear and like that bubble I might fade away to some unknown land! No one will say 'aha'—none will mourn with 'uh-oh'! To me, the thought of death is pleasant and serene of some kind.

Let me remind you that from now on, I have to be just as combative and merciless a soldier when on duty, and continue to be the murderous, blood thirsty monster on the loose, mightier than the crashing waves of the sea. My subordinates should learn how to obey my commands like robots. I do not want even the slightest negligence and discredit in my performance and my conduct. There cannot be a greater disgrace than this for a soldier. But as soon as the working hour ends, I become their ever singing, cheerfully-smiling, loving bhai. The same fiery eyes then radiate warmth and care, as if this wooden voice of thunder turns affectionate and soft like kheer, and my songs soothe and cleanse their spirit of any discomfiture! But little can they see through the opaque veil I have created to cover my inner weeping frame under my outward appearance. They can try a thousand times but will never succeed!

Khoda, let me hide my fervid, heavy sighs beneath the happy tunes of Poorvi raga—this is what I want from you now. And lest this unknown old ache cause pain in an irrational mind, then let that someone silently join in my prayer and say, 'Aha, Let it be!' This is true for those who crave for affection—those who do not have anyone to shed tears for them at the time of their death; those who detest pity but earnestly keep longing for a drop of affection and sympathy—there is nothing much to give them, or even if there is, they do not want anything more. Just a few cordial words, like a white moonbeam glistening against gloomy cave-breasts, give them consolation.

* * *

It was a moonlit night, one of the kinds that happen to remind you of your lover, reviving a profound tenderness at the core of your being. The sandalwood breeze was drunk with the intoxicating aroma of mallika and malati flowers. The strong but languid fragrance of tuberoses was filling up my heart with an unknown and unspoken dread and forlornness. . . .

It was then she came into the tendril-garden, her feet adorned with jingling anklets! In her left hand she carried a wicker-basket of culled flowers. She had tied her hair in a bun, on which mango buds dropped, but then missing it, slid and fell on her breast, as if in a drizzle of nectar oozing out of flower petals. The lazy night's zephyr brushed the pollen off her loose ringlets, and stealing the sweet smell, her aura stirred the world by spreading the news, 'O you all, wake up! See, the dream-bahu[4] has arrived, crossing the desh of sleep'. Sleeping flowers awakened and danced on the branches with excitement! I felt beads of sweat forming all over my forehead, and my heart was shaken by some paralyzing dread! I began panting and the jasmines I was carrying dropped from my hand. It seemed as if a princess from the land of sleep had personified the dream girl I had cherished for so long, who now stood before me in full bloom and cast a dream-web in my eyes! Afraid, I lifted my enchanted eyes ever so slowly and saw her—shaking like a

[4] Bride.

lean rattan cane, her eyes still downcast. The moment she noticed me watching her, she seemed to turn and leave. I wasted no time in asking her, in a voice nervously quavering, 'Who are you—Pari?'[5]

She glanced at me with her big, beautiful eyes and stopped suddenly! I could see in the clear moonlight that her gorgeous dark eyes were full of tears. In a moment, the tiny bells of her anklets sent out a worrying note—runu-jhunu! The euphoric rhythms of Hindola raga ceased to rock! She collected her slack and unruly aachol. The loosely-draped woman's shy cheeks turned crimson in the likeness of a blossoming pomegranate! With a pause in the breeze the murmuring ripples of a lake came to a halt and two red lotuses bloomed amid its darkly green leaves. Her eyes were anxious and hesitant, trembling like a frightened doe. She took her time before finally saying, 'You—Sir, when did you come here?'

'Today', I said. 'Have you been doing well, Pari?'

She forced a faint smile saying, 'Yes. Ma along with the rest of the family members came here for an outing. Bhai-jaan[6] has renovated this garden, you see! They are over there, at the ghat of the pond, chit-chatting.'

With my momentary trance soon waning, I stood up and asked, 'Oh! It has been two years since we last met, hasn't it, Pari? You seem thinner than before. Are you sick?'

She stared at me for a while with hurt and pitiful eyes, and whispered almost inaudibly, 'No!—'

Suddenly, as if she remembered something, I heard her voice choking with exasperation, 'You! Why are you here again? Please leave! . . .'

It felt as if the bright full moon in the sky had been totally eclipsed! This sudden turn of events caught me unprepared. Benumbed to the bones, I couldn't move for a long time. I didn't know how a sudden dizziness seized me and I fell; or how the area below my left eye was hit by the arm of a nearby bench, making it bleed profusely; or when Pari tore a part of her aachol and used it as a bandage to stop the bleeding! Later as I came to my senses, I could see Pari sprinkling water over my wound, but along with that was the swifter flow of tears

---

[5] Pari is the Bengali word for fairy.

[6] 'Jaan', meaning 'dear as life', is an affectionate form of address.

from her eyes! That was the moment when all my pent-up hurt found expression.

Standing up straight with the speed of lightning I told her in a hurt voice, 'It was a big mistake, Pari. Do forgive me!'

She stood there and waited—seemingly lost in a deep thought—with her fingertips gently tapping on the yellow rose petals across her chin; she then mumbled something I could hardly grasp!

I could not keep standing anymore and said, 'Let me take my leave then, Pari!'

She too, responded sobbing, 'Ah! go ahead then!'

But her legs seemed to be as insensitive as the moonstruck night, and hence, veiling her timid face, she stayed motionless like a piece of rock. When I saw the teardrops silently streaming down her cheeks like pre-winter dew, I struggled to stifle a breast full of sighs that almost came out into the open. I sensed the sharp spikes of an extreme pain impaling every nook and cranny of my body. It seemed that the vast bosom of the moon-proud night was producing the tunes of raga Sahana that could melt stone and make it cry disconsolately. And the night was gazing deep into the sky, full of twinkling stars, with teary eyes—thinking that even in the sky there are stars that shine, with crores and crores of fire inside them, driving deep into the night's heart, with a heat stronger than that of the sun! Like unmoving lightning, they burn bright in blazing rage—dhu–dhu–dhu!

* * *

It also occurred to me once that day, ah! how wretched I had been! Why couldn't I be happy with what I already had?

Those shy, romantic eyes that adored me from a distance; the tremulous, tender glances we both stole and returned while we pretended to be busy with some work; an accidental touch once in a while; the bashful, lingering goodbyes; a silent confession of mutual understanding reflected in our sparkling eyes as we tried to hide our happy smiles; our earlobes turning red at the very thought of unsaid affection—all these little bits and pieces of intense delight that poured inebriating enchantment in my mind and intoxicated me, I never wish to have anything more than that. Why did she then insult me so much?

I have loved her—I do not remember from which date or time—but with all my being. I loved her, but never desired her. I used to think before, as I still do, that my life lost its purpose when she was never mine, yet I have never been able to set my heart to yearn for her. And if there was even a slight chance of impure thoughts—that rough aspect of uniting with her or possessing her—invading my mind, my entire heart would shudder in shame and disgust. Should we allow our love that fills the entire world to turn stale in a matter of days? Chhi chhi! Na na!

It dawned on me that day—the kind of attraction that only brings two bodies close to each other and unites them cannot be called love; it is at best infatuation or yearning, or something else. Perhaps this infatuation could metamorphose into true love, eventually, through the maintaining of distance. But a momentary coupling would instantly pollute that love with outrageous ugliness. A union of sacred love is not meant to culminate in such ugliness! I knew that my life was going to be a futile one but even then, I decided never to make love with her. Bowing my head down, I have loaded on it a life-long grief and painful humiliation, but even then, I could never think of shamelessly taking the dark path of a worthless coupling and disgracing my beloved. I know one day I will get her in a way that not many can even imagine. Without anyone prompting me, I do believe that what I consider failure now will one day flower into a blossom of success . . . Holy hell! I have ended up writing such irrelevant things! Yes, what was I saying? Did she reject me because she could not understand that I avoided her only because I loved her? Hai! You will never understand, Pari—never!—the amount of pain and distress I had to go through in order to gather the strength and patience to keep from being intimate with the image of my soul! What hurts the most though is your failure to comprehend the depth of my love for you. I hurt you by giving you away to someone else, but you would never know how unfathomable a pain I had to endure in silence and how I had to suppress my own misery. Had you known this Pari, you couldn't have hurt me by remembering that episode, the way you did that day. . . .

I know dear, that the day will indeed come when the entire saga, all the hopes of my cursed life, will no longer remain hidden, at least from you. You will understand all of it by yourself without anybody else explaining it to you. But on that day, will I be able to know in my lifetime that you have not misunderstood me? If not, then it's a pity dear, such a pity! . . .

You see! It's all muddled again, like having a thousand kinds of dreams in a slumber! Inconsistent and separate, they don't make sense, yet the dream-queen is weaving and joining them together in a fine thread without making her presence felt! All these words of mine seem like a messy garland of lakhs of random flowers!

But occasionally, it seems to me that my meeting her or talking with her the way I did was not right after all. For she might have taken it as an attempt to show her my pride in the sacrifice I had made, heightened by false ego. That would have filled her with bitterness and made her act in that unforgiving manner. Unfortunately, a couple of sweet gestures from someone can make affection-hungry people like me cross the limit, which forces that person to make us come to our senses. We then take it as an affront and feel afflicted. We have only ourselves to blame.

Once the mind betrays what it is supposed to be safeguarded from revelation at all costs, the feeling of shame is unbearable, and I pray to Khoda to spare me the unforgivable discredit—please spare me! Rather, burden my head with the penalty for my actions even if it is merciless and cruel.

I am still speaking in a wakeful daze. The human mind works in mysterious ways—it's one weakness is that it avoids confronting what it finds discomforting; it pretends, foolishly, not to see what it sees! Yet surprisingly, it is the unkind, uninspiring aspect of things that someone forces me to confront. It is probably done by the relentless force that lies hidden behind the mind's facade.

You see how comical it is! My subconscious mind already knows that the lady loves me more than I love myself. But why did she show me the door so rudely that day? Oh, how painful it was, so painful! She is too self-conscious to rise above her ego which made her so unrelenting, although it hurt her the most. Otherwise, why would a flood of tears have flowed from her eyes down to her bosom just after she had uttered those words of dismissal! Everything else could be a lie, but not that—not what I saw in her eyes.

Oh! sightless me! If you could understand the depth of her unbearable pain and see where the source of her heart-rending pain was, you could have avoided this meaningless trauma! And if she too was not so quick to take umbrage, she would have placed her head at your feet like any other simple woman and cry out, 'O you unkind lord! It is enough! You have shown enough magnanimity; don't bother this wretched woman anymore! If you want to show how godlike your nature is, then don't come to me!'

If I imagine her doing this, then it wouldn't be possible for my empty heart to be filled with the pride of this statement: 'My beloved is great!' Well done, Khoda! So well done! Hence, I say this today, right from my heart, as I say everyday: 'You are ever so blissful!' I repeat, 'Let thy will be done, my benevolent Lord!'

* * *

What follows here is a story of another day.

Pari was singing in a lonely room on the first floor of her house. Her song awakened the sleepy night's pain—but it did not awaken the four celestial girls of the sky's cardinal directions of the sky. The new Phalgun sky was covered in layers of clouds. Somewhere, a peacock cried out in joy and along with it the pitter-patter of the billowing clouds could be heard—jhim, jhim, jhim! ... The prancing dawn of each day is pensive now, brooding over things. Sitting in the rain-kissed, flower-bedecked coolness of a leafy bower, I can see that I have lost my beloved, but the next moment I realise how fully I have possessed her—possessed her indeed! And this was the night of our honeymoon. And when the night ends there will be rain as usual, and rain-washed flowers will fall, followed by the calm light of day smiling from ear to ear like an infant. O my spring-monsoon honeymoon night, don't go away again—hai! don't go away!

My sleepless ears and quiet cottage pulsated with her song, which was more of an echo of wails. I was thinking hai! only three days were left! After that, I would be losing the most melodious voice I had known for fifteen years, and a close companion with whom my twenty-year long life was intimately connected. But her impression would last a lifetime resonating like the vibrating strings of veena ... I can imagine her as mine only for these three days; and soon after that, the mere thought of her crossing my mind would be defiling her, just as her thinking about me would be an unpardonable wrong! She would belong to somebody else and move to a territory far away from here. I too would leave for a region beyond all attachments. After that a long, bittersweet, insurmountable separation....

Remembering all this, I started to sing along with the rhythm of the cloudburst—'Beloved, let us solicit, like a pair of swallows, some cool, soothing showers from the black masses of clouds. We won't want any nectar from the moon! Because we are not a pair of love birds, chakor–chakori![7] Rather, we will only expect, like chatak and mithun birds, the pure, passionate showers of rain. My love, come, let us both remember each other at this hour of the clouds and rains of Phalgun and then depart! With your melancholy, murmuring footsteps, come to my heart like the night of a spring monsoon! ... But in the end, from a distance, let the two pairs of our eyes gaze at each other and bid silently "Goodbye!"'

I don't know if she heard my song. Nevertheless, the downpour stopped; a tiny flame of a lamp entered my lonely hut through its window, flickering and trembling!

Thereafter, the clouds—stubborn, unlatched, and crazy—continued roaring in league with the storm winds above—rim–jhim–rim!

* * *

It was like an idol immersion day! The music of her immersion was being played by a group of shehnai players. An overwhelming combination of solace and a heart full of untamed pain overtook over me as I could hardly keep this fatigued body straight. It seemed as if I was about to collapse any minute like a dilapidated cottage struggling to stay erect with only a handful of posts for support...

I went outside. Even there, things looked equally difficult and discomforting. The grey sky of the summer evening had turned pale and listless and had thrown itself into the bosom of the earth. Gradually the suffocating pain grew thick and turned dark. The mango buds and a

---

[7] The chakor, according to Hindu mythology, is intensely in love with the moon because the glory of the goddess Amba is revealed through the full moon's face. During the full moon, drops of the nectar of immortality or amrut, drip from the goddess Amba as she rises from the ocean. And the chakor drinks that nectar. It is also believed that the chakori only drinks raindrops that fall during one particular moonlit night. The chakor–chakori pair is also regarded as a symbol of unrequited love.

gulancha arbour in the graveyard nearby emanated a despondent aroma that took away all my restraints. I could not hold back my tears. Oh, how futile but powerful the force of those tears! Remorse coupled with a calm weariness foamed inside me, almost rising to my lips!

* * *

Pari got married... She exchanged her vows and glances with another man. Her sampradan[8] was complete. Afterwards, I could no longer keep it a secret that I was going to war. Everyone present agreed that indeed, the military is made especially for us, the drifters, bereft of family, friends and relatives. I nodded in approval thinking, 'If you say so', while some so-called friends and relatives went to the extent of faking a tear or two in mock sympathy.

The only woman to shed true tears that day was a distant sister of mine. She said, heartbroken, 'Leave then bhai-jaan! Perhaps, this is the last time I get to see you. But the cause is surely so great that it would be a selfish sin on our part not to let you go. No sister can stop her brother from the noblest pursuit of self-sacrifice for the sake of their motherland! This land might not have sheltered enough war heroines, but many a lucky sister of warrior-brothers we have. Undoubtedly, they wouldn't hesitate to dress their brothers in robes of valour and send them off to protect the nation. Do not forget bhai-jaan that the blood of a hardy Muslim clan is flowing through us as well. We too have come from the same origin! This blood is never to run cold!'

I loved this sharp-tongued sister of mine. What she said that day filled my heart with pride! While I was trying to hold back tears, her eyes were already welling up! I had never seen her cry before. She gathered herself quickly however, and in a tear-soaked voice carried on, 'The fact that no one is here to stand in your way might disappoint you, but bhai-jaan, let it be known that there are quite a few like me who are secretly crying over your leave-taking!—Yes, one other thing! Visit the house of my soi,[9] Pari, just once. There is no loss of face in these final

[8] A ritual in a Bengali Hindu marriage where the palm of the bride is placed on that of her husband, symbolising that the family of the bride is handing her over to the family of the bridegroom.

[9] A term of endearment used by close female friends in rural Bengal to address each other.

hours bhai! Pari feels terribly lost and has begged one last time to let her see you, just once more.'

Hai re! sisters; the wellspring of our solace in this household-desert! Forevermore you are the sanyasins who distribute heaps of love and warmth from home to home. It's unfortunate how, more often than not, you go unnoticed. Only an unfortunate with no sister knows what he is missing! We hurt you but as we do, you see right through our pretences, correctly recognising the changing ocean of love and admiration we hold inside, just as you do. Knowing this makes you smile, and I wonder how immediately you reduce that protective love of yours to dust when situations demand it!

I could not find the words to bless this sister of mine whom I loved and felt so proud of that day. Only a couple of my warm teardrops that fell on her bowed head, betokened my silent prayers and good wishes for her.

Surprisingly, it was not difficult to meet Pari. I wondered at my own dispassionate contentment in that moment. How could it be? . . .

Dressed as a new bride, Pari touched my feet to offer salaams and I saw the flood of tears in her eyes that was mightier than a river swollen by the monsoon rains! In a moment, an outburst of uncontrollable yet silent cries threatened to break my heart apart! Desperately fighting my tears and steadying my voice, placing a hand on her head, I spoke calmly and sweetly, 'Live long and prosper! Be happy!'

She stood still for a while! Then she left gracefully, like a queen.

As I looked around my broken hut one last time, it appeared as if my mother-village was saying goodbye, gently waving soft drumstick flowers at me! Looking at the shimul tree by the riverside, I felt as if the bloodied hearts of hopeless lovers were hanging from its branches! . . . I watched the Mayurakshi flow—its clear, teary stream flowing like mother's milk!

In a dreamlike reverie, I could hear the heart-touching melody of half a song, sung as if in a stupor, in a faraway land of music:

Plentiful words exchanged over plentiful time and roused feelings, tied with a suffering-knot

Are coming across and filling my mind at present![10]

---

[10] These lines are taken from a Rabindranath Tagore song (*Swarabitan* 16).

I left that place for an unknown horizon with a heart full of the sanctity of peace! I looked back at my empty house one more time, teary-eyed, and murmured, 'Jai! triumph of the unknown. Jai!'

PARI'S STORY

Mayureswar—Birbhum

It's the solace of an old song he sang many moons ago I now remember more than anything—

> When a rare bit I get amid the many I gathered,
> That summons the southern wind,
> The days follow each other, as if drifting along their route,
> They proceed and retreat, greeting me as I go out;
> I wait for a dawn to arrive and make its home where I stay,
> This is what I'll seek till my last day.
> In lost light, I cull flecks of what I found,
> And it's the wreath of my life that they surround;
> Sewn are the bright bits of days gone asunder,
> While with all these, I adorn my salver.
> 'Tis the thrill of a glance, the flash of a lamp aflame,
> The half-sung song on a lute now does claim![11]

My one recurring thought these days is how the scattered soul I once so carefully handpicked in a lost luminescence, piece by piece, is now deeply etched into the medallion of my life! Those stray beads of a shining pendant of days gone astray, that I gathered and mended, now garnish my platter of penance, and oh! with such ardour! . . . For what auspicious day and for what man?

* * *

On the day he came to offer me his blessing, it felt as if all the shackles holding me back had shattered into pieces! Oh Khoda! Thanks to you we learn to live through waves of pain and exhaustion wearing heavily on our chest, and if it wasn't for the sheer patience with which you

---

[11] This is a Rabindranath Tagore song (*Swarabitan* 16).

graced our heart, nowhere could we hide the shame of failing you—the unthinkable infamy! Surely, had I failed to restrain myself that day it would have betrayed my womanhood, and I could never hope to stand tall or hold my head high! It is the strength of the mind that you have provided me O Lord, that I can unhesitatingly take pride in my achievement, although it comes with so much pain!

Perhaps it was my love that was proving to be an impediment for him in performing his duty. Why shouldn't I, then, stay away from the path that leads to his happiness and satisfaction? After all, the greatest consolation is that I could be the reason for his contentment by giving up everything of mine for his sake, which in itself is enough!

But what I find most painful is the fact that now I have to get him out of my mind. I feel torn apart as the norms and mores of society and my inner self fight against each other for ascendancy. Be it society or religion, a mightier force flares its nostrils at me, fuming with an angry and distorted expression and telling me: whatever you are thinking is preposterous, an act of unforgivable transgression!

The subconscious pulls up a placid smile in response—why would I comply with a lie? The truth rests in my heart, and so it survives, to evade the inevitability of which would be a sin. It's not so much a matter of social theory as it is a truth to be deeply contemplated.

In fact, if we believe that, in accepting the profound truth of the soul we hurt society and religion, it would be a big mistake on our part. For, it is only the shell of social and religious principles that we clasp to our bosom, ignoring their intrinsic truth, and think of ourselves as serious seekers of truth. This blind faith is a pure lie we are living, and nobody knows that better than us. But the fault is never to be admitted; instead, we will bring forth thousands of pesky witnesses in support of our false testaments! But if this were the truth, how could I flee from the verity of my heart, avowing words of consent that came out of my own mouth, accepting a complete stranger as my husband?

Met with pure dismay and revulsion, the mind then protests—yes, you have made a magnificent compromise, but at the cost of a greater truth, and the punishment for that indeed is the most severe. The fact that you can never think of him again is precisely what you deserve!

I could not help weeping at the vehement reasoning of this self-reflection. It began to occur to me that it was I who avoided the man deliberately, consumed with denial and resentment! It was a personal grievance I would likely entertain upon my inamorato from this life to the next.

* * *

Last night was my wedding night, each exceptional hour of which betokens more than a passing euphoria for most women. The exquisite memory of the idyllic event shines brighter than the morning star, softly sweetening the sad tales of a woman's daily life!

Despite the blithe spirit of that night, I could not stop a spontaneous overflow of tears. My husband took my hand in his and asked in a tender voice, 'Why are you crying, Pari?' He sounded distraught.

With much hardship I hid my shameless eyes among the pillows, murmuring to myself silently, 'Weary is my heart!' I felt his warm tears falling on my hand. To assume what affliction could make a man shed tears like this made my heart skip a few beats. He paused for a minute and said in a quiet, soft tone, following the same train of thoughts I was whispering to myself, 'I do know what hurts you, Pari! How will I be able to bring any comfort to ease your pain?'

It was as if I came back to my senses in a split second. I found myself sitting straight, asking, 'You know everything?'

He forced a pitiful smile and replied, 'Perhaps, you don't know that Azhar and I go back a long way. We spent almost the entirety of our student lives together. He shared everything with me before taking his leave. I know him, you see—an honest man, innocent like a child. It's true that I know the whole affair, but it feels as if I have done him more wrong in my attempt to help him out. Now I assume that not only have I failed in making him happy, his sorrows and pains have increased because of me. I don't think the poor man would even die a peaceful death after this! This must be the first and also the final sin I was to commit in my lifetime. He held onto my legs and begged for release. A release of what sort, I didn't understand then! I did keep my promise, Pari, but it brought me more self-hatred than gratification, for I felt trapped in one of those situations where trying to make everyone happy ends up in failure! . . . Azhar did promise, however, that he would never open his mouth about this a second time. I trust his honesty. He insisted that I take a vow to make you happy. Tell me, Pari, how can I do that?'

I threw myself at his feet and said, 'Don't let me out of your sight even for a second; let me stay like this, my face clasped tightly against your legs for eternity. This torturous pain is beyond endurance!'

He sat still like a statue of stone for a long time and then pulled me close to his chest, saying, 'No Pari, your place is not there, it's right here in my heart. Just wondering what made that unlucky fellow forsake a fine gem like you and leave to me!' He chuckled.

In a moment I felt a great agitation in my heart. I felt an intense pain mixed with reverence for this simple, sincere man. But I could not help telling myself that, how great a capacity for intense love one must possess before sacrificing it in this manner—is it a common capability of the plains folks? He seemed to think about something and then told me, 'Let bygones be bygones, Pari. Don't blame yourself for what happened in the past. He is a hero, he is gone to serve his country, don't call him back. Think of it this way—whatever happened has happened only while you remained half asleep.' He gently guided my chin in his direction and then broke into a tune,

Married or widowed, with pride and head held high
Rise, O hero's lady, with hair tied and eyes dry.[12]

What mystery is this, Khoda! Give me strength and firmness of purpose, so that I never betray this man, this god! I feel like sobbing loudly like a child now. Khoda, let peace find its way to this man, the other man, and to all the citizens of the world!

Aha, to think of those who love only to return bare-handed! A life of sheer tragedy it is, a tale of never-ending trauma. The heartbreak, however, is not of the sort where one may complain against the person who never acknowledged the affection. One cannot force love in someone's heart.

Can I ever love again? How do I forget? He who took his leave in such a triumphant manner cannot just be forgotten in a lifetime! Had he lived near me and made his life successful in some other way, I might have been able to forget him. But losing everything that mattered to him, he has made his life forlorn only for the love of this unfortunate

---

[12] These lines are borrowed from the song 'Jaytha giyachhen tini shawmoray' ('Where he has gone to war'), from Act I, Scene IV of Dwijendralal Ray's play, *Shahjahan* (2011), p. 29.

woman, hai! How can I go on pretending that I can forget you? Is this how little we women have learned of love?

My husband, on the other hand, kept singing with a smile on his face,

> Lift your eyes and let me see my love,
> Why your eyes are still half asleep![13]

---

[13] These lines are taken from one of Rabindranath Tagore's songs from the musical drama, *Mayar Khela* ('Game of Illusion', *Swarabitan* 48).

FIVE

INSATIATE DESIRE

Translated by Sreetanwi Chakraborty

As I walked down the path in the twilight, it occurred to me that at the end of the day, in the home of this wretched man, if there was not a dear, young face waiting for him with 'an intense yearning in her black eyes' and an evening lamp burning to welcome him back, then nothing could be worse than the accursed and embarrassing life that he lived!

Tinged with the colour of my anguished melody, the evening star on the western horizon of the sky looked at my face and affirmed the thought with its teary, tremulous eyes. The sonorous chirping of crickets across the silent stretches of field echoed my jaded thoughts that reminded me—'Only that evening star can understand your pain!'

During dusk, when such a melancholic person keeps walking alone along the narrow bunds of a field and travels from one hamlet to another; and then, when the evening star emerges like a heart ripped open, only he can feel the heart-wrenching pain that lacerates him.

Nothing can be heard across the vast stretches of this dusty field, except the intermittent whistling of a bird shaking dust from its wings. The bird's songs weave the strains of a Baul song whose gossamer threads touch my distraught heart! Just as one or two stars have started to twinkle in the firmament's courtyard, some insistent thoughts and long-lost memories have started to rise in my mind …

I have nothing new to say; it is all about the same unfathomable pain that is inflicted upon me again and again in ways that are hard to describe. There seems to be no respite from the pain! This heart of mine could never really evade the intense sweetness of pain! Just as a serpent cannot traverse the circled halo that its cobra-pearl creates, I too could not avoid the rubied tinge of pain in my heart and its inexplicable connection with an amorous touchiness that couldn't be redeemed!

From afar, I could hear the rustic strains of a song sung by a melancholy country-bride returning from the village market along lonely roads and fields,

> My heart weeps for one who is an other,
> Hai! Can the other be mine ever?

I said to myself—hai! her wretched soul, the other can become one's own; but most people do not realise that. When one remains a bit aloof from the most prized possession, then people misunderstand and say—'Can the other be mine ever?' There is someone who made the same mistake and left me forlorn; and that pain can never be forgotten!

The soulful song of the aggrieved, rustic woman reminded me of a sensitive, proud and hurt soul. Her memory is so overwhelming and obsessive that it constantly bobs up and down in the Jamuna of my heart like a rudderless dinghy!

It was not that we knew each other from childhood—it seems earlier than that; but neither of us can remember the day of our eternal acquaintance. . . . Her house was in our neighbourhood.

I always had a special need for her, since she was there whenever I felt an uncontrollable urge to beat someone up! It was strange that I did not beat anyone when there was a legitimate reason; I only felt the urge to beat up a person if there was no reason for me to do so. I do not quite know how she felt about the beating, but if there was a gap of two days, she used to come to me, and say with a smile, 'What happened bhai, you didn't beat me these two days?'

I would feel a sense of pain and say, 'No Moti, I shall never beat you ever again!' After that, I gave her anything that I could lay my hands on, as if my heart derived a profound comfort from this act! I thought, maybe this could compensate for the pain that I inflicted on her.

Pages with pictures torn from my books were the most precious gifts that I gave her. For this, very often, in my village pathshala,[1] I was made to hold my ears and stand all day long as punishment. But all the insults that I had to digest at the pathshala vanished when I saw her hide the gifts under her aachol and carry them home. She used the

[1] A primary school in a village, usually set up for imparting basic education.

pictures to deck her doll's bed, or else, stick them on the wall of her playhouse with rice paste. Her lovable kitten was a real eyesore for me; I could not tolerate it because of the love she had for it and the way she caressed it all day and night. Sometimes, just to make me angry, she would stick the best picture that I had given her on the back of that little kitten! But then I used to beat the world out of that fondled little creature of hers.

Sometimes I would also pull a trick on her when she sat brooding, her face sullen and ashen: I thumped on her back till she started crying. Nobody could imagine my ecstasy at that moment! The more she cried, the more I made faces at her, made her cry more as I stood there and laughed. There were days when I used to beat her black and blue, which left scars on her back! It was quite amazing though that after such a beating she would forget everything the next moment, come to me with tremulous eyes and a buoyant smile, take my fingers into hers, twist them and then say lovingly, 'The mischievous fingers of your unruly hand should be snapped right out! Then I will see how you strike me again!'

Seeing her laugh like that, I would plant a solid kick on her back and blurt out, 'Then I'll land some more kicks on your back and break it like the ripe tal palms of Bhadra!'

She continued to cry and went to her dadiji to complain about the injustice I had meted out to her. Dadiji used to chase me with a wooden stick, which made my girl burst into a peal of riotous laughter! My body would then seethe in anger and humiliation. To avenge the wrongdoing, whenever I found time, I used to give her back her due by beating her left and right.

On some days I would just intrude into her prized play zone and would break everything that belonged to her playhouse into pieces. This would really infuriate her, and she would give me a huge blow with a wooden stick and then go into hiding and not show up for another fifteen days. I felt very sad during those times. Phew! Could that slender stick have any effect on my buffalo-skin? And even if it hit me hard, so what! But then, why should that monkey of a girl be fooling around and stealing herself from me like this? After I swore and tempted her with all kinds of promises that I wouldn't repeat what I had done, she would come out, run her fingers through the parted lines of my long hair and say, 'Look bhai, I will never again strike you! If I do, may my hands be plagued with leprosy; may ticks infect me!'

Then suddenly, she would say, 'Just think for an instant, how nice it would have been if you were girly like me—isn't it?—Bhai, now let me tie those unruly locks of yours with my ribbon.' In fact, there were days when she would really play mischief by braiding my hair into plaits that took me almost an hour to undo and release my unruly mane.

'What happened after that?'

The eternal listener nestling in my heart, who was accompanying me as I crossed the empty field, asked, 'Yes bhai, what happened after that?'

For a few moments, the storyteller in my heart lost their train of thought amid the frozen stillness of the tranquil evening! Suddenly, he broke the silence and spoke thus, 'Na na, I love you! That day I lied to you, Moti, I lied!' This awkward remorse of his struck an intense discord in the late evening air like the alaap of Todi ragini! The storyteller in my heart again composed himself, as if to generate the melodious, mystical cadence of raga Poorvi in his surbahar! The forever longing, eternally thirty soul of mine was now trying to satiate itself with the elixir of melody!

This is how our days passed. When she was around eleven, she was forced into the dark corners of the inner quarters of her household.

What fretful, restless moments we both experienced then! It felt as if the tide of my life had come to an abrupt halt! If a running stream loses its rippling variety, only the stream can understand its pain; the dammed, still water of a lake would fail to fathom this excruciating pain. When an attempt is made to put the liberated one into shackles of bondage, then, instantly the surging waves no longer retain their sweet agility but erupt into querulous aphorism instead. That is what we experienced as we faced hindrances and became rebellious, confronting every obstruction that lay in our way. Who would dare to stop the eternal upsurge of an agile, restless life? So I put all my efforts into getting near her. After many days, I once again discovered the wave of life!

Till the other day, when she was out and we could meet any time we wanted to, my soul had no inclination to possess her. But the moment of sudden separation tormented my soul with extreme pain, and it said adamantly—I have to get that person I want, somehow, anyhow.

It was the cry of an affection-deprived soul with an intense longing for an unfulfilled desire that aroused nothing but reckless insanity. Then this soul started to reinvent his most desired refuge in an altogether new manner. In the deepest recesses of his heart he understood, without her as his companion he would lose speed! He was lacerated by the conflict between bondage and liberation, which took a toll on his health. Society admonished, 'Leave aside your thought of liberation—see here I have erected a wall that you can't climb over!'

The heart banged its head against the stone wall and bled like the carmine waters of the Ganga, but alas! who can break a stone wall!

And on the other hand, nobody could restrain me! Going against the tide and the much-trodden way of the multitude was what I sought forever. After even their best efforts failed to put me in the cage called school, everyone remarked, 'If this lad gets educated, then why not the companions of Sugriva,[2] the scalded-face members of the monkey clan? What shortcomings have they?' So they gave up on me, and I heaved a sigh of relief.

Breathing easy, I realised that the more I tried to keep her out of my mind, the more she became close to my heart, entrusting me with all her dependence.

The Jamuna was flowing toward the ocean; the ocean too, with its tumultuous waves spanning the horizon, rushed to meet her with millions of eager, outstretched hands! Both of them had become impatient thinking about the moment—oh when they would be able to kiss in the confluence of their love, and merge into each other! . . .

After this, we never ever met or talked. The only word we exchanged remained unspoken—an evasive eye-contact, or thirsty glances we could steal across the narrow openings of a window! It is beyond my capacity to explain how in those fleeting glimpses we could ask each other all the questions we had and feel the aching joy that overpowered us!

* * *

Five more years had gone by!

One day I heard that she would be married off to the son of a very big zamindar who had passed the BA examination. The feeling that after marriage she would leave for her in-laws' house and even

---

[2] According to the *Ramayana*, Sugriva was the younger brother of Vali, the king of Kishkindha—the kingdom of the Vanars.

our momentary visual communication would be lost forever, left a deep, painful scar in my heart! The intense pain of separation began to lacerate me and vanquish me to the core. But then, all of a sudden, the thought surfaced in my mind like the resplendent noontime-sun in a cloudless sky: she would be happy! The thought showed me a new way. I said to myself—No, since I have never bowed my head in front of anybody in my life, even today should I not be the triumphant one? And why should there be any sadness at all? She will be the wife of a rich, educated man; she will have everything that can transform the life of any miserable girl and give her comfort. But hai! the inconsolable heart would refuse to accept this unpalatable truth! I felt that she would not get the kind of love that I could give her!

This heart-wrenching feeling filled my eyes with tears and I began to weep profusely. I remembered my outward penury at that time, but the glory and veracity of my feelings for her made me stand tall. In a moment of defiance and arrogance, I promised myself that I would take revenge by sacrificing my own happiness. It would compensate for my wretchedness.

Amid such conflicts, the profundity of the thought that 'my beloved will be happy' began to make deep incisions in my heart; and then all of a sudden, all the boisterous waves, tempests and pain of my heart receded into a placid silence! In the magnanimity and the nectar of divine consolation, my bitter soul was soaked with bliss. Ah! Where were you all these days, the anodyne to all my pains? After so many days, tears of relief calmed me like never before!

Which sorcerous strain emanating like a magnetic effect from Orpheus' flute pacified the tumultuous sea of my heart into deep sleep? . . . Hai! Where was this magical flute melody all this while? On that night, therefore, I looked at her casement and sang,

I have innumerable cravings
You saved me by not fulfilling those!
I treasure this cruel pity of yours
As my life's eternal abundance.[3]

Bah! I find I have almost traversed the entire road across the field and reached the border of the village! From the distance, fleeting glimpses

[3] These lines are from a Rabindranath Tagore song (*Swarabitan* 24).

of earthen and kerosene vapour-lamps can be seen flickering, the lights drawing my attention to the lit village households! It feels as if beside one of those flickering lamps, there is a young, veiled face waiting with expectant eyes turned toward the pathway. As if she is startled even by the sound of a falling leaf stirred by the south wind; as if the long-awaited treasure of her life has returned! She is intoxicated by the swirling feeling of hope and despair that is occupying her heart at the moment!

The eternal, indefatigable and lovelorn listener nestling in my soul goaded me and said, 'Think about all this later but do tell me what happened after that!'

By then, an impenetrable sense of peace, just like the affectionate look of a mother's bowed eyes. had already descended upon the village. A feeling of melancholic pain combined with a divine softness instantly moistened my eyelashes!

With tremulous eyes I recollected the rest of the story …

A few days before her marriage, we met stealthily one night. That was the last conversation we had. She said, 'What good will this marriage bring me, bhai?'

I said, 'You will be happy!'

For a moment my easy explanation and casual voice made her forget her age, my age, and our age gap. The star-studded sky above us chuckled silently. She then grasped my fingers just like in our childhood, and cracking them one after another said, 'How will that be possible? I have to leave you then. I shall not be able to see you anymore!'

After all these years, I was hearing her speak in such an affectionate and emotionally-charged voice! The deep, long eyelashes of her big, wide eyes reflected a faint light, indicating that she was crying!

I said, 'I can understand what you're saying Moti! But the person who will marry you will love you even more than me; when you go to his house, you will forget everything about us!'

But the thought that someone else would love my beloved even more than me was simply unbearable. Maybe he was more affluent than me, more handsome and more educated, but can he really love the most beloved person of my life more than me? Did I say that? Well, if I did, it was because I was in terrible agony and pain, and my voice was made hoarse by an outburst of sobs. There was no power that could stop me from crying my heart out! Almost near to fainting, she took my palm, pressed it hard against her eyes, and said in a loud, wailing voice, 'Na—Na—Na!' What was this 'No' for?

I emphasised in a loud tone, 'It has to happen Moti, it has to! You have to leave me!'

By that time, my heart was already filled with disgust and an unspeakable agony against an unknown deva! She fell onto the ground and asked, 'O! You have been hitting me hard all this while. Are you not satisfied even today? Then hit me, hurt me—hurt me as much as you want!'

The memories and pain of so many days filled my heart! But the next moment an intense feeling of hurt and pain brought back my arrogance and began to stiffen my resolve to hold my ground! My heart said—I have to be triumphant!

I smiled a cruel, ruthless smile and told Moti, 'Hmm! You won't budge, will you? Then let me confess the truth—Moti, the fact is, I don't love you!'

The words pierced my heart more than they affected her. Resembling a meek doe struck by a sharp, pointed arrow, she startled and said, 'What?!'

I said, 'All this while I have deceived and betrayed you with a lie that I love you. I never had any genuine feelings for you!'

My voice became husky, like dry wood. She looked like an injured snake and glowing with impassioned rage, she roared at me, 'Go away, go!—I do not want you, move aside! You are even crueller than the hangman! unfeeling!—Go away, leave! I fall at your feet, go away, do not insult my love any longer!'

She covered both her eyes with her palms and rushed out like the blustery nor'wester winds! As I reeled, losing my balance, I heard something—or somebody—crashing through the canopied awning of the courtyard and the thudding sound reverberated throughout the house that was about to celebrate a wedding. There was a terrible, heart-rending cry of affliction—'Oh ma!'

* * *

As my vision stretched to a long, long distance, I found the weary boatman sitting at the ferry crossing with an eternal cry bubbling out of his weary heart, as if it reiterated the words of my soul—

> O heart-oarsman, take back re! your oar,
> Now I can't row anymore.

O! oarsman-brother of my heart, I can't row this tiresome boat of my life anymore! Now take me to the anchoring shore or else to your peaceful lap for good!

The intense pang of pain still remains in my heart, but she couldn't possibly feel my pain! She could not understand that in a bid to hurt her, I have ravaged my own heart and tattered it with thorns of pain—if only Moti could see it! Oh! If even my beloved misunderstands me, then what do I live with? What is the meaning of this empty and abject life? Hai, nothing in this world is as doleful as this feeling!

* * *

Now I have entered the mango-orchard in my village. There stands my closed, dark abode. All around there are lamplit homes that are resounding with affectionate voices, and amidst this my lonesome hut remains enveloped in darkness: a venomous, cursed arrowhead. Returning home at the end of the day of work or idleness, the one thing that comes to mind everyday while I unlock my door—today is no exception—is that my loneliness will never be redeemed. The thought sets a wild bushfire to the painful wilderness of my soul!

One by one all the homes surrounding my hut will be illuminated with earthen lamps, only my lonely hut will never see the light of an evening-lamp; ever! Nobody with a pair of compassionate black eyes full of yearning will wait sleeplessly beside that pale, flickering light, for me to return!

And then, outside my dilapidated door, nothing else except the desperate wailing and Karbala-like mourning of the billowy wind could be heard. It bellowed in an excruciating wail,

> Hai! unhoused, hai! rough sleeper, hai! dispossessed!

I could feel the eternal coupling of heaven and earth now wailing bitterly in the funeral of my heart—

> Hai! unhoused, hai! rough sleeper, hai! dispossessed!

SIX

LETTER FROM A POLITICAL PRISONER

Translated by Anindita Mukhopadhyay

Presidency Jail, Kolkata
Liberty-Day, day's end

My very own and dearest Manashi!

Today is my day for finally bidding you farewell. One by one I have taken my leave of everybody. You are the only one left. I had wished to not inflict any pain upon you on this day of parting. But all that I had to say remains unsaid. I just couldn't control this irrepressible longing of mine, even though I know you will be hurt. You, of course, will not be able to blame me for this, as you have always believed with deep conviction that, when it comes to selfishness and jealousy, I am second to none in the whole wide world.

You have never liked what I had to say (I will come to that later); what I say today will be no exception. Still, Lokkhi,[1] glance through this letter keeping in mind that it is the last cry of a wretched, lost wayfarer as he prepares to travel into an unknown sunset land. Today I am really remorseless, really cruel. I have no idea how many deep scratches my words will leave in your pristine heart! But my dearest, unbearable pain—indeed unbearable pain—has driven me to become this sworn rebel, this raving lunatic. Even today I have come to make you cry. You too point out: today I am an executioner; today I am a murderous butcher. It will give me some relief.

---

[1] The endearment Lakshmi, or 'Lokkhi' as pronounced by Bengalis, is a typical Bengali endearment applicable to either gender, carrying within it a world of affect—gentle persuasion, love, and closeness.

My mind is totally distracted. Perhaps I will not be able to say anything coherently. Anyway, don't go looking for disciplined and well-knit prose from one who has spent a lifetime offering puja to indiscipline and chaos. Maybe the point from where I will begin is actually the end, and where I will close will signify the beginning! The real thing is, it is enough if you understand; I don't care about the others. It is you who can fill the empty spaces that the incomplete and unsaid words of my heart have left behind, and you must do it with your pain and your own heart's language—Now listen.

The first thing I remember is what you asked me one evening (you will not be able to recall it now, perhaps), 'What can be done to make you get better?'

Heavy pain churned in my breast, and an emotional anger surged within me when you put this heartless question to me on my sickbed!

Hai, my inept feelings of hurt! Hai, my insulted, unrequited love! I couldn't answer your question. Neither would it have been justified! The despairing cries of a hundred thousand young sanyasis mourning their hopeless and blasted youth were ringing in the pained mandir of my heart, in offerings of accumulated and endless pain. The very person, for whom I was suffering so intensely, had to come and ask me, 'What will cure your pain?' ...

It seemed to me, you deliberately said those words knowing full well how they would insult and taunt me. The pain in my chest swelled ten-fold. I hugged the pillow next to me and lay face down. My greatest shame would be for you to see my unruly tears, in case you realised that my heartache had increased again! Could there be anything as intensely shameful as shedding unstoppable tears and being overcome by pain in front of someone totally indifferent to my pain? I could not even speak; I was terrified my tear-drenched voice would betray my grief before you.

But Bhagwan protected me from such peril. You stood quietly for a long time pondering something, and then softly tiptoed away. Maybe if I told you that when you left, I thought I heard you heave a brief sigh, you would probably laugh. Hai re, this blind and deaf beggar's heart of mine! If that had really been the case, what could have prevented you from even casually asking me why I had taken to my bed so suddenly!

After you left, my heart seemed to collapse because of the overwhelming sense of hurt. In fruitless anger and stung by pain, I burst out crying. By then evening had settled. The doctor arrived; friends and relatives arrived. They soon found out my heart was functioning most irregularly. 'The condition . . .', the doctor continued, 'the patient has suddenly—umm—become emotionally overwhelmed for some reason. It is very serious. This may even cause . . .'

While the doctor hesitated to say more, I completed the sentence for him—'. . . the lamp to be snuffed out; the house to be darkened! Isn't that right doctor babu?' I tried to laugh but my sudden tears made it plain to many that I was crying. Indeed, my voice was trembling, my lips quivering, my eyelids moist. I turned and again lay face down. Nobody could persuade me to sit up again. My friends reproached me for my stubbornness for some time and then they left. I silently thanked Khoda.

Hai, why would these cruel people not allow me to cry in peace? . . . Some of them were still sitting around my bed: some near the head, some at the sides. Suddenly I thought you had come and taken my hand in yours. In an instant all my pain disappeared. Once again I had tears in my eyes, but these were tears of happiness! Not that these tears didn't hide my unvoiced, hurt feelings, but just that tiny, imagined touch of yours flooded me with joy and made me forget all my pain, insult and humiliation. I thought, you were mine, mine and only mine! Hai re! this eternal beggar! This forever-thirsty, poverty-stricken soul of mine! With such crumbs you desire to fill your heart and the void with your own feelings! But you never could attain your heart's desire.

In a little while I began to chat and laugh with everyone around me as usual, which made everyone heave a sigh of relief. But nobody understood, perhaps not even you, how and why my seething heartache had been stilled in an instant. That happiness and pain only my Maker and I knew. Do I dare tell the truth? It had seemed to me perhaps that you too could feel my pain. See what a beggarly mind is mine! You must be really sneering at me! Aha! my Lokkhi! If only you had lied just once and had said that your heart knew my pain, my life would not have been nipped in the bud this early! My life would not have been a repeat of the despondent Devdas's![2]

---

[2] A tragic hero who suffers the pangs of unfulfilled love, turns into a drunkard, and ultimately dies in the novel *Devdas* written by Sarat Chandra Chattopadhyay (1876–1938).

Huh! I was forgetting the main issue.

Yes, that day I remained intoxicated with the joy of that slight warm touch. The next day I constantly toyed with the desire to pull you aside and tell you why my heart ached so. The whole day I expected you to come and just ask me again, 'What can be done to make you better?'

* * *

Hai re! the unfortunate's hope! You didn't even absentmindedly come and ask me the question that day. The whole day I grappled with acute anxiety and finally at the end of the day my soul seemed to wilt. In deep sorrow I began to sing one of my favourite songs with great feeling just to push away the agony of my impoverished soul,

O Omniscient, the One who surely perceives
That my mind has ever been on obscure pathways.
My thoughts have never found a nest.
On the currents they always tend to float,
But I still retain hope and anticipate,
That they will stay at your feet, O holiness.

Tears and smiles have alluringly beckoned,
But each time the silken mesh did not hold!
Everyone calls me an unfortunate—
'When evening comes where will you lay your head?'
There is always your lap, I understand, I understand
Wherever, my head bows down in due course.[3]

My voice, my eyes, all became heavy with the weight of my agony. I cannot deceive the external world while I sing. The tune quaveringly cries out through my song, and that tune, that weeping does not come from my throat, but from the beloved who resides deep in my heart and cries. As I sang, I felt that in this world, even for a ne'er-do-well like me, there was one friend at least who would certainly know of my flaming soul's torment and whose eyes would moisten with empathy as he listened to my song: the Omniscient One. Just then, it flashed across my mind that if I did have a beloved in truth, she would have

[3] This is a Rabindranath Tagore song (*Swarabitan* 39).

listened to the pathetic bit 'Everyone calls me an unfortunate,/When evening comes where will you lay your head?' and instantly erased all the distance between; and lovingly placing my head in her own lap, would have said in gentle and tearful recrimination, 'In my lap, dearest, in my lap!' Her young voice, throbbing with pity, love and reproach, would have quavered, 'Chhi Lokkhi! You cannot sing such a song!'

Do you see how disgustingly greedy I am? By now you must be rolling about in laughter at such puerile emotional immaturity. Maybe you are thinking how such an arrogant and completely unshackled force can, in an instant, kneel in subjection at your feet; how could a world-conqueror be defeated so surprisingly easily. I am myself mystified. But occasionally I fear, my dear, that your pride may one day crumble in an instant 'and your eyes will stream with endless tears'. That day you might understand the pain of my unrequited love. You would know the meaning of my present defeat.

Never mind; coming back to what I was saying. As I sang, I somehow felt that the all-knowing God was standing silently before me with brimming eyes. When I wiped my eyes and looked up, 'Oh Khoda! Who are you, gazing at me with such compassionate eyes? Aha! these fickle eyes have lost their teasing gleam and mischievous twinkles and are frozen in pain. Those maddening eyes with their ink-black lashes are heavy with moisture. Oh! my Omniscient One! Are you really revealing yourself to me in this fading twilight? Hai my deva! Has this evening worship at your altar not been in vain?' I forgot everything, and like a sleepwalker, said, 'You cannot love anybody else more than me! Yes?'

Wordlessly you came and hid your face on the pillow over my lap. Why? In embarrassment? In happiness? In pain? I do not know. That's the reason for my agony and torment. Never have you conveyed your heart's desire with just a simple word, and so my chest aches with this agony of unknowing. After a lot of persuasion, you raised your face, but you still did not tell me why you had hidden your face like that. If you only had uttered a small lie that day, if you had said, 'O my dear one of my entire life! Who . . .' Na, na, let it be!

Let me tell you something funny. Sitting in this lock-up, I have a strange conviction that I am a poet. Wait. Don't start laughing. I know far better than you that Bhagwan has left nothing undone to knock out of me all the qualities needed to be a poet. My interior and exterior are very much like the Bihari khotta bhaiyas[4]—the crude brothers of this arid and passionless place. Still, had I been a poet, I would have expressed my present state of mind so beautifully:

> Only disdain, only indifference, only insult!
> Love? It is just hocus-pocus re!
> Just to procure disgrace! The soul you offer will be crushed underfoot!
> Only disdain, only indifference, only insult!

Let it go. What I could not be, I can never be at any cost. Let's only discuss whatever I am or have become.

Wait! I might be insulting my wounded feelings when I am displaying them like this. Is it not so? Like me, maybe you are also thinking: whom is all this wounded feeling directed towards? Who has given me the right to display so much confused love, longing, anger, rejection, hurt? I never got a drop of love, but I am self-indulgently hogging a veritable ocean of wounded feelings! You will be really surprised to hear that I am indeed wallowing in wounded feelings. The person to whom this feeling is directed, is free to either acknowledge it or trample it underfoot. I don't care. I do not even consider if she would at least honour my love—because blinded by the pride of my love I only think that she also loves me! That is why I am humiliated everywhere!

There have been many female travellers who have wanted to soothe the pain this traveller felt; perhaps they even loved me (do not laugh), but I never even turned to look at them. I even felt proud of my indifference. When I felt one of my fellow travellers was falling in love with me, I thought the girl would never be able to keep pace with me. Why should I pointlessly ruin her young life? I used to find it inconceivable that anyone could win the heart of this freedom-loving rebel with such ease. Whenever I got the impression that some unfortunate girl was growing fond of me, I would immediately withdraw—to a great distance indeed. From there I would assess if the attraction she had for me was truly love, or pity or just an infatuation.

---

[4] Bengali parochialism has always considered Biharis to be crude, physical, and devoid of all sentimental excesses.

There was another reason why I would distance myself: I did not want either of us to end up regretting the mistake.

I have one great weakness: no one surrenders to affection as easily as I do. So the thought that somebody was becoming affectionate towards me would make me run away fearing entanglement. From a distance though, I could see how many of them were wrong. Apparently many have loved me, yet I could see through their exaggerated claims of love because of the objectivity distance provided me. None of them wanted to have me all their lives. I am a wayfarer and they merely wanted to have me for a while as we travelled together. And so, none of them ever found me within their reach. Many tell me that this was also because of my wounds. I don't know. There have been one or two instances when I forgot myself and got close to someone, only to see the person kicking my devata—my love—really hard. Would you still say that was my unreasonable wounded feelings?

You should remember something else: all those who wanted to have me in their lives have loved me first. I have never loved them. Even though I received such bounties, my mind always stepped back and said, 'This is not the one, not the one!'

Hai, my unsatisfied heart! Whom do you really want? Who is that dearest one? Who is that proud beauty standing in her courtyard with a garland in her hand, waiting for you? I could not love anyone because I failed to have the darling of my heart, my Manashi—the lady of my dreams! Just thinking about the number of young hearts I have trampled even before my life had properly begun, troubles me intensely. Still, I find some comfort in the belief that I never insulted anyone's love. I never tempted anyone with my love and then discarded her. On the contrary, I have begged their pardon with folded hands from afar. I have requested them not to love me and removed myself from their paths forever. I have never trodden their paths in case I became an obstacle for them. Many have cursed me for this ruthlessness, yet others have called me out and told me how arrogant and haughty I was.

I have driven my chariot along various roads of my own choosing, like a victorious warrior. Then one morning you and I met. Suddenly my chariot stopped. My heart cried out in unfathomable joy, 'I have found her! I have found her!' The wayfarer inside me came out and said despondently, 'Farewell, my friend! Now you are no longer mine;

you are your Manashi's! Your road has now ended.' Then I saw him disappear into the dark horizon at the end of the road!

Hai, what was happening to me! For so long, female travellers could not stop my chariot, no matter how hard they tried. Some even laid down in front of me, but I drove my chariot over them, laughing. But now my chariot refused to move! You only slightly raised your eyes to mine—you did not even request me 'Traveller! Stop at my door for a while!'

Still I did not feel sad. I lost my self-respect. I got down with the precious garland I had strung together over many lifetimes and placed it around your neck. You stood in silence with your head bowed. I had no power to understand the language of your silence. My soul fluttered in great distress. I could not understand if you were happy or felt pain. Then, in my breast that harboured an everlasting hurt, I felt a huge pain. Why hasn't Bhagwan given one human being the power to read the mind of another? But no matter how much I felt hurt, I had no complaints against you (not even now).

I have loved you without wanting to know about the state of your heart. I have always been victorious but finally I have adorned you with the garland of defeat—you are my Manashi, my dearest! The image that my heart had cherished through many lifetimes, to find which I turned into a restless nomad for eternity, that Manash; I recognised the instant I set eyes on her. It never occurred to me to wonder whether you would accept this defeated rebel's garland of oblation with a smile or you would push it away with your foot and leave. If you cannot love me, how can I blame you? I know, I know very well dearest, that no one has any control over their mind. Whoever a person wants to love, if he considers that love to be his duty, his mind will refuse to obey him. His mind cries eternally for the woman who lives inside his mind, so he cannot love anyone else. I have searched for you for so many lifetimes, just like this, but you have not allowed yourself to be caught. This time too, you did not surrender. Who knows when, in which lifetime, we will build a home by some nameless village. I do not know when you will love me. Still I will love you, and so I place this huge burden of wounded feelings on you.

Now suppose that this hurt of mine is not true that you indeed love me, then you might be wondering why am I deliberately misunderstanding you and tormenting myself. Why am I tormenting you like this? Just to answer that, I read the few letters—kind gifts you had written to me a few thousand times last night—but I did not find anything that would dispel my cruel conviction, my firm belief! Full of pity for my misery you have sent me much consolation. You have written of so many things. In some places you have even brought tears to my eyes, but not even absentmindedly have you written 'I love you'. There is nothing in your letters, not even a circumspect eagerness or hesitation, to hide that admission. Hai, my blind belief! And still, I kept writing to you as if it were my right and with so much wounded pride. The shame and humiliation I felt has increased hundredfold, but I still cannot leave you and go away. Because this time it is I who have loved you first! The person who loves someone else first has to face such misfortune and humiliation quite often.

And so today, like the disbelieving atheist that I am, I am going to die announcing there is nothing like love in this world. In this uncaring earthly realm, if you love someone, there is no guarantee your love would be returned. Only an atheist understands how powerful the blows have to be to drive someone towards total disbelief. I know that if one has loved, then contentment comes from self-sacrifice. I also believe that if you truly love somebody, you can never forget her even though she has insulted you, hurt you and inflicted pain on you a thousand times. The torment and hurt attains a certain sentimental value. Still, if anyone claims that the starving and agonised heart does not want its squandered love returned, he lies.

Men have tried for many lifetimes with all sincerity and devotion to win the hearts of women but have failed. The inner world of a woman is like a labyrinth—complex, mysterious and secret. A woman can give you everything, but is reluctant to hand over the key to her inner sanctum. I have heard that she only does it when she loves someone with all her heart. Do you know why my hurt is directed against you? Because you have quietly put up with all the excessive love I have showered on you without any protest, but you never gave me a hint if it really made you happy or hurt you. I have never seen you with smile on your face in those times. Today, just thinking about my excessive emotional demands on you makes my chest constrict painfully. Perhaps you forced yourself to suffer these excesses in silence. But you never once wrote to me about it. It seems to me that what you really wanted was to somehow bury the whole thing and let it remain out of sight. Let it be so! Now the time has come to bury all these pains and mistakes for all time. I will never dig them up even if I return, no matter how it lacerates my heart to leave it be. If I do return, I will make one last attempt to become a rebel against myself. But hai! to whom am I saying these things! Is it a stone image of a mute devata who is listening to my bitter weeping? Let me return to what I was saying.

Do you know why I cannot be content? It is because I cannot be content like ordinary people with a simple experience of love. All around me, everybody is happily eating, drinking, quarrelling with their wives, and then immediately making up—they are living their lives with an equal measure of joy and sorrow. But I cannot tread this path of the ordinary; forget about being happy, I could not even be unhappy like them. They marry, have children, and when they grow up, they marry them off and welcome home sons and bahus—ah! what more could one want? Confined to their limited space they laugh and cry and do everything that is needed. They are content with what they have. But I think that nine out of ten of these poor things do not know—and do not want to know—that they never possessed the hearts of the person with whom they have been living their lives. Neither do they have any understanding of each other's minds, nor do they consider such an understanding a necessity. Despite such physical closeness, mentally they remain in two different countries, totally unknown to each other. The day I spotted this trickery, I lost the courage to set up a home with a companion. I am constantly afraid that my life companion would rest her head on my breast one day and think of someone else, heave sighs for someone else and quietly endure my professions of love. Ooh! I shudder to even think of it! Just so that it doesn't happen to me, the first thing I would do is to find out if her heart has recognised the inner being within me, and only then would I set up a home with her. Until that happens—no matter how many lifetimes it takes—I would either continue to be my mother's Lokkhi chhele[5] and lie on her lap, or pick up my blanket and water-pot and embrace a life of renunciation, just like I am doing now.

I have always prided myself on my ability to divine someone's thoughts the moment I set eyes on them and in many instances I have

---

[5] A term meaning 'boy' or 'little boy'

been right. But who would have known that all my pride would drown in tears when it came to you! Indeed,

> Traps of love are laid throughout the world, who knows when one gets caught!
>
> All pride, hai, is lost in an instant, tears gush out of the eyes that are wet![6]

That is so true, for you have made this reckless daredevil cry like a child! Can you tell me, my Lokkhi, why you are so transparent with everybody else and so opaque to me? And oh yes, let me offer hope—when you are really tired of life; when you see your love demeaned and the billowing wounded pride in your heart tossed into the mud; when hopelessness eats like a canker into your heart (Khoda forbid), that day take comfort from this thought, dearest, that there lived someone in this world of sorrow who loved you with all his heart. He did not get even a grain of love in return, but he did not leave any residual pain for you nor did he make any complaints to you. Had he got you, he would have placed you like a crown on his head. He had all the ability, all the desire, to make you an empress. If you had reciprocated his love he would not have wasted his early youth, so full of hope and expectation, and left it all behind! He had it in him to achieve something great and amaze the whole world. In great agony, he spent his whole life in rebellion and reckless action.

Imagine that even in the other world, he would not get peace but wander as a restless spirit through unknown paths carrying the garland meant for you and looking for you; that he would be in readiness for all time to hold you to his heart. To prove that he truly loves you, he has cut his own neck with a cleaver. Keep in mind that the person you thought of only as an obstacle in the path of your happiness, the curse of your life, has quietly removed himself from your path for ever to save you from all harm and misfortune. Remember! The person you have been indifferent to has been much sought after by many girls who vied for his attentions, but who never even turned to give them a smile in case you, his beloved Manashi, felt pain or took umbrage.

I have just remembered something else. I have no idea what you will think of me when you read it, but this is one of the reasons

---

[6] These lines are from Tagore's *Mayar Khela* ('The Game of Illusion').

why I am taking my leave of you with a heart full of wounded pride directed against you. It suddenly struck me yesterday as I was reading your letters. You know, I am a very jealous fellow. I cannot stand the thought that somebody else would love you; forget seeing it happen. I certainly feel very proud and privileged when people praise you and praise your goodness, but that does not mean I will allow anyone to love you. I want you to be wholly mine, inside and out, and I would surrender myself to you and be blissfully happy. But someone else cannot love you, no, never. So whenever I saw someone looking and smiling at you and were looking back at him with a smile, I felt like plunging a knife into his breast.

But Khoda has endowed you with so much beauty and virtue it is inevitable that everyone would love you at first sight. A love-hungry human heart would be compelled to love you. I have thought so many times that I would run away with you to some deep forest where there would be just you and me, no one else. Whenever I would open my eyes, I would see you, and you would see me. My love seems to be like Rahu.[7] Is it not so? The thought that you may love someone else and not me, is more heartbreaking than what I feel now. And so I have begged you not to love anyone else more than me.

But you have never given any response to my most heartrending pleas, never even offered me consolation with a smile and a gentle lie and said, 'Yes, oh, yes!' You have only remained silent and still. Now I am in such great torment because I couldn't understand the reason for your silence. Today I would have died in utter bliss if, on this final day, I knew what you really had in mind. Now, perhaps even if you wanted to let me know, it will no longer be possible. If you could, you would have, perhaps, pitied this eternally hapless person and uttered a few words of compassionate consolation. But my dearest, you cannot deceive this traveller who is on his way to eternity. I won't give you that opportunity. When you read this letter of mine, I will be totally out of your reach.

---

[7] Rahu and Ketu denote the points where the paths of the sun and moon intersect in space. Rahu and Ketu are called, respectively, the north and the south lunar nodes. The fact that eclipses occur when the sun and moon are at one of these points, gives rise to the popular understanding of the sun and moon being swallowed by these two serpents. Rahu is deemed responsible for causing a solar eclipse, in his attempt to eat the sun.

Today it is clear to me that there are no idiots quite like men, at least to women. It is amazing the way men rush to women for a bit of love. It seems as if even Bhagwan would not be able to quench such universe-devouring hunger, but you can dupe them so convincingly with a small, sweet word. Even this insolent daredevil becomes as tractable and docile as a small boy if you just place a palm on his forehead or hold his hand with a sweetly uttered 'my Lokkhi'! He does not want to even see what is on your mind; just that little token of regard intoxicates lovelorn men. Still, you do not completely surrender yourselves to men. No matter how hard one tries, it is impossible to know what is in your mind; and getting all of your love is like running after a mirage. No one knows the depths of your love! I have thought and thought about it in amazement! Do not think that everyone has these questions on their mind. I am simply telling you about my immediate thoughts as plainly as I can. This is how men have been tricked by women through the ages. No matter what fame they have achieved in the world as scholars, as warriors, or as doers, to you they are just plain stupid. It is no exaggeration to say you regard them as nothing more than lambs. Even Bhagwan will not be able to figure out what you keep hidden in your minds, I say this loudly and with complete conviction. You are women, and it is your nature to be affectionate, to care for and to nurture whosoever it may be, and you weep when you see anyone in pain and offer comfort. That gives you great pleasure and deep contentment. Here you are all goddesses and sanyasins. Because you desire to bring succour to the wounded and wipe away tears of suffering, you sacrifice self-interest, but you cannot—and do not—love everybody. It is here that men make a terrible mistake. They mistake your care and compassion for love and they give you their hearts in return. Even if you know someone loves you with all his heart but you cannot love him in return, you make all kinds of sacrifices for him, you take care of him, nurse him, give him solace in his distress, shed tears of pity—but you cannot love him. You can sacrifice all worldly happiness for him, but you cannot make him king on the throne of your heart.

Ignorant and blind men take your natural compassion for love and become needlessly happy and contented. Hai re! poor unfortunates! Later, they suffer for this, because a lie is revealed as a lie one day. The truth dawns on him one day when, at night, holding her close, he realises that the person who is nearest to him is indeed farthest from him; that the woman lying on his chest is no longer his own. 'I have lost her, I have lost her for life!'—this realisation is so acutely painful, only those who have suffered it will understand. Many have felt their hearts break when the truth comes out; their lives forever rendered barren. In merciless anger, they begin to punish themselves in every possible way and pay the women back for their mistake. They commit suicide, not with one blow, but bit by bit, by slow degrees!

I hold the female race in very high respect. I desire their welfare from the depths of my heart, but my consistent complaint against them is that they do not give much value to men's love, and ignore and insult their feelings. They are themselves not happy in their lives and cannot make others happy. This is what lies behind much of what society is afflicted with. The proud woman, glorying in her youth and beauty, tramples underfoot one who would have given her the status of queen and devi in his heart and home. She walks over the bleeding heart of the hapless man and applies alta on her feet with his blood. I know she has to repent for it the rest of her life. Once she insults someone's love like this, she can never get the same love in her life. Her life becomes unbearable and bitter. Perhaps she then remembers him more—the one who with even an iota of her love would have lifted her high over his head and danced with joy. Perhaps you would frown and tell me how wrong I am. Well, say it, but I am only telling you what I have seen for myself. You will come up with something like this: women are hungry for love. If somebody gives them just a little love, they fall in love with him inside and out. . . .

I feel like laughing at such declarations. Not to belittle love, but haven't I cherished you, loved and caressed you like a little bird holding it next to my heart for many lifetimes together? But did you give your heart in return? I am giving you just this one example and I may very well end here. There are a whole lot of us luckless ones, who are aimlessly roaming the streets—you just have to look to see them. Unless you have sworn to be blind, you cannot help but see them.

Let it pass. I have unnecessarily digressed from what I was saying about my jealousy. I wanted to confess that I have deliberately flirted with girls and caressed them right in front of your eyes, but you have never felt jealous. You have never flinched or felt distressed, and there has certainly been no outward show of any feelings. You know in your heart you are not mine. You cannot love me, so it does not stir you if I ostentatiously show affection for anybody—it does not matter. When you have laid no claim to me, how does it matter to you if somebody loves me or I love somebody?

Do you know what I am thinking?

If I had been a girl even more beautiful than you are, then I would have taken away the man you love and shown to you how much the heart aches, how painful it is!

Do you know why I have rambled on and on for so long? Today I am a political prisoner. I am sitting in a cell in Presidency Jail and writing this letter to you. Tomorrow is my trial. At the end of it, there will be at least a two-year rigorous imprisonment for me. In a coincidence, one of the jail officials is a childhood friend of mine. Today there was an amazing meeting between us. In school, there used to be stiff competition between us, as to who would be first in class. Thanks to his kindness, I have got the materials and time to write this letter, otherwise I would not have been able to inform anybody before disappearing off the face of the earth. I hope Bhagwan takes care of his well-being!

You may think that, if it's just a two-year jail sentence, why such a tearful farewell? I would be back again after doing my time. But I know I am not going to return. I have not told you till now—I had hidden it from you—but I am letting you know before I leave, although I know how you will suffer when you find out. I have tuberculosis, which even Lord Shiva cannot cure; or so they say. The doctor has begged me not to exert myself; my friends have all begged me to rest for a few days, but I have, of course, worked at twice the pace. If you had forbidden me just once, not out of pity but with love, I don't know what I would have done: but you had no idea about this dreadful disease of mine! Then maybe you would have gently persuaded me to get better out of sheer pity . . .

Still, I am obeying all your injunctions till my last breath. No one else in this world but you can make me listen to instructions, rule over me, or force me to obey commands! If I have committed any wrong against you at any point then please do not forget it, but forgive me, knowing that the person whom you could never love has obeyed all that you told him till the last day of his life; that he considered those commands to be more sacred than Khoda's sacred words. Let my words bring some happiness to you. Feel a little proud that you conquered someone as free and reckless as me.

Even if I am given just six months of hard labour instead of two years in jail, I have no hope of coming back. Tuberculosis has eaten into my body and pain has hollowed my breast. Add to it the labour in the jail. I cannot tell when my heart will stop. Even now, after a little exertion, blood spurts from my nose and mouth. I might have still lived, given my strong belief in my life force and my will power. But Lokkhi, I no longer have the desire to live. Even if you came to take me back with you, I could not return with you. I would have to say with much sadness, 'You came at the wrong time dearest, at the wrong time!'

Moreover, if I had some hope of doing something great in my life, then there would have been some meaning in returning to life—but there is nothing like that. I did try a lot but I couldn't find anything. So today I am giving up and surrendering: 'It is evening now, time to hold me to your breast.' I did not dream in my wildest dreams that I would get caught so easily and so soon. I had really hoped that I would achieve something great before embracing death. But I could not do that. Not that I didn't try. And I think it is pointless to delve into the reasons for my failure now. So, let me say good bye. But as I leave, I curse you: that you meet someone whom you will love with all your heart even for a day, and then he spurns your love so that you may then feel my pain! The person who blighted your life is now leaving this world! No more fear!

And, yes, if you can, please bless me so that in another lifetime, I am that someone you will love! Oh! It is so dark! . . . Yours truly

The curse and misfortune of your lifetime
Shri Dhumketu[8]

[8] Dhumketu is both a self-reference and a reference to Haley's Comet. In Bengali folk culture, Dhumketu is associated with sudden and cataclysmic events.

THE AGONY OF THE DESTITUTE

SEVEN

THE AGONY OF THE DESTITUTE

Translated by Jackie Kabir

A

Birbhum

Ah! What a spectacle unfolded before me today!

Scores of young Bengalis, charged with boundless enthusiasm, were eagerly waiting to sacrifice their lives in an unknown, unseen land for the sake of their motherland! My brothers! What fiery souls lay hidden behind their drab khaki uniforms! They were adorned with thousands of garlands of flowers: garlands of victory blessed by our mothers, and affectionate, tear-soaked tokens of love and pride given by our sisters!

The flowers were moist but bright! Their colours suggested the bittersweet pain everyone felt! They were not mere flowers, but teardrops that flowed from the holy corners of the hearts of our sisters, our mothers! And the tears that rolled down our cheeks! There is nothing greater than this!—Oh! these are tears that have flowed from time immemorial!

The rain had stopped, but it had bored through the sunshine for a short stretch of time and drenched their khaki uniforms, making them look even drabber. The raindrops were like someone else's tears! It was as if their mothers' prayers had touched their innermost being!

They left. The hissing of the steam engine resounded with the pride of successfully accomplishing the demands of the time, while there rose on the air a sad song of hope that could be heard above the waiting engine:

I will come back to my cottage, after a long absence,
I will see the sweet smile of reunion on her sad lips,
The silent voice will sing the song of reunion—
The hut's queen is but the queen of this heart of mine.[1]

The surroundings became serene and a kind of tranquillity pervaded the atmosphere! The moment of their departure shone crimson with the light of the sacrificial sun all over the sky and the winds of Bengal. Who says the mother-soil doesn't have a soul?

See! The moment that was drenched with love and tears has become a past event; who knows if it will come back ever again? Even if it did, how long would it take for it to repeat itself?

We have always praised those who have sacrificed their lives. But should that be all? What did *we* do? Did we exhaust our ability to do something concrete by just verbally praising others?

Can they do it? The brave boys of Bengal? Would they be able to really sacrifice their green, tender young lives to ensure the well-earned reputation of the nation? If yes, then please come! 'Come, the fresher! Come, the newcomer!' You are our hopes and dreams for the future! Don't listen to the elderly! They are good at giving fiery speeches to inspire you just so that they become popular. But when a passionate youth decides to sacrifice himself, they mock him and secretly curse him! They assume that 'these hot-headed boys are really dumb.' Please shatter the bonds that tie these people to their narrow self-interest, my brothers!

After a long time, the slogan resonates everywhere in the country: 'Jago, Hindustan, jago! Wake up! Beware!'

Nannur

Ma! Ma! Why are you stopping me from leaving? Tell me, would you be able to stop the inevitable eruption of fiery lava from a volcano just by shutting its mouth with boulders? Achcha ma! Would you prefer to be a mother of a mere graduate than the mother of a valiant soldier? In

---

[1] These are the concluding lines of the song 'Jakhon shaghano gagan garojay, borishay korokadhara' ('When the dark sky roars, and ice falls from the clouds') sung by soldiers in Act III, Scene I of Dwijendralal Ray's play *Chandragupta*, 1953, p. 61.

a country where people are lethargic and laidback almost all the time, how many mothers would be lucky enough to have a valiant soldier for their son? Why are you indulging in your blind love for me when you know very well what is more important? My gracious mother! Let me go! Let me! Set this crazy boy free! You can't hold me back anymore. Fire is like my brother, it beckons me! It can't remain hidden under your aachol. And one who doesn't want to stay back will invariably tear all bonds and leave. He is really an insane one; there is no asylum that has been made as yet that can keep him!

O! the madmen break the doors
Of the mental asylum
And let them
Go out, run away, loosening all their shackles!
There is no enemy in the world like your kin!
Go! Run! As fast as you can!

* * *

Today, I received the letter asking me to join the war! How a bird is filled with bittersweet joy when it finally gets rid of the chains!

Ah! When my mother gave me permission to join the war, and gave me her blessings for the last time, her voice was so deep and tearful! We both felt desolate as our impassioned tears flowed ceaselessly from our eyes.... After all, she was my mother!

After the sky silently sheds all its frozen vapours, a calm, serene and soft ambience pervades its infinite and quiet expanse!

I was doing my bachelor's degree; and since I am my mother's only surviving child, she had so many dreams for me! But I have crushed them all mercilessly. What else can I do? This is the only thing from which I cannot run away at a time like this.

Everyone has started rebuking me, as if I have committed a terrible crime. They say, 'Who will look after his poor, helpless ma?' ... How can I make them understand that my mother had already been mounted on a royal seat!

How can I tell people that if you are a millionaire, giving away ten thousand taka can't be considered a sacrifice! It is only by giving away all their possessions that someone can set an example of sacrifice. No one can come anywhere near the heights my mother has ascended with this lofty act of sacrifice. Only the All-Knowing knows the magnanimity of her secret act of sacrifice!

This is—this indeed is—the true Muslim mother who has dressed her only son in combat uniform and sent him to offer his blood at the feet of the motherland.

Is this an idol immersion or an achievement?

Salar

I had never looked at my mother or my motherland with such sad and tender eyes, the way I did on the day I left them.... Maybe, the last look is always like that: intense and sad!

No! I was tired of such an excess of devotion. It was as if I was some exalted, larger-than-life personality! People came to visit me both day and night. Even those who had seen me a thousand times came to see me again. I was quite strange! I wondered how, surrounded by my childhood friends, I had suddenly become a king in one night—like the proverbial Abu Hussain! I was really sad seeing my bosom friends' reverence for me. If friends start showing reverence, why, they allow a huge mace to strike at the base of friendship. The more I told these fools not to do this, since too much respect is actually what thieves pretend to make their job easy, the more they thought I was being humble! ... It was difficult to go out of the house! Whenever I did, men, women—even children—stared at me and brought everyone up to speed, 'See there, that good looking, tall boy is the one who is going to war!'

I wondered what they saw—my inner self—or my exterior?

B

On the train
Near Andal

Thank God! I was safe from the crowd of devoted admirers at last! Uff! Wasn't it like a war before the real war? A duel of sorts! I feel so relieved now.

Often the delight and satisfaction of a good deed is ruined by words of praise coming from others.

The largest crowds were in Kolkata and at the Howrah Railway Station. Oh my goodness! There was such a multitude of people, and they were all eager to have a look at us! I felt as though we had descended from Mars or somewhere near heaven! People with whom I never had the opportunity to get close were also hugging us and bestowing their blessings in an impassioned voice. There were thousands of women from the city whose tears, pouring straight from the sacred fountains of their heart, augured our future wellbeing! Everyone looked at us with such kind and compassionate eyes!

We were overwhelmed by the spectacular outpouring of peoples' love at every station, where they converged with gifts and their farewell wishes! We had so much food; we had no idea how to finish it! But then again, if their souls were gratified by giving us food, if their hearts were filled with pride, so be it!

Mind! You must understand why there is such an outpouring of admiration and respect. Think about the huge responsibility you've taken on yourself!

In my heart I could still hear the chant 'Bande Mataram!'[2] resonating ever so often.

On the train

Daybreak

The rain-washed sky looks so beautiful! What a soothing, silent daybreak it is! All of nature is lying in bed with sleepy eyes. A thin, misty film covers her tired, motionless body like a fine pink muslin cloth. In a short while, nature with all its beauty will wake up and resume its usual diverse gestures, and then it will all be like any other day; full of humdrum.

The same morning

It feels as if the whole country has woken up from bed and is looking at the sky with indifferent–idle eyes; a sky which appears to be more considerate than the whole lot! The eyes are heavy with sleep! Sudden gusts of wind blow like an occasional yawn!

---

[2] 'Bande Mataram' is a poem written by Bankim Chandra Chattopadhyay in 1875, and later made into a song by Rabindranath Tagore.

The train is chugging along with a steady rhythm, like the eight beats of the Kaharwa taal[3]—it sounds like 'chop the lamb meat, give me a bit'! I feel like singing a Bhairav or Todi raga with the Kaharwa taal, but my voice is out of tune at the moment.

Madhupur

Towards the end of the night, our faces look so pale and sad by the light of the gas lamps! The eyelids of my soldier-friend shine in that light as he sleeps! What are these tears for? The sorrowful separation? Who knows!

A young, pale, ashen face, just like the gas-lit dawn, keeps peeping into my heart from time to time. Her eyes were moist like the misty haze that has spread everywhere now, amid a play of light and shade! She never said anything—she couldn't say anything. I too couldn't bring myself to say anything—no matter how much I tried! Some kind of hesitation or shyness kept me from uttering those words. Even then both of us somehow came to know the secrets of each other's heart. Oh! How sweet and profound was the first love of our youth! Even on the day I took my leave of her, I couldn't disclose any of my feelings! A lump of frozen teardrops had choked my voice! She didn't say anything either, but shed tears in secret for as long as I was there! Then, at the moment I left, she stood holding the broken boundary wall with all her strength, staring at me with bloodshot, sad, anxious eyes!

My mother—as if she could somehow see the blood flowing from my hidden wound—told me, 'Go, my son, and see Shahida one last time. The girl is crying her heart out and getting sick!'

I answered with feigned nonchalance, 'No ma, let her die! I will never go to see her.' Alas! That was the groundless petulance of a whimsical man!

Today, in my moment of sadness, I am reminded of my favourite song:

Both of us met on a charming night—
Why without a word, did you slowly move out of sight?
In the garden, the southern wind sighed 'alas alas'—
Beckoned to you the climbers and the leaves!

---

[3] A taal of eight beats having a 4/4 rhythmic structure or metre.

We both shed furtive tears—
But the words died in our hearts;
Couldn't meet ever again, we remained alone in the world,
Ever since at the bank of Jamuna, we parted ways for good![4]

Uff! How dull and mirthless Bengal appears this morning! Even the newly awakened birds' chirping sounds so mournful and teary!

The dhang–dhang of the station bells announcing the departure of the train, sounds so deep and heart rending! Just like the death knell of a church announcing the passing of a helpless person!

Near Lahore
At night

The fanatical steam engine chugs along like the hefty Mahishasur,[5] its mind fixed only on the journey. Move on, move on, you goliath of fire and steam! And rock–rock the young brothers who are riding you! Run you crazed Titan! Run and squash the iron road that you are moving on! Wake those sleepy men and women up, who are lying on both sides of the track with the noise that you make....

This eccentric monster, crazy in the head, bores through the dark night, frightening the quiet forest. But my mind is being hurled a million times faster in the opposite direction, to the village whose benign darkness is being torn apart by the muffled cries of my beloved! My heartbeat is keeping pace with her breathing. Her protracted sighs are cruelly rebuffing the gentle breeze rising from the field! I can clearly see with my mind's eye her dishevelled, curly hair, her sloppy garments smeared by dust, and her tear-drenched pillows! And my heart is being filled with a kind of pride by these honeyed imaginings!

It feels as though a giant mother is wailing and lamenting her son's death as we rampage through the forest of sal and piyal, 'ou-ou-ou!' Like a baby giant who lost his mother, the train is also crying, 'Oo! Oo! Ooh!'

---

[4] A Rabindranath Tagore song (*Swarabitan* 32).

[5] An asura and the son of a buffalo, Mahishasur considered himself immortal because of the boon Brahma had granted him—that he could not be killed by a god or a man, but only a woman. Mahishasur thought that he was too powerful to be killed by a woman but was ultimately killed by the goddess Durga.

C

Nowshera

Come, my mute friend! We have met after a long time! Had I not placed the burdens of my soul on your chest, then my neck would have been broken by now!

Ah! What pain it is! Even in the middle of such hard labour, such backbreaking work, the pain of that intimate, blind memory did not release its stranglehold on me! . . . It's time I got rid of it! O heart, be strong—the cord must be cut! The one who was never yours, the one whom you never held in your arms, the one who might never be yours and yet the memory of whose undeclared love has been giving you pain—you must forget everything about her. Shahida's face must be erased from your memory once and for all. Oh! Can you do that? Are you brave enough? You can't say no. You must do it! Do you remember the gifts your sisters and mothers gave you? Did you realise that those were not only gifts, but the burden of a duty to be performed, a responsibility to be fulfilled? The whole nation's fate now depends on our actions. We must be tough and resilient like a touchstone; only then will the people of the world find out that Bengalis are from a brave nation. This is not the time to yield to a secret pain that might enfeeble you. You cannot lock it up, so you must forget all about it! You must give away everything that you have, cleanse yourself of all your desires, before you can experience the destitution that will reveal the full extent of your victory! Many might have sacrificed their lives but held on to their sweet memories. You must make that impossible possible! Can you do that? Do you have that perseverance? If you cannot, then why should you brag so loudly and rend the sky that you are 'free', 'destitute', 'brave'? How can a self-indulgent liar who retains secret longings make a false claim to sacrifice? It would be a crying shame! What right does the coward have to insult the helmet of a valiant soldier? Those who would sacrifice their lives for the country would first have to become celibate, forgo all sensory passions!

My mother, from her exalted position, is looking at her soon-to-be victorious son with hope and expectations. And at his feet, a young woman is supplicating him with her tear-filled words, 'Please don't go, my dear, don't go.' What will you do? Of course you can do it! You are a tough soldier devoid of compassion! . . .

Be strong my heart! Be strong! It's your day of sacrifice! You must make your heart bare like the arid land that lies near the Kabul river. Only then would you be able to sacrifice all your thirst, all your sorrows and pains in the yagna of renunciation and sing the song of true destitution:

O Needy! how you've turned me needy, like yourself
What more do you want?
O Beggar! you are the beggar whom I possess,—
Instantly I've offered all at your feet, nothing is left.
What more do you want?[6]

* * *

Kurdistan

Accomplished—accomplished! After one whole year, I can feel that my heart has been filled with complete emptiness! . . . How hard I fought with myself this whole year! The war has caused so much loss! But how relentless is the war within! Many may win a battle on the field, but how many can truly win a battle of the mind? A fiery resilience has gradually spread throughout my frame. My heart has become boundlessly empty! Is this what is meant by being destitute? No pleasure, no sacrifice, no thirst, no contentment, no love, no separation—it is a state of benign indifference! No bhai, this emptiness loaded with bitterness would make my life miserable! I didn't want this pitiless burdensome freedom! This is like a lifeless temple made of marble!

Yet, from time to time in my marble-hard mind, someone's calm and gentle glow shines like the glimmer of waxing moonlight on marble. Yes, it touches the heart, but the heart doesn't melt anymore! See! My proud heart wants to say that it's just a tiny white spark of the undivided happiness that came from sacrificing the self! But it is not yet ready to admit that it's the sparkle of love coming from an idol being immersed!

Ah! The bare nature of Arabia in this cloudless night, with moonlight shining on its face and bosom, looks like a nun dressed in white! Moonlight in this region is really something to enjoy. I don't think

[6] This is a Rabindranath Tagore song (*Swarabitan* 35).

any other country in the world has such intense and bright moonlight. If anyone saw my photographs of the moonlight here they would hardly believe it, but assume that these were taken in the golden sunlight of an autumn morning.

Oh yes! I have another problem here! A young Bedouin woman with the beauty and glow of pomegranate flowers has asked me to marry her! And she is so insistent, almost forcing me to say yes! The more I say 'No', the more she says, 'Yes, of course yes!' She has told me that she has really fallen in love with me; I told her that I did not love her at all! She replied that it didn't really matter much to her; that she loved me and took me to be her companion forever. She didn't care about my objections or excuses. The more I requested her to forget about it, the more she burst out laughing, and said, 'Bah! I love you, so why can't you love me?'—Hai! What kind of torture is that!

Listen! You, the unfettered! You wretched! Do not fear, do not fear! Your heart has become so dry and barren that a thousand years of rainfall wouldn't make anything grow there—no grass, no flowers! It's like the sapless Sahara: full of sand, but no love.

How can you make someone love you if he is not willing to love? How can you bind someone who wouldn't be chained?

> The one who would try to bind me,
> whose only sadhana would be nothing but this,
> can the person accomplish it so easily?[7]

Karbala

This is the stage where an unrelentingly tragic drama was played out; the place whose very name brings tears to every Muslim's eyes! Whenever anyone comes here, even a millennium after the tragedy, they remember the story of thousands of brave young soldiers sacrificing their lives with smiling faces and becoming 'martyrs' for the sake of their religion and country! The river Euphrates still flows, for a drop of whose water a baby named Asghar[8] had closed his thirsty eyes forever in his father's

---

[7] A Rabindranath Tagore song (*Swarabitan* 9)

[8] A martyr of the Battle of Karbala, Ali Asghar was the youngest son of Husayn ibn Ali, grandson of Prophet Muhammad. A soldier named Hurmala had hit baby Asghar's neck with a three-headed arrow.

arms from the wound of a poisoned arrow! God knows how many more brave fighters' sacred blood has spilled on this bank of the Euphrates and mixed with the sand of this desert. Ah! A mere touch of these grains of sand seems to have sanctified my heart.

There were a few stone huts still standing quietly on the sand, frozen in time. The desert stands embarrassed with her sandy aachol spread everywhere, like the generous endless sky. Two thirsty baby lambs are crying 'ma—ma' and are running towards the Euphrates. A few girls, beautiful like dewdrops but extremely hungry, have waded knee-deep into the river and are out of breath after drinking palmfuls of water in an attempt to satiate their hunger. The sand and the wind seem to be engaged in a restless game—all this has created a mournful picture of Karbala.

Karbala! Karbala!! Today I am as barren as your wind, your sky, and your mind: filled with a vast emptiness!

I met those Bedouin women a couple of days ago. Among them was this unruly, childlike, young woman who was following me around! Every time I went out, I saw her riding an Arab horse and singing ghazals along the bank of the Euphrates! The tunes of her songs were so piercing that they stung my heart just as a khedong arrow[9] would!

I told her, 'Chhi! Gul, why are you acting like this? Are you losing your mind? I don't have any love left inside me, so it's impossible for me love anyone!'

But my words only made her laugh her heart out. She said this was news to her. She had never heard of people who didn't have love in their heart.

I was annoyed and told her, 'Well you have no right to love me, Gul!'

She took my hand and put her tender lips, trembling like leaf, on them, her face turning redder than a ripe pomegranate. She said, 'How do I love then if I have no right to love you, O handsome?'

What could I say after this simple argument?

---

[9] A kind of arrow used by the Bedouin.

D

Azizia

How troublesome it is! That was Karbala and this is Azizia! And I am here after all this while! . . . But Gul has found her way here! How?

I heard that beautiful women in this country are very independent and stubborn. Once they love someone, they don't ever forget them. This is true love, unbounded love, which has no falsehood, no deceit! But I am not comfortable with this tough 'snake–mongoose' game of love. It would certainly destroy my pride at being destitute.

When Gul passed by me on a horse yesterday, I could see a painful urge in her trembling eyes, eyes that have the look of nargis flowers! As she cast a quick glance at me, I could hear the unspoken, tearful words of her eyes telling me, 'You have hurt me deeply, O merciless one!

I repeated, 'I am unfettered! No one can bind me! I am a destitute! There is nothing I can offer you!'

In a split-second, she tied my hands with her turquoise scarf and said, 'See! I have bound you! . . . You say you are destitute, O handsome? That's fine with me, because I will fill up your empty heart with a portion of my love that I have stored in a pitcher!'

The more I said, 'Na—Na', the more she repeated, smiling, 'Liar, liar, merciless!'

It was true! What kind of recklessness was Gul evoking in me? Why are you awakening my arid heart? No!—I must leave this place too. I just remembered something: 'In a moment, all my pride, hai! vanishes, only tears flow from the eyes.'[10]

O you free bird of the sky! O enchanted bird! Why are you letting yourself be chained?—Avoid her! Avoid the golden shackles! 'People may die from sweetness, like birds do, stuck in glue.'

Kut al-Amara
The last night of spring

Ah Khoda! I wonder how you saved me from two imminent attachments. My eyes are filling with tears and I feel disturbed as I sit here and think

[10] This line is quoted, with slight alteration, from Tagore's *Mayar Khela* ('The Game of Illusion').

about them! This joy of freedom is but filled with pain! No one can feel the agony of the destitute like me unless one moves back and forth between getting his hands tied and setting himself free.... Yes, along with it, I can't stop my mirthless laughter after seeing the distressing outcome of these two failed relationships. So, tonight I am singing a song with a demonic laugh,

> Merciless, what you have done is pretty fair!
> This is how you should burn my heart with your fire!
> What you have done is pretty fair![11]

Let me tell you what happened.

The other day, I received a letter which informed me that my secret admirer, Shahida, had got married—She was happy, finally! I felt as though I was liberated.

No, no, I won't lie anymore! At that moment my heart was filled with envy and anger. So, for the last few days, I have been running around in a murderous rage, but peace has eluded me. No matter how much pride we take in our body and the mind inside it, how much of it survives on the outside? We severely thrash and discipline our mind till the mind falls in line, and then we feel as if 'we have become dervishes'. But all of a sudden—and we can't understand why—a starving desire takes hold of our mind, wailing for recognition! Even if we can make sense of it, we try to cover it up! Alas, human existence! Maybe our true freedom lies in this attachment. Who knows? . . . Forget everything, hapless Shahida!—forget the past, forget all the pain of remembrance, all hidden desires, everything. Why would you wretched ones desire someone you will never have, while you remain prisoners in the dark cells of society? Why would your charmed and foolish hearts pour all their possession at someone's feet? That too, at the feet of those who would never be yours! Why this blind desire? ... Even in the innermost heart of the world, dreary springs of unrequited love flow like undercurrents of the Phalgu river. Your heart is being torn apart as you try to preserve this ignorant love, and the social fabric is smeared red with blood from your broken heart. Even then, society did not indulge your spontaneous love or provide any space for it to grow. That is why

[11] A Rabindranath Tagore song (*Swarabitan* 38).

this society is still carefully guarding you like a stone deity with a huge baton in its hand!

You must forget me Shahida! You must replace your old love with the joy of your new love! You do not have the right to love a personality; you are forced to love husband-hood! …

Ah! Look at the moon tonight! The soft light of the moon, appearing just after the full-moon night, has torn aside the cloud-curtain and assumed such a melancholy shade! I remember what happened last night; it now torments me with so much pain!

Last night, around this time, I was out inspecting my encampment. I was commanding a small group of soldiers with a revolver in hand. Suddenly, a sentry from behind me shouted, 'Halt! Who goes there?' He repeated his command, 'Who's there? Halt! Don't move!'

This was followed by a cry 'O ma!—Ooh!' There was no sound after that, just a muffled groan that rose in the air. I ran as fast as I could towards the source of the noise and on reaching there, I found a soldier lying motionless and cold on the ground while an Arab woman attired in a red dress was trying to escape with his rifle. In an instant I understood the mystery of the missing rifles and dead soldiers that had baffled us for the past few weeks. Oh! how daring these Bedouin women were! I stood firm and shot at her but missed the target. As I fired a second round, the woman realised the danger she was in and turned around in a split second to face me, carrying the rifle on her shoulder and aiming it straight at me. There was the sound of the bolt closing; then I don't know why, she just threw the rifle away and started to tremble! Then she quietly sat down. As soon as I heard the sound of the bolt closing, I had dived to the ground to save myself. And when she threw away the rifle, I jumped up. What I saw next made me drop my revolver. The veil had fallen off the woman's face, and the white light of a full moon, shining through the clouds, fell on her face in an endless stream! I clearly saw, it was the Bedouin woman Gul, sitting with her legs spread out. From her stunned eyes flew a stream of tears that were brighter than the moonlight. She seemed to be shaking all over in bittersweet joy. The words of her heart were written in her teardrops. Her eyes seemed to speak to me, 'Oh! You heartless man! I see you after all this time! Chhi! Why did you make me cry so much?' I felt as though someone had cut through the stone that my eyes had become and released a few teardrops!

Oh Khoda! What trial are you putting me through? After I recovered from my initial shock, I asked myself, what should I do? I feared that all my restraint, my determination to sacrifice and persevere would be washed away by her tears.... I remembered Shahida; she too has such a tender face, washed by tears!

A voice echoed from the desert and mountains of Kut al-Amara, 'Beware! Soldier!'

At the same time, I could visualise our dear Bengal blessing us, and with garlands of victory soaked in tears in her hand, waiting for our return with anticipation in her eyes! How could I sacrifice my duty at the feet of my love? No, no, never!

Without any further thought, the stoic in me exclaimed, 'Khoda! Give me the strength of mind! Give me strength in my arm! Let me be steadfast in carrying out my duty! Let every vein in my body wake up to the call of duty!'

The blood in my body began to boil and animated me with the strength of a battle-hardy warrior. I held the gun straight in my thunderous hand. There came a command from somewhere that shattered the silence of nature with the force of a thunderbolt: 'Shoot!'

Boom! Boom! Boom! There was a painful groan!

'Amma!–Ma!!–Ah!!'

Everything went silent.

* * *

I forgot myself! ... I ran to Gul's body that was lying on the ground and held it to my ever-thirsty chest with all my might! Then I pressed my yearning lips on hers which trembled with pain, and called out, 'Gul! Gul! Gul!' Her teardrops fell on my face and my chest like a bunch of shiuli flowers shaken loose by a gust of damp wind!

With a great deal of effort, she placed her benumbed arms around me and drew me close—a bit closer—to her until she lay motionless! The moonlight hidden behind the clouds shone on her tormented face, which was suffused by a tender, melancholy and ethereal beauty! I knew that the pitiless memory of the moment would forever remain with me as my only treasure—the travelling allowance for the rest of my roads!

After a while, with one last effort, she opened her eyes, looked at me, and closed them again. With the hint of a smile she said, 'O my handsome! The death of the beloved by her lover's hand is so desirable and pleasant, don't you think?' I just sat there like a stone. And I saw the sad smile slowly disappearing from her lips! Her last smile of fulfilment did not quite play out on her lips, rather it left like a massive shudder from an earthquake! The blood from her heart was mixed with my teardrops! She held me tight till the very last moment and her tender face was filled with a serene and content look! Was that what she wanted? I wondered. Did she feel that her life as a woman was complete? I called her once again—just one more time—as I pressed my dry lips on her cold, lifeless lips, 'Gul! Gul! Gul!' There was an echo in the air that seemed to mimic me saying, 'Untruthful! Untruthful! Untruthful!'

The moonlight tore the clouds apart. I fell unconscious onto Gul's lifeless body. At that moment, a middle-aged Bedouin woman appeared like a huge gust of a storm and snatched Gul from me. She started crying like a mad woman, 'Gul—Amma—Gul!'

* * *

As the middle-aged woman held Gul in her arms and started wailing in grief, I screamed and fell on her lap like someone blacking out and cried, 'Amma—Amma!'

She kissed my forehead as though she was my own mother and cried out, 'My son! My son!'

A stream of tears that were more forceful than the stream of the Kaveri fell on my head . . .

Ah! How miserable was the cry of a mother who had lost her daughter!

* * *

Gathering all my strength I got up and yelled out to her, 'Amma—amma—ma!'

A voice muffled with tears called back, and the gale carried it to me, 'Son!' . . .

From far away, from beyond the hills, the mournful cries of a mother echoed, ‘Ah!—Ah ah!’ . . . An Arabian horse raced past, and the clatter of its hoofs reverberated all around—khawt–khawt–khawt!

E

Karachi

A cloudy evening by the seashore

Am I a pauper or a king? A prisoner or a freeman? Affluent or destitute?

The questions came to my mind as I sat contemplative, by the shore of the Arabian Sea. Once in a while, rain fell from the vast sky above—jhim–jhim–jhim!

EIGHT

AUTOBIOGRAPHY OF A VAGABOND

Translated by Amita Ray

A

[A headstrong young man from the Bengal platoon told me this story in a state of inebriation. I am recording it here. The young man died while fighting in Baghdad.]

‘Well bhai, won’t you leave me alone? Will you cling to me like clay? Shame on you! I find you more tenacious than sticky molasses. Frankly, though we are buddies sharing a drink from the same glass, I feel uneasy sharing these stories. Khoda had made a great mistake at the time of my birth; he made my skin thicker than an elephant and my heart softer than clay! Naturally, if my skin is bludgeoned by hired goons, I would gently stroke my moustache and say, “Go ahead, I don’t care.” But I would shout in pain like a little girl if anyone hurt my delicate soul! The heavy blows that you land on my thick skin produce no response except for a feeling of pleasure. But the moment you nudge me and say, “Bhai you have to open your heart to me”, my heart starts thumping and the geographical truth of the earth spinning becomes true to me. You also cannot deny that only in such miserable circumstances does a person realise that unbelievable things can happen; that mustard flowers can bloom or fireflies glow in one’s eyes.’

B

‘Well, I don’t quite remember my childhood days. The little that I recollect is blurred and devoid of the romance of variety! I was brought up like most other children, cuddled in the excessive affection of parents. I was a total failure in my studies, but was unmatched in the game of dandaguli.[1] I was an incarnation of Nandadulal Krishna[2] with all his naughtiness and mischief and an undisputed junior version of Alexander the Great among our gang of boys. I cannot honestly say if everyone in my village was happy with my acts of kindness and provocation, but I am very well aware that all of them prayed night and day for my wellbeing. There is a saying which goes, 'mischief makers face the music, sooner or later'. Needless to say, in my case there was no exception; it proved to be more than true. When I eventually had to move away from my mother's care and landed on the world's busy thoroughfare, hundreds of booted legs trampled over my ribcage—so many, the number easily defeats mathematical wizard Shubhankar dada's ability to calculate. Well, let me not irritate you with those insipid tales. Will you listen to some fun?

One day, sitting in a classroom in my pathshala, I was enthusiastically reciting a poem. I was entertaining some boys by imitating the character of Muchiram Gur from a story written by Bankimchandra,[3] 'Oh touchy Radha! Lift your face just once and have some tobacco!' I didn't get the chance to know whether the coaxing appeased Radha or not because the panditmoshai's[4] hand landed on my shoulder like a slithering serpent and roared, 'You scoundrel! You depraved little creature!' This naive little boy had no way of knowing that the fearsome teacher was hiding behind the curtain like the formidable Bhim[5] in folk dramas! I could feel that he was seething with even more anger than the wrathful Durvasha[6] when he hurled himself towards me like a huge ram, and started banging my head hard against the wall furiously while holding my small ears. True, there

---

[1] A game played in the Indian subcontinent with two sticks, also called gilli-danda; the large one is used to hit the smaller one.

[2] Nandadulal is a name for baby Krishna.

[3] The famous Bengali writer Bankimchandra Chattopadhyay (1838–94).

[4] 'Pandit' refers to a teacher or a scholar; 'moshai' is a form of respectful address.

[5] In the *Mahabharata*, Bhim is the second among the five Pandava brothers. He is known for his great strength and stature.

[6] Durvasha or Durvasa, according to Hindu mythology, is an ancient hermit/ sage known for his short temper.

was no new electric reaction to the violence he inflicted, but I couldn't deny a current shooting excruciatingly through my body. This sturdy frame of mine had withstood severe beatings in its life so far, so the pain I experienced was much less than what my mind felt on being so viciously maligned. He assaulted my forefathers with unsavoury remarks and accused me of some relations which were absolutely impossible. His 'tuft of consciousness' or pigtail of moderate length, was dancing on his head like an animated tadpole. At the same time I felt like laughing because I thoroughly realised the potential meaning of his rising 'consciousness'. Gradually when I found that the poetic rhythm of the beatings inflicted on me was unpunctuated, I couldn't stand it anymore! You know very well that the wrath of a male is transient, so with the intention to make a final settlement then and there I gave his aquiline nose a moderate punch and left for my home like a hero. But I didn't feel I would be safe at home. So, out of fear of my father, I took refuge in the rice granary thinking no one could possibly discover me in that solitary place.

But who on earth knew what was in store for me! A little later I could hear from my hiding place the voice of the panditmoshai, who had arrived by then, explaining lucidly to my father, using the choicest of metaphors, that the most basic education would forever remain unattainable to a reckless vagabond like me. Moreover, for the crime of dealing a hard blow on his nose and for speaking ill of his spouse I would have to meet the fate of Lokhutthuto—which meant that I would be afflicted with leprosy. He added that he would pray to Ishvara to ensure that 'special' punishment was meted out to me in hell! At first I became a bit perturbed fearing that his curse would befall me. I could not understand how I had spoken ill of his wife, but later I learnt that the name of the panditmoshai's better half was Sreemati Radha, and that she had a habit of chewing tobacco. Of course she did not do it in front of her husband. I was supposed to have seen her in the secret act, come to my friends and with tobacco in hand, enacted the scene in front of my friends when I said, imitating Muchiram Gur, 'Oh touchy Radha, do lift your face once and try this tobacco' (which our reverend teacher had heard this from his secret hideout).

I could not tolerate this false allegation anymore and became restless inside the granary. It was so hot that I was perspiring profusely. I absolutely did not know that the panditmoshai's wife's name was

Sreemati Radha; the fact that she chewed tobacco was also absolutely unknown to me. It was difficult to keep calm any longer. So I leapt out from the granary and landed right in front of my father to declare my innocence. I started defending myself with irrefutable logic and proof in a voice bathed in tears. But my infuriated father, ignoring all my appeals, held the long tuft of my hair that resembled a horse's mane and gave me a sound beating. To be honest, I never expected such bashing in my life. Using both his hands and his feet as well, he landed all sorts of blows like slaps, smacks and kicks on my face and back like 'a torrential shower of the monsoon months', as described by Robi Thakur in his song.[7] The experience of that day's whacking made my back realise the significance of it being called 'back'. The bashing was nothing short of what 'pedie Brindaban dekhiye deoa'[8] signifies. I might not have seen Brindaban, but the very next day my father took me to Bardhaman and admitted me to New School! Seeing no way out, I helplessly started to endure everything and became resigned to my fate.'

C

'After arriving in Bardhaman, for the first few months at least, a stubborn village boy like me had to face some humiliation; especially from the pranksters in the neighbourhood. The wicked boys looked at a boy from village as their prey, just like an owl considers a rat fair game. But within a short period of time, I became adept in the ways of the townsfolk! Gradually this backward rustic from the village became an expert leader in their group. Those mischievous boys who had pestered me before now began to hold me in esteem. They were afraid to bully me as they were convinced that I was a hard nut to crack, being made of a combination of eight metals. As the days passed I made little progress in my studies, but progressed admirably in the research of all types of pranks and tricks. Then the sacred place of Bardhaman became scared at the very sight of me.

---

[7] A reference to a Rabindranath Tagore song, 'Sraboner dharar moto poruk jhore' ('Let your music be showered on us like the monsoon rains'; (*Swarabitan* 11). Robi Thakur is a common appellation for Rabindranath Tagore in Bangla.

[8] To beat one until one sees Brindaban (or Vrindavan), a sacred place in India; but meant more like 'beating the hell out of someone'.

Gradually a big gang of boys was formed. The police made a covert deal with us after they were plagued by us for some days. In this manner I slowly became one of the noted bad guys. But though we were daredevils and into mischief making, I can't say that we were not involved in any good work. Our activities supporting different charitable organisations for lepers and during the famines, far surpassed the activities of the other innocent goody-goody boys—they could not achieve even one percent of what we did. From where would they get such indomitable courage and mettle like us? They were only bookworms.

When Bardhaman was flooded, we were the ones daring enough to save one-fourth of the townspeople; many from our gang sacrificed their lives to save the flood-stricken! We were the ones to organise and take the initiative to collect subscriptions for conferences and meetings. It was due to our efforts that cultural activities and organisations like 'sports', 'gymnastics', 'circus', 'theatres' and 'clubs' existed and flourished.

Though my father did not earn much he used to send me money each month on time. He never thought that his son would do the things he was doing and make such 'progress'; he also did not have much information about me. That was because I managed to get promoted in all the classes. Even after much scrutiny our headmaster could not find out how a good-for-nothing and impudent boy like me could score pass marks in all the examinations. Bhai, herein lies the test of genius! There is a saying that 'cheating is a great skill if one does not get caught'. During the examinations, four to five pairs of investigating eyes remained focused on me, but a boy like me who could not be detected by the three collective creators of the universe—Brahma, Vishnu and Maheshwar[9]—could never possibly be caught cheating by such insignificant entities! Moreover, is it just enough to master the art of cheating? One has to rack one's brain for it. This humble self had also mastered the manner in which the answer script could be changed in the examiner's house through his son or other relatives in exchange for a silver coin, or how to steal the question papers from the printing press, and the like. If I go on narrating all this, you will be highly astonished! By hook or by crook I managed to step across the threshold of Class Eight.

---

[9] Another name for Shiva

I hardly visited home because the village did not appeal to me anymore. My father too did not mind because he had faith that this time I would definitely do something great. From our village I was the only one who had gone to study in an English school; moreover, I was jumping the hurdles of passing each class like a winged horse! Only my affectionate mother awaited my homecoming! A mother's loving mind does not understand the world's complications, so if I didn't go home for two months she used to cry her heart out! I did not receive any affection or pampering from anyone in this world other than my mother. When I was beaten black and blue or taken to task for my wickedness, it was my loving mother who held me to her bosom and consoled me. It was as if she preferred my naughtiness to anything else. After such a beating left its marks on my back, she massaged it with oil while shedding profuse tears! This happened on many occasions.

When I was promoted to Class Eight, it was probably at my mother's insistence that my father turned me into a four legged creature: that is, I got married. I came up with a lot of excuses for not marrying, but in the court of my mother and her tearful pleadings all my excuses were swept away. When the ritual subhodristi[10] was over it couldn't be undone!

Moreover, the choice of the bride was not bad. It is hard, in fact, to find one like her among the village girls. She was about thirteen years old. My mother had found an adult in that adolescent girl and had tried her best to get me married to her! I was also nineteen years old by then. Thanks to this, my mother had to hear a lot of disapproval from the womenfolk of the village. At first my newlywed wife used to sit silently like a clumsy bundle in a corner of the house. It was the custom that a newly-married girl should not look around with her eyes wide open; so she often kept her eyes closed. But to keep one's eyes closed all the time was also a tedious thing. So when others were not looking, she quickly stole a timid look around. If she were caught in the shameful act then it would amount to defiling the *Mahabharata*! When her glance fell on me she quickly covered herself with her sari or scarf, and like a turtle, got lost in a shell. Then it would be impossible even for the most experienced, probing eyes to find out if she was a person or a bundle

---

[10] A Bengali wedding ritual where the bride and groom see each other for the first time.

of clothes. But the moment I looked elsewhere she would cast a glance at me from behind her Banarasi sari; and when my eyes fell on hers she instantly closed her eyes and sat with a serious face. I smirked, ran away and loudly proclaimed my wife's shamelessness throughout the house. My mother burst into a fit of laughter. She said, "Oh dear will you remain crazy throughout your life?" But my sisters were playfully adamant; they demanded explanations from my wife. I was amused at the thought of her being embarrassed thus and had a hearty laugh. I somehow started liking this game. Gradually I had a feeling that my adolescent spouse had started to like me. But I never gave up playing tricks to pester her. Fearing my crazy behaviour, the poor girl could not look straight at me; but through a chink in the door, her beautiful eyes with a fleeting, tender gaze kept watch over me. I could sense it and hummed a note—

> With her pitiful eyes, she arouses compassion
> What does she wish to say, why does she leave it unspoken.[11]

Gradually my love for her expressed itself little by little through such playfulness. Then with the examinations drawing near my well-meaning father did not deem my presence at home to be safe. The day I took leave of her I could not hide my feeling of love with my cheekiness. While I laughed, my eyes were full of tears which rolled down my cheeks. I held her hands and said, "My dear, forgive all my naughty behaviour and do remember me." She could not utter a word, but her tears spoke of how much she had fallen in love with me. When I let go of her hand, she flung herself prostrate on her bed and wept silently. Pressing the handkerchief on my eyes, I somehow tried to hide my weakness.

Who ever knew that my first meaningful conversation with my wife would be my parting words—my first kiss would be my last! I did not see her after that. Two months after my departure she breathed her last in her father's house, leaving me grief-stricken for the rest of my life. When I heard the news I just couldn't believe it. How could she go away leaving me in the gloom of sorrow? My broken heart cried aloud, 'No never, she can never die! She can never go away like this

---

[11] A reference to a Tagore song 'Shokhi protidin hai eshay phiray jaye ke' ('Hai, my sakhi, who comes and goes everyday'); (*Swarabitan* 50).

without informing her husband. Everyone has turned against me and has lied about you.'

In a fit of madness I appeared in Rabeya's house. On seeing me, the family's grief was renewed. There arose a heartrending wail in the house which struck my heart like rumbling thunder. I fainted—oh dear! will not her silent tears bathe my stony heart anymore? She couldn't even speak a single word to me! She can't go, can never go away like this. 'Hai offended one! Come back! Come back!'

She did not return. At midnight when no one was awake, only a fox barking to make my heart palpitate, I went to her grave and fell on it—'Rabeya my love! Get up now, I am here, I have forsaken my mischiefs. In my heart I have painted your portrait and I have come to this graveyard in the dead of night to show it to you. Rise, my sweetly delicate Rabeya, no one will see, no one will know.'

I cried the whole night clutching her grave but Rabeya did not rise from her eternal sleep. I was caught in a whirlwind which went on whimpering; the dew-drenched flowers from the small jasmine tree showered on my head. Were they Rabeya's tears or someone's consolation? From one or two graves which had collapsed, wild fire flickered. A wave of fear rolled through me. But then it became dawn. Letting out a sigh, and with my body smeared with the soil from her grave, I returned to Bardhaman. Hai! She was gone, but the flame of memory she had kindled in me did not die. The fire spread gradually and consumed me. Besides the burning memories she had left no trace of herself with which my soul could find some solace.

The blow I received at her death left my heart totally broken. I could not put it together ever again.'

D

'Days passed; time never comes to a halt. My days were drab, spent somehow. Gradually I was promoted to Class Ten. By then I had amended my ways a lot. In the meantime, Bardhaman New School closed down and I went to study in a school at Raniganj in the hope that the environment of a new place would have a healing effect on me. My previous headmaster was then holding the post of headmaster in Searsole Raj School at Raniganj. He looked at me affectionately as I was his old student; I too paid a bit of attention to my studies.

But soon another calamity befell me—I got married again. You will be surprised to know that I didn't object to the marriage. At that time I had neither the enthusiasm nor the stubbornness to resist. With Rabeya's death I had transformed into a little boy totally dependent on others, without a will of my own. I used to agree with what others said nonchalantly. I totally lost the ability to look into the depth of things or express my independent views at all. All my craziness and all my laughter vanished from my life.

Seeing all this, I presume my mother was so eager to get me married again. Moreover, I thought that maybe I would get back my Rabeya in my newly married life; and the touch of her affectionate hands would probably bring peace to my grieving heart. But hai! One whose life is destined to be sorrowful has no way out other than through 'patience' and 'gratitude'. Ill luck is bound to accompany him. My new wife Sakhina was not a paragon of beauty, but she could certainly pass as pretty; besides, considering my own looks, it was unfair and shameless to expect an angel as my wife.

She was more accomplished than me and did not have any flaws. Nowadays, young boys shamelessly choose their life partners. Their own complexion may be darker than ebony or their body more rugged than timber, but the wife must be fair complexioned; she must have eyes like those of a deer or at least be almond eyed; her waist should be like that of a lion; face as beautiful as the moon; voice as sweet as the koel; and her gait as graceful as a swan. In addition, she should have rosy feet, for if a situation did ever arise where his sweetheart's pride is hurt and she had to be appeased by holding her legs in praise, then God forbid if the legs were hard as wood like Gadadhar's aunt! Then the husband would be deprived of some pleasure and it would spoil all joy.

The list of superlatives doesn't end here, as poets would remind us, but I seem to have forgotten them. These fools do not ever think that girls may be guileless and devoted to their husbands, but they too have their own likings. They too wish for a worthy match. We the men are a selfish lot and we turn a blind eye to their sufferings. I do not approve of the fact that women keep silent, even when their hearts break with sorrow! If the poor women cannot, at least indirectly, express their opinion about their life partner then one should agree that it is justified to call them porakopali—utterly luckless. But I am afraid that the learned might not pay heed to such crafty words coming from an insignificant person like me. Moreover, they might shave my head, pour some special substance over it and drive me out of their territory. So I shall just go on narrating my own story.

My newlywed wife had admirable qualities, but I failed to love her. I rehearsed a lot, but somehow could not make myself love her truly. I did not like this fake play of love with her heart. Moreover, you may not believe it but Rabeya was ensconced in my heart like a queen on a throne; no one was permitted near the throne. If extreme devotion to one's love did not turn a person eccentric, then the famous romantic hero, Qays would not become the legendary Majnun[12] (one who is crazy in love and a vagrant), and seek his Layla in forests and mountains; or Farhad[13] would not meet with his tragic outcome.

I could understand the intensity of Sakhina's pain but alas, could not do anything about it. The guilt of neglecting my wife pricked my conscience. My mother was displeased; my sisters blamed my wife and made her carry out their orders. But I couldn't understand who was at fault; I just failed to love her. She shed tears profusely but my heart was not swayed. In sorrow at my repentance and at being maligned, I fled from home. I could not bear the blow dealt by Rabeya's death, and in addition to that—Oh Khoda! what a stupid thing I did like an immature person! Why did I bind myself to this unfortunate woman's life? An intense anguish tormented me and like a sharp knife kept poking at the agony that was already tormenting me. I almost went mad.

Meanwhile, I went to Raniganj and appeared for my 'test examination'. The whole year was spent in turmoil. How could I hope to get through? I was not inclined to cheat in examinations any more—so it is quite clear that I was not allowed in the test; I guess I don't have to tell you that? But when the news reached my father he wasted no time in writing me a long letter, addressing me by all kinds of bizarre names, and telling me that he had known all along that an unworthy son like me would not be able to pursue his education beyond this point. He also told me that he had spent a lot of money on me for no use. My life turned bitter.

---

[12] The literal meaning of the word is someone who is 'possessed'. When a seventh century Najdi Bedouin poet, Qays ibn-al-Mullawah, became almost mad in his love for Layla, the people of his community started calling him 'Majnun', or 'possessed'.

[13] A famous character in Persian literature whose love for Shirin is legendary.

Disgusted, I wound up all my work, and then began to do anything that I fancied. People voluntarily advised me to go to Baharampur. I gave a damn about their advice but clearly lost my way. The boarding superintendent didn't say anything for a few days but then one fine day he roughed me up and drove me out of the boarding house. I returned to Bardhaman. The hooligans belonging to the gang I used to lead, which had by now dispersed, welcomed me.

On receiving this news my father disowned me as his son. A year after this, I learnt that Sakhina too had died. The news of her death seemed like a cruel irony. Even while breathing her last my unfortunate wife had cried for blessings from a sinner like me; she died hugging an old, torn photo of mine. As the days passed, I became free from all attachments. After another six months my mother too breathed her last. Laughing boisterously, I started emptying bottles of liquor. Then one fine day I joined the regiment with the name of Kedarnath[14] on my lips! Can you give me another glass of water, bhai?'

[14] Another name for Shiva.

NINE

MEHER NEGAR

Translated by Marzia Rahman

A

Jhelum

The flute was playing, and my heart was choked with tears. We parted ways on a sultry evening in the month of Boishakh,[1] to the strained notes of Pilu-Barwa ragini thrumming its sad tune. Our hearts were wracked with pain and the melody of that simple wooden flute expressed it vividly. After the tune lost its way around the supine field, its distracting echoes kept resounding. Meanwhile, a koel was worried, exhausted, searching for his naughty beloved, and in a vain attempt to stop his uncontrollable tears, he repeatedly rubbed his eyes and turned them red as liver. By then, the female must have felt bad for hurting her mate so much—because right then, she peered out from behind a bunch of green mangos in a mango tree nestled amidst the banana plants and called out playfully 'koo–koo–koo'. The poor koel immediately let out a squawk from the branch of an ashoka tree to convey his utter delight, but his voice was sore from calling out to her for so long. Yet the sorrow caught in that broken voice struck the evening breeze, which in turn incessantly stirred the kash forest by the banks of the Jhelum.

I called out, 'Meher Negar!' Swinging thousands of white shoots, the kash forest ridiculed me, '. . .Aa . . .rr!' Rebuffed by the high sand banks across the river, my cry rushed back and conveyed to me, with bated breath, 'Meher—no—more'.

---

[1] The first month in the Bengali calendar (between the second half of April and the first half of May).

The pyre of the sun in the west was burnt and blown out. The cries of the flute came to an end. The forest of sandalwood-winds and parul flowers heaved a deep sigh. The parul said, 'Uh–uh'—the sandalwood said, 'Aa—h—ah!'

I puffed out my chest, ruffled my hair and chided my heart as I made my way back, singing an Anandabhairavi alap—a lot of poor souls like me tread this painful path. Even with my trained voice, the melodies kept stumbling and were dying of shame. I was not ashamed though. I found my friend with a tanpura in his lap playing Shree raga. Smiling, he said, 'What is it, Yusuf? Is the imminent evening your chosen hour to sing Anandabhairavi alap? You seem to be delightfully contradictory!'

I felt like crying. Yet, I retorted with a smile, 'Bhai, the time for your playing Shree raga is over too.'

'That's right!' he said, 'But why does your smile look so melancholy today—like the smile of a stone statue, ice-cold and frozen?' I turned around and strode off.

Like a sad, pampered bride, the evening's face was slowly turning darker. At that point, the starry sky of the second day of Krishna paksha[2] surrounded her and asked, 'Shondharani, evening queen! Why are you sulking? Don't get so impatient dear, look—the moon-lord is about to make his appearance.' A faint glow of a forced smile played on the lips of the poor, unguarded evening.

The moon walked in with a clumsy, drunkard's gait, his eyes and face red. And the moment he appeared he forcibly lifted the evening-bride's veil. Evening laughed. Sitting in a bakul tree, a bird (like the prying womenfolk) turned red in shame and teased, 'Chhi—chhi!' Shortly afterwards, an altercation broke out between the moon and the evening; a shower of dew rolled down the evening's cheeks before she turned cheerful again and regained her playful mood. And soon, except for a few shameless stars, everyone took leave.

I returned to my empty abode. The moon had risen, so I didn't light the lamp. Even had I lit it, the dim, smoky leap of the flame could

[2] According to the Vedic lunar calendar each month is divided into two lunar fortnights; each phase is called a 'paksha'. The period of the waning moon, that is, from full moon to no-moon, is called the 'Krishna paksha'. Krishna is also used as the Sanskrit word for 'dark'.

hardly drive away the dense darkness of my room. It would rather hide behind the leaves, in the corners of the room, at the back of all other objects; turning into a shadow, it'd keep me at the centre and revolve around me. And no sooner had I closed my eyes, than it'd rush back like flash floods—just when the light would have shifted a little! Oh, my darkness! No, I wouldn't chase you away again. From today, you will be my friend, my brother! See! Bhai Darkness, I had wasted all these years needlessly going after the light.

'O Meher Negar! I absolutely need you', I told her, 'Or else, I won't live. You are mine. And that is why I recognised you as my own among so many people. You are the companion I found in my dream! You are mine, of course you are mine!'

Startled, she stopped suddenly and looked at me with her beautiful black eyes as big as palash flowers. She stood still with the pitcher on her waist, right there at the bend of the road, for a long time and then said, 'Ok,—you are mad!'

I gulped, pushing back my tears and nodded, 'Hmm!'

Tears welled up on her thick black lashes! Then, as she began to pick up the pace, she said, 'Achcha, I am yours!'

A sudden surge of an unimaginable happiness numbed me; I stood transfixed for a long time. Startled out of my reverie, I saw her turning at the bend of the road and going far away.

I ran after her, calling out 'Meher Negar'! She did not reply. Clutching the pitcher to her waist, she walked fast, swinging her right arm rhythmically. She washed her feet at the steps of her house, threw me a pale, disapproving glance and went inside. Before leaving, she said, 'Chhi! Do not call my name in public! What will people say!'

Because I was running too fast without looking at the road, I had stumbled and cut my nose; it was still bleeding heavily. I hid it with my left hand and said, 'Ah, yes of course! I will not call out to you like that again!'

See yaar, Darkness! One who is born blind does not suffer as much as the one who loses their eyes in an accident. That's because those who are born blind have never seen light; so, there is no reason for them to feel upset about missing out on things they have never known. But to be deprived of light after seeing it once—oh how much crueller and more pathetic that is!

How you punished me for leaving you! Bhai Darkness, let me not leave you again! Oh! how much I suffered for thinking you small and insignificant!

I met her again on the banks of the Jhelum that dawn. She was returning after bathing in the river. Her wet, black tresses and thin, violet odhni embraced her body passionately. Her fresh, lovely face amidst the nest of her hair looked like a newly-bloomed lotus in the black water of a pond. Sitting under an olive tree in the distance, a naive shepherd boy was singing in his own language,

> Softly tread, O damsel, lest the water in the pot spill out—
> Pitcher on hip, pot on head,
> Strain not your dainty waist, aha, strain not;—
> O damsel, softly you tread!

I joined in, echoing his song, 'Oh fair damsel, tread softly—slowly! Water will spill out of your pitcher. Your dainty waist will be sprained by the weight of the pitcher. O, young damsel, tread slowly, softly'.

As she saw me, her earlobes turned vermillion-red. Throwing me a shy, reproving glance, she said, 'Chhi chhi, go away! Why are you acting crazy?'

I called out in a hurt voice, 'Meher Negar'

She threw a quick look at my dishevelled hair, sad pale face, ragged clothes and dust-caked body; she thought of something and stood quietly for a while. Then, she asked with a faint smile, 'O man! Who said my name is "Meher Negar"? Why do you call me by that name? Who is she to you?'

I saw some strange fear and incredulity choking her voice. Her fearful heart started beating faster. I was also taken aback. My gaze began to blur. I leaned against her body and asked, 'Ah! Aren't you that girl?—No—no, you are the one—my Meher Negar! The same face and eyes—the same eyebrows, the same gaze, the same style of speaking! No, dear, no, do not deceive me anymore. You are her! You—!'

She said, 'OK, where did you see Meher Negar?'

'Why, in my dream!', I replied.

Her face lit up at once. Blood seemed to appear in her pale, white face again. With a laugh like a rippling water fountain, she said, 'Achcha, are you a poet, or a painter?'

Embarrassed, I replied, 'I love painting, but I am not a painter. I write poems too, but I am not a poet either.' She laughed her head off this time.

'Look, how terribly naughty you are!', I said.

She said, 'OK, I will not laugh again. What kind of poems do you write?'

'Of love!'

Wringing the edge of her wet cloth, she said, 'I see—whom do you write them for?'

I slumped to the green grass right there and said, 'You—Meher Negar! I write them for you!'

Someone seemed to have daubed her face with abeer.[3] Balancing the pitcher on her waist once again, she said, 'How long have you been writing those poems?'

I said, 'From the day I saw you in my dreams.'

She looked at me with awe and wonderment in her eyes. 'What do you do here?', she asked.

'I learn music.'

'Where?'

'From Khan Sahib.'

She said with great enthusiasm, 'I will listen to your song one day—will you sing to me?' As she prepared to go, she suddenly turned back and asked, 'Achcha, where is your home?'

'In the mountains of Waziristan,' I replied.

With her big eyes, she stared at me for a long time. 'So, you are not from this country?' she asked softly, 'A newcomer to this place?'

Looking into her eyes, I said, 'Yes—I am a foreigner.'

She left abruptly without saying a word.... My throat started to hurt terribly as if someone was strangling me. Flinging myself onto the green lap of the grass, I called out to her again. Her pitcher fell with a thud and broke. Throwing me a blazing look, she snapped, 'Don't call me like that ever again!' I saw two streams of tears rolling down her cheeks!

---

[3] Coloured and scented powder with which the spring festival of Holi is celebrated

B

Even after relentless effort, I could not tune the surbahar that day. Like a pampered girl throwing tantrums, it continued to stubbornly crank out off-key notes. Never before had this favourite instrument of mine behaved in such an unruly manner, nor had it cried so unwaveringly. Just like a mother, who having failed to pacify her daughter with love and care would slap her twice as hard, I too ran my hands on the strings harshly. It started to growl in jumbled tunes.

Ustadji, my music teacher, intoxicated with grape-liquor, was watching my activities in a lighter mood. In the end, he said with a laugh, 'What is it bachcha? You are not feeling well today—no? If the tune of your heart does not work, the tune of your musical instrument will not work either. If your heart plays off-key, the instrument will do the same. It's a simple fact. Give it to me—let me tune it for you.'

No sooner had ustadji gently rubbed the ears of the unruly surbahar a couple of times, than it started to tune like a calm, obedient boy. Handing me the instrument, he cut off two hot seekh kebabs with a knife from a plate before him and said, 'Achcha, sing the alap of Bageshri ragini once, bachcha. And yes—the precise time for the rendition of this tune has almost arrived as well. What time of night is it? And haan, listen bachcha, try to delineate the gamaks with your voice; it'll sound wonderful then.'

But my voice, it seemed, was full of pain. I had buried the tune under the sands of the Jhelum's banks earlier that day. Hence, when I went up to the third note with great difficulty, my voice cracked and what came out was only the sound of weeping. Under the influence of liquor, ustadji said, 'Move bachcha, more ... two frets higher till the fifth...' but stopped mid-sentence and asked affectionately, 'What happened to you today, bachcha? Give it back to me.'

The whimpering of Bageshri was soon heard in ustadji's deep voice in the ascending and descending notes—delivered through proficient gamaks and meends. He sang, 'The veena player's instrument stirs no rhythm in the heart of the forest today. Tears have gripped her throat. Hence, the melody is stifled. Oh dear, the strings of her higher and lower notes have been torn apart.' However, my mind was not there at the moment. It was with the young girl I met in my dream.

Oh! what an absolute delight to recall the dream, filled with such sweet intoxication that even remembering it a thousand times could not satisfy me. A thorn of discontent has pierced the bottom of my heart, oh my dream-devi! That thorn has festered and my heart now throbs with unbearable pain. Oh, my dream-queen of the sleeping world! Where is that country of yours with flowers reaching to the sky and its air brimming with pollen and nectar? Where is that hut of yours, glowing in moonlight, where your alta-dyed feet leave prints on the leaves of the roktoraag plant? Where is that hut—behind which forest?—on the banks of which bubbling, murmuring fountain?

Oh, how beautiful that dream-image was!

That evening, I wrestled for a long time; and when I lay in bed, exhausted, a world of sleep numbed my whole body with gentle strokes on my eyelids. Shortly afterwards, a sudden, passionate kiss of someone's soft lips consumed my senses! I was startled! Who came in and lined both my eyes with soothing kohl! I saw a young girl playing veena where the earth and sky were kissing each other. She looked as lovely as moonlight on ice on a full-moon night. The veena player's youthful loveliness burst forth through her thin, blue, muslin gown—as glorious as the morning sun in a rosy-blue sky. She called to me, waving her hand. The colourful fog of sleep pulled a thin, muslin-like veil over my eyes. Like secret words whispered into the ear of her beloved, the veena player with her humming love-words, sweeter than the veena's melodies, disclosed to me, 'See—that shore by the river, sparkling in the moonlight—that's my home. I play my veena there. The simple tune of your simple flute wrung pain from my heart, and that is why I've come. We will meet again in the pale, waning light of sunset. And we will be united in the lap of this open sky on one such rosy, crimson day-break—when the cries of Lalit and Bibhas will be pouring from the farewell tune of the flute.'

Overwhelmed, I touched her aachol and asked, 'Who are you, dream-queen?'

She replied, 'Didn't you recognise me, Yusuf? I am your Meher Negar!' ... The joy of getting so many things, unthinkable and astonishing, all at once filled my heart. I asked in a choked voice, 'How did you recognise me?—Yes, it's only you I have desired—but I did not know your name. Don't others call you too in the spring of their lives? Have you appeared only before me, and not to any others?'

Curving her thin, rosy lips as if dyed by paan she said, 'No—how am I supposed to know you? I roam everywhere, floating on this light wind. When I was passing by yesterday evening, I heard you playing the flute, pining for me! And that is why I've come to see you ... and yes, I only appear in front of those who cry their heart out for their unknown beloved in their prime ... nonetheless, I am only yours!'

Soon, the figure of the young damsel faded into the clouds.

I woke up. The cuckoo cried out, 'U–hu—u'! Papiya asked, 'Where's Piyu, the beloved?' Bulbul shook his crest, puffed up his throat and replied, 'cl—ue—less'. The last scent of the withered henna flowers, and the morning breeze brimming with pollen and nectar, heaved a deep sigh close to my ears, 'Hu–hu–hu!'

C

The strings of my love and affection snapped in the strong wind like an old, tattered sail-rope! And then, floating in the waves—out of place, out of home—I came here to the Jhelum! I saw the Punjab of Hindustan for the first time—a land of heroes and five rivers, billowing with waves. In this land every grain of sand was stained with the blood of heroes—where people's thirst was quenched only by the blood of traitors and enemies of the nation.

* * *

No matter which branch of the tree I tried to hold, it broke and fell on my head! Therefore, like a helpless man grasping at straws, I took refuge in music—a useless man's work—as my sole activity and consolation!

Oh, this strong muscled body of mine—unfeeling chest as hard as a steel door—I could not put it to good use even after putting in my utmost effort, Khoda! It couldn't perish for the good of this country either! My dear mountains of Waziristan! What a happy death it would have been if while trying to save you, the rocks of your mountain fell on me, shattering my ribs! It would have been the greatest achievement of my unfortunate life! Since there was no one to cry for me, no man would have shed tears for me, but a plaintive, wordless tremor would have been felt in your rocks, desert-warm breeze and withered branches! And it would have satisfied my soul! Ah, would such a day ever come into my life!

Oh, the great creator of the unseen! Why are your creations full of such lovely complexities? A water fountain flows in the heart of your rock mountain, and you have hidden a fountain of love in the hearts of stone-hearted people like us! And if you have created love, then why did you hide despair behind it, like a shadow beneath the light?

Anyway, what hurt me most was the incident that took place yesterday!

It was a little before evening when I met her again suddenly. The bank of Jhelum was buzzing with the chirping of crickets. Just like the young damsel of my dream, she called to me, waving her hand, 'Come here!'

I asked, 'Meher Negar, do dreams come true?'

'Why do you ask?'

I told her about my dream: 'It was you who came to me at daybreak the other day and you also told me your name! . . . You are mine!'

She heaved a prolonged sigh; it shook the cloth on her chest! 'Yusuf, I am not Meher Negar,' she said, 'I am—Gulshan!' And then she began to cry.

I said, 'Never mind, you are the one! . . . I will call you Meher Negar.'

'Come', she said, 'Aren't you supposed to sing me a song?' 'You sing, I will listen.'

She sang,

> On being put to the test, oh Saki! my beloved, my own blood I have drunk as liquor
>
> I have roasted my heart and devoured it as kebabs in the searing heat of dolour.

Ah! Whose smouldering heart is undergoing such restiveness? The separation from my beloved made me drink my own blood as liquor and roast my heart as kebabs and eat them. Oh darling—why continue? It took a long time to end the jingle of the esraj.[4]

I sang, 'Oh dear, if she asks about me, tell her: he has waited his entire life for her, though he's become tired now, he is still waiting for her, sitting outside the door of heaven!' She broke into tears. Placing

---

[4] A stringed bowing musical instrument popular in Indian subcontinent.

her hand on my lips, she said, 'Na—na, you should not sing this kind of song!' After a while, she said again, 'Achcha, you enjoy playing music a lot, don't you?' Once again, my sorrow and anger against some nameless, cruel entity made my heart whimper. And I began to sing,

> Is there any peace for me in this whole wide world?
> Distress strikes me, stroking the veena for its sound!
> Forever soul-searing songs keep flaming in me and burning,
> Is this what makes you happy and is that why you are garlanding
> Me, with tunes so fragrant and so overpowering?[5]

At the time of our parting she tried to smile, but she cried instead. 'Achcha, you love me,' she said, 'so, I am begging you . . . Promise me, you won't love me again, you won't even ask for me.'

She knelt at my feet and the moonlight at once disappeared behind the black shadow of a colossal cloud! I could only manage to utter, 'Why?'

She paused for a few minutes, and then pressing her eyes with the edge of her sari, she said, 'Listen, worshipping something holy is done with things that are holy as well. If one worships it with an ungodly offering, the worshipper's sins will be grave. This love of yours, even if it is full of exhilaration and intoxication, is pure and profoundly sacred! It is not in my power to denounce it. Don't you know me? The name of Khurshedjan Baiji[6] that you hear in the town, I am her daughter.' As she said this, she stood up while her whole body was shaking! She continued, 'Since I am the daughter of a prostitute, I am hateful, impious. Oh my dear, dirty, tainted blood runs through the veins of my body! Make an incision and you will find the colour of my blood is not red; it is blue like a dying man's poisonous body.'

I watched her tears pour like fiery sparks down her cheeks. Not a soothing, scenic fountain, but a huge discharge of boiling lava erupting out of a volcano!

I felt a stinging pain, like that of a scorpion bite, in my heart. I pondered—it is not the flower's fault if it emits an odour. And if

[5] These lines are borrowed from a Rabindranath Tagore song that begins with the line, 'Kanna haashir dol dolano poush-faguner pala' ('Seasonal changes play the ups and downs of tears and smiles', *Swarabitan* 16).

[6] 'Baiji' was an appellation used for a courtesan skilled in singing and dancing.

it is a fault, then the fault is the creator's own. However, it requires someone extraordinary to examine the scent it carries in its heart; ordinary people will press a handkerchief to their noses or snicker when they go near it.

Like a mute bird, I said in a hurt voice, 'Let—let it be, Meher Negar! It's not your fault. Can't you walk on a righteous path if you want to? There is no injustice in the creator's creations. He showers his pity and sympathy on those who are less fortunate, and that is something we can't help but contemplate! . . . And you have truly loved me! There is no pretension in this love; I can feel it with my own heart. And except our two hearts, no one else in this world will be able to grasp whether the love is real or fake. Yes, when a creature cries in love, the person rises at a much higher place; while people down on earth ponder, "The fall of this man is certain." The man knows it too. That a little slip may cause him to plummet to the ground. Hence, he keeps climbing up carefully without heeding anyone . . . No, Meher Negar you must be mine.'

She sat still, and then weakly, she said, 'You are right, Yusuf, many others have approached me too; but I have never cried like this before. Whoever has come and stood before me with hands full of garlands of flowers, I used to feel, ah! I love him. But none of those were true. I know now that what happened on all those occasions was nothing but a passing infatuation and excitement of the nerves. But the day you came and said to me, "I am yours", all my heart and mind responded to your call at once, "Oh yes, I am all yours". Oh! what a deep and profound joy flooded through the veins of my body! It's a wonderful feeling which a human being experiences only once in their lifetime—I can't even frame it clearly! But what I can say for certain is that this love of ours and a saint's love have the same depth, if that love is eternal.'

Resting her head on my shoulder she said slowly, 'Even after knowing I have you, I am driving you away because I have loved—I have loved you with all my heart! My . . . my heart is shattering, Yusuf. But I must give up the hope of getting you. I cannot disgrace the very man I love so dearly! And this much sacrifice, yes, I can bear it. We, the unfortunate women, have to make far greater sacrifices than this. No matter what you people call it, to us it's neither unusual nor difficult . . . Oh, why did you cross my path? Why did you stir my hidden love with a stroke of your golden wand of pure love? ... No, even if I do not get you, you will always be mine. And now, we must get away from each other. The heart which carries love holds desire too, waiting in ambush. One should not trust a woman's heart, Yusuf. It is too tender and even a little heat can melt it. Who knows, if we stay in touch it might lead to our downfall someday from this higher abode! No, no, dearest! I cannot let your clean, uncorrupted image fade in this corrupted air any longer. We may not meet again. But if we do, we will be united where the sky and the sea embrace each other in double infinity! Goodbye, dearest! Goodbye!' Saying this, she kissed my hand and ran away like a mad woman.

There was a storm blowing and howling—shon–shon–shon. Injured, the bamboo forest nearby cried out 'ah–uhh–ah'! The joints of the bamboos snapped as if their nerves were being ripped apart.

I returned with a heavy heart! As I was coming back, I remembered with teary eyes, my dream-queen's final words: 'We will be united in the lap of this wide, open sky in one such blooming, crimson day-break, when the songs of Lalit and Bibhas will be cascading down the farewell tune of the flute!'

D

That day when my motherland suddenly sprang a surprise on me by asking for my blood, I could not put into words how my heart began to stir! Later, I came to know that both the British and the Emir of Kabul were greedily eyeing our free mountainous nation. Moreover, some evil traitors, divided into two groups, were trying to hand our country over to others. They had forgotten the truth that no one would ever be able to subjugate us—the homeless Pathans. We had always been independent—free. And no matter what, why would we accept their domination? Shackles made of gold are still shackles. No, no! as long as even a drop of blood is left in this body and the head is still connected to the shoulder of this Yusuf Khan, no tyrant ruler would be able to lay his hand on a grain of sand of my motherland! Oh! how come Khoda, this world in your free empire is full of injustice and intolerance? All these contemptible people beat their own drums and call themselves 'superior', 'great', 'big'! Oh! had it been true, then why is our condition similar to those free birds in the sky that were caught and put into a cage made of iron bars. Oh, how all the nerves and muscles of my body are swelling up!

It also came to my notice that both parties were trying to scare us. Hah! hah! hah! If showing his rifle, a hunter threatens the birds in the trees and orders them, 'You all must come to me at once, or the bullets will fly!', would the birds obey his order? No, never. They would rather die but they could not be captured—just couldn't be! The birds knew that the hunters had hidden knives on their bodies. They didn't need anyone to teach them that. And yes, if we joined the battle to safeguard our freedom, we would thrust our swords and direct our thunderous fists wherever we'd see injustice. My motherland had never been desecrated by the footsteps of any conqueror, nor would it ever be: 'We will give up our lives, but not our freedom.'

I solemnly swear in your holy name, as I take this sword in my hand, Khoda, it will never drop! Give strength to my arms! I will purge the thirst of this sword—first with the blood of evil traitors, and then with the dirty blood of the enemies of this country! Ameen!!!

* * *

Yes, I have a feeling that a brother from my own country will turn into a butcher and kill me ... Let it be so. I will die in utter delight because I'll be sacrificing my humble life at the feet of our country!

'Khoda! I hope you accept this sacrifice of mine.'

* * *

Well done! Ably done! Befittingly done!!

While I was making my farewells yesterday, I don't know why I felt the urge to see that unfortunate girl for one last time. I could not resist the wish. And when I reached there, I found her abandoned house covered in dust and weed, wailing like a recently widowed woman! And—and what was that? Whose grave was that in the courtyard? As if a heart full of pain was lying upturned there. As if someone's mountainous sorrow had solidified, and having lost consciousness was clinging to the soil right now ... With whose blood were those words written on the marble headstone: 'Do not hate me, oh traveller, even if I have taken birth in a tainted womb! Shed a tear praying for my wellbeing—I do not know if I am impure or not, but a pure love had once touched my heart! And O! lord of my heart! If you ever come here—ah, you will surely come— do not cry remembering me. No matter where I am, my love, we will surely be united. The end of such an eager wait cannot be settled in this world alone! Because Khoda is all-loving! The unfortunate one: Gulshan!'

My tears fell on the faded, blood-drenched writing on the gravestone, making them brighter . . .

And whose misty, plaintive melody was battering me from the other side of the Jhelum:

> I would have lavished the garden, were I the gardener,
> Taking the hand of Bulbul, I would unite it with the flower.

Hai, foolish singer! If you were a gardener, you'd have taken Bulbul's hand and united it with the flower—oh dear! Impossible. That was impossible. Perhaps, Khoda had not given you the power. But those who had the strength, oh brother, far from materialising it, they would not even utter that wish of yours. And in case you had the skill, then perhaps you would not have the ability to sing this song!

* * *

And yet, I found that song on the day of my farewell, heart-touching and melodious.

TEN

EVENING STAR

Translated by Priyanka Chatterjee

Meeting Evening Star again was quite an interesting event. The tiny hill sprouting out of a beach of the Arabian Sea is covered with skeletal seashells of varied colours. It looks like a graveyard of shells. Spreading my legs across the skeletal shells without anyone around, I was musing on something that can sometimes be heard in the trembling voice of distant travellers; in the doleful call of doves lamenting the loss of their mates; and in the mumbled utterances of distressed poets ringing like the receding sounds of home-bound birds.

On that day, a profound tiredness at walking a long road was making every atom of my inner-self lethargic. Lifting my tired, dry locks away from my eyes with fingers that were like buds of rajanigandha, the princess of the dreamlands coaxed me lovingly, 'Sleep now, my dearest!' So saying, she gently cradled my tired head close to her warm bosom. Waves of music arose in the voices and veena of her female friends,

> From the far end of the river of tears
> The ghat is visible beside your doors.[1]

The touching song sent waves of pain through me like the sorrow-pangs of a recent widow. I implored in a sleepy and entreating voice, 'Please don't ask me to sing that song!' My thirsty soul floated along the tune of the song and was lost somewhere in the directionless north. Then . . . no one was there. Alone—alone—all alone! Oh! Where is my river of tears? Where are its far-away banks? Where is the ghat? At whose door? The endless horizon embodying the fathomless depth of the whole world's

[1] These lines are taken from a Rabindranath Tagore song (*Swarabitan* 16).

tears silently indicated another infinity, 'Oi—there—in that direction!' ... Hai! Where? in which direction, precisely?

Caressing my entire body with a lazy, preoccupied look, someone bade me goodbye in a sad voice, 'Get up, O traveller! It's time for me to leave!'

Clutching the ends of the dream princess's skirt, I implored yet again, 'Na, na! my time to get up has not come.... But who are you, dear? Why does a tearful melancholy prevail over you?'

Her voice was choked with emotion. Fighting tears, she said, 'My name is Languor, I spent some intimate moments with you today ... now I must go; try to get up. Come my soi Sleep, leave him now!'

I woke up to find myself alone. The black, peacock-shaped barge of the evening queen had already set sail, dancing on the bosom of the sea. My heart sank with gloom ... Those who had embraced me in my drowsiness—didn't I lose them when awake? Why? This lonesome life of consciousness is so bruised by pain, so full of unrelenting bitterness! On that day I realised with what agony the listless cries of the distraught evening song echo along the wasted dusk-paths of the tired traveller—

> My day was spent expecting you,
> I wait alone at the empty ghat,
> Ferry me across O! boatman, along with you![2]

Oh! indifferent traveller! Everything you do is doomed to fail, bhai, doomed to fail! Where is the boatman, bhai? Which boatman did you call out to with your heart-rending cries? Where is he? Who did you wait for all day long? Who is that yet-unfound but most-sought-after treasure of yours—not only in this life, but in the endless cycle of rebirth? Which river ghat are you sitting at all alone and weaving the tapestry of this tune? Did she ever lift her veil and cast a suppressed, joyful look like that of a new bride at you while returning home with her water pitcher, filling your eyes with inarticulate desire? Or did she ever create rangoli of memory in your bosom with her wet, lotus-foot prints? Are you so disconsolate because all your life you could not claim anyone as your own, bhai? O! traveller to distant shores, not a speck of dust from the feet of the Lakshmi of your mind, who came close to you once a long

[2] This is a Rabindranath Tagore song (*Swarabitan* 10).

time ago, is there for you anymore! Futile is your search for miniscule bliss all over the place, O! bhai, futile indeed!

But this inconsolable heart wishes to hear nothing of this, tries to understand no logic. It is filled with an insatiable urge to repeat—like that mad Mansur's exhortation 'Anal-Haq'[3]—the eternal cry 'Oh! this lost treasure of mine! Hai! my lost Lakshmi, my Lady Luck!'

It is better when I am asleep. It is only in my dreams that I can possess my Lakshmi, a thousand times in thousands of ways! The intense desire that I have to possess her during my awakened state—to hug her closely and press my lips against hers—I can realise in the garden of my dreams in the land of sleep. The human mind is a huge puzzle. Like a weighing scale, the mind tips to the heavier side depending on what is put on it. Therefore, I sometimes think that to possess is to be on top of everything; to possess is to taste success. But then again, I think, no—not possessing is to possess in the real sense; that in not possessing lies the essence of possession. This dilemma remains unresolved. Yet, both paths lead to the same goal. Both streams flow with the resolve to empty themselves along with all their motion, speed and currents in the infinite bosom of the beloved ocean, then forget their own existence and become one with the ocean. But the words 'every part of me cries for every other part' are so intoxicating that it is agitating the adolescent desire of my mind, saying 'there is freedom in bondage'. Is this eternal message of the human heart entirely untrue? No, this problem eludes all solutions.

My mind boggles yet again.

My heart has never been able to resolve the conflict between the epicure and the ascetic in me and so I have no one in my life whom I can call my own!

Then? . . .

Despite finding no one, why does the primitive, lovelorn-self inside my heart rush from land to land driven by pangs of separation? Like a madman desperately looking for a philosopher's stone, what cure-all am I wandering around aimlessly hoping to find? Which goddess of luck

[3] Mansur al-Hallaj (859–922), a great Sufi poet and a mystic, was executed for his apparently blasphemous utterance 'Anal-Haq' or 'I am the Absolute Truth'; an utterance which was the outcome of his spiritual annihilation of the ego and complete unification with the Almighty.

has tied it to her aachol? Which young woman is wearing it around her neck like a protective pendant?

These thoughts brought tears to my eyes. In a teardrop someone's playful smile suddenly shimmered. Startled, I looked up and saw in the vast expanse of the sky, lowering her veil to cover half her forehead, the Evening Star standing with an earthen lamp in her hand. At the corners of her eyes, in the lines of her face, on her lips, a sportive smile played hide-and-seek. And as she tried to hide the bashful, quivering smile of her lips in vain, the flames of the holy lamp in her hand flickered wildly with my desire to plant kisses on the beautiful lady's warm cheeks. The wild wind lifted the edge of her dress that covered her bosom again and again, making the poor one more embarrassed.

She fixed her gaze on me; I, too, kept looking at her. I had lost all words.

She was retracing her steps slowly towards the horizon where the sun was setting. Her eyes gradually became gloomier and tearful. As she sighed heavily, her kachuli[4] trembled like a tender leaf fighting the wind. As she kept climbing up her heavenly path, moving towards the darkening horizon, her eyes and her face became pale like someone blacking out. Then, standing at the last bend of the road, looking at me with a last steadfast gaze, she bid me goodbye with a salaam and disappeared into emptiness.

In every niche of my heart, my desperate plea reverberated with these words that have remained unspoken like that of an obtuse person—'Hai Evening-Lakshmi of mine! Hai!'

It struck me all of a sudden that I don't remember when I first started gazing at the Evening-Lakshmi every day. I can only remember that, a long time ago, I used to gaze at the Morning Star rising at dawn. My entire morning would be filled with intense pleasure as if anticipating the arrival of a beloved. Every dawn she would come, scattering red-dyed pollen-dust all around, and then, looking at me with a bashful but contented smile, she would say, 'Oh my dear friend awaiting my arrival, I am here.' I could read the language of her eyes; I could hear her words of desire. Then as soon as the Sun god would glare at us with his blood-red eyes, she would run away like a frightened girl, and climbing the heights of the sky-complex would disappear at its peak.

[4] A cloth used as an undergarment to support the breasts.

How she laughed all the way! All day long I could hear the clinking of her waist girdle, the jingle of her gem-studded bangles and the tinkling of her anklets as she hastened to run away from the sun.

That was how my days passed ... One day I said, 'Won't you come down to where I am, my beloved?'

She looked at me for a while, and then blushing—her cheeks turning red like a sindoor-ripe mango—said in a quivering voice, 'No, my dear. If you want me, you will have to be one among the stars. I cannot come down; you have to climb up my path.' As she spoke, she twirled the end of her Banarasi sari around her little finger unmindfully, just like her longing gaze and her words were entwined with an unbearably pleasurable pain. I understood that while she wanted to become one with me, she also needed to uphold the eternal law of nature. She could not muster enough courage in her tender heart to take off with me to pursue a life of abandon. No matter how much she loved me, she would not be able to take my uncertain routes—she would not dare bear my colossal weight along a fearsome path strewn with ambiguity.

But was it like that?

Maybe I am mistaken. Because one day she said, 'Darling, this confused path of yours isn't a path of wellbeing. I have to hurt to turn you back. If I am not able to bring you to the path of wellbeing, I cannot be your Lakshmi, your Lady Luck!'

These weren't words spoken recently. I heard them on some unknown night through sleepy ears. I understood nothing of them then.

Just as I couldn't accept the stubbornness of her traditional thoughts, she also did not step down to tread upon my path.

Even on the day she bade me adieu, she wore her usual familiar smile. She seemed to mock me again and again with her sweet, playful look. She just added one new thing, 'We won't meet again on this path, my dear. We will now meet on a new path and with new identities so that we can know each other fully'.

I have always ignored her sighs when she said goodbye to me, but today I could feel the tremor of pain in the air as she sighed before leaving. Now it is difficult for me to even breathe that air ... When will the air I breathe be used up for good, my dear?

As she bade me goodbye, I chose not to see her teary eyes; but now in the eyelashes of a million stars across the sky I can see the droplets of her tears. Now even their laughter seem like cries, and only cries!

I came every day after and left when the wait was over, but the path of dawn was no longer painted with the rangoli of her alta-reddened feet! Nowadays the sun emerges laughingly. I find his laughter unbearable. His beaming tone, similar to the melody of Bibhas raga, of the morning bird, stings my ears like the notes of raga Poorvi, with melancholy . . .

I said, 'Hai darling! I have lost you.' I found the sky and the winds reverberating with my cries, 'I have lost you!'

It was evening—on that seashore.

Whose voice do I suddenly hear? The voice that was familiar to me? Whose is that known gaze I see? Who is that?

I said, 'Darling, where do you go dressed like a bride today?'

She said, 'On the path of the setting sun.'

She then told me that she would come every day in the heavenly courtyard of the dark horizon to unveil the evening light. But she didn't want to see me there.

I realised that as long as she remained a bride in the country of the setting sun, I wouldn't even have the right to look at her. Even today she was following the age-old conventions of her world. She couldn't be a rebel. She was a woman—auspicious, benevolent! She was the one who had put the world at ease and kept its eternal flow uninterrupted with her undiminished sense of symmetry.

I asked her, 'When will I get to meet you again? When will I get you again?'

She said, 'At dawn, at that very path of sunrise'.

Now that she is a bride, I haven't looked at her evening path.

I have no idea when and on which dawn path we will ever meet again. But I still have hope; I will meet her again, I will surely get her.

* * *

When I reached my home after crossing the seas and stood in the yard tired and alone, my sister-in-law asked, 'I hear that you have married?'

With a feeble smile I said, 'Yes.'

She laughed and asked, 'That is a good thing you have done. Where's the bride? What's her name?'

I sat in silence for a long time. The dark veil-shade of a dim evening, stricken by the tunes of Shree raga, began to cover the face of the west-facing earth, as if wrapping it in a shroud. I looked away.

Then, with much effort, I pointed towards the western horizon and said, 'The Evening-Lakshmi of the setting horizon'.

My sister-in-law's long eyelashes seemed to get moist; her eyes dropped in inexplicable pain. The darkness of the evening began to grow thick!

ELEVEN

RAKSHASI

In the dialect of the Bagdis of Birbhum[1]

Translated by Sutanuka Ghosh Roy

A

For the past two years, I have constantly been thinking and asking myself this question in utter bewilderment—why do people run away when they see me? The same menfolk who raise a ruckus behind the curtains of the women's quarters in their houses and terrify their children with their yelling and shouting, quietly leave their verandahs with hookahs in hands, as if they feel a sudden urge to visit their family inside! Women drop the pitchers from their waist and run to save their lives! The children get so scared that they end up grunting and grimacing! From a distance they scream 'Baap re! Oi the madwoman, the rakshasi slut is coming, run, run! She'll get us, eat us!'

Why? What have I done to you all? Which ugly, oven-faced fellow's chances of fortune have I blocked? Which rascal's face have I burned? Which helpless, blind woman have I targeted for punishment? Whose body did I put a stake through? Which children's tender heads did I feast on? Tell me bon,[2] do they run a 'government' that they can say whatever they feel like? What relation do they have with me?—Killed?—Fine, I have killed my own husband! Yes, I have slain him with a cleaver! Why are they so bothered? Why should that make their hearts burn? I haven't snatched anyone else's husband; neither

[1] The Bagdis are an oppressed caste who used to enjoy the status of great warriors at one point in time. Nazrul states in the subtitle that this story is actually written in the language spoken by the Bagdi people of the Birbhum district in West Bengal. However, the uniqueness of the language is lost in the process of translation.

[2] Younger sister.

have I killed any of them! Why should they bad-mouth me then? Are they my close acquaintances, or the guests of my seven-generation-old ancestors? If they continue like this, then one day I may really become a rakshasi and chop off their heads, wrench the hearts out from the women's chest and crush them like mustard seeds!

Who turned me into a maniac? These are the people who have done it, aren't they? I started afresh—as if nothing had happened—and became busy with my family life. But day and night, near my house, in and around my neighbourhood, on roads and alleys, in social gatherings and majlis, everywhere, they labelled me a rakshasi, teased me, maligned me, pestered and threatened me—no wonder I cracked! They forced the inscrutable pain that was buried deep in my heart to come out in the open! Tell me bon, who is responsible for my frenzy? If a person is constantly poked at till they become frenetic, then does the blame lie with the innocent soul, or with the sane ones who drove the soul crazy?

My husband was a simple and straightforward person who knew nothing of the crooked ways of the world. He was a farmer and happily tilled the land. And I spent the whole day fishing, husking paddy and winnowing rice. There was no other way to make ends meet. We had three children by then—the eldest son had grown up and we needed to arrange a marriage for him to keep him from going bad; the middle one was a daughter who was also growing up fast; and the youngest daughter was just a baby learning to speak a word or two! We didn't make much, but managed to run the household smoothly, with blessings from all of you. I, this Bindi, used to gather enough rice for our meals and also collect fish, cockles, periwinkles and other such things to eat along with rice. Besides, my son, with your blessings, had also started earning some money on his own. Even my daughter used to go out with the wives in our neighbourhood to collect leafy vegetables and fish which also fetched good money—enough to buy salt and cooking oil. We had enough rice to last us throughout the year, from which we could also save some. There was peace and happiness in the family. It was as if Lakshmi, the goddess of luck, had been kind to us!

Everything that I and my husband did was for the children, right? So I cooked just enough rice to feed the children and my husband so that I could save the rest. While the others had the rice, I was happy to eat the starch we strained from the boiled rice! That was enough luxury for a woman, and in any case, if the children remain calm, then mothers too feel content! We were no zamindars for sure, but we were also not beggars or thieves. We lived on what we earned. On a few occasions, we too invited guests and fed the fakirs. Aha! That gave me great satisfaction didi! People used to call me a miser as I was not a spendthrift. But what could I do? Not that I cared! They didn't know what a great burden I was carrying on my shoulders. I had two daughters who had to be married off when the time came. My son too needed a wife. And then the bahu and the two sons-in-law would be a part of our family! My clay hut would turn into a paradise! Besides, some of their wishes had to be met. Add up the expenses, and that's a pretty sum! Would anyone spare a penny for us if we were in trouble? Baap re baap, I knew very well even if we had snakes wrapped around our necks, no woman that I knew would give us even a morsel of broken rice! Hadn't this Bindi understood that how they were so full of themselves—their words sounded so hollow! But also I realised how this little happiness of ours turned many of those whores green with envy.

This is how we were spending our days in happiness! I was hoping to live my days looking after my husband and the children, and having grandchildren around me when I died—as a married woman, and not as a widow! But the god of charred fate could not tolerate that. So my treasured household became a cremation ground! And all my happiness and hopes were thrown into the pyre!

Listen, didi, listen to everything that I tell you! If you find any fault with me, then beat the poison out of me with your broom, or throw the ashes from the cooking fire at my blasted face! Even stones melt like wax when they hear my sad story, but the heartless people of the village do not care to offer any consolation. What they do instead is even more painful. They spread all kinds of lies about me which makes me so angry. I feel like telling someone the whole story, not missing a word, then cry my heart out and feel relieved. But whoever I approach feels threatened, as if I am going to eat them up! As if I am less than even a witch or a sorceress. This humiliation and panic makes my head burn like a furnace. As a consequence, I start acting more frantically! This is why, my language is so full of invectives and swear words! Please listen to my story bon, and then you are free to flatten my face with a mighty kick!

B

You knew all along didi, that Panchu's father was a simple, uncomplicated man and never understood the roundabout ways people took—their twisted arguments and their pretensions. He was forthright and could not understand why people would put their hand round their head only to touch their nose, without doing it directly. This was the reason many devious women made him work without paying him a single farthing, or swindled him out of whatever money he had by sweet-talking him. I had cautioned him plenty of times, given him good advice, but nothing seemed to work. It is said that a 'habit doesn't end even with death'. One of his bad habits was his addiction to alcohol. He was a confirmed drunkard. I told him so many times, 'It's no problem if you drink, but be careful that the drinking doesn't get you!' Whatever he used to earn he spent buying alcohol. But again I took some consolation from the fact that many men also had the same vice, and I forced myself to come to terms with it. But I couldn't believe what he did next—and neither can you, bon. Someone took advantage of the naivety of my Shiva-like husband and made him take something that completely changed the innocent man he was! I had no way of knowing what it was!

Do you know what Ratho Bagdi's notorious daughter—the one who married two or three times—did? Well she raised hell for some time. The chhori[3] never spent time with any of her husbands, but roamed around with the younger boys in the neighbourhood and infected their immature souls like woodworms. And what can I tell you about her parents! Chhi, shame on them! But instead of the parents, it was me who felt like taking poison and ending my life! O ma! I began to hate the whole Bagdi community!

Makhon Di, you know that the villagers and the Bagdis all believed that we had a lot of money! Besides, there were also these daughters of child-killers who spread a rumour in the village that we had got our hands on some hidden treasure. Tell me bon, doesn't it make you laugh?

Yes, that bitch, that 'wanton gal who became the stud bull', went after my Bholanath-like[4] husband—like a bull always accompanying

[3] A somewhat dismissive term for a woman; here used in a derogatory tone.

[4] Shiva as the god of simplicity is also known as Bholanath.

Lord Shiva—to get hold of the so-called treasure. And to tell you the truth, my husband was quite a good looking man! Clad in dhoti and shawl, he did look like a perfect bhadralok.[5]

The day I came to know about their affair I felt so low; it's something I can't make you understand, bon. I don't know if, when struck by thunder, anyone feels a bigger shock. That night I beat him up with a broomstick! O bon—the man I had known all along, the gentle soul who would never utter a single sound even if someone gave him seven slaps, caught hold of my hair and beat me at length with a wooden stick. Oh! how inhuman! More than the stick, it was my back that bore the brunt of his beating! And while he was carrying out his act, it was not the physical pain that I cared about—I hardly took note of it. The pain it caused inside me was even more! That night I knew my husband was no longer mine! I could plainly see my luck running out. I felt as if someone was searing my heart with red-hot iron—I started sobbing!

All my anger was then directed at that haramzadi beti.[6] I wanted to tear her up with my nails. But I could not find her. She always escaped when she saw me!

C

My cad of a husband began to overdo things. He began to avoid coming home! He would often sleep at his employer's house where worked and got his meals. All of us—me, my son and our good neighbours—tried our best to make him come to his senses. But hai! we couldn't bring him back; the gal had cast a spell on him! He had become a silly lamb! I felt that it was a late-life, stupid outburst of desire in my husband; and that trollop had really turned the scoundrel on. Else, how could a man eat away his own eyes of honour! One day I fell at his feet and told him what a big mistake he was making. He kicked me in my face and left. My entire body was emitting something fiery like a ball of fire. I realised that he had walked the green miles towards the hell from where there was no chance of redemption.

---

[5] A Bengali middle-class gentleman.

[6] Bastard daughter.

On top of that, everywhere I went people blamed me for what had happened and said nasty things to me. I felt insulted and outraged. I'll take my revenge, if my name is Bindi, I told myself!

Another day when I came back home after working in the fields, I found out that the scoundrel had broken into my cash box and had helped himself to whatever savings I had made. I also heard that he was going to marry that chhori in a couple of days. He had handed over my entire savings to his would-be father-in-law. The hard-earned money was dearer to me than my blood! And it was about to be spent like this? How could someone stoop so low? There was no time to waste. Whatever had to be done must be done within those two days. I started mulling over the idea. A devata-like man was descending into hell, one step at a time, and there was no way out. If I killed him, would that be a sin? After all, I was his wife; I did have certain responsibilities towards him. With my husband heading towards hell who else, other than me, should bring him back? And if he chose the road to hell, I would also have to answer for it to my Bhagwan. But if I finished him off before he went any further, he would be free from all sin while the burden would fall on me. Well, if the wife didn't take on the burden of her husband's sin, who would? A ghost who dwells on a sheora tree?

So I made up my mind and told myself that I needed to kill him, whatever that entailed—'Bhagwan, you are my witness! Before my god enters the door to hell I will sacrifice him and offer him at your altar like hibiscus flowers. Absolve him from his sins and punish me instead. That will make me happy.'

That day, after it drizzled lightly towards the evening, the sky cleared up. At that point, I saw my husband sitting alone under the tamarind tree behind the house of that wicked woman. With his hacksaw he was working on the cot leg with a great deal of concentration! Within a second I made up my mind! I cast a furtive glance around and saw that nobody was around. Like a madwoman I took out the cleaver; the red rays of the falling sun shone on its blade. Just then, it started drizzling again! A group of small, naked kids were frolicking in the rain beside the house, singing,

> When it rains while the sun shines hot
> It's time for the foxes to tie the knot!

I hid the cleaver under my aachol, sprang like a tigress and sat, O! how firmly, on his chest. Even though he tried hard, he could not wrench me off! I raised the cleaver and struck his neck hard. Immediately I felt my hand going limp! He somehow freed himself and ran for his life, but fell in the jute field nearby. But I was thirsty for blood! So I followed him and struck him twice. Now his head was severed from his body. I was in a pool of red—red blood encircled me and danced around me. Then I blacked out!

When I regained consciousness I discovered I was in a new place with people who looked different! What surprised me most was seeing myself pressing a millstone with all my strength. After so many days I saw sunlight—beautiful, white sunlight! Before that, all I saw was the play of red light in front of my eyes. After I asked around, I came to know that I was in Shiuri jail. I had been sentenced to seven years of imprisonment. And only three months had passed. I was told that I had confessed my crime to the magistrate. My punishment would not have been so rigorous if I had not beaten the police inspector with a broomstick after he had gone to my village and kicked up a fuss; and I had the nerve to tell him to spare the poor villagers! It was because of the policeman who pleaded before the judge sahib that I ended up with such a strict punishment.

Oh ma! What hard labour I was set to in jail! Didi, it was fine as long as I had no recollection of the event. After I got my memory back, it became unbearable! Whether I was at work or having a moment of respite, all I saw before my eyes was nothing but blood—blood spilling and dancing like flames! Oh, I didn't know blood had such power! Baap re baap! Whenever I think of the blood leaping up like flames, I lose consciousness! When his head was chopped off, his body twitched and jerked like a catla fish on land! I never knew that there was so much blood in the body of a small human being! After that evening, I was scared of darkness because either his severed head or his headless body would appear in front of my eyes! Oh!

Then what happened didi, was that a judge or someone who crossed the seven oceans and thirteen rivers came to Delhi and sat on the king's throne, and all the convicts were released! I too was let go.

You see didi, there is a Bhagwan after all who knew that I had done what was correct and nothing wrong! I had stopped my husband-devata before he entered the gates of hell. Whichever way the menfolk interpreted it, I and my Bhagwan knew it was a plain, truthful act of justice! But men shout like that in any case—because for centuries they had seen only women being decapitated for their crimes. I am not sure if the women, in the beginning, had protested against that kind of injustice, but over time they had surely got used to it. If I were the one who was sleeping around and my husband disposed me off with a cleaver, I am sure the men would have not uttered a single word then. And the women would have joined them in denouncing me. 'Such a bad woman deserves such a death', they would have said, because they had been used to seeing men being forgiven for all such crimes.

But the punishment that the other people gave me was nothing compared to what my inner self inflicted on me. Tell me bon, who could feel the pain and torment that I felt ever so often? Although I slaughtered him with my own hands, he was my own husband! I heard about a judge who had sentenced his own son to death by hanging. But didn't the man—even though he was a hardy soul—feel a wrenching pain in his heart when he did so? Oh! when I was straddling his chest and striking him with the cleaver like a ferocious rakshasi, he was making piteous moans—entreaties to spare his life! There was a frightened look in his eyes which seemed to seek my forgiveness—Ah! Ah!

In prison, throughout the day I used to busy myself with all the work I had to do and didn't have time to think about anything else. I didn't let my mind wander and the loads of work helped me keep my focus. When evening came, I was so exhausted that sleep easily overpowered me. The day I was acquitted my heart cried out in agonising pain! I was quite fine in jail! My mind was at peace! Where would I go after my release? Oh! Getting my freedom back turned out to be a burning pain of poison!

I came back to my home! My son had married by then—his wife was a shy, pretty girl. But when the villagers heard about my return, they all came running.

'She will bring a plague to village. Baap re! The devil woman, Taraka[7] rakshasi is back! We are doomed—we will all be sent to the land of Yama', they said.

At first, I ignored them and the things they said about me. 'Let them say what they want to', I told myself, 'I will turn a deaf ear.' But

---

[7] The character of Taraka appears in the *Ramayana*. Taraka was born as a beautiful yaksha princess. But one day the rishi Agastya cursed her, and as a result she was transformed into an ugly and demonic rakshasi.

after some time, it was impossible to ignore them; they were relentless. I picked up the pieces of my life and made a new start with my son and bahu. But as people began to hound me, my life became miserable. I wanted to marry off my daughter but no one was willing to accept her. 'A rakshasi's daughter can only be a rakshasi—that's the truth', they said. The pain that I had suppressed for so long was now cruelly dug up by these people and held up in front my eyes! My darling son, a real golden moon, did not pay any heed to their nasty talk—he also never once asked me what drove me to that desperate act! Rather he left the task of running the household to me. He seemed to have realised that in seeking redress for his father's loss, he would lose his mother! But these hateful barren women—none of whom were my kin, even in seven generations—day and night, with their stomach empty or full, were out with a vengeance to destroy me! They came as the curse of the devatas and destroyed all our peace! They ostracised my son. But that didn't satisfy them. For the last two years, the people of this village have been harrying me without a break! Let me tell you, didi, even pariah dogs are not treated with such hatred! This is enough to make even a good person lose their sense; you can imagine how a devouring rakshasi like me would react! Still didi, I suffer in silence and don't react or use swear words if they do not cross the line. It is only when pain becomes gut-wrenching that someone begins to curse!

Now tell me my didi, who is to blame? And please, use that clay lid in your hand to crush my head—let me be punished for all my sins—Oh Bhagwan!!

TWELVE

SALEK

Translated by Fakrul Alam

A

Dawn brought to the city that day, a dervish no one had seen before. As if a sea in spate—streets, docks and fields started overflowing with excited, voluble people—all open spaces were filling up. The harems of the jananas[1]—where the women were supposed to stay, so deep inside their houses that they were not polluted even by the touch of the sun—however, were as quiet as ever; as if every day the whole world stirred in one direction only! Outside was tumult. Inside though, life throbbed on!

On everyone's lips there was only one query, 'Who was he? Who could have appeared so suddenly at sunrise like an aubade sung by the birds chirping away, and generating ripples of delight like that of an agomoni song[2], set to Anandabhairavi and Bibhas?'

Men and women, young and old, all jostled against each other to get a glimpse of the dervish. And yet there seemed to be no end to the line of people wanting to take a look at him. Like Dushasana who tried to disrobe Draupadi[3] in public, these people robbed the dervish's privacy who sat unspeaking, with a bemused look—and their numbers kept increasing all the time. There seemed to be no beginning nor end

---

[1] Females

[2] A kind of song sung in Bengal to welcome the arrival of Durga or Uma from her in-laws' house at Mount Kailash to her ancestral home in the plains.

[3] Dushasana is one of the Kaurava brothers in the *Mahabharata*, who dragged Draupadi by her hair into a hall full of the sires of the kingdom and attempted to disrobe her, after Yudhishthira had lost her in the game of dice. Draupadi was wife to the five Pandava brothers.

to the queue. Hey, there exists an invisible devata who would not slight those who had veiled themselves from the public eye!

But the dervish said not a word—he was completely silent!

Many insisted that they would like to have his blessings by becoming his disciple. But the dervish evaded all their pleas. Only to someone who was absolutely unrelenting in wanting to be blessed by him, the dervish said, 'Take your clothes off and come.' The man shed his dirty clothes and put on a unique suit of expensive clothes and came to him. But all the dervish did was laugh and laugh; he said nothing more to the man.

The Kazi[4] heard about what was going on. Soon, he himself began to frequent the dervish's place. The more the dervish appeared to ignore him, the more resolute Kazi sahib became in seeking his attention. The dervish realised, here was someone who was not going to be shaken off easily. His face eventually showed traces of a tired but empathetic smile.

B

The dervish said, 'Listen, Kazi sahib, will you be able to accomplish all that I tell you to do?'

Kazi sahib said confidently, 'Yes sir, your sidekick is ready.'

The dervish smiled and said, 'Look, tomorrow is jumma, the weekly Friday afternoon prayer. The emperor of this realm will be coming here. He will tell you to lead the congregation when he comes. Could you do one thing then?'

Kazi sahib said, 'Certainly huzoor, certainly! What can I do for you sir?'

The dervish said, 'You'll have to carry a liquor bottle under each of your armpits; when everyone has lined up for namaz, fling the two bottles on the prayer mat so that they shatter into pieces there.'

Kazi sahib's face paled immediately! Trembling, he said, 'Huzoor, you will end up being free of me surely, as my head will be severed from my body—but will I be able to flee the scene?'

---

[4] The city magistrate

The dervish said, 'You've freed many people from worldly pain in your lifetime; why not pursue the path of freedom from all worldly cares at least once?'

Kazi sahib returned home. He thought, 'Let what will be will be. I'll take two bottles of liquor to the mosque tomorrow. No doubt the dervish is wiser than I am.'

C

The emperor arrived. With him came his retinue—ministers, officers, soldiers—all of them! The jumma prayer began. As an imam, Kazi sahib led the prayer service. In no time at all, two bottles of liquor dropped from where he had concealed them under his armpits! Needless to say, the awful smell of liquor filled the mosque as did the sound of the bottles smashing into pieces on its floor. Everyone agreed unanimously that the whole wide world did not have a drunkard as rotten as Kazi sahib and that no one ever would be able to match him in this regard. Someone who consumes alcohol could be forgiven, but someone who is consumed by alcohol should not be shown any mercy and let off leniently.

A meeting was called. What punishment did this supremely brazen drunkard deserve? Except for the minister of state, everyone said in one voice, 'What is there to deliberate upon in such a case, O Emperor? Crucify him!'

The minister, however, said 'Your Highness, forgive this servant's impertinence for speaking in front of you! But in my estimation a death sentence is not punishment severe enough for a sinner of this magnitude. The harshest punishment that can be meted out to him will be to take away his position and title, and to confiscate all his property. A death sentence would merely be a quick-fix solution. But when he is subject to a lifetime of reproaches and rebukes and will feel his disgrace forever, he will die a slow, searing death.'

The emperor and everyone else present in the assembly concurred, 'This is a great idea!'

A madman who was passing by at that time was saying things that did not seem to make any sense at all—things that seemed to be floating randomly like straws in the air. He kept babbling, 'Such a punishment is like marking one's forehead with sandalwood paste! Nothing can be smeared that way; all it does is soften things!'

D

After Kazi sahib had been humiliated and abused in this manner in the emperor's court, when he had been stripped of everything he had and stood in the bend of a dark road, even the roadside dog would begin to whimper. As the proverb goes, 'When the elephant is sprawling in the dirt, even the titmouse will give it a kick.' Perhaps those whom he had punished justly when he was the city magistrate were now seizing the occasion to flay him any which way they could to let him know that no one could enjoy good fortune forever. And those whom he had punished unjustly were now taking their revenge on him in such cruel ways that it would have been better for him to have been crucified than face the ruthlessness with which they were taking revenge on him.

But amidst such humiliation and abuse, someone seemed to touch him softly and gently, just as a beloved woman would tenderly touch her lover's fever-scorched forehead. Kazi sahib clasped his shrivelled chest at this and burst out crying, 'Khoda! Is this how you decided to drown my pride in tears? Oh dervish, where are you now? In which faraway land could you be?'

That evening, like a reptile, with great effort and pain, Kazi sahib crawled towards his destination—the dervish's dwelling place. By the time he reached the place his eyelids were drooping in sleep's gentle embrace. And yet he cried out soulfully at one point, 'Dervish, initiate me in your ways! I've come and am running out of time!'

No one would feel the melancholic quivering inside him, not unlike the doleful sound created when a player strums the notes of the evening's raga, Poorvi, on their stringed instrument!

Someone's peaceful and cold lap seemed to beckon him, 'O my child! Come to me! Here all your worn-out clothes and fading pride have been washed in tears and purified fully.'

The dervish now stroked his surbahar and sang these lines:

> Make your prayer mat wine-coloured, if this is what your spiritual guide wants;
>
> Only 'Salek', the one who shows the way, can tell you where the path begins and ends.[5]

---

[5] These lines are taken from Hafiz's poetry.

As with a girl whose mother had passed away and who had been driven out by her stepmother, who consequently had tear-filled eyes and a moist face, a thick cloud gradually plunged everything into darkness.

Kazi sahib now gathered all the strength that was left in him and said in a voice that seemed to be cracking, 'Who is it? O my companion in the road ahead of me! Who are you?'

For a long while nothing broke the silence that followed. Across the quiet of the riverbanks reverberated a solemn echo, 'Who—are—you?'

As the boat rowed across the water, a very soft voice said tremulously, 'Drunkard Hafiz!'

THIRTEEN

THE WIDOW

Translated by Sudeshna Majumdar

A

Oh! What parching thirst! Salima! Can you give me some water, bon? And you ask me, what happened to me and how I encountered such a misfortune—na? But what's the use of paying heed to my laments and sighs, bon! I bless you; may your husband remain alive forever! Misfortune might strike you dear, if you listen to the story of my miserable life! May Khoda allow women to die before they become widows, or may all girls enter their graves before marriage! If you give birth to a baby girl, Salima, kill her by forcing salt down her throat right after her birth, get it? Or else, you will have to spend the rest of your life with embers of grief smouldering within your heart.

It's been ten years since you left this village, so you know nothing of these incidents! You left at a very tender age and now you have come to visit your parents with a son on your lap! . . . Everybody stays away from me, thinking me insane. But you know me well dear, and you can see me even now. Tell me, have I really gone mad? Yes, you are right, I am not mad—na?

Long ago—I can't recall the exact year—the creator's curse had stricken this little peaceful village of ours in the form of cholera and smallpox. Under this curse, so many mothers, siblings and children vanished into the land of no return, leaving a great void at the heart of this prosperous village. As I recall those days, O ma!— my heart twists in seven turns and aches in pain. So many homes were emptied and locked, all their inhabitants dead. Just as the dwellings were deserted one by one within the village, the number of graves increased in the graveyard so rapidly that it was hard to even look at it.

Achcha bhai, this graveyard by the deep pond with thousands of graves, are these nothing but the silent agony tugging at the heart of our village? Did these undercurrents of sadness, like the subterranean river Phalgu, solidify only to emerge as graves? Or is it our Mother Earth, aggrieved by the suffering of her rustic, poor and disease-stricken children, who has covered them affectionately beneath her aachol of dust and hiding them in rest? No grief, pain, suffering or torture can reach the kingdom below! This is a region marked by an infinite calm—the silent and inert repose of weary mankind. It is the realm of sleep and the kingdom of silence. Nobody in the village knows how many people from a remote past are asleep in this graveyard. The number of people I have seen dying is insignificant in comparison. When these ancient people died, I was wandering in a similarly invisible land perhaps. Afterwards, somebody threw me onto this earth and my eyes were dazed in the scorching light of this world. I cried aloud for sure in a strange indescribable tongue: 'O, why have you brought me into this world of clay and stone? Why, oh, why?' Soon after, as I lay on my mother's lap and sucked her milk, my mind was deeply consoled! Forgetting my entire past in the blink of an eye, I fell asleep.

Those gravestones are age-old. It was the Badshahi era and this small village of ours was a small urban settlement called 'Olinagar'. The small hillocks you can see nearby are known as Rajar Garh and Ranir Garh. The king and the queen along with the prince and the princess built their mansions there. They were known to have slept in diamond beds and feasted on red gemstones. But this golden city was burnt down by the curse of a pir, whose dargah was situated in the western part of the graveyard. The entire family was gone; their homes were burnt down along with the entire city and nobody remained to carry forward their line. Maybe, their ashes were scattered on this graveyard by the west wind. Look dear, such is the grace of Khoda! The king who has so much wealth and power turns to dust after death, and the beggar who dies starving in his thatched cottage embraces the same fate. It is a good place indeed, bon!

You have rightly said bhai Salima, there's no use crying and brooding over this! Events that are not written in the stars won't take place, and things that have been lost won't be back. But this inconsolable mind of mine can't accept this fact. I have sobbed through many nights sitting alone in this graveyard, but all my tears and entreaties failed to get any little response from him. Is he sleeping soundly? How profound is his repose? Not one bit of my heart-rending moans and sky-splitting screams entered his ears? Oh! what touch of a wizard's magic wand has put him into such a deep slumber? Why can't I become as insensate and still as him? Why doesn't my life get an equally cool and soothing touch of death? Why can't I become still and solitary like the graveyard at midnight? Only then will this abysmal past of mine not suffocate my heart any more like a heavy stone! The harsh memory from long-lost days won't singe my wounded heart with its heated rod anymore! Oh, how long shall I suffer and burn like a sacrificial beast? Why doesn't death engulf me as a blessing from my mother? Whose welfare is being achieved by our Gracious Lord tormenting a hopeless one like me? I keep thinking over and over again—my miserable train of thought seems to have no beginning or end. How things were—how things ultimately turned out—this remains a big mystery to me!

One morning a shepherd boy was singing a very plaintive song as he walked along the bund by the paddy saplings, while chewing a raw mango. I can't remember the exact lyrics of the song, but its inner theme is something like, 'How many mornings have turned to evenings and days merged into nights, how many seas have dried up into deserts and rivers lost their courses and how many mountains have turned to dust, and yet, O my heart's desire! you never arrived!'

As I listened to that song, I was wondering how the shepherd's lyrics succeeded in giving voice to my ardent cries. The same way, the great tides of time ebb in the blink of my eye and I make my earnest entreaties for a glimpse of a person who would never come, nor would respond. The pensive humming of flies in midday sun I hear in this graveyard—is that the sound of his mourning? The relentless moaning winds across the graveyard through the days and nights—is that his sigh? The heady whiff of shirish blossoms at night—is it the fragrance of his lovely body? The dewdrops that fall from evening till morning, soaking the shirish, shefali and henna bowers and the verdant undergrowth of durba grass and bhnui-kadam of the graveyard—are these his melting sorrows? The intense flash of lightning that dazzles my eyes—is that his parting wild laughter? The deep rumbling of clouds that follows the lightning—is it the throbbing of his stony breast? The gust of wind that dances around me time and again as a storm—is it his invisible, eager embrace? The air that ruffles through the white kash-blossoms on the banks of the Kunur flowing by the graveyard—is it his trembling voice that calls me? Why can't I merge into this infinite universe like him and feel his presence? Why can't my mind feel the presence of this absent man in each and every entity of this world? Oh, when will the finite be absorbed within the music of the infinite? Now that the day is winding down, listen to the swan song of life sung by the tired boatman—

As the day wraps up, no more sings the bird,
As the tired wind ceases to blow,
This is when I am engulfed
By the firm dark shadow![1]

B

This graveyard, where the devata of my life is laid to rest, was my favourite place since childhood. Those three little graves you can see nearby, almost levelled to the ground and covered with new durba grass, are the graves of my younger siblings. They died at a very tender age, just as green mangoes drop in the harsh hailstorms of spring. I planted the bakam plants you can see at the head of their graves when I was a small girl. Now that place is filled with shrubs, creepers and undergrowth. The bakam and shirish blossoms shed their yellow pollen through autumns and springs on the graves of those who were tender and pure like these flowers. Along with the pollen, I shed a fountain of tears gushing out of the river of my heart, pining for those three little companions! My father held my mother in his arms and guided her through that narrow path on melancholy summer evenings and told her, pointing at the small grassy graves of our Tunu, Tahera and Abul, 'See, they are asleep here and they will never arise. After some time, we shall come here as well and lie beside them—our neighbours will make similar earthen chambers for us.'

On those mournful and pensive evenings, my heart was infused with a melancholy mood and a shadowy perplexity which I could not express in words and so I fell sobbing while looking at my father's face. Embarrassed, my father picked me up and tried to console me, patting me. I became so attached to the spot that I came here every day, stealing away from my mother and gazing at my siblings's little graves!

---

[1] The lines are from Song 157 of Tagore's *Gitanjali*.

Oh dear, is the attraction of blood so strong? Then why was my mind so eager to see that painful and sombre place where the bodies of my little siblings, precious like flowers, had mingled with the earth? I have heard that the place from where Khoda takes the earth to mould us is the same place where we are eventually laid to rest. That's why we always feel a strange tugging in our heart for that spot.

Nowadays, Tahera's grave has broken open and a white bone can be seen poking through it. After many years I feel my grave, too, will collapse the same way and all my bones will lay bared naked to scare others! Hai! such is the end of man and yet man is so proud—why? I keep wondering! And yet, sometimes I think I have to go to an unknown land, leaving this beautiful earth behind. This very thought tugs at my heart with terrible pain. Oh! what sort of blind and vain attraction do we feel towards this earth?

Soon my father too was laid to rest beside Abul. That bigger grave beside the larger hedge belongs to my father. After my father died, I started visiting the graveyard more than ever and sat in silence as I waited to hear words of mute affection from my departed friends. A deep pathos filled my eyes.

My mother was wasting away day by day through grinding pain, humiliation and poverty. Moreover, she could no longer endure the blows that battered her. Gradually she caught tuberculosis. I sensed that my misfortunes had begun and that my mother was leaving me as well, for she was summoned by death. I did not even dare to look forward to the future—ooh, it was pitch-dark gloom!

Such was the time when mother's bosom friend Soi-ma[2] visited us one evening and holding my mother's frail hand said, 'Soi, my son has come home for his summer vacation. With your blessings he has passed his BA examination with great success. My plan is now to get him married and leave the task of running the household to the bahu. Moreover, I'm the only one who lives in the house: no daughter, no daughter-in-law; the empty home feels abandoned. Khoda hasn't even bestowed upon me a daughter so that I would enjoy a few days with her and a son-in-law. My son had insisted all along that he would marry only after his graduation. Now Khoda has fulfilled his wish. If he had married earlier, wouldn't there be one or two grandchildren by now?!

[2] A soi or best friend is called 'Soi-ma' by her female friend's children.

And my house would have looked much better. But we cannot decide our fates until the appropriate hour arrives. And since this quiet, gem of a girl is ready at hand, why should I look for a bride elsewhere?'

Saying this she drew my head close to her bosom with affection. My mother and I were looking at her awestruck, for her words appeared to us more like mad ramblings. My mother began to breathe faster as her heart throbbed in excitement. Soi-ma took some ointment and massaged my mother's chest, while talking unperturbed, 'I have always trusted my son, because he has never disrespected any of my wishes. I told him, "O Aziz, your Soi-ma is going to be your mother-in-law. I would like to bring Begum home as a bahu; hope you would like her as a bride! I am asking you because you children of these days no longer marry according to the choice of your parents!" I need not elaborate more, for he happily replied, "Alright Ma-jaan, I have never been disobedient to your words, and I am really happy that you are going to save a poor and destitute girl instead of arranging my marriage to a zamindar family. I feel like boasting to the entire world, what a big heart my mother has!"

My Aziz is a crazy mamma's boy. As I have fulfilled all his demands since childhood, I have become the best mom in the whole world! Jokes apart bon, I would like to bless Begum this very day, because we can't foresee our death—you too have such a critical health condition, we do not know, what fate has in store for us. I am planning to take your daughter home as a bride within this very month. We should not delay an auspicious act, as some villagers might create some unnecessary complications. Soi! Let Begum come and fill my empty home!'

I can't recall what else Soi-ma said on that day, as my head was reeling and a shrill excitement filled my brain—it is as if somebody had benumbed my entire body with a sudden jolt of joy infused with pain.

C

Our wedding took place amidst a lot of merriment. By merriment I do not mean 'fireworks', 'bands', 'dancing girls', 'theatre', or all those profane entertainments. If merriment means the exchange of pure joy between people, there was no lack of it. The poor people of the village were heartily fed for seven days. Many broken houses were rebuilt. Those who had no farm animals to till the land, were presented with cows. The two weaver families in the village were given looms to encourage the production of traditional textiles. Five thousand rupees were donated to an orphanage in Kolkata. Besides, my mother-in-law sent money to a number of places, which I don't remember in detail!

The happiness Soi-ma felt in making me her bahu was surpassed by the discontent felt by her neighbours and kin. Many of their relatives did not even attend the wedding as they felt betrayed by my mother-in-law's choice of a girl from a lower-class family as the bride. On this issue the bond of kinship was severed forever with many of their relations. Many well-wishers turned into enemies. And since money talks everywhere, many shrewd characters of prominence maintained an apparently amicable relationship with them, while trying secretly to harm them. Though the family was not fully excommunicated, nobody visited them without a purpose, which was usually driven by self-interest. The helpless poor people of the village who survived on the benevolence of this family were apparently scared of proscriptions by other prominent members of their society. They knew these powerful people could do them a lot of harm. The weaker a person is, the more they are smothered by society. If a person is powerful enough to challenge society, it is the society that becomes pliant and pampers them, keeping mum about their wrongdoings. So when my husband and his mother said, 'Since we have never been a part of society, who will excommunicate us?', society kept quiet like a submissive kid and never responded. But the poor people who visited my husband's family were expressly prohibited by the society bigwigs from visiting them.

My in-laws were not at all shocked by the conduct of such people; rather they were very relieved. Their hearts were touched by the smiles and the glow that lit up the teary-eyed but delighted faces of the poor villagers. This, however, burnt the envious ones with jealousy!

Oh, what an immense strength filled my mother's battered chest on the day I took her leave! Tears of happiness gushed out of her eyes! No matter what task she had to perform on the wedding day, she never lost her smile although it was laced with tears.

My life became radiant and blissful on that day—when I came to know that the lord of my heart had accepted his mother's blessings wholeheartedly, and all my secret prayers at the feet of my devata had been answered!

I only longed to place my head on his feet and say: 'O swami! O my devata! Pray don't give so much happiness to this famished woman; do not let the heavy shower of love fall on this parched heart—do not envelop my entire body and mind in your eager and strong embrace of earnest love! This little heart of mine won't be able to contain so much love and happiness!' But alas, as I fell into his arms, I forgot everything. I was oblivious of my past, present and future! It was like visiting fairyland in a dream and falling asleep with one's head on the beloved's breast. As the throbbing of the heart stops and the flow of blood becomes suspended—the feeling of only 'You' and 'Me' remains—it is a moment of total submission, like a drop of water losing itself in the infinite sea!

While his all-consuming love was reflected like a glow in the darkness of his eyes, I only kept musing, what heights man can attain through love! A mere touch makes the serene and pure river of tenderness flow across the innermost regions of the world's soul. Is there any entity called devata? Certainly not. Only human beings can attain such heights by immersing themselves completely in fathomless love, where the subjective identity no longer prevails and everything becomes beautiful and joyous—it is only then that a human being becomes devata! There is no separate existence called devata.

* * *

Anyway, let's leave this point now—what was I saying?

Right, such an unnatural incident as my wedding raised a great furore in the village. The marriage of a bright graduate boy from the Sayyid line to a girl from a lowly-born destitute family like ours was as amazing as the fairytale marriage between a shahzada[3] and a pauper girl! The village belles looked at me in utter amazement and thought, 'Holy hell, how fortunate the girl is!' They also kept spreading rumours about how a simple girl like me had captivated my spotless moon of a husband by casting the trap with my beauty. Even after spreading all these rumours they were not at all tired, and together began to proclaim

[3] Son of a shah—a monarch; a Mughal prince.

how could a high-born family like this ever get rid of such a blemish. Such excess wouldn't be taken kindly by fate, never ever. They kept talking and waited for the moment when a calamity would strike our family to their utmost satisfaction and their prediction would come true. But I paid no heed to their words, because oblivious to everything I discovered my lord each day anew—this was my devata who had turned my whole world into gold with the touchstone of his heart, and all my being along with all my desires had become immersed in him. I neither had anything to think, nor say. It was that auspicious moment of my passage towards the zenith of sheer bliss! But hai! the cruel hand of time exposed before my very eyes the harsh facets of this world even before that auspicious hour arrived. Even before I could immerse myself in peace and tranquillity everything fell apart. I did have a chilling apprehension of this calamity within the deepest regions of my heart! I felt as if a thunderbolt would strike and annihilate all my happiness. As if my fool's paradise would collapse and fall apart! The momentary gift I had received, which was a piece of sheer joy delivered in a dream, would be rudely taken away and the collapse of the dream would lead to eternal darkness!

Soon after giving my hand to my husband, my mother again became bedridden. As she had finished all her duties and met all her goals, she felt free! Thus, leaving me in my Soi-ma's care, she left for the land unknown. It was as if my father waited there, teary-eyed with their children by his side. Oh, what serene satisfaction glowed in the smile that played on my mother's wasted lips at the time of her departure! As I fell crying on my mother's breast saying, 'Oh ma don't leave me. I have no one else in this world,' my mother put her hand on my lips to stop me and said, 'Never, never say such things Begum! What do you lack? You have a ma-in-law who is more affectionate than your own ma. You've got a husband who is mightier than a devata. Even then, you rakshasi, keep on lamenting that you have no one? Chhi ma, don't utter such unlucky words!'

Mother was laid to rest beside my father's grave. Just the way the graves of Abul and Tahera have merged with the dust, after a certain time, my mother's grave would become flattened to the ground. But would the terrible grief that is tightly knotted in my breast, dissolve ever?

Since then, the recurrent blows of grief gave way to a terrible malady of seizures! I often became unconscious and when I came to my senses, I saw my dusty head resting on my husband's great, trembling breast and held in his eager embrace. Oh, what a frightened and compassionate expression showed in his eyes! His ever-charming face was filled with profound sympathy! Then I thought, what else can a woman desire? For us ill-fated race of women, what can be more ethereal and desired than this? Hai! why didn't my last breath mingle in the air at that moment with my head on my husband's lap?

D

The account of my life I am narrating to you, my bon, is a kissa.[4] Who would believe my words and who would listen to it at all? Moreover, my brain is supposed to have gone into a manic phase, and that is why I show off my knowledge through confused lectures. Nobody likes my chattering and leaves annoyed after listening to me for a few moments. Tell me bon, can women talk in a precise way? And isn't it their nature to talk a lot! How can I express all my experiences through only a few words? You may say, who has forced you to tell your story? True, no one has forced me. But if I don't share with others the words that are churning in my guts and paining my heart, they make me restless and my heart becomes heavy, which is also a strange malady.

* * *

Soi-ma was so reserved in speech and manner that everybody was respectful of her. She was the head of the family. No one dared disobey her. That is why, in spite of taking such a disastrous step—making a destitute girl like me a royal bride—nobody dared to open their mouth in opposition. When other ladies came to inquire in an oblique way about my baser origins, she told them off with these words: 'What shall I do with status and caste, wash and eat them? Does one have one's caste and class identity written on one's skin? The person who behaves in a gentle way is a nobleman. On the day of Last Judgement,

[4] A tale

Khoda will never say that as you are born in a Sayyid family all your virtuous acts will be forfeited and your fate will take you to hell! What I look for is quality in a person, irrespective of class. Let all of you take a look at my bahu—such glowing charm, more well-behaved than a noble person, educated and efficient at household work—who else can boast of such a Lakshmi-bahu! Why should I bring a high-class girl into my family? Whatever good looks and qualities she would bring would be accompanied by bigger boasting about her family name and great discord! Let my gem of a son remain alive and bring children into this home. This happy sight will let me die in bliss.' Hearing these affectionate words, my heart was filled with joy! Tears rolled from my eyes. Maybe, the language of gratitude and devotion is expressed through tears of love!

Genuine love from my husband and profound motherly affection from Soi-ma had left nothing unfulfilled in me. Whatever I looked upon in the world, everything bloomed in beauty. I have never seen this earthly world glow with so much beauty. Oh, what power does this spell of love have, so that all ugliness turns to beauty!

There was so much happiness and yet this unfortunate mind of mine seemed to fold upon itself. The one comment from my neighbours that haunted me and pierced my ears was, 'This will not last, this will not last!' Just as 'the mind of a thief hovers round his stolen goods', perhaps it was the same way the ominous whistle of misfortune pierced my ill-fated mind! The blow of intense love made me embarrassed! Honey tastes very sweet, but an excess of it creates a burning sensation within. I felt like banging my head against their feet and say, 'O devata! O heavenly devi! don't engulf me in so much love and affection, for I can't take it anymore! My heart breaks under the weight of affection! Scorn me a bit, speak ill of me, hit me hard, or else my heart will bend!'

That very moment the same monstrous form emerged before my eyes saying, 'This will not last'.

I don't know how two years passed this way. Then came the sudden double blow of cholera and smallpox—as I had mentioned at the beginning of my story—and consumed our entire village like demons. Their stomachs were hard to fill. What insatiable hunger these demons had! The entire village became as desolate as a burial ground. People fled wherever they could to avoid death. When a flock of sheep is attacked by a wolf, all the sheep gather together in a circle, close their eyes and bury their heads, believing that the action would make them invisible. But a human being cannot flee leaving a fellow human being in such a distress. Our in-laws had the same human instinct and the same humanity and they possessed a greater power within, for they empathised with the sorrow of others, and were happy to share the distress and grief of others. This gave them a sense of deliverance.

As all the inhabitants left emptying the village, only we remained; my husband said, 'Where is such a country without death for us to hide in?' While everybody stopped even walking on the street in fear of the epidemic, he braced himself and went down the streets saying, 'My work beckons me now.' And gladly he took to the service of sick people. At that time, he was studying Law after completing his Masters. He had come to the village to escape the searing heatwave that was afflicting Kolkata at the time. What charm of inner strength filled his glowing face on that day.

Again those ominous words, 'This will not last, this will not last'.

Through days and nights, without food or rest he ran around to take care of the cholera and smallpox patients. He was more restless than the sick themselves. I fell at his feet and pleaded, 'O my devata! Stop, please stop, the whole world belongs to you, but I have none other than you. O my sole support, stop, please stop!' Hai! who could stop the man obsessed with such a mission? His heart was given to the welfare of this world. Did the sound of my little sobs echo in his great, world-spanning heart? Even if it did, it could merely touch him, but never could move him.

The smallest apprehension of evil, which had so long lain suppressed at the innermost corner of my heart and filled my entire breast with fear, that little shadow took a full embodiment and stood before my eyes in its terrible form. What an ugly look it had!

Mother never stood in his way so he was free to do whatever he wanted. One day after her evening namaz, with tears in her eyes, she dedicated her most precious wealth, her only son to Khoda. Oh, what a divine glow filled her teary face with the grace of renunciation on that day! The grace of Khoda seemed to rain in a thousand showers like a fountain on mother's head. My heart too swelled in pride that suppressed a dull pain.

Such a person is called a devata—na?

E

That day my right eye had been trembling since morning. An owl hooted three times in broad daylight on the ashwatha tree behind our house. A black lizard continuously called above my head, making my mind more restless and agitated. Did they have any connection with my fate?

My husband went out at dawn with a corpse on his shoulder. Throughout the day I kept looking his way restlessly, but there was no sign of him.

In the afternoon dark clouds gathered in the sky, accompanied by a heavy storm and rains that felt like a duel between two immense forces! Oh, the clouds contained so much water and hailstones within! Then a sudden harsh clap of thunder about twenty feet away from our house made my head reel and I fell down in a swoon.

* * *

When I regained consciousness, I sensed a storm lashing through the house. I heard wails all around and the sound of incessant rains. I felt a huge thunderbolt darting towards me, aimed at my forehead!

My husband-devata was tossing and turning in bed as his ma kept staring at him, like a stone-idol. Drops of tears were lining her eyes. There was a strange, inexplicable brightness in her gaze coupled with an unwavering fearlessness.

What I heard was, on that day he was returning home after treating some patients and burying ten to twelve people who had died of cholera in our neighbouring village. On the way back, he began to show symptoms of the disease. He fell unconscious under a banyan tree and was carried home moments ago. The rain had started pouring again and the entire firmament seemed to collapse under its force! Jham, jham, jham . . .

Nobody had the strength to hold him back—his work was finished, why should he stay anymore? He was gone! People wept as much as they could. The neem tree in our courtyard shed all its leaves, jhar jhar jhar! The cow ran away from the cowshed, making a moaning sound. The parrot at our door gave a loud cry and hung lifeless from the cage with its head down. A piercing wail from his dying mouth was heard from all around. A horrid sound of crying pervaded the air, dominating all other noises! The inner cords of the entire world seemed to twist in sobs, while tears gushed out through rains—jham jham jham.

Mother alone stood still and colossal like a mountain!

In his departing moment she only said, 'My son, I am not supposed to cry at your parting moment. You are no longer in my possession, for I have sacrificed you to Khoda! I have no right to mourn over the offering I have made to Khoda! Let's move baap, for you can't stay without me even for a moment and I have never let you go out of my sight. If your work is done in this world, my work too is complete.'

Some people are so brainsick that a moment seems to them an eternity. Has my mind become that deranged? Else why do I feel that these incidents took place aeons ago in the time of Father Adam, and I have been keeping vigil at the graveyard since then. But you say that this happened just the other day. This means I have really gone mad!

What did you ask? why have I come to this graveyard?—Aha, what a question to ask! Where shall I go then? To this graveyard where genuine human beings are resting, or into the jungle infested by beasts that have hands and feet like a human being but have hearts that are darker than the devil itself? I can clearly recall, as his dead body was brought out from the house, a certain relative of my husband dragged me out by my hair and said, 'Get out, you devil woman, get out of this house right now! Didn't I tell you, poking your nose into the noble family would bring you nothing but bad luck? They brought you into the family and now no one remains to carry on the family name. Get out, you rakshasi, and never show your face in the village! Or if you fancy it then come, we can arrange another nikah for you!'

All the beatings and verbal abuses never affected me the way that single mention of nikah did. That ugly word beat in my broken heart like a big blow. O! what do you mean by nikah? Is it a mere custom of putting a garland around another person's neck a second time in life? The custom of nikah is written in scriptures, but for whom? See dear, those driven by poverty and necessity insult their love—do they not have a thing called a heart? Still they can be forgiven. But those who, driven by desire, trample purity and womanhood, can never be forgiven. For, those who soil that heavenly flower called love through their lustful breath, no hell is fit for their souls.

My words will make the maulvis angry, they will not even conduct my funeral prayers, but there is a vast difference between a common man and a maulvi—between the call of the heart and the rules of scriptures.

F

It is, therefore, much better to stay in this world of the dead, away from all sorts of humiliation.

* * *

Oh dear, why do you look so startled? Is it to see me blacking out? You say I have taken poison? Then you too have gone mad! Perhaps you thought I have taken poison, seeing my body turning blue. No dear, no, I may be mad or whatever, but I don't have that weakness in me. Burning themselves in kerosene, drowning in water, hanging themselves and taking poison have become a malady of the female race! Though I have been stricken by fate, I scorn such 'cowardly deaths' from the core of my heart. Bon, through such a death you lose both the world and the world after death!

After you took fright and left me last night, my vomiting started! Then I passed out and regained consciousness just a while ago.

I have realised bon, I have no time left. No one's tears can stop me anymore from embracing my death. Oh! after such a long time the lazy melody from the riverside has touched and soothed my heart. Oh! how pensive it is! Tears have filled my eyes, bon! I can feel its gentle touch on my eyelids. What a thrill fills every pore of my body!

Oh! what a thirst, what parching thirst! Give me some water, bon! Na na, that will do. Look there, you can see my husband, the lord of my heart standing with the cup of sharaban tahura[5] in his hand! Oh, what an intense look his eyes have, moist with compassion, melancholy and affection! Ah, O ma! Ah!

---

[5] Divine nectar in Islamic culture.

FOURTEEN

THE RESTLESS TRAVELLER

A vignette

Translated by Dhrubajyoti Sarkar

He was walking through an impassable thorny way. At one stage he turned back and saw millions of steadfast gazes fixed upon him. An incandescent lustre of seething excitement and expectation radiated from those gazes. It filled the traveller's heart with an intoxicating pride. With a smile of profound satisfaction, he asked in fraternal confidence, 'Bhai! Where did you get such a powerful gaze?'

Millions of lustrous eyes replied, 'O brave traveller, we got it by looking at the long stretch of road you have travelled!'

Someone's sorrowful yet tender glance sent him a message, 'Hai! This treacherous road leads a youthful traveller only to inevitable death!' Millions of others cried loudly in desperation, 'Shut up! You coward! This is the eternal and true path of the soul of humanity.'

With both of his eyes wide open, the traveller deeply drank in the beneficence of the million gazes. Just as a perfectly tuned veena comes to life at the touch of a finger, the dormant truth of the traveller's heart also responded with an animated resolve: 'Fare forward!'

The sylvan expanse filled the traveller with its impulsive youthfulness and announced, 'Let me put on your forehead the mark of youth's sovereignty! This makes you immortal with everlasting youth.' Distant skies stooped down to kiss his head in benediction. The distant horizon showed him the blurred outline of freedom. The wayside trees waved their branches at him in greeting. Across the entrance to the free country, the fiery awakening call of the flute attracted the traveller like a captivating deer. Guided by the tune, he started running towards the path to freedom, shouting, 'Ho, where is your grand gateway to freedom? Open the doors, open the doors—show me light, show me the way!'

The mantra of universal beneficence engulfed him and said, 'It's still far away, keep walking!'

The startled traveller said, 'Hey, you are the one I want!'

The unknown companion replied, 'To get me you have to cross that lofty portal ahead'.

The restless traveller quickened his unrelenting pace, and said, 'Yes bhai! That is my destination!' The unbounded sky momentarily peeped through a parting in the distant forest, and millions of young voices from behind him thunderously echoed his resolve, 'We too have the same destination; move forward bhai, be in front of us—we too are following your footprints'.

Showing the pride and satisfaction of a pioneer, the traveller reminded them: 'But, this road leads to death!'

Agitated, the fiery youth roared back, 'We don't care! This is not death; this is the beginning of a new life'.

Far behind, a group of feeble-hearted, older people was shivering in fear of death. Sitting astride on their shoulders, someone with a grimacing face mocked them, 'Look at me, I am Death. I am here!'

Nearby, a fragrant pyre had been lit to create an illusion for the dim, old eyes! Trying hard to suppress derisive laughter, someone drove them to the burning pyre and said, 'Lo and behold! That is your path to salvation. Why do you risk your lives on this long and rugged track at such an advanced age? It is just a matter of time before the restless traveller and those who are following him are killed'.

Raising both their hands up above, the elderly people said, 'Yes sir, of course!'

A mischievous voice repeatedly cautioned, 'Oho fools, never beg for anything! They will slowly burn you to death in the pyre.'

Their shepherd suppressed another bout of laughter and advised them 'Na, na, don't listen to them. Their path is a frightful and long one, and is filled with troubles, obstacles and misery. Your liberation is close at hand.'

The restless traveller was still following the tune of the entrance-flute, overflowing from the land of freedom ... The phantom called

Horrors of the Road now started to torment him. The traveller could see traces of a few faint footmarks still pointing the way forward. The phantom held out a skull to the traveller and said, 'Look, this is what happened to those before you on this path'.

Placing the skull on his head, the traveller announced: 'Aha! They are the ones who have called me! I too want such an end. My death will not be my end. Instead, I will live among those countless youth walking behind me'.

When the phantom asked him, 'Who are you?', the traveller replied with a smile, 'I am the eternal seeker of liberation. Those whose skulls are strewn here are not dead either; each of them has invigorated me with new energy, new life and a new glow. The clan of the liberated souls has become immortal.'

The phantom trembled and desperately cried out, 'Don't you know me? I am bondage personified. Whatever you say, my goal is to destroy you; to put freedom in chains is my goal. You have to die at my hands!'

The traveller paused and replied, 'Kill—tie up—but you can never really confine me. Death cannot destroy me! I will keep returning!'

The phantom blocked his path again and declared, 'As long as I have any strength left, I will kill you every time you return. If you have the strength, kill me; otherwise, you have to endure my torment.'

Far off, from the wide-open terrace of the state of freedom, the past martyr-travellers of the road appeared in the effulgence of eternal youth and welcomed him! The traveller asked them, 'Does the significance of life lie only in giving it away?'

A free soul on the free terrace replied in a voice full of tenderness and empathy, 'Yes, bhai! For ages life has sung the paean of such death. The significance of your death lies in rejuvenating millions of lives. Your death achieves its immortality and eternal consciousness by arousing others to life!'

The young traveller bared his mighty chest and stepped forward. 'Swing your scimitar,' he said.

The youths who followed him hoisted the lifeless body of the restless traveller above their head and cried out loudly, 'Come back again!'

From the far-off horizon, a symphony of voices rang out,

> Your kettle drums have delighted the far-away lands with their solemn beats,
>
> Here comes and gathers around your seat, a group of the valorous![1]

[1] These lines are taken from a Rabindranath Tagore song (*Swarabitan* 16).

THE SHIULI MALA

FIFTEEN

THE LOTUS-COBRAS

Translated by Sucharita Sarkar

1

In front of everyone's eyes, the fortunes of Rosulpur's Mir Sahib and his family grew and swelled exceedingly rapidly. People began to whisper among themselves that they must have got their hands on a treasure belonging to some djinn or yaksha. Otherwise, it was not possible to amass such enormous wealth in the span of only two years, unless one possessed Alladin's lamp.

Although it was certainly true that even ten years ago, the condition of Mir Sahib's family was not inferior to any zamindar in the country, within a few short years their zamindari—like the saying, 'it was a husk lever but cut short into weighing scale, cutting it further short nothing remained after a while'—disappeared through overspending.

It is said that their misery began when they started to compete with the nawabs of Murshidabad in their lavish display of luxury. People say that they used to attach golden anklets even to their khadams or wooden clogs. Apparently, the present Mir Sahib's grandfather had collected a square-dozen beautiful young women from various provinces of India just to give him oil massages before his daily bath.

Soon after Grandfather Mir Sahib passed away, his golden Lanka became a charred Lanka.[1] The situation was so dire that his son was surviving hand-to-mouth by running a small maktab[2] in the same village.

---

[1] According to the *Ramayana*, Ravana's kingdom of Lanka was made of gold. It was burnt down by Hanuman, Rama's devotee and boon companion, when he travelled to Lanka to rescue Sita.

[2] Muslim elementary school.

Surely, the grandson of such a grandfather could not marry into any aristocratic family. However, the family of the girl he married had a lineage that was no less prestigious than his—rather, it was significantly more.

The name of the luxury-loving Mir Sahib's grandson was Arif. His bride's name was Zohra. The fame of Zohra's beauty had already spread to the surrounding villages. In spite of such beauty and such family prestige, no nawab's son showed any interest in marrying the daughter of the penurious Sayyid Sahib.

Yet, it was intolerable to her parents that their daughter should become an aging maid tied to a post. Hence, in spite of some reluctance, they were relieved to marry her off to the maktab teacher Arif, the son of Mir Sahib, who had recently gone broke.

Although nothing else remained of Mir Sahib's family riches, the wealth of their beauty was still very much undiminished. The resplendence of their beauty had, in fact, put to shame even the renown of Kutubpur's Sayyid Sahib's family in this regard. Thus, it was a sight for sore eyes when Zohra and Arif stood side by side, dressed as bride and groom. It looked like a competition between two moons.

Although Zohra's father still had some reservations about their match, her mother felt a deep sense of peace when she saw the joyful, glowing faces of her daughter and son-in-law. The couple's wide eyes became wider with happiness, love and adoration during the exchange of glances at the subhodrishti.

For quite some time, Arif's mother had been ailing and was confined to bed. With the arrival of her bahu, however, her condition started to improve speedily. Overjoyed, she kept repeating, 'My bahu has brought us luck, so I recovered; now our home will once again be filled with riches.'

Soon, word spread around the village that the Lakshmi of Mir Sahib's household had returned.

I do not know whether human beings have any such attribute as 'luck', but it was true that after Zohra set foot in Mir Sahib's household, there was an inexplicable change in their fortunes, rising rapidly from good to better to even better.

Initially, the news spread around the village was that the new bride of Mir Sahib's household had found the buried treasure of their forefathers, and this was the reason behind the unforeseen change in their fortunes.

This rumour was not entirely baseless, though. One day, out of curiosity, Zohra had been examining a strange crack in one of the walls of her in-law's dilapidated mansion. Maybe she felt the desire to search for hidden treasure, so on an impulse she poked the fissure in the wall with a stick. Immediately there came a hissing sound, like that of an angry snake, from inside the crack which scared Zohra and made her run quickly to her husband and report the entire incident.

It goes without saying that Arif had fallen overwhelmingly in love with his new bride. Not just Arif, her in-laws also regarded Zohra in a very favourable light.

At first, Arif scolded Zohra for her recklessness, but when he went to check it out himself, he heard with his own ears the loud hissing of the snake coming from inside the crevice. He went out and called his father. The father was somewhat more daring than the son. He said, 'That snake has to be killed, otherwise it might come out and bite someone. From its loud hissing, it seems as if it is a venomous breed.' Saying this, he mildly reprimanded his daughter-in-law.

The place surrounding the crack in the wall had become overrun with weeds. After cautiously clearing some of the nearby weeds, the father–son duo poked a stick into the crack a few times, and soon enough, an enormous milk-white cobra came out. It had a vermilion circular mark on its hood, which looked like a pair of khadam-prints. When Arif readied to kill the serpent, his father objected, saying, 'Don't kill it, it is a baastu-saap.[3] Can't you see that it is a lotus-cobra?'

The upraised stick remained in Arif's hand. The lotus-cobra that had been the house's baastu-saap, disappeared into the jungle nearby.

As everyone began to move away from the spot, Zohra called Arif aside and told him, 'When you were poking at the snake, I heard a strange sound coming from in there. I'm sure there are things inside, possibly made of brass or bell metal.'

Upon hearing this, Arif's eyes glistened with unshed tears of joy! When he told his father, initially the old man could not believe his ears.

---

[3] A snake which lives in someone's house or property; it is believed to guard the inhabitants of the house.

He said, 'Where is it son? No, I don't think I heard any strange sound.'

Arif responded, 'We were so scared of the snake that perhaps we failed to notice any sound.'

When the father and son carefully removed a few bricks from the wall, they could clearly see something sparkling inside the crevice. What the extremely enthused father–son duo brought out after a few hours of toil could not perhaps be called the treasure of a yaksha, but it was definitely not insignificant. Especially, considering their current straitened circumstances!

A medium-sized brass pot filled with Badshahi-era gold coins.

Yet, they nearly killed themselves in trying to remove the pot from the crevice. When Arif was about to bring out the pot, he noticed another lotus-cobra coiled around the upper end of the pot. Leaping back ten paces in fright, Arif exclaimed, 'Oh my god! The serpent has come back there!'

Zohra responded in a low voice, 'No, this is another one. Most probably they are a pair. I saw the first one going that way.'

Whether this snake was the same or a different one, it refused to move away from the pot. But killing a lotus-cobra was out of the question. It was not done. Remaining tightly coiled around the pot, the lotus-cobra intermittently spread its hood wide to scare off the intruders.

On a whim, Zohra went and brought a bowl of milk which she fearlessly kept near the pot. The snake uncoiled itself from the pot and quietly began to drink the milk. In the meantime, Zohra picked up the brass pot and brought it out. The snake could have easily bitten her hand, but it did not do anything. Instead, it kept drinking the milk with utmost concentration, making a low sound like the chirping of crickets. Soon after, another lotus-cobra came to the spot and also began to drink the milk.

Zohra spoke up, 'That's the snake we saw earlier! It still has the mark where it was poked with the stick. Poor dear, see how the bruise has turned blue there!'

Arif and his parents were looking at what Zohra was doing in bafflement. Scared and astonished, they had completely forgotten that Zohra could be bitten by the snakes at any moment. Suddenly coming to their senses, they dragged her away from that place.

So overjoyed were they to find gold coins in the pot, they did not know how to applaud or thank Zohra enough. Eyes wet with tears of gratitude, Zohra's in-laws repeatedly said, 'Truly, dear Zohra, the Lakshmi of the Mir household has returned home with you!'

The news of this event remained within the family of four and did not spread in the village. When they secretly took the coins to Kolkata and sold the melted gold, the money they got in exchange was more than sufficient for the small Mir family to live a life of ease. However, emboldened by his bride's 'luck', Arif decided to move to Kolkata and use a portion of that money to start a coal-trading business. This business gave them larger-than-expected profits.

Within two years, the dilapidated mansion of the Mir family was completely renovated. The household once again filled up with maids and servants.

After some time, Arif managed to become a contractor with Kolkata Corporation and began to earn huge sums of money. The family lacked nothing, besides Zohra gradually becoming a cause of great concern for them.

2

Soon after the family came into possession of the unexpected wealth, Zohra became inordinately fond of the pair of lotus-cobras, and the serpent couple also seemed to become attached to Zohra. Or perhaps, they followed her around because of their greed for the milk-and-bananas they were fed.

Zohra's in-laws lived in constant fear of their lives because of the snakes and began to suffer horrible visions of death. Baastu-saap were guardian serpents, so they could not even kill them, lest the divinely bestowed riches suddenly vanish.

The snake duo moved all around the house in such a calm and quiet manner that there was nothing to fear. Still, they were a venomous breed! If they became angry and struck even once, death would be inevitable.

In a way, it was impossible for the family to leave their ancestral house and go elsewhere. They were at their wit's end, unable to decide what to do.

If Zohra was cooking, all of a sudden one would see the serpent pair come in and lie down at her feet. Seeing this, her mother-in-law would scream aloud in fear. At this, the bride would reprimand the snakes and the pair would glide away soundlessly.

The mother and the daughter in-law would be sitting down to eat, when suddenly the guardian serpents would slither in and straightaway sip from the bride's bowl of dal. When the snakes would find out that it was not milk, they would start hissing angrily and Zohra would quickly get up, asking them to wait. The snakes would lower their hoods and lie down, and when Zohra brought them milk, they would drink it and disappear into the unknown.

Stiff with fear, her mother-in-law would feel the cooked rice shrivelling up into hard paddy grains inside her stomach.

Even this would have been bearable, but the snakes started pestering them so much that Zohra's husband was forced to escape to Kolkata to save himself.

In the dead of night, Arif's sleep would be broken by an ice-cold touch on his skin. Waking up, he would see right beside him the pair of lotus-cobras seeking shelter on his wife's breasts. He would scream and run out to sleep in the outermost part of the house. At Zohra's scolding, the snakes would go away, but soon they would come back and press themselves around her feet in mute supplication. Zohra's eyes would fill with tears and she would find herself unable to scold them again. Like a practised snake-charmer, she would pet them fearlessly and allow them to sleep beside her.

Within a year of Zohra's marriage, she had given birth to twins who died right away inside the lying-in room. Their faces were fresh in the canvas of Zohra's memory. Her famished maternal heart imagined that her own departed twins had come in a different guise to deceive her! She was surviving the pain of her children's death; even if the snakes bit her, this pain would be nothing compared to the agony of that loss. The love-starved young mother's heart and soul overflowed with affection and compassion; her fear vanished, and like one possessed, she cuddled the snake-children, put them to sleep, scolded them lovingly.

The husband fumed with helpless anger, but there was nothing he could do. He could not bridge the distance created by the raised hoods between himself and the wife he loved more than his own life. He died a thousand deaths from his fruitless rage.

His wife had brought them luck—he could not possibly get angry with her. How could he be angry, she had not committed any wrong.

One day, in a fit of rage, he told her, 'Zohra, I do not want this treasure if it means losing you! Let us kill those two! My poverty was so much more peaceful compared to this.'

With an unspoken plea in her tear-filled eyes, Zohra let her husband know her disapproval! 'They are my sons,' she said, 'they have not harmed anyone, they do not even know how to bite others!'

Arif became furious and said, 'They may not bite you, but I am dying from the sting of their venom! You will not be able to comprehend how much harm they have caused me! If they had bitten me instead, it would have been a far happier outcome than my present anguish!'

Zohra did not reply and silently wiped her tears! She really believed that her dead sons had come back to her in another form, but societal norms prevented her from admitting this aloud.

Her husband and in-laws finally decided that Zohra should be sent away to her father's house for a few days. Perhaps once she was there, she would forget about the serpents. Also, upon finding her gone, the pair of snakes would probably go away.

One morning, Arif's father called Zohra and told her, 'Ma, you have not visited your parent's home for a long time, and I have been wrong to turn down your father's requests a couple of times. Today Arif will take you, and you can go and spend some time there.'

Zohra understood everything, but she did not protest. She left, silently wiping away her tears. While leaving, she could not see the serpents anywhere.

After taking Zohra to her father's house, Arif went back to Kolkata to look after his business.

Zohra's parents had been used to seeing her unadorned. So, when she stepped into the house, golden-complexioned and decked in gold ornaments, her impoverished parents could not believe their eyes. Overwhelmed, they were unable to decide where to keep their daughter and son-in-law and how to treat them.

Within a day or two, however, Zohra's parents noticed that the smile on her face had vanished. She seemed to be always thinking about someone else. Even when she talked or was busy with work, her absent-mindedness became very apparent.

One day, her mother drew her aside and asked, 'Should I write a letter to Arif and ask him to come?'

Dying of embarrassment, Zohra exclaimed, 'No ma, he is coming this Saturday anyway!' The son-in-law came, but Zohra's former lustre did not return to her face.

Her mother asked her, 'Tell me the truth, Zohra, did you and Arif have a quarrel?'

Zohra smiled a pallid smile and said, 'No ma! He loves me as much as he did before! I am feeling sad because I have left my two sons behind at home.'

Zohra's mother did not know how her son-in-law had suddenly acquired an enormous fortune. She did know, though, about the death of her daughter's newborn twins, and how they had been laid to rest in the graveyard in front of the house in keeping with the family tradition. Assuming that Zohra was remembering her dead sons' graves, she wiped her eyes in secret and went back to her chores.

Six months passed by quickly. But no one talked about Zohra's return to her in-laws' house. She was frustrated and angry, more so than her parents. She could not fathom what her fault was. Her husband visited her every Saturday, but Zohra's hurt pride prevented her from asking him any questions.

Her mother, though, could not bear to stay silent for too long. One day, she said to her son-in-law, 'Baba, Zohra has almost stopped eating. I don't know if she has caught some disease—day by day, my daughter is withering away!'

On hearing this, Arif's heart seemed to skip a beat. He could not even imagine that a human being could love venomous serpents so obsessively. He began to doubt her sanity. Then, he suddenly remembered that Zohra's grandmother had been a renowned expert in the field of snakes. Maybe that same expertise had somehow been reborn in Zohra!

During these six months, Arif had made many visits to Rosulpur but had seen the snakes only a couple of times. But each time, they were no end of trouble to the family! It was painfully obvious to everyone that they were searching for Zohra!

The snakes had raised hoods and venomous fangs! Yet, how they slithered around in desperate supplication! The snakes would seem to throw themselves at Arif's feet, then his father's and then his mother's, but they would run away, scared for their lives!

Arif did not reveal any of these to Zohra, nor did she, in her hurt pride, ask him anything about the snakes.

When his son-in-law did not show any willingness to take Zohra back, her father told Arif, 'Baba, you well know how poor we are! My daughter has taken to bed! With such bad times falling upon the country, we can barely feed ourselves let alone arrange for our daughter's treatment! If she stays here, she will die without medical treatment, so it would be better if you take her back to your home or to Kolkata. Then, when she recovers, you can bring her back here again!' While saying this, his eyes filled with tears.

It was decided that the next day Arif would take Zohra to Kolkata and visit a doctor there; after she recovered a little, he would take her to Rosulpur.

3

That night, Arif woke up from sleep to an unfamiliar noise. The moment his eyes opened, he saw someone standing near his head with an unsheathed sword and another person—possibly a woman—in the next room, who had broken open Zohra's box and was stealing all her jewellery. Scared stiff, he lay motionless, pretending to be asleep. He felt as if his ability to shout aloud had been stolen from him.

Although he was terrified, he had a suspicion in his mind. That female robber! Opening his eyes a little, he tried to recognise her but pretended to be deeply asleep all the while.

The bedroom where he and Zohra slept had a small room adjacent to it. In that room there was a steel trunk containing Zohra's ornaments—ornaments worth almost twenty thousand rupees!

Zohra had pleaded with him several times to take the ornaments back to Rosulpur, but Arif never paid heed to her requests. He would say, 'Your luck has brought us so much wealth and gold, if ornaments of this much value get stolen, let it be so; at least you cannot be stolen. These are yours, so you should keep them with you! Besides, your father is a pir of this area, no one would dare to rob his house!'

Arif could not believe his eyes when he realised that the female robber was none other than his mother-in-law—Zohra's mother.

A storm that raged two days ago had blown away some of the straw in the thatched roof, and through the gap the rays of the waxing moon of Shukla dwadashi[4] entered the room. The moonlight fell directly on his mother-in-law when she turned to leave, after tying up all the ornaments in a bundle. Arif could clearly see the face of the one person he had respected even more than his own mother. The darkness of the no-moon night descended on his face, in his eyes, inside his mind.

How ugly is this world!

He did not utter a word. Using all his willpower, he controlled himself. The sword-carrying robber followed his mother-in-law out of the room. When they went down to the courtyard, he rose up and saw through the window that the other robber was none other than his own father-in-law.

Arif was aware that in the past months, his father-in-law's financial condition had worsened considerably. The entire country, too, was in the grip of a near famine. He somehow knew that sometimes his father-in-law had to pawn household utensils to buy food. So, he offered to lend some money to his father-in-law, who refused to accept it from him. Even when Arif had given money to Zohra to give to her parents, he had seen his father-in-law unwilling to accept it.

Frail and listless, Zohra was slumbering deeply. Arif did not wake her up, but fear, disgust and anger made him unable to get back to sleep. When he finally fell asleep it was almost morning, but he was soon awakened by the sound of someone crying. His mother-in-law was wailing loudly that robbers had left them destitute. The noise woke Zohra up. She hurriedly got up and looked around in mute astonishment. Arif could not stand it anymore. With daylight, his fears had also vanished. Coming out of the room, he spoke loudly, 'Don't cry any more, ma, I know who has stolen those ornaments. If I want, I can get them right now.'

Needless to say, his mother-in-law stopped crying immediately. She and her husband kept looking at each other in dismay. Arif was about to go out, when his father-in-law caught his hand and asked, 'Who is the thief, baba? Have you seen? Really seen him?'

Arif smiled contemptuously and replied, 'Ji yes, I did. Since this is Kaliyuga, everything has turned upside down. The person who has

[4] The twelfth lunar day of Shukla paksha.

been robbed should catch hold of the thief's hand, but now it is the thief who is holding the hand of the robbed.'

Looking anguished, his father-in-law released his hand.

Arif called Zohra and narrated the night's events to her, and he also seemed to insinuate that she had been involved in the plan! Zohra blacked out! When she regained consciousness, Arif told her that he would be leaving immediately. He would not stay a moment more in this hell. It was as if Arif's in-laws had been turned to stone; even when Zohra fainted, it was Arif who tried to revive her. Her parents had not come forward to help. The moment Arif was preparing to leave, Zohra fell at his feet, crying out, 'Please take me along with you, don't leave me here. Khoda knows, I swear on your life, I have not committed any crime.'

At Zohra's tearful entreaties, Arif agreed to take her to Kolkata with him. Obeying his instructions, Zohra did not ask her parents any further questions.

4

When they were leaving, Zohra's parents began to cry, holding their hands. They pleaded that they should not leave with an empty stomach—that they should eat at least something before leaving. Arif was feeling suffocated, as if there was a putrid smell in the very air of this house! Yet he agreed to eat something before leaving, just so that he could see the limits of human hypocrisy. The more Zohra vowed that she would not touch a drop of water in this house, the more Arif insisted that he would not leave without eating.

Zohra kept her vow and did not eat anything. Arif, however, started vomiting minutes after eating. Zohra fainted again. Before losing consciousness, she looked at her mother and uttered one word, 'Rakshasi!'

Arif did not fail to understand exactly what he had eaten! But he could not let himself die by simply staying there! He needed to narrate the history of his death to his parents. He desperately began to run towards the railway station.

On reaching the station, he began to vomit blood and somehow clambered onto a train that had just started to move. The station master ran after him shouting at the top of his voice, but he had no time to listen to his warning. Inside the compartment, a suit-clad Bengali gentleman yelled at him, 'This is a first-class compartment, get down, get down!'

Before Arif could give a reply, he started vomiting blood again. By divine coincidence, the Bengali sahib turned out to be a renowned doctor from Kolkata. Arif was able to speak in a feeble voice, 'They have poisoned me, my . . .'

Then he lost consciousness and fell down. The doctor sahib had gone to see a patient 'on call'—a rich zamindar who lived in a mofussil town. So, he had his medicine kit with him. He immediately called his attendant from the servants' compartment and, with his help, made Arif lie down properly. Then he checked his pulse and gave him an injection. After two or three injections, the patient began to feel better. His vomiting stopped. The doctor had decided against stopping the train because any delay would have made it impossible to save this unfortunate man. When the train reached Kolkata, the doctor put Arif in an ambulance and sent him to a hospital.

Zohra was indeed the harbinger of good luck, because Arif had a narrow escape from death.

Back in Kutubpur, when Zohra regained consciousness and heard that her husband had left, she started howling like a madwoman. Falling to her father's feet, she kept insisting she should be sent to her in-laws' house. The neighbours who had gathered around could not understand what was going on, and they kept asking question after question in bewilderment.

Zohra's parents explained to their neighbours that all of Zohra's ornaments had been stolen the night before which had driven her crazy, and that their son-in-law had gone to the police station to file a complaint.

The crowd moved away, suppressing their curiosity because they feared the curses of the pir.

5

After three days and three nights, when Zohra refused to take even a drop of water, her father sent her back to Rosulpur in a palanquin; and then went on a pilgrimage to Mecca to reclaim some virtue. On the same day, Arif also returned home from the hospital in Kolkata in a motor car!

Surprisingly, after he came home, Arif did not say anything to his parents! He had been thinking over things during the past three days as he battled death. If his father knew about it, he would surely rush over to kill his in-laws. That would be the end of his in-laws, but he was afraid he would also lose his father. Eventually, Zohra would also take her own life!

Zohra! Zohra! These five letters seemed to contain the world's entire store of honey! When he was in the clutches of death, he had promised himself that he would not blame anyone except providence. Neither in front of others, nor within himself!

Zohra still didn't know that he had come back home alive. And whom would he accuse as offenders? They were the closest relations of his beloved! Coming back from the brink of death seemed like a rebirth. It was as if this was a new life! The touch of death had turned him into gold.

On seeing Arif's face, his parents exclaimed, 'Oh my goodness, why have you turned so blue? What has happened to you?'

Asif calmly replied, 'I had cholera, Asiatic cholera. It is enough that I have survived, that's all.'

His parents started crying, embracing him closely. They donated money to a hundred poor villagers and performed other acts of charity. In the evening, they arranged for a Maulood Sharif[5] in their house.

The sun had not yet set when the palanquin bearing Zohra stopped in front of the house. She got down from the palanquin with a pallid, deathly face and, seeing Arif in front of her, fell to his feet, crying loudly, 'Oh you are alive! You have returned alive!'

Saying this, she collapsed. With the help of his parents, Arif lifted her up and carried her inside. When she came to and felt a bit better, Arif's parents started crying, 'Have both of you returned from the jaws of death?'

His mother sobbed, 'Who has done this to my golden idol?'

---

[5] A Muslim ceremony in honour of Prophet Mohammad, consisting of recitations from the Quran and prayers.

Arif drew Zohra aside and told her everything. Zohra laid her head on his feet, and cried, 'No, no, you must punish me! All of you must hate me, hit me!'

Arif bit Zohra's lip and told her, 'Take this, this is your punishment!'

6

Even in the midst of this storm of trouble and sorrow, Zohra had not forgotten her lotus-cobras. For so many days, she had tried not to think about them, just as she tried not to think about her dead sons! But was it the same as forgetting them? The slow-burning fire and the poison inside her had pushed her to the door of death! She constantly thought of herself as a snake-charmer, as the daughter of a snake-charmer! Awake or asleep, she dreamt only of serpents. She imagined that her husband was the lord of the Land of Serpents, and she was Snake-Mother, Queen of Snakes!

When she did not ask anyone about the snakes since her return, her in-laws heaved a sigh of relief, thinking that the bride had perhaps forgotten about them.

Late at night, Zohra had a dream: she saw her dead sons come and tell her, 'O ma! we are so hungry, you have not given us milk for so many days! We are lying in the grave; we cannot get up anymore. A little milk! Ma, a little milk! We're very hungry!' Screaming and sobbing, 'My son! My sons!', Zohra woke up. She saw that her husband was still asleep. She lit a lamp and started to look around. But there was nobody there.

Tonight, she is a madwoman! She is a bereaved mother, she is a mother who has lost her sons; her lost sons are calling her, they have not eaten anything for six months!

Like an insane woman, she opened the door and went out. Right in front of the house was the graveyard of the Mir family. Holding a feeble lamp, the deranged mother went and stood near the two graves. Two small graves side by side, like twins lying in each other's embrace. At the head of the graves, there were two krishnachura trees that Zohra had planted with her own hands. They were in bloom. The graves were covered with their blood-red flowers. The mother cried out with a loud sob, 'Oh my sons, my sons! Who has given you so many flowers my dear? My sons!'

Whether she fell down in a faint or whether sleep overcame her while she was crying, clutching onto the graves, she did not know—but when Zohra awoke, she instantly noticed the pair of lotus-cobras lying curled up on her chest. Like a maniac, Zohra shouted, 'Sons, my sons, so you have come! You remembered your ma!' Zohra passionately embraced the serpents to her chest, and the pair of snakes also coiled around her neck and arms like a necklace.

By that time, it was dawn.

Zohra noticed that the lotus-cobras no longer had their earlier milk-white appearance—they had become somewhat thin and pallid. They were repeatedly flicking their tongues in and out, as if reminding Zohra of their hunger and thirst—Ma dear, we're so hungry! You were not here, who would feed us? A little milk! We are very hungry, ma, very hungry!

Hugging them to her chest, Zohra went inside the house. No one else was awake as yet.

Entering the kitchen, she saw a big cooking pot full of milk. The moment she put down two bowls of milk, the famished snakes leapt towards the bowls as if they had been starving for ages and drank up the milk! Tears streamed down Zohra's eyes.

When her mother-in-law woke up and saw what Zohra had done, she stood dumbfounded. The moment she realised Zohra had noticed her, she exclaimed, 'Oh dear, what will happen now? Where have these pests been for the last six months? They must have sniffed the smell of your body and came over immediately!'

Zohra replied in a deeply hurt voice, 'God forbid, why will they be pests? They are my sons!'

Her mother-in-law did not understand what Zohra really meant, but she laughed and said, 'They really are your sons! After you left, I gave them milk a couple of times. You will be surprised to hear this, they did not even touch the milk! They just went away! Snakes also recognise humans! What stranger things will we see in this Kaliyuga!'

By this time, the snakes had gorged themselves on the milk and were lying down at Zohra's feet motionless.

7

Later in the day towards late evening, one of the housemaids suddenly screamed, 'Oh ma! A ghost is after me! The king of the djinns! A ghost djinn!' She fainted immediately. There was a huge hue and cry all over the house.

This happened in the middle of a conversation Arif's mother was having with her son. 'Why didn't you tell me,' she had asked Arif, 'that our bahu is pregnant again? She is having labour pains!'

Arif had replied, 'But it is not yet time for her to get labour pains, it has been only seven months.' Right after he had said those words, he heard the maid shouting, 'Ghost! Ghost! A very long-bearded ghost!' and the hullaballoo that followed!

All the housemaids and servants swore that they had seen it with their own eyes—a living ghost! So tall that his head touched the skies! Standing under the mango tree inside the house compound!

Arif and his mother came out with lanterns. It was true, there was somebody standing under the tree like a ghost. Right behind them, Zohra had also come out to see the ghost, but nobody had noticed her.

Suddenly the ghost yelled, 'O baap! Snakes are biting me!'

Zohra shouted, 'Baba, it's you!'

Arif's mother exclaimed, 'What! it's our beyai?'[6]

By this time, Zohra was screaming, 'It's really a ghost! Not my baba! He can't be my baba, he's a ghost! Beat him up! Beat him up and throw him out!'

All of a sudden, she could hear the ghost beating someone mercilessly with a sturdy stick, and shouting, 'Oh my baap! Snakes are biting me! I am being bitten by snakes!'

Like a madwoman, Zohra snatched the lantern from her mother-in-law's hand and rushed forward, crying, 'Oh, he's killing my sons! Catch him! Catch him!'

Everyone followed Zohra and rushed towards the mango tree and when they reached there, they saw that the ghost was none other than Zohra's own father. The pair of baastu-saap were biting him furiously and he was hitting them back even more furiously.

---

[6] The father-in-law of one's son/daughter.

Zohra cried out 'My sons!' and then again, 'Baba!' and blacked out.

When Zohra regained consciousness, she called Arif. When everyone moved away, she asked him, 'Where are my sons? My lotus-cobras? My baba?'

Arif broke down into sobs, 'Zohra! Zohra!! Nobody's left! Everything's gone! They are all gone! Your baba died from the bites of the lotus-cobras! Your mother died of cholera! They were going to Mecca. Your ma died while on the road, and your repentant baba came to have a last look at you in secret. Perhaps he would have also gone away secretly. But suddenly the maid spotted him and screamed out, "Ghost!" At the very moment, your cobras chased and attacked him!'

Breasts heaving, Zohra breathlessly said, 'Serves them right, they have gone to hell! Good! Now tell me, where are my lotus-cobras—my sons?'

Arif said, 'Your baba has killed them.'

Exclaiming, 'What! my sons are no more!' she lost consciousness again!

By the time it was dawn, the news spread all around the village that the golden bride of the Mir family had passed away after giving birth to a pair of dead serpents.

SIXTEEN

THE KING OF THE DJINNS

Translated by Saurav Dasthakur

1

On the bank of the river Arial Khan in the district of Faridpur, there stood a small hamlet called Mohanpur. Most of the villagers were Muslim farmers. On the edge of the village, at a distance from them, lived a few Kayastha[1] families. They kept apart as if to save themselves from the impurity of the Muslim touch.

Just as the black tassel on the Turkish fez wishes to live amicably with the holy tuft of hair worn by Hindu brahmins, but never receives any respect from them, the attempts of the Muslims in the village to make friends with the Kayasthas were always rebuffed, for the latter looked suspiciously at them as if they were scared of the approach of evil spirits.

Among the Muslims of the village, Chunnu Byapari was a man of influence. He was a headman, but that did not stop him from toiling hard on his land. He was helped by his three wives and seven sons. Only he knew what stood in his way of attaining sunnat[2] by taking one more wife. The village-folk of course would gossip among themselves that his third missus was a shrew with a dreadful temper, and that it was because of her menacing verbal armoury that the prospective fourth wife could not make it into the Byapari household. This upset Chunnu Byapari terribly. He would often grumble to his friends, 'This is what you call—Khoda proposes but man disposes! Indeed, Allah

---

[1] Kayastha represents a high-caste Hindu community whose profession is mainly related to writing—writer, accountant, clerk, et cetera.

[2] The way of life including deeds and customs followed by Muslims; marrying more than one wife is practically non-existent nowadays.

Miyan has commanded you to take four wives, hasn't He! But what can you do when fate conspires against you!' Stopping for a moment and swallowing, he would say, 'Marrying that evil woman was my undoing!' And then he would hastily add, 'Now, don't you go and tell her all this. That deadly little bitch would raise a ruckus and make my life hell.'

It is the third offspring of this third wife, Allah-Rakha, who is the hero of our story. And like the heroes of stories, he was a dreadful daredevil of a boy. He was of course known in the village by the soft sobriquet 'Keshranjan babu'. This name was given to him by a girl in the village, Chan Bhanu, that is, Chand Bhanu.[3] More on this later.

When Chunnu Byapari's third wife was blessed with a son after giving birth to two daughters, the wary mother christened him 'Allah-Rakha' (one who is protected by Allah). At least the mother, if not anybody else, was relieved of her worries by entrusting Allah with the responsibility of protecting the child from untimely demise. Allah perhaps had a good hearty laugh that day. He had transported many such Allah-Rakhas to graveyards, but in this case He seemed to have cracked a joke by keeping him alive indeed! He said to Himself, 'Wait, I'll make sure he lives on, but the rest of you will burn alive!'

I have no idea if he would die later, but in these twenty years the village-folk have had the misfortune of seeing him alive and kicking. Exasperated with the eagerness with which he gave them ample proof of his existence, they would say—the rascal had better been a mamdo-ghost[4] than Allah-Rakha. Even ghosts couldn't be this devilish.

The Muslims would refer to him as 'son of Iblish'[5] and the Kayasthas, 'the new moon monster!' His father would call him 'son of a bitch', and the doting mother 'Aflatoon'—the charming master maverick!

Now let me introduce Chan Bhanu, the girl who named him 'Keshranjan babu'. She was the daughter of Narad Ali Sheikh, of the same village. Now the name Narad Ali was not meant to signify

[3] 'Chand' is the Bangla word for moon. In the villages the final sound (in this case 'd') is often dropped during the pronunciation of words with final nasal syllables. Hence, 'Chand' is pronounced 'Chan'.

[4] A Muslim ghost.

[5] Satan.

Hindu–Muslim unity[6], for he had been named way before the surge of the Non-Cooperation Movement. The movement was a mere toddler of the height of his knee; I choose not to say, 'the left knee', for that would be exaggeratingly diminutive.

One would, however, still come across quite a few people with names like Narad Ali, Sheikh Ramchandra, Sita Bibi and the like in villages! I am not sure though, if there are names too like Hanumanulla, Bishnu Hossain and all.

Though not a man of high standing in the village, Narad Ali was by no means a poor fellow. His days were spent living quite easily off the produce of his land. Neither would he borrow, nor lend.

Quite a peaceful man he was! But he was not quite comfortable with the mock quarrels his wife would often make, just to have a hearty laugh at the expense of the unsuspecting man. She was a trickster of a woman who liked to provoke people. Failing to get the drift of her tricks, her opponent would fly into a rage and she would keep up the squabbling game for a while, until all of a sudden she would put a basket upside down at the centre of the yard, as if to hush up the subject by shoving it under the basket. Then she would blurt out, 'Let our spat lie here under the basket for now, I have to go have my bellyful, and then you'll see the fun! In the meantime, the one who removes the basket, will have to endure what Allah has ordained for her—a nikah with her husband's elder brother.' The dramatic way she would secure the basket in the yard and say the words would make the person who was quarrelling with her, along with the fun-seeking onlookers, break into laughter! The opponent's fury, though, would not calm down in the process.

Their only child was Chan Bhanu, named by the adoring mother after the heroine of a kissa from a punthi[7] to which she had once listened.

Chan Bhanu was almost a slightly modified and enlarged version of her mother! She was a chatterbox, would scamper around like a hare on village paths and fields, and fearing her, the waters of the river Arial Khan would flow swiftly away.

---

[6] Narad is a Hindu name and Ali is a Muslim surname.

[7] Literally a book, but more specifically a type of manuscript in circulation in eighteenth and nineteenth century Bengal, often read out to illiterate rural listeners.

She had crossed fourteen, but the mother refused to discuss her marriage even if the father would try to broach the subject. How will we survive in a joyless hell when Chan leaves, said she. If Narad Ali persisted, his wife just snubbed him, 'Don't be a pest, my daughter won't marry till her Hanif[8] arrives—like he did for Joigun Bibi in the kissa!'

The prince-charming 'Hanif' did not take long to arrive for the Joigun Bibi of Mohanpur, Chan Bhanu; and he was none other than our Allah-Rakha.

One fine morning while reading the punthi of Sonabhan, it occurred to Allah-Rakha that it was Chan Bhanu who was the Sonabhan Bibi of the story and he himself was Gaji Hanif, for there was no girl more beautiful than Chan Bhanu in the whole village. He continued reading while contemplating Hanif's triumphal march towards the conquest of Sonabhan—

When the Bibi heard Hanif's arrival sound,
She gorged on a breakfast of around eighty maund!
With a thousand-maund shield and the courage of a lac,
On twelve horses together, she roared, 'I'll break your back!'

Baap re! This lady is Hanif's nemesis! She crams a breakfast of eighty maunds and rides twelve horses together! Will Chan Bhanu do anything like that? Allah-Rakha was totally flabbergasted. Hanif initially kept losing, but he won the jackpot at the end of it all, didn't he! Let there be whatever there is to be!

Parting his curly mane by combing once through the middle and once each through both sides of the head, applying Keshranjan[9] oil to his hair, massaging some on his body and even sprinkling some on his shirt and stuffing a few paans into his mouth, Allah-Rakha ventured out to conquer his Sonabhan, alias Chan Bhanu.

It should be mentioned here that our Allah-Rakha grew into as modern a cad as one could be by reading books. He would not exactly live like a farmer's son. Putting on a clean dhoti, shirt and shoes and

---

[8] In Arabic, Hanif means a true believer or a righteous man.

[9] There actually existed a brand of hair oil called 'Keshranjan tel' ('kesh', 'ranjan' and 'tel' being Bangla words for 'hair', 'pleasing' and 'oil' respectively). 'Ranjan' is also a popular suffix in modern Hindu names for men.

neatly parting his long hair, he would loaf around on the village paths chewing paan, smoking cigarettes and devising ingenious plans of playing mischief upon people. However, in spite of having long crossed the 'frontier' of adolescence and attaining manhood, he never did any harm to women. His targets were mostly old people; fruits and crops in fields and around homesteads; the topmost branches of trees and the highest points of thatched roofs; and bamboo groves, tamarind and palm trees and so on during night-time.

He didn't contribute much to his father's farming activities except by beating the oxen for no reason or by letting the oxen loose, which made people swear at his father. He went to look after the crop twice in his life—once he set fire to the ripened paddy, and the other time he harvested the crop only to leave it on somebody else's land. Never again did his father ask for his assistance.

When his mother stopped shelling out money to meet the expenses of his foppishness, and his father, when asked for the same, chose to settle the accounts with an entirely different coin by giving him quite a few lashes on his back with the cattle-truncheon, he neither cried or fled from home, nor did he complain to anybody.

That night Chunnu Byapari's house caught fire. Allah-Rakha lit his cigarette in that fire and said, blowing out smoke in a quite unperturbed manner, that he didn't have the money to buy a matchbox that day; and it was sheer good luck that their house had caught fire and he could light his cigarette for free.

When his father was beating him black and blue, he stood quiet and still and said that he had set fire to the house only to warm up his body that ached terribly because of the thrashing he had received in the morning. If the fresh night-flogging caused him much body ache again, he would have no other choice but to set fire to somebody else's house in the neighbourhood to ease that ache.

This simple submission dried up all the smacking energy that still remained in his father's arms. He kept striking his head violently at his son's feet and saying repeatedly, 'I implore you, you filthy rogue, you son of a bitch, please don't do that one thing! We all will go to jail if you do!'

Finally, an agreement was reached that night through the mediation of the village people to the effect that his father would keep bearing the cost of Allah-Rakha's dandyism, at least for the sake of the village's safety. Allah-Rakha declared with due solemnity, 'I am my baap's son, what I say I never fail to do!'

Everybody laughed, and the father whose son he was broke into tears of anger and distress. Kicking his son to the ground he shouted at the top of his voice, 'Listen to what the son of a bitch says! The son of a bitch says, like baap like son! I piss in your baap's mouth!' This time even Allah-Rakha couldn't help but laugh!

Well, to get back to the point. Allah-Rakha entered Narad Ali's courtyard unhesitatingly, all decked up and bellowed, 'Narad fufa,[10] are you home?' The three people inside the house were startled to hear that familiar voice.

Chan's mother exclaimed, 'That wicked fiend has come!'

Chan Bhanu, at that point of time, was seated in the veranda and was busy making the best use of a heap of ripe karamchas by mashing the sour fruits with salt and green chillies, and savouring the mix with a slurping noise of complete contentment made with the tongue and the palate. She rolled her large eyes a couple of times, and casting a sidelong glance at Allah-Rakha's tripartite hair arrangement screamed, 'Keshranjan babu is here, please bring the cot out!' Then she spoke in a musical tone,

> Here's the cot, come O! friend, sit,
> There's the river-ghat, go wash your feet,
> I'll break your back with a thick wooden slat!

After the recital, she started giggling and ran away into the inner quarters of the house

Allah-Rakha was not quite prepared for this sort of a dramatic welcome. He took to his heels instantly. This was the first defeat in the life of the Hanif of Mohanpur!

Narrated by Chan Bhanu's mother and then through word of mouth, the story spread across the entire village. From then on, on seeing Allah-Rakha, everybody, girls in particular, would say, 'Look, there comes Keshranjan babu.'

It was Chan Bhanu who affronted Allah-Rakha, but it was the village people who paid for it. Allah-Rakha had drawn a bunch of village boys to himself through a constant supply of paans and cigarettes and

---

[10] Husband of the paternal aunt.

trained them almost to perfection. The boys placed at the doorstep of every household at night, a generous amount of a substance whose very sight—let alone smell—would induce terrible nausea!

Even a prolonged and intense research by the village-folk failed to yield how so many cholera patients came to grace their village together in a single night. Nor did they have any idea that eating tamarind leaves caused severe indigestion. It was not that challenging to figure out the chemical composition of the innovative concoction of cow dung, 'human-dung', filthy muck and gandal leaves, but how the hell did tamarind leaves feature in that mixture?

But it did not take them long to resolve the mystery, for they soon discovered that even though removing all the other components was not very difficult, tamarind leaves stuck stubbornly to the doorstep! When, after a lot of importunate hard work went in vain and they succeeded in getting rid of the tamarind leaves finally by shovelling some of the doorstep soil out of the mud floor, everybody said in agreement—no, this bloke is really gifted! They became aware of the gravitational pull of tamarind leaves from that day on!

Only one household in the whole village escaped the wrath of this demon that day—Chan Bhanu's house. The girl and her mother did not fail to realise why Allah-Rakha, who did not even spare his own house, chose to ignore Chan Bhanu's—an awful grudge against whom was the driving force behind his handiwork!

As if he wanted to put across the message, 'You saw my prowess, didn't you! I could easily avenge your insult had I wished to, but chose not to! I forgave you.'

Contemplating the subject the next morning, Chan Bhanu suddenly broke into tears! Her bright, full-moon-like silvery face assumed the reddish hue of the rising new moon of the dark fortnight. Seeing the daughter cry, her mother felt jittery and said, 'Why are you crying Chan? Has your baap scolded you?'

Being an only child, Chan Bhanu was showered with affection and she was also quite touchy. Her mother had assumed that before leaving for the field her father had scolded her for some reason.

What Chan said amidst a more intense bout of sobbing was this—by making an exception of them while everyone else was a victim of his prank, Allah-Rakha wished to convey to them that they were not worth his notice; that they could be forgiven! She would have much rather preferred a direct affront.

Her mother consoled her and tried to explain to her that the whole thing was triggered by the welcome he had been given the previous day. Chan Bhanu, however, didn't regain her composure. Allah-Rakha stuck to her mind like an itchy thorn in the flesh.

Like Hanif, Allah-Rakha was an expert archer. His first arrow had hit the bull's eye.

That day while Chan Bhanu was going to bathe in the Arial Khan, Allah-Rakha rejoiced in triumph seeing her sad gloomy face, even as he felt a slight prick in the chest. Ah! Her face looked so joyless! No. Chan Bhanu was no less an archer than Sonabhan. Her invisible arrow had also hit the target bang on.

When her eyes met Allah-Rakha's however, the glum Chan Bhanu felt like breaking into a smile. She was not at all prepared for this smile. Such a devil with such an innocent, desolate face, that would tickle even a dead man!

But even as she laughed, her face reddened in bashfulness. What if Allah-Rakha reads this smile differently, she thought. Chhi! Chhi! What a shame! How awful!

But Chan Bhanu didn't have to carry the burden of this awkwardness for long. No sooner had the knife of her smile showed a hint of its glitter, than Allah-Rakha turned his back promptly on her. He apprehended that the lightning flash of that smile would immediately be followed by the crash of a massive thunderbolt. Right before Chan's eyes, Allah-Rakha swiftly scaled a huge, ancient peepal tree and perched right on its topmost branch. What a daredevil! Everybody said venomous snakes lived on the tree! If he gets bitten by one, if he crashes down along with a broken branch! Chan Bhanu briefly observed his acts of daredevilry before making her way down the river ghat even as she was thinking all this.

Immediately after she had waded into the river, she thought, chhi, chhi! What had she done! Why the hell did she watch the monkey for so long, standing rooted there! His audacity would cross all limits now with such indulgence! God knows what he is thinking right at this moment!

Swimming lost its charm for Chan Bhanu that day. The waters of the Arial Khan were also very relieved at not being disturbed as usual! Standing still in neck-deep water, Chan Bhanu was lost in her thoughts.

Since early morning till noontime, only one riddle had been troubling her all day—why had Allah-Rakha visited their place in such an odd manner yesterday! He usually keeps away from households, never setting his foot in the inner yards. And then, why was he staring at her with such a strange gaze! Besides, why did he choose to avenge her insult on the entire village, save herself? He was not just a monkey, perhaps crazy as well!

While she was engrossed in this train of thoughts, it suddenly occurred to her that he was watching her from the top of the peepal tree. The tree was quite far away. But still, she clearly saw that he had left the branch on the other side of the tree and was perching on one that was nearer to the river; he was staring at her with a fixed gaze. What a nuisance! Chan Bhanu felt like she would never again be able to come out of the river! She had seen him in close proximity several times earlier and had swum in the river before his eyes too, but never before did she experience this bashfulness, or this trepidation. At what inauspicious moment had he stepped into their yard last evening!

This was like a nor'wester cloud—you are as fascinated by it as you are scared of it.

But Allah-Rakha relieved her of this unease this time around too. Chan Bhanu saw him climbing down the tree trunk.

Now she was really pissed off with the rascal. What did he think! Did he think that she could not finish her bath and leave with him seated on the tree-branch? That's why he chose to oblige her by climbing down the tree? Did he think that Chan Bhanu would not be able to go to the river if he stood on her way? And was that the reason he left? Chan was seething with anger. No matter how scary a rogue he was, she would show him that she didn't give a fig about him. Her body was burning in rage under the water. Finishing her bath quickly, she walked home very fast. Should she come across him on her way back, she would show him how she could whiz past him right under his nose! She didn't even count him as a human being.

But nowhere did she even catch a glimpse of Keshranjan babu! The same insult, the same generosity, again? Chan hated him—hated him from the bottom of her heart. But what was this, was it because she didn't get an opportunity to give him a piece of her mind that she felt suddenly so dejected? Why was it that she felt so miserable just because she couldn't get a glimpse of him on her way back home? Why did her feet feel so drained of vigour? What happened to her? Was she possessed by an evil spirit?

The arrows of the god of five arrows[11] are perhaps daubed with some deadly poison, like that of the cobra. As soon as the arrow strikes, the poison spreads through the whole body and reaches the head. Or else Chan's condition wouldn't have been this wretched within these few hours! She could not throw him out of her mind, yet to remember him filled her with a burning, insufferable wrath.

For the first time in her life Chan Bhanu didn't have any appetite for food. Her mother was worried. She now realised why after a certain age unmarried girls started attracting evil spirits. She wept secretly and said to herself, 'Ghosts have cast upon you an evil glance, my girl! I cannot hold you back any longer, soon you will be out of bounds!'

Narad Ali was taken aback when his wife asked him to look for a groom for their daughter. They did not exchange another word on the subject, but a couple of teardrops rolled down their cheeks silently.

2

Chan Bhanu's wedding date was fixed. It was just a month away. The groom was the son of Chheraz Halder from the adjoining village.

The Hanif of Mohanpur, our Allah-Rakha and Chan Bhanu's Keshranjan babu, became desperate at this news. It was time to strike the final blow and clinch the deal. He had to have Chan Bhanu, by any means. He knew that her parents were dead set against her match with him. So there was no point in proposing a marriage. He was at that time totally smitten by the story of Joigun and Sonabhan. He would just carry Chan off and run away to some other land! But the problem with this last idea was that Chan Bhanu had to give her consent. How could he possibly get her consent?

As many as ten days passed, but no such chance offered itself. It was on the eleventh day that Allah probably cast a fortuitous glance at Allah-Rakha.

---

[11] Madan, or Kamadeva, the Hindu deity of human love and desire

In the meanwhile, he happened to come across Chan Bhanu several times, but on none of these occasions could he look up at her eyes more than once. Why would the one who the entire village was terrified of be afraid of this tiny little girl, was something that beat Allah-Rakha completely. But time was fast running out, and there was no room for diffidence any more. He hatched many plans, but there was no way he could execute even one.

But finally, Allah probably became kind to him.

One evening when Chan Bhanu went to the river, the ghat was absolutely desolate. As soon as she dipped the pitcher into the water, the face of an evil water-spirit that looked like an earthen pot popped up a little distance away, and spoke in a nasal voice, 'If you marry anybody other than Allah-Rakha, I'll break the necks of both you and your groom at your wedding night and drink your blood.' Hearing that bizarre voice and seeing that frightful face, Chan Bhanu let out a shriek, 'oh ma!', and passed out immediately! Considering this an opportune moment, the water-spirit came out of hiding, threw away the peculiarly painted earthen pot into the river and carried Chan Bhanu off to the bank. The water-spirit was none other than our man with a fertile imagination, Allah-Rakha alias Keshranjan babu!

On regaining consciousness, when she found herself on Allah-Rakha's lap, Chan Bhanu leapt to her feet and exclaimed, 'Where did you come from?' She was trembling like a falling bamboo-leaf.

Allah-Rakha replied, 'I was just passing by and saw somebody floating in the river, so I ran down and jumped in. And then I found it was you! Allah, O Allah! I must have been brought here by some divine spirit, or else nobody knows what would have happened! What happened to you?'

Chan Bhanu stared at Allah-Rakha's face with tears of gratitude welling up in her eyes! Then she narrated the whole story save the words of the water-spirit ...

When Allah-Rakha accompanied Chan Bhanu home and told them everything, they raised an uproar. Her parents blessed him with teary eyes. In response, all Allah-Rakha did was to smile at Chanu Bhanu and tease her, 'Why, how about breaking your Keshranjan babu's back now with a wooden slat?'

All of a sudden, huge waves of happiness rose and fell in Chan Bhanu's breast. In the gust of happiness her tongue slipped, 'I sure will, if the day comes by Khoda's grace!' Immediately a coyness overtook her, and she wished to hide her face in the ground beneath her feet and make herself invisible. Those words were certainly not unintelligible to Allah-Rakha! But Khoda would not bless her with the gift of such a day. In another score of days, she was going to the Halder family as a bride. What a stupid thing to do! Running off into her room she threw herself prostrate onto her bed. She felt like wailing aloud.

Allah-Rakha also vanished at that very moment. Chan Bhanu's parents, thoroughly puzzled, were staring at each other. What happened! What did all this mean?

Allah-Rakha sprinted down to the riverbank, beside himself with joy. The nearly full moon was rising, illuminating the horizon. Allah-Rakha thought it was not the moon, but Chan Bhanu herself, who had filled his heart's firmament with an ethereal glow!

He sat on the riverbank till ten at night and sang at the top of his voice. Then returning home, he went to think—it could not be the vision of the water-spirit alone, Chan must have reported his words to her parents too. May be they would call off the marriage and visit his parents the next day to propose a match. And if they wouldn't do that, and she would never go to the river again, the land ghost was still there to take care of things.

But when nothing of that sort happened even after two days had passed, it was clear to Allah-Rakha that because of her shyness or some other reason, Chan Bhanu did not tell her parents about the water-spirit's decree. Had she done so they would not be able to initiate the marriage rituals in such a carefree manner. Failure made him insanely furious. Delaying his plan any further would make to lose everything, so it was time the ghosts conveyed the message directly to her parents! In the wee hours that night, Narad Ali's family woke up startled by an eerie howling sound! It was like somebody was wailing plaintively out in their yard. Narad Ali thought his neighbour Sobhan had beaten his wife again and the woman was crying outside. Still he called out asking 'Who cries there; is it you Badna's ma?' There was no response even as the howling went on unabated.

Narad Ali went out with the kerosene lamp in his hand and instantly sprinted back inside, letting out a shrill scream, 'O Allah!' He bolted the door tightly. Chan's ma asked in a trembling voice, 'What happened! Who's that?' Narad Ali didn't reply; shaking violently like a malaria patient running a temperature of a 105 degrees he kept blowing on his own chest while reciting 'kulhuallah'.[12] He was so scared that even the hair on his head stood erect like the protruding spines of a porcupine. The more he huffed and puffed in mortal fear, the more he recited 'tauba astagfar'[13] and tried to take Allah's name. But he was so horrified that while saying Allah's name every time his tongue twisted at the first 'l'.

Chan Bhanu had woken up by then, but scared out of her wits she clung to the bed half-dead!

After a long time Narad Ali somewhat came back to his senses and said, 'Allah re Allah! (Now touching his nose and ear) Tauba astagfarulla! Tauba Tauba! Auzbilla[14] (not nauzbilla![15]) Bismillah! Arre I went out and saw an old man as tall as a palm tree standing with a turban on his head. His beard must be fifteen feet long! Allah re Allah! It's none other than the king of the djinns who came to our house!'

Hearing all this both Chan and her mother were on the verge of blacking out. Nobody even dared to check if the alleged old king of the djinns was still there in the courtyard. Their voices grew too feeble to call out to the neighbours for help; somebody seemed to have throttled them! Also, what if the king of the djinns took offence if they started calling the neighbours! That would be like inviting disaster! The three of them lit lamps and kept praying to Allah, all the time shuddering in fear!

That night the king of the djinns didn't trouble them any further. Moving slowly into the nearby mango grove, he made some gestures and three or four more apparitions, strange in appearance came out. They took off the garb and garments of the king of the djinns.

The garb included one very long and one short bamboo stick tied across each other; an earthen pot with a monstrous face painted on it and draped in a turban at the top that was placed on top of the long stick; and an incredibly long beard made of jute fibres which hung from the lower end of the pot. The two ends of the small stick tied across the long one were made to serve as hands, covered with loose pieces

---

[12] First verse of chapter 112 of the *Quran* that says, 'I believe in one God'.

[13] A vow of recantation and a promise not to sin anymore.

[14] 'I seek refuge in Allah'.

[15] Not abiding by Allah; apostasy.

of cloth that looked like the sleeves of an upper garment. Two flowing dhotis hung from two sides of the long bamboo stick which hid the person holding the stick firmly as he walked, giving the impression of a very tall apparition on the move. Forget human beings, even ghosts would be terrified if they saw such an unusually tall figure walking by at night!

Once the 'king of the djinns' was disrobed, out popped none other than our very own Allah-Rakha from the structure! The leader of the ghosts vanished into thin air with his gang and props, and said, 'Enough for the day; they saw a djinn tonight and will hear strange things tomorrow!'

The next morning, news spread across the entire village that the king of the djinns had visited Chan Bhanu's place the previous night. Narad Ali told the villagers that the djinn was tall like a palm tree, and the villagers went on to add to the height to finally settle on a sky-high entity. The women-folk commented, 'Now, it had to come to that, hadn't it? Will the djinns spare you with such an overage girl left unmarried in the family?'

Some of the women were of the opinion that Chan Bhanu's exquisite beauty had attracted the king of the djinns who had fallen for her. Aha, perhaps the spirit would break the neck of her poor groom right on the wedding night!

That whole day was spent in a recitation of the *Quran* by Mullahji at their place. A Maulood Sharif was arranged in the evening, wherein, needless to say, the ghosts themselves participated and gleefully partook of the shinni.[16] Sobhan and a couple of others slept there that night.

In the dead of night a siren screamed from the palm tree behind the house. As it was, everybody was too scared to sleep. Looking outside the window, they saw a thirty-foot tall, pitch-black leg coming down from the top of the tree. The huge leaves of the tree moved with an eerie rustling noise. Simultaneously a heap of rubbish streamed onto the tin roof of the house, even as six or seven betel nut trees close by shook violently together as if they were about to break. Strangely there was nothing on the trees. Nobody could relate what had happened after that the following morning, for after seeing this much they all turned deaf, dumb and blind.

---

[16] Food served at the end of a religious ceremony

Whatever little sense they managed to retain till then deserted them completely when a black cat landed near their window from the top of the palm tree.

That night the committee of ghosts reached a resolution that it would not be judicious to frighten them for the next few days; otherwise they might flee the village altogether. Shaking his long black leg—which was a long bamboo pole draped in black cloth—the chief of ghosts Allah-Rakha said, 'I have an idea.' The ghost gang was eager to listen.

What Allah-Rakha said was, briefly, this: he had decided to get a letter printed in Kolkata which would be delivered to Narad Ali's place by none other than the king of the djinns himself. That would surely do the trick.

All these quandaries forced her parents to defer Chan Bhanu's marriage by another month. Ghostbusters, sorcerers and spiritually elevated exorcists from villages near and far assembled at Narad Ali's place and worked strenuously to drive away the evil spirits! The whole locality was stirred up!

When there was no sign of the troublemakers for the next seven to eight days, everybody was of the opinion that it was these powerful incantations and supernatural rites that made the foul brood of ghosts run for their life! What a relief, finally!

Meanwhile, the morning after the second night of the ghostly activities, Allah-Rakha collected the address of a punthi printing press in Kolkata and drafted a letter which he revised, corrected and brought to final shape with great patience. Then he sent the letter along with all other print matter, over to them. The following is the letter that was sent to the manager of the press:

SriSriHaknama Bharosa[17]

Sir,

I offer you my chhalam.[18] Please print the attached matter in the most attractive and beautiful way possible. And if you will not print

[17] Literally 'God be relied upon', 'Haknama Bharosa' is a customary invocation in the Muslim tradition of letter writing. 'SriSri,' on the other hand, is a Hindu way of invoking gods, goddesses and great religious leaders. The combination of the two signifies the long history of religious syncretism in this part of the world.

[18] A rural variety of 'Salam'.

it within 3–4 days of the receipt of the letter and if you neglect the matter then you will be obliged to answer to Ishvara Himself. And please inform me of the expenses of the printing. Dear sir and my lord, don't be negligent. Also print it on high quality paper with beautiful borders on all four sides. Yours truly.

Year 1337 Boishakh 10.

Our address
Allah-Rakha Byapari
Alias Keshranjan Babu.

Should reach him:
Vill Mohanpur,
P.O. Dyamudya
Dist. Faridpur.
(Should reach the place where Arial kha river flows.)

The print matter, accompanying the letter, containing the oracular message of the king of the djinns was like this:

Bismillah Allaho Akbar
La Elaha Ellella
Oracle

O Narad Ali Sheikh
Telling you and your wife
Your daughter Chan Bhanu

Must be married off to Chunnu Byapari's son Allah-Rakha. Next, if you don't do that you will face a lot of trouble. When you go to Chunnu Byapari after reading my letter and propose marriage to his son, he might ask you why you want to do that. But you should just stick to your proposal. Then one day you invite Allah-Rakha and call a munshi[19] and make them read the Kalema.[20]

Beware Beware

Chheraz Halder of Majgan wants Chan Bhanu for his son. His mind is set on it. Beware. Beware. Khodatallah has issued an order for her

[19] A language teacher or a religious man who can conduct a wedding.

[20] A guiding principle in Islam invoked during weddings and on other religious occasions.

to be married to Allah-Rakha. And if you disobey the order your daughter will go through a lot of sorrow and suffering later.

Beware—watch out—be careful if you do not respect this letter of mine you will end up being a kafir.

If you get her married to Allah-Rakha you will see me in your dream at the end of the wedding. Chan Bhanu is like my sister. I will give her wealth. Look I tell you again and again—your daughter sincerely wishes to get married to Allah-Rakha. But if you do not arrange this marriage, you will see signs of things to come.

Sincerely

The king of the djinns
Gayabulla.

He made an earnest request in a corner of this press matter too that there be attractive borders on all four sides of the letter . . .

They say you can get even tiger milk in the city Kolkata if you are ready to pay the right price! This oracular message too was printed and came back in eight to ten days. Allah-Rakha couldn't hold back his delight!

The committee of the ghosts met again. It was decided that the letter would be delivered to Narad Ali's place that very night and that Allah-Rakha, clad in the apparel of the king of djinns, would do the job. If somebody happened to wake up at that time and catch a glimpse of that frame, he would not take much time to pass out.

That night, penetrating its thatched roof, the oracle of the king of the djinns smoothly landed inside Chan Bhanu's house. The entire village woke up to an uproar again the next morning.

Narad Ali found himself on the horns of a dilemma. Not giving consent to a marriage to Allah-Rakha, as decreed by the king of the djinns, was simply not on. On the other hand Chheraz Halder also was not a man to be taken for a ride. In spite of the rumours of supernatural interventions by djinns, spirits, fairies and so on he was adamant that he would marry his son off only to this girl. Nobody from either Majgan or Mohanpur could shake his resolve. All he said was, 'If Khoda blesses my son with life, no supernatural ass can do him any harm. He will have to die one day anyway, and if he is destined to die by a ghost's hand, who can save him?'

The thing was, Chheraz was an exceedingly shrewd and clever customer. He realised that as Chan Bhanu was the only child of her parents and beautiful too, some scoundrel must have orchestrated the whole thing for the girl and the property. Of course, it was not that Chheraz did not have faith or fear in ghosts, it's just that he thought that the man who was behind all this had hired some ghoul-expert to do things at his bidding. So once the wedding was taken care of, it would not be much of a problem to hire a ghostbuster to chase away the ghosts! Besides, what other princess—and the heiress of such a large amount of property to boot—would be waiting for his dazzling prince of a son with a wedding garland in hand!

Like his father, Chheraz's son too was a brave, clever and sly fox. He planned it like this: first let the wedding take place peacefully, then there would be time to hire an exorcist and take care of the ghosts before he became close to his bride.

The father–son duo had a talk and decided that only the wedding would take place at the bride's place. And until the ruyat, or the solemn rite of the exchange of glances, which would take place a little later, the girl would stay at her father's house. Then they would bring her to Majgan.

Narad Ali sent for Chheraz Halder, and the latter arrived promptly. He read the printed oracular message and gave it a good hard thought. Then he said in a firm voice, 'No matter what you think, beyai, I say, this has nothing to do with Gayab. This rather smacks of that rascal Allah-Rakha. The scum has got it printed from some press. Why would the king of the djinns send you a printed letter? I salute the king of the djinns but, brother, it's not his handiwork. If it's not by that son of a bitch, you may give me fifty blows with your shoes!'

Well, they had never given this side of the story a thought! But Narad had seen the king of the djinns with his own eyes. Goodness gracious! As tall as a building, his beard flowing down to his waist, a turban wrapped around his head! He begged and implored Chheraz—but couldn't make him budge. Chheraz was adamant; if that comes to that, it's his son who would die, so what was Narad Ali's problem! Ultimately, when Chheraz threatened to claim compensation on grounds of a breach of contract, Narad Ali gave up.

Chan Bhanu's mother never spoke through the entire course of this negotiation. She seemed to have completely lost her earlier verve and zest for life. The series of supernatural occurrences and vague apprehensions were gnawing at her persistently. The mother and the daughter wouldn't leave their home at all. Since the water-spirit incident, the mother would carry water for Chan Bhanu to bathe at home. Never again did Chan go to the river. Armlets, amulets, trinkets—Chan's arms, neck and waist did not have room for any more. It was like trying to save a sinking ship by tying sponge wood all around it.

Chan too was growing pale and lifeless by the day. The relentless buzz around made her believe as well that she was possessed by an evil spirit—a djinn or an aseb. She lost her sleep, forgot to laugh, lost interest in everything. But this was a funny ghost, wasn't it! If it was really a ghost that possessed her, then why would he harp on Allah-Rakha? Ghosts never act like this! They seek complete possession over the person they target. Is it then a pet ghost of Allah-Rakha's? Or, is he himself the ghost?

She could not keep Allah-Rakha out of her mind, however, amidst all these troubles and turmoil. It's as if his strange ways kept reminding her of him compulsively.

No matter how bad a guy he was, he never did her or her family any harm. Yet how rude and abusive she had always been to him! She just recalled how the other day on her way back home from a neighbour's place she found Allah-Rakha lying on the path, writhing terribly in pain. There was nobody around. Rushing to him, she asked what had happened; he told her that he had been bitten by a snake. On being asked where the snake had bitten him, he pointed to his chest. He was indeed bleeding from the chest. Chan Bhanu couldn't afford to be shy at that critical moment. It was none other than Allah-Rakha who had saved her life one day lifting her out of the river. Sucking some blood out of the wound and spitting it out, she asked him—before she would repeat the exercise—which snake had bitten him. Allah-Rakha just pointed to her eyes silently. She could not recall how she tottered and staggered all the way back home and fainted at the doorstep. But none other than the two of them knew about the incident.

Chan Bhanu did realise that Allah-Rakha had bruised his chest with a knife or some other weapon to make it bleed just in order to deceive her into touching his chest with her mouth, and the snake thing was a cooked-up story. Still she could not be angry with him. Who could or would love her more than a man who would cut his chest open for the sake of a touch by her, even though it was a touch of her mouth! Perhaps whatever her would-be father-in-law Chheraz suspected was true, but still why was it that her heart bled for a good-for-nothing loafer—an eyesore of the village people? Why did her days feel vacant without a glimpse of him!

She was indeed possessed by a djinn, a ghost—but one that loved her. It was only for her sake that he became now a king of the djinns, and then an ekanodhe—ghost of a palm tree! She started feeling like it was she who was bitten by a snake, not Allah-Rakha—the pang of poison didn't allow her a moment's respite.

Nothing evades the mother's heart. It was only she who could feel the daughter's agony, read the history of her slow poisoning and living death. She also had finally nailed the real ghost. But there was no way she could turn back now, no matter how she wished to. She had to slaughter her daughter with her own hands! Chheraz Halder was a notorious man, he would spare no effort to put them to shame if they broke off the negotiations at that juncture.

Father, mother and daughter, all three helplessly resigned themselves to the inevitable.

3

All his efforts went in vain. The one who never knew what defeat was, tasted defeat for the first time in his life. The king of the djinns and his oracle, and his army of ghosts of various shapes, sizes, creeds and colours—ekanodhe, mamdo, mother of the seventeen-eyed, behmodotti the Brahmin demon, kandhokata the headless spirit—all of them together could not save the match for him! Besides, Allah-Rakha lost his earlier enthusiasm too. The day Chan Bhanu touched his bleeding chest with that moonlike face of hers, all the poison in his blood, all his hunger, greed, envy and spite were transformed into divine nectar. A touch of the philosopher's stone gave his inner world a pure golden hue. That very instant he was exorcised of the ghost that had possessed him.

Chan Bhanu's wedding was over. She didn't get to see how the groom was. Nor did she wish to. The groom too was too scared to have a glimpse of the bride, should the djinn come and break his neck! He set out in search of the best exorcist available that very day.

The day following the night of Chan Bhanu's wedding, Allah-Rakha's parents and kin were shocked to see him. His flowing curly mane was replaced by a cropped hair; he was clad in a simple gamchha,[21] with a truncheon in his hand and a plough on his shoulder. His mother understood everything. She knew everything that had been doing the rounds in the village concerning Chan Bhanu and her son. She wiped her eyes and went in. His father and brothers thanked Khoda profusely for the good sense that had finally dawned upon him ...

Far away, staring at Allah-Rakha's peasant look from under the shade of a mhijal tree, another pair of eyes turned moist like the morning's cloud-covered sky. Those eyes were Chan Bhanu's. Running to him, she threw herself at his feet and wailed out, 'Who did this to you?'

Allah-Rakha smiled a serene smile and replied, 'The king of the djinns!'

---

[21] A thin, woven cotton towel.

SEVENTEEN

THE VOLCANO

Translated by Gulshan Ara

1

Ali Nasib Miyan of village Birrampur, was, in all respects, an Ali Nasib—a man of luck. He had plenty of houses, cars and a beard. He was in charge of all of the jute trade in Trishal.

He was almost fifty, but his complexion was as fair and shiny as the arils of a jackfruit. His forehead—which is a symbol of an individual's luck—extended to the top of the head, and one couldn't say if his baldness or his wealth was more abundant.

He was betrayed only by his teeth and hair; teeth were all gone and so was most of his hair, while whatever was left, had greyed. He considered his double setback regrettable and premature! He had tried everything to prevent the early loss of his hair, but, unfortunately, all his efforts failed. He then consoled himself saying that even someone like King George the Seventh was also bald. Whenever the subject of baldness came up, he would sarcastically say that baldness was something that only afflicted the rich, and that the coolies and day-labourers didn't have to worry about it! Besides, baldness helped flawless financial calculations by keeping the head unpressured.

Although he justified his baldness in such laudatory terms, he would always wear a cap which he hardly ever took off. If anyone made fun of it, he would say, one must always keep one's wealth and baldness hidden, otherwise people become too inquisitive about them. Well, he might have been successful in keeping his baldness hidden, but what about the remaining strands of grey hair and his white beard? He was scared of using hair color! He tried it once, but the colour triggered a severe allergic reaction and his face swelled up really badly, and the doctor advised him not to use it anymore. Since then, he never used hair colour. But his grey hair and beard worked in his favour; matching his bright complexion they made him look quite dapper. He looked like a white swan spreading its wings on a white sand bank!

Sabur Akhand, a young man of nineteen or twenty lived in Ali Nasib Miyan's household and attended a madrasa in Trishal. Miyan had generously hosted Sabur, who came from a respectable but impoverished family, and paid for all his educational expenses as well.

As his name implied, Sabur was patient and uncomplaining about everything. To everyone he was polite and deferential, and always ready to turn the other cheek. His body language sent the unmistakable message: 'I have the honour to be, Sir, your most obedient servant.'

The boys from Ali Nasib Miyan's neighbourhood were extremely notorious! They loved to bully Sabur, tease and ridicule him. Whenever they saw Sabur they would laugh at him and make fun of him. It is said that lies hurt, as does water dumped unexpectedly on someone, but Sabur withstood all the bullying silently and he never protested.

Rustom was the leader of the neighbourhood gang. Every day he would come up with a new plan to harass Sabur. They named Sabur 'Mr Owl' because he always looked frightened like an owl. Just to avoid such harassment, Sabur would stay in his small room most of the time. But whenever he went out, the boys would go after him like crows chasing an owl.

Sabur's refusal to react to the boys' bullying didn't mean that they let him go. Rather, they became more creative and would find different ways to harass him. The neighbours also enjoyed the show and had a hearty laugh at Sabur's expense, which seemed to encourage Rustom's gang. Most of the neighbourhood boys attended regular school and they considered the boys attending the madrasa stupid. In the past, no other talbilim, or madrasa student, had lasted long in that neighbourhood because of such bullying. But Sabur was an exception; he had boundless patience. That is why he had survived for three long years. If only he could manage to stay one more year, he would graduate from the madrasa.

The boys would always wait for Sabur to come out and when he did, they would start a chorus,

Mr. Owl! O, Mr Owl!
Just for once, please croak and growl!

And Rustom would blare,

Drag your feet O! Mr Owl—
Go slow as you walk and crawl.
O! Mr Owl, climb up the tree,
As the crows chase thee.
'O uncle! Return my leg'
Your bullfrog nephew begs.
You tell the frog, 'Now run away.
See the baby snakes coming your way.'
Then go and eat a dead mouse,
As you sniff with your flat nose!

The song sent everyone rolling with laughter. Poor Sabur would turn back quickly and run to his room, shutting the door behind him. Rustom would peep through the bamboo fence and sing,

Mr Owl, hoot for once from your den
Smile and sniffle if you can.
O! dear Owl, curse me if you want
But come out and rave and rant!

Sabur didn't, of course, respond. He shrugged off all the insults and concentrated on his studies as if nothing had happened. But the boys wouldn't give up and continued to sing,

How the Owl studies, come and see,
The kitten goes to Mecca, truly it's funny.

Suddenly, they saw Ali Nasib Miyan walking home and fled as fast as they could. Although Ali Nasib Miyan scared the gang away and saved Sabur, he couldn't help but laugh. He was laughing as he entered his house and noticed his daughter Nurjahan crying and complaining to her mother asking, why should the boys harass Sabur every day since it wasn't any of them who provided his daily meal!

While she was venting her frustration to her mother, the boys could be heard singing again within earshot,

As Mr Owl reads the holy book
How his beards and cooking pans shake, have a look!

Nurjahan got very upset at her father. She expected him to scold the boys and tell them off. She told herself, 'Sabur's only crime is that he comes from a poor family and can't afford regular school, so the only option he had was to go to a madrasa simply because it is affordable! What if, instead of attending a madrasa, he fell into ditch or drain—how would it affect others? Then why are they all after him and doing such mean things to him?'

Ali Nasib could feel his daughter's frustration, but still, could not stop laughing. He asked his daughter, 'Why are you so upset my Princess? You see, the boy tolerates the insult, doesn't raise his voice, and stays home most of the time—that's why they make fun of him, call him an owl.'

Nurjahan said, 'Abba, I don't want to talk to you anymore! Sitting in his room, alone, Sabur cries all the time and you make fun of him! If I were a boy, I would have slapped Rustom and his gang so hard that they would fall flat on their faces and never be able to stand up again, let alone eat another meal', then broke into tears.

Ali Nasib Miyan tried to console his daughter saying, 'Don't worry my Princess, I will tell Munshi the next time he sees Rustom, he should give him the lesson of his life! I will ask him to cut off Rustom's ears!'

This made Nurjahan very happy. She came to her father and asked, 'My dear abba, would you like a cup of tea?'

Ali Nasib Miyan said with humour, 'So now my daughter remembers to offer me a cup of tea.'

Nurjahan was Nasib Ali's Miyan's only child, so naturally, she was the apple of his eyes. She was over fifteen, but her parents were still not ready to marry her off. And if the issue of her marriage ever came up, they would say, 'It is hard to find the right boy for her! We can't have her marry just anyone which is no less than throwing her into the water while her hands and feet are tied!' Well, in fact her parents couldn't imagine their life after the girl, the light of the house, left with her husband. The house would certainly turn dark and desolate! Otherwise, with so much wealth and Nurjahan being the sole heiress, why would she have trouble finding a husband? They often received marriage proposals for her, but since Ali Nasib Miyan didn't show much interest, the boys' families didn't pursue the matter.

Nurjahan had been receiving schooling at home for some time and later, when Sabur came, she began to take lessons in Urdu from him. Usually, in a respectable family with good social position, no parent would allow their young daughter to go anywhere near a young man, much less allow her to take lessons from him. But Sabur had such reputation in the village as a young man of character that nobody raised an eyebrow when they knew that he was tutoring Nurjahan.

When Sabur gave lessons to Nurjahan, he sat with his head down, never even once looking at her face. Every time he entered or left the house, he would keep his head down! In the beginning, everyone used to make fun of him—but now they had become used to it.

The fact is, for the last three years that Sabur had been living in Ali Nasib Miyan's house, he had seen only Nurjahan's hands and feet, but never her face.

Now, this Nurjahan may not have been the light of the world, as her name indicates, but she could certainly be considered the light of Birrampur. Nobody had any doubts about it. Nurjahan too was quite aware of her beauty and took pride in it.

In the beginning, Nurjahan would not be bothered by the fact that Sabur never looked at her, but after sometime, it began to hurt her pride. Did it mean that her beauty had no charm? She had been taking lessons from Sabur for the last three years—but despite being so close, why didn't he look her in the face, just for once? With all her beauty and charm she could not get Sabur to show any interest in her; this definitely hurt her pride. She didn't expect Sabur to love her—but to not even be noticed by him? This was something she couldn't accept. Someone with such reputation for beauty, someone any other boy would feel blessed just to have a glimpse of—and this young man didn't even look at her even once! Is Sabur's virginity more fragile than that of a woman?

The more she thought about it, the more she got angry and frustrated at Sabur and thought of not taking lessons from him anymore! But when she saw that Rustom's gang continued to bully him, ridicule him and set mad dogs at him, she could not stay calm. Sabur was really an innocent, harmless young man, but no one came forward to defend him! He never fought back. Goodness, what kind of a man was he! No matter what you did to him, he would never react. It was strange that the world had people like him!

The more she thought about the situation, the more she felt sorry for him!

Sabur was not the masculine, he-man type that male figures were supposed to be. His looks were rather plain. He was slimly built with a brownish complexion. The only attractive feature he possessed were his eyes that were like a pair of timid birds. After casting a glance, the eyes looked down. Those eyes, and the way he looked—extremely timid and pitiful too, but incomparably beautiful! Very rarely does one comes across a guy with such big, alluring eyes!

In the three years that Sabur had been living in Ali Nasib Miyan's house, he had never been the first to strike up a conversation with anyone. He only spoke when someone talked to him. Talking to a stranger was out of the question! He would pray, recite from the Quran, go to the madrasa, return home, read some more, and go to bed—this was his daily routine. If on some days his meal was not sent to him by mistake, he would not ask for it and went to the madrasa on an empty stomach. Even if the food was not enough, he never asked for a second helping. If he felt thirsty, he would go to the pond for water instead of bothering anyone at home!

Since Sabur appeared so innocent and defenceless, Nurjahan always stayed vigilant on his behalf. If she weren't around, Sabur probably would never have got his meals on time. In spite of her care and concern for Sabur, he never expressed any gratitude or paid any attention to Nurjahan, let alone spoke to her. He never complained about anything, not even if someone gave him a beating. He would keep mum even if someone gave him a piece of gold!

2

The other day, a highly respected Maulana from the region located outside western Bengal visited Ali Nasib Miyan's place. So, it was planned that in the evening there would be a Milad—a religious prayer service—followed by readings from the Quran, and it would end with a waz or sermon. Sabur was put in charge of looking after the Maulana's hospitality. Sabur had never felt so overwhelmed and nervous in his life, so he put in all his effort to serve the Maulana.

That day when Sabur went out, Rustom's gang members also came out one by one and gathered around him. Sabur turned pale like a bashful bride suddenly coming face to face with her husband's elder brother.

As usual, the gang started to harass him with silly questions about the Maulana, like how much his turban or his beard weighed, and how many tigers were needed to eat him up. They also asked questions about who had nibbled his beard and moustache—termite or mice? Since Rustom hadn't yet arrived, the boys confined their activities to making fun of the Maulana instead of Sabur!

At that moment the Maulana came out and asked Sabur in pure Urdu, 'What do you do?' Sabur replied with great humility that he was talib-e-ilm, meaning a student at Islamic school. Immediately, a gang member, Yusuf, asked, 'What did the owl say, Fazle?'

Fazle burst into laughter and said, 'The owl said he is talbilim.'

Rustam had made his appearance by then and immediately joined the fracas. 'Who's the talbilli? Our Mr Owl?' he asked.

The boys now began to laugh and roll on the ground. 'Well said, Rustam,' they said, 'Talbilli! The cat from the palm tree! Illa billa! Talbilli—hi hi ha ha!' This was followed by bursts of laughter!

Poor Sabur was so embarrassed at being ridiculed in front of the Maulana that he ran into his room and locked the door, forgetting all about attending to the guest. Rustom instantly composed a song which he began to sing,

> The owl is now a talbilli
> He'll go to Deoband and then to Delhi.
> When he returns he'll cry shrilly—
> Puppies and hillbillies!

The situation made the Maulana very angry, and he began running after the boys chasing them away. Seeing the big muscular body of the Maulana the boys took to their heels. But while fleeing they kept singing,

> The Ulu[1] has come from Lahore
> To teach us the letters and more!

The Maulana, forgetting his scholarly Urdu, began to yell at the boys, calling them names in slangy Hindi.

Ali Nasib Miyan, after hearing everything, called for the boys. He was planning to give them a good thrashing in front of the Maulana. But none of the boys were to be found anywhere.

By that time, the boys were three to four miles away near a large water pond, looking to catch frogs. They had become very upset at

[1] Slang for maulana.

the Maulana for chasing them away and planned to spoil the waz, or sermon, he was scheduled to deliver that evening. Their plan was to go into action at the peak of the waz. It was decided that one boy would squeeze the stomach of a frog so hard that the frog would croak like it had been attacked by a snake, another boy would release a second frog in the middle of the congregation, and as the frog would start to jump up and down, the third boy would scream, 'a snake, a snake!'

This would surely spoil the waz!

So, after a great deal of effort, they finally caught a few frogs and came back.

On their way back, they saw Sabur going to the lavatory near his room, leaving the toilet wash pot, filled with water, outside the door. Bari asked Rustom, 'Should I filch his wash pot?'

Rustom gladly ordered it so and Bari very carefully removed the wash pot and kept it by the side of the pond.

Hours passed as Sabur kept sitting inside the lavatory! He didn't come out, or shout for somebody to give him another wash pot! As the gang noticed Ali Nasib Miyan walking towards his home, they fled in a hurry!

Ali Nasib Miyan noticed the boys and thought that they must have done something to Sabur again. He looked for Sabur everywhere, but he was nowhere to be found. So he entered his house and asked about Sabur, but no one seemed to know where he was. All they could say was that the boys were bullying him yelling 'Talbilli'.

After two more hours, they found Sabur. He told them everything. But the result was just the opposite! Ali Nasib Miyan started to yell at him saying he could have come out and asked someone to bring him a wash pot. After hearing the story, Nurjahan, instead of getting angry, started to laugh thinking how was it possible that someone could be such a simpleton!

A few days back, she had also laughed seeing Sabur in another such mortifying situation. While Sabur was having a haircut, Rustom bribed the barber with one rupee and asked him to leave a tiki—a thin, ponytail-like tuft of hair, typical of Hindu brahmins—on Sabur's head. The barber obliged. After the haircut Sabur took a shower and went for his lunch. Nurjahan was home at the time and when she saw him with the tiki, she burst into laughter. But she also realised how much her laughter had hurt Sabur!

This time too, after she had had her fit of laughter, Nurjahan could feel how this would pain Sabur. She became quite emotional and, who knows why, her eyes were suddenly filled with tears . . .

In the evening, the Maulana began his waz, but his admiring audience's inability to understand most of what he said was compensated by a show of fake but overpowering devotion. Suddenly, from a corner of the congregation came the helpless grunting of a frog! This startled the audience. After some time, a bloodied frog was hopping throughout the room and flying over the heads of the devotees, as if a hound race was going on! Then someone screamed, 'Snake! Snake!'

Everyone ran off and the room was emptied in a split second. The Maulana jumped up on his chair and began to shake his dress. The waz ended there . . .

Later, as the Maulana sat down for dinner at Ali Nasib Miyan's house, they could hear the boys singing from a little distance,

'Say something, Ulu', said the snake
The Ulu said, 'Oh for my father's sake!'
Would there be another session tomorrow?
The Ulu said, 'No no, I don't think so!
Let me gather my baggage and swiftly run'
Ulu! Return to your homeland, the job here is done!

Hearing the song, the Maulana choked on a chicken bone and Ali Nasib Miyan began to fume with a futile rage.

3

The other day an elephant that belonged to the zamindar of Gafargaon was strolling majestically along the road. Nurjahan was watching the elephant from behind the fence. Sabur too came to the road, unable to resist the temptation of seeing the elephant. Rustom and his gang were also watching the elephant from a distance. Pointing at the elephant Rustom shouted, 'Hi there Mr Talbilli, see, the calf is going through the road, go catch it'.

People on the road burst into laughter. A girl standing on the road said in reply, 'You bastard, the elephant is not a calf, you are the calf!' Luckily for her, Rustom didn't hear her.

That incident made Nurjahan furious. But she was angrier at Sabur than the boys. She promised herself that she would give him a piece of her mind when she met him next. She wondered, 'What kind of a spineless man is he! Even worse than a woman!'

That evening, when Sabur went to teach Nurjahan, she began to berate him without wasting any time, 'Aren't you man enough or what? Those devils insult you, humiliate you, and you turn your tail. Why? Hasn't Allah given you hands and tongue?'

By mistake, Sabur cast his pitiful eyes on Nurjahan! But what he saw made him forget all the shame and indignity he had suffered for so long! His eyes, rewarded with such prettiness, were filled with boundless astonishment! So this is you! Suddenly he blurted out, 'Nurjahan!'

Nurjahan, too, was looking at his eyes with a mixture of bewilderment and surprise. Who is this frightened deer from the woods?—she seemed to ask herself. One whose eyes are so frightened like those of a deer has to be faint-hearted. Nurjahan had never seen Sabur look up. He would talk or walk with his eyes cast down. She saw for the first time how someone's eyes could also make that person incomparably handsome.

Hearing Sabur saying her name, Nurjahan blushed as if the moon on a rainy night had been encircled by a mystical rainbow.

The invariably quiet Sabur suddenly became restless and voluble, as if a cyclone was churning through the calm Pacific Ocean. A mountain usually stays silent but, when it breaks its silence, it turns into a volcano.

Sabur's face began to glow with the beam of manhood. He looked at Nurjahan with shining eyes and said, 'Would you be happy if I teach those boys a lesson?'

Nurjahan responded, casting her shining eyes at him, 'Who? You? You'd teach them a lesson?'

Sabur did not reply to her sarcastic remark but went out, leaving a burning imprint of his eyes on Nurjahan's heart. Nurjahan couldn't move but kept sitting in the posture of someone who had forgotten who she was. She couldn't remember anything of Sabur except his alluring eyes and their even more alluring looks! Everyone was surprised to see Sabur, who never looked up but always cast his eyes down, moving around with confidence and resolve; his eyes gleaming with a light no one had ever seen before.

Rustom's gang was returning home from their regular round of mischievous activities. All of a sudden, Fazal yelled at Sabur, 'There goes the Talbilli'.

Sabur rolled up his sleeves and waited.

Bari smacked him on the head from behind and said, 'O owl, start croaking'.

Without saying anything, Sabur slapped Bari so hard that he lost his balance and fell on the road. The gang members were stunned by Sabur's unexpected response and stood there, not knowing what to do.

Without wasting any words, Sabur started to walk towards home. Bari had sat up by then and yelled, 'Sala! Where did the bastard go?'

Bari's angry voice made the gang members grasp the situation and they ran after Sabur, but this time Sabur fought back with incredible courage. No one could ever imagine Sabur possessed so much strength. He grabbed each member of Rustam's gang by the throat and threw them into the nearby pond.

The pond belonged to Ali Nasib Miyan and had been freshly dug, so the soil around was still slippery. So, those who were thrown into the pond were not able to climb up the steep banks. The harder they tried the more they slipped back into the pond. One by one, five to six of the boys, including Rustom, were thrown into the pond. Amir brought out a knife from his pocket and attacked Sabur. Luckily Sabur evaded the first knife-charge pointed at his chest, but in the scuffle, the knife left a deep cut in his arm. Sabur grabbed Amir's hand and twisted it with all his strength. Amir fell on the ground and the knife pierced his chest all the way to its hilt! He cried out in pain once, 'ooooh!', and then passed out. The rest of the gang ran off as fast as they could and spread the news in the neighbourhood. Everyone including Ali Nasib Miyan came running to the scene.

Sabur, in the meantime, with his arm bleeding and blood all over his body, lifted Amir, pulled the knife out of his chest, and pressed the wound with his palm.

Ali Nasib Miyan could not believe what he was seeing and he covered his eyes with his hands.

A short while later both a doctor and the police arrived. Amir was taken to hospital and Sabur was taken to the police station.

Before the police inspector did so however, at the request of Ali Nasib Miyan, he sat down with Sabur in Ali Nasib's house so that Sabur could tell his story. Sabur told him exactly what had happened without exaggerating anything. No one had any doubts about the truth of Sabur's story. The police inspector said to Nasib Ali Miyan, 'The case isn't that serious, the boy would survive! I'd ask you to go for an out of court settlement, Sahib.'

To that suggestion, Ali Nasib Miyan said, 'I have no problem with that, but you know the boy's father—a very stubborn man, will he agree to a deal?'

The inspector said, 'Well, in that case, I will have to take Sabur to the police station. That's my duty'.

By that time, everyone in Ali Nasib Miyan's household had heard the news, realised the gravity of the situation and began to cry. When Nurjahan heard the news, she fainted. But when her father brought Sabur and the officer into his house, she fell near Sabur's feet and cried out loud, 'Why did you do this? Who asked you to do this?'

Nurjahan's mother loved Sabur like a son for the qualities he possessed. In the absence of a son of her own, she poured all her motherly love and affection on Sabur. Clasping his head to her bosom, she told her husband, 'This is my son. I'll give you ten thousand taka, please just tell the inspector to let him go.'

Sabur picked up Nurjahan with his bloody hand and said, 'I have to go now, but I wanted to prove that I am a man too! And if I hadn't done this you would have always hated me. May Allah make you happy!' He then bowed down and touched Nurjahan's mother's feet with reverence and said, 'O Amma, for the last three years you made me forget the pain of losing my mother.' He choked back tears, unable to say anything more.

Then he touched Ali Nasib's feet, asking for his blessings, and walked out the door with the police inspector without showing any emotion. The inspector refused to release Sabur even for such high bail money, because he feared he might lose his job for giving bail to a murder suspect.

Sabur's last statement 'you would have always hated me' kept resonating in Nurjahan's ears. Even if she hated him, why would that matter to him? She asked herself, why was Sabur so desperate to please her? If she hadn't teased him that badly, maybe he would never have reacted so violently! He tolerated all the harassment and bullying for long three years. But today, it was just because of her that he was taken to the police station! After a day or two he may be sent to jail or sent to a penal colony—or even worse—hanged! 'Ooh', she wailed and blacked out.

Ali Nasib Miyan seemed to discover a whole new world today. With his misfortune, Sabur seemed to have made Miyan's remaining happy days bleak indeed. For a while he thought he had raised a poisonous snake; the next moment he realised that Sabur was not a snake, not a snake! He was the most innocent young man with the purest of souls! Even if he was a snake, he was the most majestic kind, with a gem in his crown!

Suddenly Ali Nasib Miyan remembered that although in recent days Sabur had been surviving on Miyan's kindness, he really came from a much higher social class. He may be poor now, having lost both his parents, but once some of Ali Nasib Miyan's ancestors used to work for his family. Besides, in exchange for the lodging, food and clothes that he had given Sabur in the last three years, Sabur had taught his daughter Urdu and Persian. Indeed, Nurjahan had picked up the languages much better than if she had been taught in the madrasa. Ali Nasib Miyan was a product of madrasa education, but he had to think twice before starting a conversation with his daughter about Urdu and Persian. So, Sabur had really repaid all his debts. Ali Nasib Miyan's heart was filled with admiration and fatherly affection for the boy! He vowed he would save Sabur at any cost!

Not only for himself, but for his daughter, who was dearer to him than his own self! By now he had realised how Nurjahan felt about Sabur. All these years, he had been afraid of giving away his daughter in marriage and sending her to someone else's house but now, if he could get Nurjahan to marry Sabur, it would make her happy and there wouldn't be any need to send her off to some other house! Sabur would live with them like their own son. High educational status? Sabur had already finished his final exam from the madrasa—and probably would score the highest marks. Then he could be sent to a college for higher education.

Ali Nasib began to console himself and his daughter by imagining such a happy future. That night Nurjahan did not have any fainting spells, but she also could not sleep. Piercing the darkness all around her those two eyes glowed—Sabur's eyes, like the morning and evening stars.

4

Amir could not be saved from death; Sabur could not be saved from a prison term.

Amir died on his way to a hospital in Mymensingh. Amir's father refused an out of court settlement. He complained that because he was trying to arrange a marriage between Amir and Nurjahan, Sabur killed Amir when he came to know about it. Sabur did that because he was having an affair with Nurjahan. In support of his claim, Amir's father brought quite a number of witnesses who had seen Nurjahan crying, holding Sabur's feet on that fateful day! Besides taking advantage of tutoring the girl, Sabur had plenty of opportunities to get close to Nurjahan!

Nurjahan and Ali Nasib Miyan felt like sinking into the earth with shame! The story caused a scandal that spread far and wide. Most people who heard it believed it.

Despite his repeated attempts, Ali Nasib Miyan could not convince Sabur to take the help of a lawyer. Sabur told the court that he would defend himself without the help of any lawyer or witnesses. Many lawyers, expecting generous fees from the wealthy Ali Nasib Miyan, tried desperately to convince Sabur to hire them, but he wouldn't budge. As a last resort, Ali Nasib Miyan, along with his wife and daughter, met him in jail and repeated his request. Once again, he failed. Upon Nurjahan's request, Sabur told her he had already harmed them enough, and now did not want to cause them more financial loss to add to his debts. 'Forgive me, Nurjahan', he said. 'I want this forgiveness from you so that you never forget me!'

In the court session, Sabur gave a detailed account of the event, from the beginning to the end, as truthfully as he could. The judge believed him, but the jury didn't. Consequently, Sabur was sentenced to seven years rigorous imprisonment. He refused to appeal the sentence, although everyone told him he would certainly be set free if he did so. Sabur smiled and told them he didn't want to be free—since his hands had Amir's blood on them, if he could wash off the blood in seven years, he would consider himself lucky.

The judge wrote in his judgment that he had never felt so much pain sentencing anyone before.

The day the proceedings ended, Nasib Ali Miyan was present in Mymensingh with his family.

The same day Nurjahan requested her father to take them to Mecca. Incidentally, Ali Nasib Miyan had been planning to go on Hajj for quite some time, but it never materialised thanks to various preoccupations. Naturally, Nurjahan's proposal made him feel that he had got the moon in his hands! Ali Nasib Miyan delightedly said, 'My dear child, this is the best suggestion you have ever given me, let's go to Mecca and spend the next seven years there. We don't want to stay in this cursed village anymore. But before we leave let's tell Talbilli that he should come and visit us after he is out of jail, if Allah is kind enough to let me live until then.'

After uttering the name 'Talbilli' Ali Nasib Miyan burst into laughter and the next moment, began to cry like a child.

Nurjahan's mother did not protest. She realised the way they had all been disgraced and Nurjahan's character smeared, it would hardly be possible to get her to marry someone in their village. Besides, living a life here of shame and disgrace was impossible.

It was decided that they would sell all their assets including their home, take the cash with them and move to Mecca. Accordingly, Ali Nasib Miyan met the bank manager on that very day and arranged for the sale of his property. The bank agreed to give him the cash in advance and get reimbursed by selling his property.

The next day, they went to the jail to see Sabur. After listening to their plan Sabur began to cry. Then he wiped his tears with the sleeve of his prison uniform and said, 'Abba, Amma, I will visit you all after seven years—I promise'.

Then he looked at Nurjahan and said, 'Even if Allah doesn't allow me to see you again in this world, I promise, I will find you wherever you go.' He then choked up and was unable to say anything more.

Nurjahan also burst into tears and touched Sabur's feet. Drops of her tears fell on Sabur's feet! She said, 'Pray that your words come true.'

Then, the prison door closed behind them with a loud bang. Looking back, Nurjahan felt that the door to her paradise of happiness had slammed shut forever!

EIGHTEEN

THE SHIULI MALA

Translated by Pritam Bandyopadhyay

1

Mr Azhar is a reputed young barrister in Kolkata. Butler, steward, errand boy, doorman, gardeners and servants keep his house bustling all the time.

But the house lacks its real decor. Mr Azhar is unmarried.

Though a reputed barrister, Azhar doesn't accept too many cases. Not even after a thousand pleas. People say it is yet another strategy to hoard money.

But the chess players of Kolkata know that if Mr Azhar really has a strategy, it is one that he uses while playing chess.

To this day, no one has managed to beat him at chess. His friends at the chess addas know, it is this chess that has stopped Mr Azhar from becoming an even more successful barrister. But it has made him a man with a noble heart.

When rich barristers read their 'weekly notes', Azhar deliberates on the games of Alekhine, Capablanca or Rubinstein, Réti or Morphy and thinks of their strategies with his eyes closed; or reads a chess-magazine.

In the mornings he doesn't get time, but in the evenings, a chess adda takes place every day. Most of the famous chess players of Kolkata join him. They chat, play and discuss the game.

Azhar's greatest regret is that a player like Capablanca could be defeated by Alekhine! And yet this Alekhine himself had been defeated as many as five times by a player like Bogoljubov!

Mr Mukherjee is a die-hard fan of Alekhine's. Even today when Mr Azhar expressed his regret like all other days, Mr Mukherjee quipped, 'But whatever you say, Azhar, Alekhine's defence—it seems unmatched in the world. And Bogoljubov? Hasn't Alekhine made mincemeat of him three times five, fifteen times in total? All world champions lose such games twice or thrice like that during world championships. Bogoljubov won five times out of twenty-four. And Bogoljubov is no ordinary player either!'

Azhar laughed and said, 'Arre, enough of your Alekhine. This time he is playing with Capablanca again. Just you see what a sorry state he will be in then. And even the other day Bogoljubov was beaten into a bagel by the Italian Monticelli. But yes, this Grünfeld guy knows how to play.'

One of his friends was annoyed. He said, 'Don't you people have anything else to do? Who are these bagel-bags or ashpits, Alekhines or an egg of horse?—What a bother!'

Mukherjee chuckled, 'Why Ajit, you play grabu[1] so well. In this mushy monsoon why don't you pay a visit to your wife's sisters? These chess moves are not for your intelligence!'

The young lawyer Nazim yawned and snapped his fingers, 'Thank goodness that thing hasn't entered my intelligence. Better Mr Azhar sahib sing a couple of songs before we head for home. Then you may sit with your king and knight.'

Any objections from the chess playing lot did not hold water. Azhar had to sing. He sings thumri really well. He had a large stock of thumri songs in the pure Lucknow style. And he sang them with such feeling that any listener was bound to be moved. But today he only sang ghazals.

At other times, Azhar would not sing ghazals so easily.

Mukherjee laughed and said, 'Is your heart overflowing with the pangs of separation today? You're singing just ghazals. What's the matter? There seems to be a splash of colour somewhere?'

Azhar too smiled and said, 'For once just take a look outside.'

At last, everyone noticed the spectacle unfolding outside. The sky had been washed by monsoon rains a while ago and resembled a huge, blue lotus. Enfolded within it, the autumnal moon glowed like a lotus-gem. All around it the stars were like lit fireflies.

Beside Lake-Road, the house looked like a painted picture.

---

[1] A card game.

The wind, laden with a mixed fragrance of shiuli and rajanigandha, was occasionally wafting into the hallway dispensing a languid and intoxicating charm.

It was a treat for the eyes as well as the mind for everyone.

Sitting straight, Nazim said, 'These things would surely have remained unseen had you busied yourselves with the chess pieces.'

Azhar sighed unmindfully and said, 'True indeed.'

Mukherjee commented, 'Nah, this goddamned shiuli flower won't let us play chess today.'

Azhar replied in astonishment, 'You too like shiuli? Hey! Is there anything special related to these flowers?'

Before they could speak it was Ajit who remarked, 'Arre chhi! Chess player and romance? The poor guy's only love affair has been with his wife! Imagine falling in love with one's own wife! Oh Rama! Even that wife has left him for her father's place, disgusted by his obsession with chess! Fancy linking him with the shiuli flower!'

There was a roar of laughter. Mukherjee shot back, angrily, 'Stop it, Ajit. Crazy talk isn't always funny.'

Ajit pretended to have lost face and quipped, 'But I wasn't joking dada. You have indeed fallen for your wife—and people are spreading scandals, which is why I also mentioned it. How is it my fault if they laugh at it?'

Azhar laughed and said, 'Is this your way of trying to pin the blame on Mukherjee, Ajit? How do you know that a chess player can't get involved in an accident with anyone other than his wife?'

Ajit answered, 'I know because I saw Mr Mukherjee, and then you!'

Azhar burst out, 'Arre, I haven't married as yet.'

Ajit blurted, 'That means your condition is even more miserable. This poor guy at least has a wife to fall in love with, but you couldn't even get yourself a wife.'

Nazim banged on the table and shouted, 'Bravo! Long live Ajit babu! Well said this time!'

At that moment the gardener entered and placed a lovely pair of large shiuli garlands on the table. Ajit hung them from the coat bracket with a show of seriousness, which made everyone laugh. Turning his face away, Ajit spoke in a theatrical voice, 'O bracket beauty! On this autumnal full moon night these shiuli malas —'

Azhar protested with a pale smile, 'Please Ajit. Don't mock those garlands bhai! They are not mine.'

Ajit was stubborn! Concealing his surprise he said, 'Then whose garlands are these, my friend? I mean—for whom, my friend?'

Nazim remarked, 'See? And someone was claiming that a chess player doesn't have romance?'

Azhar said, 'Each year, on this first day of Ashwin[2] I float shiuli malas on the water. These garlands belong to the water—no one else.' There was a sad smile on his face.

This made even the gang of chess players sit up straight. Ajit hailed the attending boy with a yell and asked him to bring tea. He then arranged his clothes neatly and turning his chair to face Azhar, spoke, 'So then, my friend, what's it all about? Seems quite serious, doesn't it? The first day of Ashwin, floating shiuli malas on water every year! It'll be an excellent story! Out with it. Or else we'll all begin a satyagraha here.'

Everyone laughed but supported Ajit's proposal.

After a lot of coaxing Azhar said, smiling, 'But even that began with chess!'

Ajit jumped, 'Not an issue. We'll manage to eat the bitter palta[3] curry somehow; towards the end there'll be sandesh and sweet curd.'

Mukherjee blurted out, 'Hey, I bet this game of chess will have more checks from the rook than others! The bishop and knight will capture each other! Don't worry!'

2

After everyone had another round of tea, Azhar lit a cigar and blew out smoke for about a minute. Then he began to speak—

'The story starts when I had just passed the bar and was on a visit to Shillong. It was the month of Bhadra. The Durga puja vacationers hadn't started crowding the place yet. Only a handful had begun arriving. Right from my childhood, I had much too much of a fascination for the game of chess. That fascination increased when I went to England.

---

[2] The sixth month in the Bengali calendar.

[3] Leaves of the potol or pointed gourd plant, bitter in taste. They are deep fried or used as ingredients for preparations such as shukto.

There I played with quite a few famous players like Yeats, Michael, Winter, Thomas and others, and won many a game too playing for Cambridge. In Shillong I looked for chess players and promptly came to know one or two. But none of them were big players. They were constantly losing to me. One of them told me one day, "There's an old, retired professor here, a mighty chess player. It's said that no one can beat him—want to go to play with him?"

Immediately I got up and said, "I'll go right now. Let's go. Where is he?"

The gentleman said, "Why not? Come with me, I'll take you there. He'll be very happy to find a player like you. He too is addicted to the game like you. The old man is a strange player. Moshai, he plays blindfolded!"

In Europe I had seen many a chess player's 'blindfolded' game. I, too, had played like that several times. So, I wasn't very surprised by this.

It was almost evening then, with a slice of moon in the sky, probably that of Shukla panchami.[4] It looked like a sign of some new hope. The whole sky seemed to have launched a rowing competition among the white cloud-vessels. The moon and stars were all making frantic efforts to keep afloat.

We reached a colourful bungalow surrounded by eucalyptus and deodar trees and soon enough I spotted an aged gentleman, dignified and composed, playing chess with a young girl.

That was the first time I saw a woman of my country playing chess.

The moment I cast a look full of surprise and admiration at her she got up and said, "Baba, look who's come."

Seeing his daughter get up before the game was over the old man looked at us with what seemed like a bit of irritation. But the next moment he was up smiling, and said, "Oh, I see it's Binoy babu! Who are these people? Please come and be seated. And they are . . . ?"

As soon as Binoy babu, who had escorted me there, introduced me, the old man jumped to his feet and hugging me, said, "Mister, I mean you are that Azhar? Arre, I've found your name in chess magazines and newspapers plenty of times. You are such a great player!

---

[4] The fifth lunar day of Shukla paksha.

Winning a challenge against Yeats is no small achievement! And at this young age too! Oh! so happy I am—so happy! . . . O ma, Shiuli, a mighty chess player's here! Come and see! Bah, it seems happy times are ahead of us. Even at this age I have too much of a craze for the game and finding no one else was playing with my daughter. What to do!" And with that he filled the quiet evening with the reverberations of his loud, spontaneous laughter.

Shiuli made a namaskar and quietly sat down beside her father. Seeing her I felt she was truly a shiuli flower of the autumn season.

With her fair, spotless face shining against the dusky hue of her sari she was looking as beautiful as the white shiuli flower on its yellow stalk. Maybe the length of my gaze was longer than expected, but I was brought back to my senses by the old man's words.

The old man seemed to be impatient to start a game. As soon as a servant brought in arrangements for tea, Shiuli began to prepare the tea. She smiled and said, "Can't bear any more delay, right baba?" Then she looked at me and said, "Don't mind. Baba is just too fond of playing chess. The very idea of missing a game makes him sick!" She promptly handed me the cup of tea and said, "Now begin while you're having your tea and let us watch the game."

Binoy beamed, "Yes, it'll be face to face combat now. You know Miss Chowdhury, he thrashes us badly every day."

The game began. Everyone looked on with interest, a few offered some advice about smart moves. The way Miss Chowdhury, alias Shiuli, pointed out one or two of her father's mistakes, it was clear to me that she was as good a player as her father.

Playing for a while I realised that Professor Chowdhury was a better player than many I had played against in Europe. I knew Professor Chowdhury as an eminent chemist, but not as someone who could play such superb chess.

I captured one more of his pieces and the old man immediately slapped my back, commended me and began playing defensively. He profusely praised my moves with the bishop. Shiuli kept looking at me with astonishment and admiration. But even with one piece less the old man kept congratulating me over and over again, "Did you see it ma Shiuli? Our players believe that the bishop doesn't play like the knight. Did you see what a game that pair of bishops presented? You play just too well baba! I either get beaten or win the game; a draw is rare to come by."

Shiuli smilingly said, "But baba, haven't you been unbeaten for several years?"

Professor Chowdhury smiled and replied, "No ma, I have been beaten. That was almost fifteen years ago. A gentleman from the countryside—not educated in the modern sense—had come and defeated me. Oh, haven't seen such a player since."

As soon as the game began again Binoy commented with a grin, "Why doesn't Miss Chowdhury play with Mr. Azhar this time?"

The old man happily remarked, 'Why not? You play ma. For once let me watch.'

Embarrassed, Shiuli exclaimed, "How is it possible for me to play against him?"

But at everyone's request she sat down to play. In the middle was the chessboard, on one side sat Shiuli on a chair—on the other side was me! The fragrance from her hair was making me intoxicated. My body and mind seemed poised to succumb to some addiction. When I made a few wrong moves, Shiuli looked at me and lowered her eyes. I thought there was a hint of a smile at the edge of her lips. The smile seemed meaningful.

With another mistake I was under pressure and lost a rook. The old man seemed a little surprised. Binoy babu and his lot commented with a laugh, "Now is the time for Mr Azhar to face checkmate." The laughter seemed mixed with sarcasm.

Now I composed myself and started playing with concentration. I launched such an offensive game with my two bishops and the queen while advancing the pawns of my court, that even Professor Chowdhury couldn't save the match. Shiuli lost! Though beaten, she had played so well that I couldn't resist praising her. I said, "You see, I have even played against the women's world champion Miss Menchik but didn't have to face so much trouble. I was almost at the point of losing."

I saw that Shiuli was blushing like a lotus in joy and embarrassment. I was relieved. I considered it enough good luck that on losing the game she hadn't felt offended.

There was another match with Professor Chowdhury. Again, it was a draw.

The old man was over the moon with joy. He said, "Yes, after all these days I've finally found someone with whom one has to plan at least eight moves in advance."

It was decided that hereafter a little adda over chess would take place every day at Professor Chowdhury's house.

While getting up the old man suddenly said, "Ma Shiuli, I'm sure Mr Azhar is exhausted after playing for so long. Why don't you sing for him?"

I immediately sat down and said, "Wah! Why was this unknown to me!"

Shiuli shyly said, "I've just started learning since the last few days; can't sing well yet."

Shiuli's unwillingness to sing didn't last in the face of our protest. She began to sing.

I began to feel that whoever might have penned the song, it was the expression of nothing other than Shiuli's soul—a tribute of her sorrows.

Some people have voices that challenge one's ability to judge whether they are good or bad. They are so laden with passion and are so sincere that the listener forgets to even praise them. They are far above aesthetic judgements. They boast of no burden of duty, nor do they display austerity, but nevertheless touch the heart. The praise surges up in the eyes, not in the mouth!

This was such a voice! I was enchanted. I didn't want to say anything. Only for once and that too for courtesy's sake, I tried to say, "Excellent!", but my voice failed me. Shiuli noticed the tears in my eyes. She seemed to be searching for the meaning of those tears with teeming amazement in her wide eyes.

Hai! If only she knew—words written in ink can be erased, but not those written in water.

What did people think of me that day? I didn't give it a thought then, neither do I think about it today. What I think is that if the shiuli flower could sing, perhaps this is what it would be like. Such was the passion in her voice, the intensity in her notes.

Whatever little artistry she displayed in the tunes was a mixture of thumri and tappa. But I realised that it was not something she had learnt from her training—this artistry of her voice was spontaneous. This was quite similar to the way the lotus arranges its petals delightfully around its scented pollen without knowing anything about it.

At the end of the song I commented, "If you learn thumri you can become the unrivalled musical artist of this country! What a wonderfully melodious voice!"

Joy and shyness blended in Shiuli's looks, making her appear as beautiful as the lustre of a shiuli branch lit up by moonbeams.

Overcoming her shyness Shiuli protested, "Na, na. My voice is a bit broken. Anyway, I have a feeling that you can sing. Since you can, why don't you sing?"

I was in real trouble. I thought I'd say no. But on the other hand my voice too was tingling to sing. I said, "I'm not exactly a singer, just an aficionado! And whatever songs I know are Hindi ones."

Professor Chowdhury happily exclaimed, "Aha ha ha! You should have said this earlier! Then I'd first hear you sing. And music is not complete at all unless it is in Hindi. That language seems solely meant for music. You see, the language of classical music just cannot be Bengali. Except kirtan, Baul and Ramprasadi,[5] songs in other styles don't go with this language."

I replied, "Though I have no stock of Bengali songs yet, I don't have such despairing thoughts about the Bengali language."

I sang. Professor Chowdhury straightaway requested me to begin training him in music from the next day. Shiuli's eyes were glowing with the radiance of the unspoken words of her praise.

I saw that even Binoy babu's lot preferred classical music. At their request I sang a few khayals and tappas. Professor Chowdhury lavished so much praise on me that half of what I sang couldn't be heard. Towards the end I sang mostly thumris.

As I finished singing, I saw some ladies standing behind us. Shiuli introduced them, "She is my ma—she my mami—these are my younger sisters."

The next day I was invited to lunch at Professor Chowdhury's house. While returning I noticed Shiuli's eyes after the usual exchange of namaskars. My eyes smarted. I thought, if a mere grain of sand

[5] Ramprasad Sen was an eighteenth-century Bengali poet who set his religious verses to simple music that became renowned as Ramprasadi songs.

can make the eyes burn so much, the pain of looking into the eyes of someone must be beyond imagination.

3

I was in Shillong for a month and a half. After just a week or so I had to leave the hotel and put up at Professor Chowdhury's residence. My days and nights there flowed like a stream. The only activities I had were playing chess and singing.

The problem was with Professor Chowdhury. Playing chess with him was part of my work, no doubt, but teaching him music proved to be the most arduous task.

Shiuli too began learning music from me. Within just a few days my stock of songs and taans[6] was all but exhausted.

It seemed as if my musical training had fulfilled its purpose. I emptied my voice of its entire savings and poured it all into her voice.

There was no exchange of garlands between us—nor will there ever be. But we exchanged voices! And hearts? Well, that only the heart knows!'

Ajit interrupted and said teasingly, 'Baba, was it an exchange of kanttha or kontthi?[7] So your tale ends with the love of Neraneri?[8] Chhi!'

Without saying a word Azhar lit another cigar and went on—

'Early one morning, Shiuli's voice roused me from my sleep. She was singing,

No more can I wait,
Open, open the farewell gate.[9]

---

[6] Taan refers to the embellishments created by weaving together notes in a fast tempo following the norms of the raga. A taan is often delivered through the vowel sound 'aa'.

[7] 'Kanttha' refers to voice or throat, 'kontthi' refers to necklaces made of tulsi or holy basil. These basil-necklaces are worn by members of the Vaishnava community and are exchanged between a groom and bride to solemnise the wedding.

[8] A branch of the Vaishnava community that conducted its religious pursuits through simple and spontaneous methods, skirting those of institutionalised religion. They used to shave their heads (nera/neri is a man/woman with a shaved head) and did not follow any caste or other social distinctions. Their practices involved unrestrained mixing among people and of passions.

[9] The lines are from a Rabindranath Tagore song (*Swarabitan* 6).

Listening to this song, it seemed that my entire ribcage was in pain. In spite of my efforts, I couldn't get up. My eyes brimmed with tears.

All the agonies of her heart seemed to be pouring through the melodies of the third and sixth flat notes of Asavari raga. Today, for the first time, I heard a hint of tears in Shiuli's voice.

There was a clanging sound and I turned to find Shiuli with her leafy palms placing an offering of shiuli flowers on my table. There were tears in her eyes.

When our eyes met, she made no pretence to hide her tears and asked, "Are you leaving tomorrow itself?"

While attempting to answer her question my voice choked with tears. Restraining the heart's passion with full effort I slowly said, "Yes bhai!" I wanted to say something more but forgot what I had to say.

Clutching the shiuli flowers in her palm and absentmindedly pressing them against her lips and cheeks, Shiuli said, "When will you come again?"

With a pale smile I replied, "That I don't know! But then, I might come again."

Putting the flowers down Shiuli left. She didn't ask me another question.

My heart seemed to cry out piteously—O foolish man, the most auspicious moment of your life arrived just the once and you lost it carelessly. This fortunate moment won't come again in your life ever, ever.

I had been at their place for a month. What wealth of affection and caring! What warmth I received! We mixed freely and without restrictions—there was no prohibition, no shame, no obstacles, no suspicion. And precisely because these were not there, I suppose neither of us had any physical contact, even that of our hands, despite staying so close for such a long time. Perhaps this freedom was our most insurmountable obstacle. Neither of us judged the other's mind. No question ever arose in our minds. One of us was the infinite sky; the other a bottomless ocean. No words—no questions, simply one looking into the other's eyes.

Nobody stopped me, nobody blocked my way. As if she too knew that I would have to leave; and I knew it too.

The only truth is that the river flows—the twin banks of the river look at each other in silence. There is no longing; just helpless staring with tearful eyes.

After she left, I picked up the offering of shiuli flowers and was about to touch my face with them. Perhaps even without my own knowledge I pressed them against my forehead and put them back on the table. It seemed that these were the flowers of a priestess, not of a beloved. This thought shattered my mind with unutterable pain.

Lifting my eyes, I saw Shiuli standing there with a smile on her face like the one she had every day, and asking me, "Won't you give me music lessons today?"

I said, "Come, but today's lesson is not going to be the last one of course."

Shiuli fixed me with her doe-eyed look. I was too scared to try to comprehend its meaning.

She was like the sensitive kamini flower and I was the timid morning breeze—the more the love, the more the fear. It was as if she would crumble to dust with a single touch.

It was like the dreamy fantasy of fairyland—opening one's eyes would break the dream.

It was like the deer of illusion—pursuit would make it vanish into thin air.

I taught her a song; not a song of parting. A song about all else except parting. The moment of departure was bound to arrive; why spoil its sweetness and its anguish by discussing it?

That evening was unblemished—cloudless, bare. I told Professor Chowdhury, "Hasn't the evening today dressed up in a surprisingly unassuming manner? No finery at all!"

No sooner had I uttered that than Professor Chowdhury took the words out of my mouth and said, "The evening is a widow today."

From this one comment I understood the state of his mind. I realised what a storm had been brewing inside the heart of even this calm and gentle person. I silently said, "You are a resolute mountain, one ought just to meditate at your feet. Storms can never touch you, can they?"

The old man seemed to have had listened with attention to my unspoken words. With a pale smile he said, "I'm a very insignificant person, baba. I'm just an anthill, not a mountain. Still, the respect people like you have shown me makes me wish to become the king of mountains."

Before I could reply Shiuli came and stood before us. All of a sudden, I found myself saying, "Here's the evening devi!" And I felt so embarrassed immediately.

That evening Shiuli's golden body was wrapped in a blazing red sari. Never had I seen her wearing a red sari before. It seemed as if the evening had deprived the entire sky of colour and had come down in human form to the earth. Her body was covered in a blood-red sari; her heart was bleeding. On her face were the dark shadows of the approaching night. My eyes burned, and my mind resounded with flutes playing Poorvi raga.

I had learnt a few Bengali songs from Shiuli. I asked, "Can I sing a song?"

Shiuli sat down on the grass near my feet and said, "Sing!"

I sang,

> The golden sky is flushed with
> The hues of marriage re.[10]

Professor Chowdhury got up and left. While leaving he said, "Babaji, today we must play for one last time."

When Professor Chowdhury had left I said, "Can you tell me bhai Shiuli, what should I do when another such Ashwin month, another such evening, comes again?"

Shiuli seemed to empty all the words in her eyes into my eyes. Then slowly said, "Float shiuli malas on water!"

I silently agreed: it will be done. I asked her, "What will you do?"

She said with a smile, "Shiuli flowers fall down in any case by the end of Ashwin!"

The evening star glistened with our tears.

At night the chess party began. Professor Chowdhury lost to me. I lost to Shiuli! That was my first and last defeat. And the defeat remained as treasured as a necklace around my neck from then on.

When I took leave in the morning, the willow trees around their bungalow were covered in a coating of snow!

---

[10] From a song by Rabindranath Tagore that begins with, 'Amar godhuli lagonelo bujhi kachhay' ('It seems the twilight hour of my setting life is approaching', *Swarabitan* 33).

We haven't met again—and never will. She stays so close to me that I can touch her if I reach out just a little. Still, I don't dare touch her. The shiuli flower is very tender and very timid. It withers within minutes of wearing it on the neck. That is why when the Ashwin of the shiuli flower arrives, I string garlands in silence and float them on water!'

UNANTHOLOGISED STORIES

NINETEEN

LETTER FROM A LOST BOY

Translated by Ketaki Datta

Ma,

It was the morning of a day on which people are discouraged to travel that I set out again, facing the east! From the gateway of the rising sun in the east, came the baleful notes of Sohini–Bibhas ragas, with striking resemblance to raga Poorvi, that won me over! The notes seemed to gently touch the veena strings in my heart. The unknown veena-player, a lady from a far-off land beyond the oceans, had her dark eyes awash with tears. I failed to make out the silent pleas in those tear-soaked eyes that day. I took the dark, charming shadows of her long, thick eyelashes as beckoning signs from a mute girl, begging me to go down the streets to reach her. So, I stretched my hand to the boundless east, standing firm on the pathless way! It was the moment that was considered inauspicious to venture out on a journey. It seemed to me that glistening Venus in the fathomless depths of the blue sky's eye was, in fact, the pupil of that eye. The plaintive note of its glow seemed to fill me with a wandering-woman's sadness, filling me with profound sense of melancholy. Your fugitive, itinerant child has set out on a journey again.

As I moved forward, it occurred to me that it was indeed the 'measureless distance' I was in search of—the friend whom I had never met, but whose flute's melodies have turned me into a perplexed Baul and made me a traveller who has lost his way; not allowing me to settle down anywhere! Just like a little bird which lost its nest on a squally night, I kept flying, sidling up to the horizon in search of a refuge! I cast wistful, avid glances downward at my place, but tears welled up in my eyes in revolt, in inexplicable pain. I could neither win that haven, that shelter, nor a home. No one came forward to take me, an arrow-struck bird, in her hands like you! Yet, why am I keen on bounding out . . . what for? Which ignored feelings, what pain kicked off such never-ending cries of anguish in me, typical of a motherless child? When even close and distant relatives, holding a knife to his throat like a butcher, failed to drive him into tears; the one for whom Bhagwan was the first and foremost enemy, and who withstood the curses hurled at him by Lord Rudra, along with all the conflicts and imprecations of the world—how could you make him cry like a helpless child? Why did you make him cry? And again, why am I shedding these desolate tears? Why do I feel that today is the day to cry and wander around the streets once again? I am reminded again how anyone who had come to take me in their folds of love was burnt to ashes! And speechless in wide-eyed wonder, saddened with no definite reason, I cast my tear-filled eyes at the hard-hearted Almighty, wanting to ask him something vague!

Just at that moment, the emotion-stirring melody of the moist, tender voice of that veena player from that far-off green path, beyond the sal and piyal trees drove me to tears,

Can the man who is filled with fire
Survive, if he is ever nabbed?
His blood dances in joy in evading
Being trapped![1]

But am I truly filled with fire? Does the flame of my fire burn down the peaceful households of contented people? But why? I have never harmed my enemy, even by mistake! I am a tramp, a wandering beggar; I am as homeless as ever. Who could be my enemy? And who would I harm? I never want to afflict a heart with pain; I only want to give people joy. I consider myself Neelkantha[2] who drinks all the poison of evil meant for the men and women of the world and replaces it with pure joy. Who is the ruthless power then which erects barbed wire barriers to block my way? Yet ma, do I have to admit that there is a Supreme

[1] This is borrowed from the Rabindranath Tagore song, 'Amare bandhbi tora shei baadhon ki toder acchay' ('Do you all have such ties by which you can confine me', *Swarabitan* 16).

[2] The word means 'blue-necked'. Shiva is supposed to have drunk the poison which surfaced as the gods and the demons churned the Ocean of Milk, and while drinking the deadly poison, his neck turned blue—hence the name.

Being, 'Goodness Personified', who governs the universe judiciously? No—not at all; there is no creator-controller of this universe!

Let that be, for the moment. What was I talking about? Well, it was a Sunday, the twenty-first day of Chaitra,[3] in the Bengali year 1327. The day was not auspicious for travel, but at the crack of dawn I chose to start my journey to the east. There was no particular reason for me to do so, no invitation to work, but I set out anyway. I did not even tell my best friends about the journey lest they held me back. I was possessed by wanderlust and the road beckoned me, right then! I have seen this strange thing happening to me: if I hear such a call when I am busy with work, I don't respond to it, but if I am called for no particular work, the stir-crazy one in me dances in sheer delight!

Why was I going out? Chasing what hope? Who caused me such pain that the nest I had built with the pleasure of a wayward traveller, I razed to the ground just to be footloose. I do not know . . . Concealing the pain in the deep recesses of my heart, I am desperately trying to make sense of what the journey really means. But no matter how hard I try, the meaning eludes me and the vain effort leaves me numb in my head and my chest—as if someone was pounding my ribcage with a hammer of fire.

A little foundling sister of mine, whom I am so fond of, had sent someone to get me—her fugitive brother—and at the point of death, cast a tear-drenched look at the road which was supposed to bring me back to her. But my wanderlust kept me so obsessed that with extreme cruelty, I disregarded her. She just cried and silently observed how her affectionate demand was trampled by someone she had loved! Her studied silence has been my punishment—it whiplashed my insides, leaving scars everywhere! I don't know if she would ever forgive me! Even though she did, I would never be able to forgive myself. I don't think there is any forgiveness for trampling on someone's right to affection.

Hai! How deeply attached I become, with these foundlings on the road, with the ties of woe, anguish, hope and dependence! And how fondly and firmly I embrace them to this lost and timid bosom of mine! Again, how in a moment's capriciousness and error of judgment I pull apart the bonds of sorrow that tie us with inexplicable ruthlessness and

---

[3] The last month of the Bengali calendar.

rush towards another unknown destination! That proves to be such a colossal blunder that even lifelong penance cannot compensate for it. What an uncomfortable, accursed, restive life I have been living! Who makes me commit such a heartless blunder? Who has blown away my roadside hut with a gust of squally wind, again and again? Who could that be? Why was such mindless villainy inflicted on me?

Severing bonds one by one, I now realise it was I who had been the worst victim, and it is I who has suffered the most. It has lacerated my heart. I have not untied these knots but have ripped them apart. And because I was tearing them off with brute force, each time a tough knot ruptured it got entangled in my heart! That, I believe, has created the heart condition that makes it difficult for me to breathe, even though I don't fully asphyxiate!

In my heart of hearts, I was aware of a dreadful urge for slaughter and murder—turning everything red and red! Blood spilling out everywhere! The more the bonds I snapped, the more they lodged themselves in my heart. And the more laboured my breathing has become like the northerly winds whimpering through the acacia trees! Ooh, it's such an intense pain, ma!

Even then, I had to leave. The plaintive note carried by the gust of wind from the east blew me away, rebuffing the doleful cries of everyone's love and affection! It kept singing, 'Oh cautious wayfarer, keep wandering, losing your way once again!'[4]

My mind was being assailed by a resounding wail from all corners. 'Get out right now, otherwise you will never have a chance to meet the "Unexpected"!' What a pity! Who would the 'unexpected' be? Which near and dear one would I get to meet now? Which lost mother would call for me? Well, wouldn't that affection which has beckoned me, that charm of home that has drawn me to the road, reveal itself to me now? Isn't it also walking the road hoping to meet me? But then, I heard an echo in the wilderness of my mind—'No, my dear crazy soul, no! It moves far away; its journey stretches over eons. Now you must go and search for that.' I kept crooning the tune of the easterly wind on my way forward,

I shall not wait for you to appear,
I shall venture out instead,

[4] Opening line of a Rabindranath Tagore song (*Swarabitan* 16).

The leaves from the dry flowers disappear
Not a moment is to be wasted![5]

Then going down the road, I saw the grass flanking the thoroughfare and the rows of kash waving their blades like a conceited little girl, crying aloud, 'Na, Na, Na!' The young paddy saplings flashed a verdant smile and shaking their heads and raising their finger reprimanded me, 'Na, Na, Na!' Far away on the outskirts of the village that merged with the horizon, the bamboo plants, coy like young brides with their eyes downcast say in a trembling voice, 'Na, Na, Na!'

Dipping the pitcher she had been carrying into the water of the pond, and standing on the last of the steps leading to it, a young wife from the hamlet glanced wistfully at my chariot and seemed to ask with a tinge of sadness in her voice, 'Where are you going, O stranger, O traveller from afar?' That child-bride, perhaps, was imagining my residence to be near her baap's! Perhaps, she thought, I would take the road that ran in front of her father's house! Hai! She had quite a pile of messages for me to deliver to her baap–ma, to her siblings! Tears welled up in this homeless wanderer's eyes as he kept looking at the wisp of a girl! What a pity! A dear 'homeless' sister of mine, plucked from her mother's lap! Oh sister, I do not belong to your land, but I do not know why I feel like crying just looking at you! In your eyes, I can see a world of pain writ large, suffered by child-brides throughout Bengal, who had to leave their own homes behind! The attraction of one's own home is so filled with pain! I saw her wiping her tears with the end of her Moynamoti sari,[6] and disappearing like a spec among the columns of betel-nut trees, crossing the paddy-fields with the pitcher held firm on her waist. I was reminded in that moment of a conversation between 'Kumar' and 'Ila' in the play *Raja Rani*,[7] when Kumar was shedding tears remembering his younger sister, Sumitra, whom he was extremely fond of. Sumitra had been married off—she was no longer a part of his family. In a bittersweet voice he was recounting this to

---

5 Lines from the same song (*Swarabitan* 16).

6 A cotton sari of fine texture, woven by the weavers of Bengal, in pre-independence days.

7 Nazrul has referred to the play *Raja O Rani* (*The King and the Queen*) written by Tagore (1889).

Ila through his heart-rending words. I also recalled the moving song sung by Ila:

> They bring the far ones near and push, far-off, the dear ones.
> The flute's tune calls them out of their homes![8]

I also saw how a nonchalant traveller was crossing the stream on a banana-raft, and how he was lost in the beauty of the paddy saplings on either side of it as though he was reading a note from someone he had been missing all his life, etched on the paddy in green letters. The eternal hawker woman of my mind-village was still shouting 'Who will buy me, who will buy me', hurting the southerly breeze.

The sunburnt, barren noontime was gasping like a thirsty raven. That was the time when our boat floated on the river Padma. I saw the dry sand bank of the river lying prostrate and panting like the bone-tired widow keeping the ekadoshi[9] fast. On the other side of the Padma, the borders of Manikganj were drawn in deep green lines. And on this side, the forests of Faridpur cast deep and verdant shades. Two lonely pigeons, a male and a female, went crying out aloud on opposite banks of the river, filling the noontime sky with their loud wails. I don't know why my heart cried out in unfathomable pain.

Ma, that day when I took my leave and cried my heart out, and made you cry too, I stood holding the railings of a steamer on the Padma at the wharf of Goalanda before the advent of the evening—I looked at the green horizons of Manikganj and my eyes filled with tears. Ma, you had told me that over there, by the blue horizon, on the other bank, we had our dwelling once. That shack might still stand there, though it should be a forlorn place now, abandoned and left to rot. I was also reminded of the memories of my lost sister, Beli, who was burnt to ashes on a funeral pyre, perhaps in that village, lying on the other side of this river; Kirtinasha!

Oh Lord! Where is that all-devouring crematorium? Where again is that dilapidated house still preserving loads of memories? These two lost sisters of mine, Lily and Beli, made me cry the most as I remembered their cremation and their turning into ashes! My greatest sorrow is that

---

[8] The lines are taken from a song of Tagore's from *Raja O Rani* (*Swarabitan* 28).

[9] The eleventh lunar day after the new moon as well as the no/new moon. Hindus often fast on ekadoshi as a means of self-control or self-cleansing.

I never got to see them after I left. Bela was supposed to have seen the Lotus-Eyed Lord[10] on the day she breathed her last. When Kamala and Pramila came to know about it, they burst into laughter. Angrily, she said to them, 'You will never get to see Him. You are liars. He never appears in person to those who lie.' Her simple worship of many years found its veritable fulfilment through her truth and grit. And that was why she was blessed with the benevolent lotus-eyed glance of the Lord and was rendered free. How could we hold back the liberated soul? So the girl, freed from all bonds, severed all ties to take her leave from us.

Just an hour or so before that, my heart felt a sudden pang when, looking at Faridpur on this side of the river, I thought about a shady homestead in whose yard my strong and affectionate mashi-ma made her evening offerings at the tulsi-altar; which no longer happen now and have been lost in the folds of time! I could not check my tears as I remembered this strong, ascetic mashi-ma of mine, who was, in every sense of the term, a daughter of Swaha![11] Well, could you please tell me what the Almighty had gained by depriving this hermit-like woman of her iron-bangle and the sindoor in the parting of her hair?! Who would answer my queries, ma? Do I still have to say there is a special deity by the name Mangalmay,[12] whose every action leads to the well-being of humanity? I feel greatly perturbed when I see these widows. No spectacle would ever be so heart-rending as that of the widows of Bengal. I offer these ascetic women my heartfelt respect as I remembered again that rebellious lady—my youngest mashi-ma.

As I looked on, teary-eyed, at the shady columns of trees lining both the banks of the river, I tried hard to locate those lost dwellings bearing the touch of my mother and aunt. Where had they all gone?

A smoky, grey dusk descended on the Padma. Evening wore on, letting down its smoky hair like a lately-widowed woman who, smeared in dust, was rubbing her hair with the cloudy aachol of aimless celestial

---

[10] Lord Krishna, as his eyes as described as being lotus-shaped, wide, and evocative of deep emotions.

[11] Swaha is the wife of Agni, the god of fire. Tejaswini means strong and radiant. Hence, she has been compared to Swaha's daughter, Agneya (meaning, Agni's daughter or 'the daughter of fire').

[12] The Almighty, who does 'good' for all.

maidens in order to remove the last traces of sindoor from the parting of her hair! Fine drops of moisture accumulated on the paddy saplings and in my eyes!

When I boarded the train at Chandpur, the evening had already intensified. The train began to move and I lost myself in my thoughts. What my lazy, distracted eyes registered was the illusion that the train was rushing backward at full speed along with the dark trees, which were becoming darker as the night progressed. From the long shadow that the train cast it appeared that a giant centipede was rushing forward.

It was already deep into the night when I got down at Comilla. A youth, exceedingly handsome, came forward, offered me his hands and said, 'Come with me'. Glancing at his lotus-like, polash-like eyes my own eyes became calm! We fell in love, without knowing each other. But, on the contrary, he kept on calling me 'lotus-eyed' and 'polash-eyed'! This brought tears to my eyes.

When the two us, like two brothers holding one another, reached the yard, it felt like the night was still awake. I noticed two or three sprightly girls. They were looking at me with a world of curiosity in their eyes, wide open.

Just then, you made your appearance and I kept looking at you, overwhelmed. Even a chatterbox like me completely lost my speech.

I instantly recognised you. I had travelled widely and had been to many lands, but I had never come across such a calm, serene and exquisite figure of a mother. My eyes were blessed by the motherly grace of Goddess Annapurna, the provider of food, the empress of the world! Again, I also recognised in a flash, your eyes as those of my mother who had lost her child. In your perplexed look I could see unfulfilled motherly feelings that had been there for many births! Didn't you once tell me that you would love to be the mother of hundreds of lost children, again and again, just to get back the son you lost, perhaps in your previous birth?

Thus, you, the Mother of the Universe, had laid a trap to catch hold of your fugitive child! That is why you have taken up all the foundlings of the street on your lap, equally disregarding the barriers of religion and society. The words that articulated inside me now reverberated all around me, saying, 'Oh dear, this time my venturing out has been fruitful, quite meaningful!' It seemed as though I would be able to 'taste freedom amidst innumerable bonds'.

Many things came to my mind then, as if I was mesmerised. The memories of those moments overcame me and I seemed to have lost my language . . . However, I had a peaceful, sound sleep that night, too happy to have cuddled up in the bosom of this house . . . And then, as if I had been shot with an arrow in my chest, I kept vomiting blood like a wounded bird and sought shelter at your door, and my aunt and you took me up with much care, to hold me tightly to your heart. You, mashi-ma and my little sisters put up a brave fight with Yama to bring me back to health. Now I wonder, with what motherly and domestic charm could you captivate the wild deer? Bless me, ma, so that I can dedicate the life that you have given me as a gift, to your service.

TWENTY

THE HAWK-CUCKOO FROM THE WOODS

Translated by Parjanya Sen

The steamer-station at Tepakhola

Embraced by a caressing moon in full glow, the Padma river reverberates, rapturously! The happiness in the river's bosom is echoed by the waves breaking on her shores.

Sitting on the shores is Romola, the wife of the deputy magistrate of Faridpur, Mr Dushasan Mitra.

Mr Mitra paced restlessly and occasionally rebuked his wife, 'Romola, it's nearly 9 pm! We need to leave!'

Romola, however, was entranced by the sight of the waves of the Padma. She did not respond. Faraway, in a boat that floated half-hidden by shadows—who was the person playing a simple tune of a bhatiyali[1] on the flute! An ecstatic Romola gushed to her husband, 'Dear! Can you feel it? The moon is Krishna, and the Padma his Radha! Her body is attired in a blue sari, and his light creates ripples within it! The sound of the flute has quickened her passion!'

Mr Mitra was somewhat afraid of his wife. She was a headstrong woman, blessed with stunning beauty. She also came with a lot of dowry and wealth from her father's house. She seemed to be happy-go-lucky. And yet, somewhere, there was something she missed! All of a sudden, without any apparent reason, she would become absent-minded. Her face gathered shadows as if a strange sense of despondency afflicted her. On such occasions, seeing her in such a state, Mr Mitra

---

[1] A genre of Bengali folksong; it is the song of the boatmen about rivers and riverside communities.

became quite concerned. He tried in vain to decipher the meaning of her despair. Unable to do so, he tried to shift her attention to worldly household affairs which often led to disasters. Romola wept loudly, took the motorcar, and went to sit by the shores of the Padma. Despite the name Dushasan, meaning 'the uncontrollable', Mr Mitra was completely unable to control his wife. After all, the motorcar too was a gift from his father-in-law and his job as deputy magistrate was made possible through the man's recommendation!

Romola, interpreting the interaction of the moonlight and the river waves as the erotic play of Radha and Krishna, kept mumbling to herself. Mr Mitra, in an agitated tone, told her, 'Romola, this madness has taken hold of you ever since you began learning kirtans!'

Romola's father was a devotee of Krishna. Every evening, there was a kirtan soiree at his house. Romola, too, could sing a few kirtans. When she sang, her mind travelled to Brindaban, and she began to weep!

Before she could respond to Mr Mitra, out of nowhere a bird suddenly descended on Romola's bosom. Caught off guard, Romola shrieked. Mr Mitra caught hold of the bird and said to his wife, 'See Romola! Such a beautiful bird! Oh, one of its wings is broken!' Romola snatched the bird from her husband's hands and placing it upon her bosom, began to inspect it. What sort of a bird was it? She had no clue! Mr Mitra attempted to identify it. 'It's a jungle babbler!' he said while Romola continued her careful inspection of the bird. The bird strangely made no effort to escape. It seemed to be already familiar with Romola. Mr Mitra kept repeating, 'Can't you see? Its wing is broken! Otherwise, why shouldn't it try to fly away?'

In a disconsolate voice, Romola said, 'Let's go home!' The bird tucked its head into her bosom snugly, as though it had returned to its lost nest its eyes were overcome with sleep. It refused to even budge!

Upon returning home Mr Mitra began frantically searching for a place to keep the bird. Romola, carrying the bird, entered her drawing room. Suddenly, she gasped! There was a blood stain on her sari! She examined the bird and noticed that there was an open wound on its neck. It had possibly been attacked by a snake or a wild animal! The bird's pain began to throb within Romola's own bosom. She immediately applied turmeric, salt and iodine to the bird's wound and hugging it to her heart, began to weep—what if it doesn't live? Back in her father's house, her elder brothers used to call her a crybaby. Upon seeing any animal or bird in pain, Romola would create a ruckus with her tears.

She began telling the servants of the house, 'Do you see? This bird seems to be my pet! See, I am not holding onto it. But it refuses to let go!' She hugged the bird to her bosom, showering it with kisses. A little later, Mr Mitra returned from town, panting and carrying a huge cage. 'Romola, see! I bought a cage for the bird. Isn't it beautiful?' He grabbed the bird from his wife and placed it in the cage. He exclaimed, 'I have never seen a bird like this before! It looks like a black-hooded oriole. It might also be a hawk-cuckoo.'

A few of the servants said, 'Indeed Sir! It is a hawk-cuckoo!'

From then on, the wounded bird would often call out 'Piya kahan? O! where is my beloved?' in its mellifluous voice.

It had been four or five years since Romola's marriage to Mr Mitra. She did not have a child. Neither did she seem keen on having one! People found her a bit strange. She didn't even have any friends. The wives of Mr Mitra's colleagues and fellow officers had tried many times to befriend her. Each attempt ended with a casual exchange of pleasantries. Romola had never made any friends. This made Mr Mitra inwardly happy. Friends would mean added expenses! And Mr Mitra was quite the miser! His servants whispered among themselves that he would even squeeze ants to extract jaggery.

A few months later it seemed that the hawk-cuckoo had become tired of its imprisoned life. It began fluttering its wings and trying to escape its cage. At first Romola was worried it would fly away if she set it free from the cage. Eventually, however, she began letting it out after securely bolting the doors and windows. She would hug the bird to her bosom and test if it attempted to escape. The hawk-cuckoo seemed to prefer Romola's bosom to its cage. It would nestle itself snugly in her arms and call out 'O! where is my beloved?' Romola would smilingly respond to it, 'Eh! How would I know?' and shower the bird with kisses. Her eyes would brim with unwarranted tears.

After a few months, the bird seemed to have become strangely domesticated. It would not even attempt to fly away! The people of the household were taken aback by the bird's ability to listen to and pick up many human words. It would call the servants by their names. On hearing Romola sing any kirtan, it would keep muttering 'Radha Krishna!' till its voice reached a feverish crescendo! Romola would immediately stop her singing, hug the bird to her heart and exclaim, with her eyes brimming with tears, 'You are a bird from Brindaban!' Mr Mitra's servants fondly named the bird 'Hari-Bola'[2] as it did not at all look like a jungle babbler. Many people came from all over just to see this mysterious bird who could now almost talk like a human!

A year had passed—the bird could now utter many words. . .

Suddenly, a strange ailment befell the bird—on seeing Romola each time, it would call her, 'O piya! O beloved!' Romola's heart would resound with happiness—a happiness tinged with bittersweet melancholy. From where did this wild bird arrive? Who taught the bird to call her 'beloved'? Was it a messenger from Brindaban? Or was it the very flute of Krishna? She hugged the bird to her chest and shed poignant tears. She could not lose sight of the bird even for a moment! Wherever she went, she carried it with her.

Mr Mitra had initially been very fond of the bird. However, each time he came physically close to Romola, the bird would cry out, 'O! my eyes are gone, eyes are gone!'

Romola would laugh and ask Mr Mitra to let go of her. She would tell him, 'The bird gets jealous! It understands everything!'

Mr Mitra would caress her even more as if to show off to the bird that she belonged to him! The bird would keep crying out, 'O! my eyes are gone, eyes are gone!' in a shriller tone. Ultimately, Mr Mitra would let go of Romola, but both of them would double up with laughter.

At first, it was the bird who expressed envy; now it was Mr Mitra who began feeling pangs of jealousy. It was as though Romola loved the bird far more than she loved him! She would obsess over the bird and play with it continuously. What would make the bird happy? What would it eat?—these thoughts preoccupied her constantly! A bird belonged in a cage! Hearing it call out once or twice a day was fine! Even occasionally petting it was acceptable! But to obsess over it night and day seemed madness! Romola wouldn't let the bird out of her sight even for a second! This became intolerable to Mr Mitra!

In exasperation, he told her one day, 'Romo, you are obsessing too much over the bird!'

---

[2] Bola is a Bengali word that means 'to say'. Hence 'Hari-Bola' means the one who can utter the name of Hari.

Mr Mitra's words lashed her like a sharp whip. 'What do you mean?' she asked!

'You know better than that!' Mr Mitra retorted.

For a second, Romola seemed lost in her thoughts, her eyes downcast. Then in a soft voice, she murmured, 'Have you ever seen me mix freely with strangers, male or female?'

Mr Mitra replied, 'No!'

Romola reiterated, 'Have any of my actions or behaviour ever given you cause for anguish?'

Mr Mitra, suddenly overcome by guilt, grasped Romola's hands and in a dejected voice, said, 'Why are you saying such things, Romo? Truly, when I see the behaviour of my friends' wives, when I see them mingle with strangers, I feel overwhelmed by disgust! The lack of restraint I see in the interaction between men and women in these modern times I never see in your behaviour! Indeed, I consider myself extremely fortunate!'

Hearing these words, Romola's eyes glittered like the pole star—she sometimes looked at Mr Mitra in this way! Mr Mitra was petrified by the look in her eyes—it seemed as though some goddess was staring at him. Overwhelmed by fear and respect, on such occasions, Mr Mitra felt like genuflecting before her!

Romola said, 'I can hear the call of the lord of Brindaban in this bird's voice! It isn't just any bird; it is the very flute that adorns the hand of Krishna! When I hold him to my bosom, I feel the Lord's holy touch! If you are jealous of him, I will be forced to think of you as a demon and I shall cut off all my ties with you!'

Mr. Mitra indeed became a demon all of a sudden! Like a python, his eyes began to flare, as he shouted, 'I know your father is very rich! My wealth, my job—everything is granted by him! True, you can leave me whenever you want! You can even remarry . . .'

Romola didn't let Mr. Mitra finish his sentence! Her whole being ablaze with an incandescent light, she began to glow like a liana vine. Confronting Mr. Mitra, she cried, 'You are corrupt, you are ugly! Seeing you, hearing you speak, makes me forget my Lord, the vision of ideal beauty! You turn this beautiful world into a hideous one! Get away from me!' These last words seemed almost a command!

Calling for the chauffeur, Romola took the motorcar and headed to Mr Dutta's house. Mr Dutta was an elderly judge; his wife loved

Romola like a daughter. If she had any friend at all, it was Mrs Dutta. Romola called her 'mother'—her own ma was long deceased.

When she returned home in the evening, it occurred to her that caught within this tussle she had entirely forgotten about the bird. The whole day she hadn't called out to the bird, or thought of it, or even seen it! Her bosom heaved with an overbearing ache. She began frantically looking for the bird. As she entered the drawing-room she saw—an empty cage, no trace of the hawk-cuckoo! Her whole body began to quiver. She fell unconscious upon the floor.

Much later, upon regaining consciousness, she began summoning the servants, 'My hawk-cuckoo! Has anyone seen my hawk-cuckoo?' The servants, however, would not utter a word. It dawned on her immediately that Mr Mitra had released the bird, or, perhaps, worse . . .

At that juncture, Mr Mitra himself entered the room.

Romola's whole body now radiated with a divine light. Encountering Mr Mitra, she stood right in front of him and asked calmly, 'Where is my hawk-cuckoo?'

Mr Mitra replied harshly, 'The hawk-cuckoo has been returned to the wild!'

Starting to unbraid her hair, Romola said, 'Fine then! I too am heading there.'

Mr Mitra's whole body shook like that of a monster as he bellowed, 'You will not find your precious bird in the wild! I have torn away both its wings and thrown it back in the woods—the place from where it had come—on the shores of the Padma! By now, it must have been released from its misery by a wildcat or a snake, or else, the tides of the Padma must have washed it away.'

Even as an enraged Mr Mitra was uttering these words Romola had removed and tossed away her bracelet and bangles. She had loosened her hair, and unadorned and unembellished, she looked resplendent. In a trance-like state, her whole being quivering, she uttered, 'You may have injured the bird; but you cannot kill it! He is the bird of Brindaban. You may be my worldly husband—but He whose messenger the bird is, is my Supreme Lord, my true soulmate! In every life, I am His devotee, His beloved. You know, all these years that I was married to you, I have never neglected my duties towards you as a wife. I served you with my body and soul. I gave you all my wealth. You can marry again with this wealth. I do not know through which deity's curse I had to endure being married to a demon. Was I Tulsi in my previous birth? That selfsame Tulsi who was the beloved of Krishna and who had been cursed to endure being married to the demon Shankhachura.[3] And yet, when the period of her curse ended, the divine Lord came to rescue his beloved. Likewise, my curse too has been lifted on this day. I shall not return to this world. No unholy being will ever touch this body of mine!

O hawk-cuckoo! My hawk-cuckoo! The one who calls me beloved! Finally, I have heard your voice, I have understood your call. I am coming—I am coming to you my love.' Uttering these words, like one seized with insanity, she ran towards the shores of the river Padma!

Already overpowered by rage, Mr Mitra made no attempt to stop her. He remained seated in one corner, shaking in anger!

Romola ran through the streets shouting, 'Hawk-cuckoo! O my hawk-cuckoo!'

It was well past midnight. High above in the night-sky, the full-moon of Shukla paksha ekadoshi seemed to weep divine tears, like the forsaken Radha herself. The streets were deserted. Romola tripped and fell again and again as she trekked through the woods bordering the shores of the Padma. Her sari was torn apart by the thorns of the wild bush, her body was bruised and bloody. Yet, her thoughts were focused on the bird—'O my hawk-cuckoo! Come back, O! my beloved of Brindaban, return to me!'

Suddenly, she heard that familiar sound echoing somewhere from the sands of the Padma's banks—'Piya! O my beloved!' Romola tumbled headlong onto the sandy shores. The wounded, near-dead hawk-cuckoo trudged weakly to her bosom and called out in a soft tone, 'Piya! Piya!'

---

[3] Tulsi, whose name was Brinda in her previous birth—or Vishnupriya because of her devotion to Vishnu—was married to the demon, Shankhachura. Shankhachura started attacking the gods and he could not be defeated because the power of Brinda's chastity functioned as a protective force. Lord Vishnu deceived Brinda by disguising himself as her husband and so undermined her chastity. Brinda was furious and turned Vishnu into the Shaligram stone with her curse, while Shiva blessed her so that she could be united with Vishnu in her next life. Brinda was turned into Tulsi and the custom of offering tulsi leaves to the Shaligram stone began from that day.

Romola hugged the dying bird to her heart and plunged into the waters of the Padma! Her open hair surged like the tide of the river. The halo radiating from her body illuminated the whole river. Her face, still afloat on the water, appeared like a freshly bloomed lotus-flower. She looked upward, towards some celestial being in the open skies flooded by the light of the moon. With both hands, she raised the hawk-cuckoo skywards from her bosom. Who knew where the waters of the Padma bore the beloved clasping Krishna's emissary to her bosom!

EDITORS AND TRANSLATORS

EDITORS

Syed Manzoorul Islam is Professor Emeritus in the English Department of the University of Dhaka. He has written extensively on literature, literary theory, cultural studies, art and architecture in journals at home and abroad. He has also published articles on Kazi Nazrul Islam and has recently edited a collection of his poems, songs, short stories, novels and works in other genres titled *Aboshyik Nazrul* (*The Essential Nazrul*). Professor Islam is also a fiction writer and has received numerous awards in recognition of his contributions to literature, including the Bangla Academy Award (1996) and Ekushey Padak (2018).

Kaustav Chakraborty is Associate Professor of English, at Southfield College, Darjeeling. He has been a fellow at the Indian Institute of Advanced Study, Shimla. He is the author of *Indigeneity, Tales and Alternatives: Revisiting Select Tribal Folktales*; *Queering Tribal Folktales from East and Northeast India*; and *Nations and Nationalisms: A Short Introduction*. He is the editor of *Indian Drama in English* and *The Politics of Belonging in Contemporary India: Anxiety and Intimacy* and has co-edited *The Queer and the Vernacular Languages in India: Studies in Contemporary Texts and Cultures* as well as *Tagore and Nationalism*. His areas of interest include Indigenous literatures and cultures, folklore, cultures of nationalism, queer studies, philosophy of intimacy, and South Asian literatures.

TRANSLATORS

Amita Ray is retired Associate Professor of English. An academic of varied interests, she is a translator, short story writer and poet. She has translated Abanindra Nath Tagore's *Khirer Putul* and a compilation of short stories written by eminent Bengali authors titled *Treats in Translation*. She is presently engaged in several translation projects. Her latest publication is a collection of short stories titled *Trail of Love and Longings*. Her poems have been widely published in various anthologies, journals and e-zines of national and international repute. She is also an Executive Committee member of the Intercultural Poetry and Performance Library, Kolkata.

Anindita Mukhopadhyay is Professor, Department of History, University of Hyderabad. She obtained her PhD from SOAS, University of London. Her areas of interest include cultural identities, state, governance and power, intellectual and legal histories, the impact of the colonial domain through knowledge/power nexus, and the political domains of texts and translations. She is the author of *Behind the Mask: The Cultural Definition of the Legal Subject in Colonial Bengal (1715-1911)* and *Children's Games, Adult's Gambits: From Vidyasagar to Satyajit Ray*. Her translation of Rabindranath Tagore's 'Sesher Kobita' has been published as *The Last Poem*. She has also translated the short stories of Sarat Chandra Chattopadhyay in her book *Stories from Saratchandra: Innocence and Reality*.

Dhrubajyoti Sarkar is Assistant Professor, Department of English, University of Kalyani. His teaching interests include eighteenth-century English literature and culture, Indian literatures of the nineteenth century and women's literatures. His doctoral dissertation at the University of Hyderabad analysed the creation of textual authority in the early phase of nationalism in colonial Bengal. His research interests are religion–culture interface, religious nationalism and issues of aesthetics.

Fakrul Alam is Director, Sheikh Mujib Research Institute for Peace and Liberty, and UGC Professor, Department of English, University of Dhaka. He received the Bangla Academy Puroshkar (Literature Award) for Translation in 2013. His publications include *Bharati Mukherjee*; *Jibanananda Das: Selected Poems* and *Imperial Entanglements and Literature in English*; and *The Essential Tagore* (with Radha Chakravarty). Other works include translations of Sheikh Mujibur Rahman's *Unfinished Memoirs* and *Prison Diaries*, as well as *Ocean of Sorrow*, a translation of the late-nineteenth century Bengali epic narrative, *Bishad Sindhu*. Among his most recent publications are a translation of Sheikh Mujibur Rahman's *New China* and *Reading Literature in English and English Studies in Bangladesh: Postcolonial Perspectives*. Forthcoming works include a selection of translations of Rabindranath's song-lyrics from Tagore's *Gitabitan*.

Gulshan Ara, professionally a scientist, received her PhD in Physics from Columbia University, New York. During her long scientific career, she has focused on the development and application of novel technologies for the diagnosis and treatment of cancer. She is also an avid Nazrul researcher and spearheaded the establishments of Nazrul Endowments at California State University and the University of Connecticut. She has also worked relentlessly to incorporate Nazrul into American undergraduate curricula. The Bangladesh Nazrul Institute has published two of her books on Nazrul: *Kazi Nazrul Islam: Life & Lyric* and *Kazi Nazrul Islam & Maya Angelou: Two Geniuses from the East & the West.*

Jackie Kabir is a writer and translator from Bangladesh. Her first collection of short stories *Silent Noise* was published in 2016. She has translated Selina Hossain's book *River of My Blood* and co-translated *The Charcoal Portrait*. She has contributed to volume such as *Kazi Nazrul Islam Selections Volume 2*, *Contemporary Short Stories from Bangladesh* and many others. A translation of one of her short stories was anthologised in *Ganthagolpo*. She has also contributed to the translation of Kazi Nazrul Islam's 'Badhon Hara' published as *Unfettered.*

Ketaki Datta is Associate Professor of English, Chandernagore College. Her debut translation was *The Voyage*, a translation of a Bengali novel by Jarasandha titled *Paadi.* She has also translated *The Last Salute*, originally *Shesh Namaskar* by Santosh Kumar Ghosh; twelve short stories by Tagore into English as *Selected Short Stories of Rabindranath Tagore in Translation*; selected short stories by Bimal Kar, Santosh Kumar Ghosh, Bimal Mitra, Sunil Gangopadhyay; and stories by Saikat Rakshit and Nalini Bera published in the volume, *Anthology of Bengali Short Stories,* edited by Professor Sanjukta Dasgupta. She is a contributor to both *Prachin Sahitya* and *Adhunik Sahitya* of Rabindranath Tagore, jointly published by CENTIL, Jadavpur University and Visva-Bharati.

Marzia Rahman is a fiction writer and translator based in Dhaka, Bangladesh. Her writings have appeared in *The Daily Star, Dhaka Tribune, Golpokotha, Six Seasons Review, Writing Places Anthology, The Book of Dhaka, The Demoness* and several online magazines. She is a member of the Dhaka Translation Centre. In 2017, she participated in the International Literary Translation and Creative Writing Summer

School at the University of East Anglia, Norwich, UK. Her novella-in-flash, *Life on the Edges,* was longlisted for the Bath Novella-in-Flash Award Competition in 2018 and her novella-in-flash, *If Dreams had wings and Houses were built on clouds,* was longlisted for the Bath Novella-in-Flash Award Competition in 2022. She is currently working on a collaborative translation project of Shahaduz Zaman's *Ekjon Komlalebu.*

Masrufa Ayesha Nusrat is Assistant Professor of English, East West University, and was educated at the University of Dhaka and the University of Nottingham. Currently she is pursuing her doctoral studies at the University of Texas, Dallas. She is a literary translator and has contributed to many anthologies published locally and abroad. *Celebration and Other Stories* (2015) is her own collection of short stories in translation. Her research interests include women's writing, feminism, South Asian literatures, English literature and cultural studies.

Nishat Atiya is a lecturer in the Department of English, University of Dhaka, Bangladesh. She was sub-editor of the literature and review page of Bangladesh's leading English newspaper, *The Daily Star.* Her research interests include comparative literature, history, narrative studies, creative writing and translation.

Parjanya Sen is currently a Postdoctoral Visiting Fellow at the School of Anthropology and Museum Ethnography, University of Oxford, and 2023 Early-Career Research Fellow, The Robert H. N. Ho Family Foundation Program in Buddhist Studies. He is Assistant Professor of English, Deshbandhu College for Girls, Kolkata. His work lies at the intersection of Buddhist historiography, colonial Bengal, Tibet studies and museum ethnography. He has co-edited *Death and Dying in Northeast India: Indigeneity and Afterlife.*

Pritam Bandyopadhyay is Associate Professor of English, Barasat Government College, Kolkata. He was sub-editor of the Bengali daily *Ananda Bazar Patrika.* Apart from his regular teaching assignments, he has also worked as a member of the Undergraduate Board of Studies of Netaji Subhas Open University and handled teaching assignments at West Bengal Judicial Academy where he taught in-service judges of the West Bengal Judicial Service. He has translated poetry as a contribution to *Word for Word: Essays on Translation in Memory of Jagannath Chakraborty*. His latest venture is the translation of stories for young adults from Bengali into English in *Timeless Tales from Bengal: An Anthology of Bangla Children's and Young Adults' Stories.*

Priyanka Chatterjee is Assistant Professor of English, Directorate of Distance Education, University of North Bengal. She has recently completed her PhD in English Literature from Sikkim University, Gangtok. Comparative literature, gender studies and cultural studies are some of her areas of interest.

Sarker Hasan Al Zayed is an academic, translator and fiction writer. He is currently Associate Professor of English, Independent University Bangladesh. Zayed received his PhD from the Department of English, SUNY, Albany, for his research on contemporary South Asian literature. He is the translator (along with Raihan Rahman) of Ian Almond's *The Thought of Nirad C Choudhury*. His academic works have appeared in journals such as *South Asian Review*, *Crossings* and *Harvest,* and peer-reviewed anthologies published by Lexington Books and Pearson Longman. Zayed is a regular contributor to the literary page of *The Daily Star*, Bangladesh.

Saurav Dasthakur is Associate Professor of English, Visva-Bharati, Santiniketan. His academic articles have been published in books and journals of national and international repute. An avid translator between Bangla and English, he has coordinated translation workshops, contributed translations of poems and fiction and non-fiction prose-pieces to several journals and anthologies. His individually published and edited volumes of translation include *Minority Voices: An Anthology of Asian-American Poetry in Bengali Translation*, *Timeless Tales from Bengal: An Anthology of Children's and Young Adults' Stories* and *Khali Haat*, a translation of Joan Larkin's *Naked Hand.*

Sohana Manzoor is Associate Professor, Department of English and Humanities, University of Liberal Arts Bangladesh. She has a PhD from Southern Illinois University, Carbondale and her area of expertise is nineteenth-century British fiction. Her short stories, non-fiction and translations have been published in *Kitaab, Borderless Journal, Asiatic, The New Age*, *The Dhaka Tribune, The Daily Star, Bengal Lights* and *Six*

Seasons Review. Currently, she is also the Literary Editor of *The Daily Star*, Bangladesh.

Sreetanwi Chakraborty is Assistant Professor, Amity Institute of English Studies and Research, Amity University, Kolkata. She graduated from Presidency College, Kolkata, did her postgraduation from the University of Calcutta, and obtained her MPhil from Rabindra Bharati University with a thesis titled *The Sleeping Beauty Wakes Up: A Feminist Interpretation of Fairy Tales*. This was published as a book in 2019 and it received the 'Rising Star' Award in the non-fiction category at New Town Book Fair, Kolkata. She is the Chief Editor of a bilingual, biannual academic journal *Litinfinite*. Her areas of interest include Indian English poetry, Indian English drama, feminism and cultural politics and South Asian diasporic studies.

Sucharita Sarkar is Professor of English, D.T.S.S College of Commerce, Mumbai. Her doctoral thesis investigated mothering narratives in contemporary India. Her current research focuses on intersections of maternity with body, religion, cultures, self-writing and media, from South Asian perspectives. She is an invited member of the Faculty of Humanities, Dr. Homi Bhabha State University, Mumbai. Her recent publications include articles in *Current Sociology*; *Qualitative Inquiry*; and *Open Theology*; chapters in *Representing Abortion; Food, Faith and Gender in South Asia; Thickening Fat: Fat Bodies, Intersectionality and Social Justice*; and *The Politics of Belonging in Contemporary India*, among others.

Sudeshna Majumdar is Assistant Professor of English, Rampurhat College, Birbhum. Sudeshna has published a monograph titled *The Serpentina within the Pyramid: Strategies of Representation in Select Eighteenth-Century Literature and Painting* and an album of paintings titled *Colours of Confluence: a Pictorial Journey into Sufism and Bhakti*. Her essay on 'Post-Partition Bangla memoirs' was published in *Indian Literature*, the Sahitya Akademi journal. Her translations have been published in volumes like *Bharatiya Engraji Kobita: A Collection of Indian English Poetry* (edited by Somdatta Mandal and Soma Mukhopadhyay) and *Timeless Tales from Bengal: An Anthology of Bangla Children's and Young Adults' Stories* (edited by Dipankar Roy and Saurav Dasthakur). Interested in creative writing, painting and music, Sudeshna has published two collections of poems in Bangla: *Akash Ki Shudhu Neel* and *Jol Chhunye Jao*.

Sutanuka Ghosh Roy is Associate Professor of English, Tarakeswar Degree College, University of Burdwan, West Bengal. Her areas of interest include eighteenth century literature, Indian English literature, postcolonial literature, Australian studies, Dalit literature and gender studies. She is a regular contributor to anthologies and national and international journals of repute like *Muse India, Setu, Lapiz Lazuli, The Statesman, Life and Legends, Kitaab*, and so on. She has guest-edited the July 2020 issue of *Setu* on Children's literature. Her poems have been anthologised and published in *Setu, Piker Press, Harbinger Asylum* among others. Her monographs include *Critical Inquiry: Text, Context, and Perspectives*; *Commentaries: Elucidating Poetry* and *Rassundari Dasi's Amar Jiban: A Comprehensive Study.*